Annie Fields

Life and Letters of Harriet Beecher Stowe

Annie Fields

Life and Letters of Harriet Beecher Stowe

ISBN/EAN: 9783337119102

Printed in Europe, USA, Canada, Australia, Japan

Cover: Foto ©Raphael Reischuk / pixelio.de

More available books at **www.hansebooks.com**

LIFE AND LETTERS

OF

HARRIET BEECHER STOWE

EDITED BY ANNIE FIELDS

CAMBRIDGE

Printed at the Riverside Press

M DCCC XCVII

PREFACE

THE editor of this book wishes to express her thanks to the Rev. C. E. Stowe for the use of the Life of Mrs. Stowe written by him while his mother was still at his side. His sequence of material concerning her early days left little to be desired; but many letters and much new material have since appeared, and the publishers believe that a complete life, corresponding to the new and beautiful edition of Mrs. Stowe's works lately issued by them, is wished for by the public.

To Messrs. Harper and Brothers the editor is indebted for the use of the Life of Dr. Lyman Beecher, passages from which, chiefly those written by Mrs. Stowe, have been used as necessary parts of her own history.

To the [friends whose letters now appear for the first time the thanks of the editor are especially due.

The moment has at last arrived when the story of Mrs. Stowe's life can be given in full. The cause to which she surrendered herself is not forgotten; one by one the figures of those who bore a part in the great sacrifice begin to shine like bronze after the smelting, and stand, cut in imperishable forms, upon the tablets of memory. Therefore it is fitting that one who led the vanguard, one who was born nevertheless to carry neither gun nor bayonet, but to bear upon her heart the weight of a great love for suffering men, should now herself be known.

A. F.

CONTENTS

LIFE AND LETTERS

OF

HARRIET BEECHER STOWE

CHAPTER I

ANCESTRY AND EARLY CHILDHOOD

THERE were generations of character and fine development behind the life of Mrs. Stowe.   John Beecher and
his mother, the first of the race who came to this country,
eighteen years after the arrival of the Mayflower, were
of the company of Davenport, a distinguished clergyman
of London, under whose leadership came a rich and able
body of men and women with the serious intention of
founding a new colony.   Mrs. Beecher was a good woman,
and useful to the company, therefore they gave her a lot
of land in New Haven, whither they soon betook themselves.   The equivalent of this land had been promised to
her husband before his death, which occurred on the eve
of their departure.   Their first religious service was held
under a large oak upon this place, and there later the
house was built, called latterly the old Beecher house.

It is impossible to understand the development of genius unless we regard the root from which it springs.   We
wonder at the beauty of the rose, but we think little of
the bush which bore it until we find no other rose to equal
it, and then we say, Whence came this wonder!

The Beecher race may justly be considered a noble one, as we trace it from this beginning; strong in spirit as well as in body, always readers and thinkers, always animated with love of the public good, and holding it predominant above private good. The grandfather of Mrs. Stowe was "one of the best read men in New England; well versed in astronomy, geography, and history, and in the interests of the Protestant reformation. Old Squire Roger Sherman, one of the signers of the Declaration of Independence, used to say that he always calculated to see Mr. Beecher as soon as he got home from Congress to talk over the particulars."

Surely it is not often that one discovers such persistence of traits and habits as in this family. One would seem to be reading of Mrs. Stowe's father rather than her grandfather, as the history continues: "He always kept a number of college students and of representatives to the Legislature as boarders, being fond of their conversation. He often kept pace with his student boarders in their studies, frequently spending his evenings in their rooms. He had a tenacious memory for what he read, but was entirely forgetful and careless as to his dress, hat, tools, etc." This grandfather was not a preacher, nor a college-bred man. He was a farmer and blacksmith and maker of tools, employing a man to do the ordinary work of the shop. Dr. Beecher used to say he himself was so like his father that when his sister Esther grew old she often called him "father" by mistake, instead of "brother."

The same strange absent-mindedness which we shall find in Mrs. Stowe is spoken of as a trait in her grandfather's character. "Your Aunt Esther," says Dr. Beecher, "has known him at least twelve times to come in from the barn and sit down on a coat pocket full of eggs, jump up and say, 'Oh, wife!' 'Why, my dear,' she would reply, 'I do wonder you can put eggs in your pocket after you have broken them so once.' 'Well,' he would say, 'I thought I should remember this time.' "

The same love of fun, the same suffering from depression of spirits, possessed this grandfather as was seen in his son and his grandchildren. Dr. Lyman Beecher's mother was of Scotch descent, a Miss Lyman. He says of her: "She was a woman tall, well-proportioned, dignified in her movements, fair to look upon, intelligent in conversation, and in character lovely. I was her only child. She died of consumption two days after I was born. I was a seven months' child; and when the woman that attended on her saw what a puny thing I was, and that the mother could not live, she thought it useless to attempt to keep me alive. I was actually wrapped up and laid aside. But, after a while, one of the women thought she would look and see if I was living, and, finding I was, concluded to wash and dress me, saying, 'It's a pity he hadn't died with his mother.' So you see it was but by a hair's breadth I got a foothold in this world."

One experience, testifying to the sincerity of heart of the Beecher family, and to their clear judgment, was common to father, son, and grandson, Henry Ward Beecher. They all married women distinguished for intellect and character. Whatever appreciation of grace and refinement may have been theirs, their wives possessed qualities born of energy of mind and piety of heart. Dr. Beecher grew up in his uncle's family at Guilford, Connecticut. It was country life indeed, but there was an excellent school where he was very early told by the teacher to come up "next the head," because he was the best reader in the school. His pride at this announcement can be imagined. It dwelt with him all his life, and came back to his memory when, being too old to write himself, his children gathered round and made him tell the story of his days.

"They say everybody knows about God naturally,"

continued the old man. "A lie. All such ideas are by teaching. One Sunday evening, I was out playing. They kept Saturday evening, and children might play on Sunday evening as soon as they could see three stars. But I was so impatient I did not wait for that. Bill H. saw me and said: —

" ' That 's wicked; there ain't three stars.'

" ' Don't care.'

" ' God says you must n't.'

" ' Don't care.'

" ' He 'll punish you.'

" ' Well, if He does, I 'll tell Aunt Benton.'

" ' Well, He 's bigger than Aunt Benton, and He 'll put you in the fire and burn you for ever and ever.'

"That took hold. I understood what fire was and what forever was. What emotion I had thinking, No end! no end! It has been a sort of mainspring ever since.

"Curious now, this thing of personal identity! Here I am an old man, telling you this story about a little boy; and yet I feel I am the same person I was then."

But the continuation of this identity as we see it in his son Henry Ward Beecher and in his daughter Harriet makes the wonder of it still more living. How like in character is that tale of Henry's childhood, when, being very angry, he rushes from the house behind the barn and after a pause, says to himself, "Damn it." Then he remembers that it is wicked to swear; what would become of him! The thought was too horrible to be endured. Sweat stood in great drops upon his forehead. After a while, he could bear the solitude no longer and went back into the house, but doubtless carrying with him an unhappy conscience for many a long day.

To show moral courage of a high order was common to them all. Lyman Beecher went to college, although there was very little money, his father having married again, and the house being full of children. His uncle helped him out; but he was very industrious, and made a good deal of money, for that time, by his own exertions. He heard a robber one night in his room, and waked just in season to see him disappearing with some garments through the window. Lyman Beecher had a hot chase, but caught the thief, brought him back to his room, and made him lie on the floor by his bed until morning, when he carried him before the judge.

Mrs. Stowe asked her father once if he was never afraid when he was a boy alone in the fields hoeing corn, and one of the great summer thunderstorms broke over him. "Not I. I wished it would thunder all day. I never heard such thunder since, except once in the hills round Marietta, Ohio."

When his college days were nearly over, he began to spend a part of his vacations in Guilford, near the large house and farm of General Andrew Ward. Here Roxana Foote lived, whom he married after a courtship of two years. He found her reading Sir Charles Grandison. "She said she never meant to marry until she found his like — I presume she thought she had. All the new works that were published at that day were brought out to the old house at Nutplains, read and discussed in the old spinning-mill. When Miss Burney's ' Evelina ' appeared, Sally Hill rode out on horseback to bring it to Roxana. A great treat they had of it. There was the greatest frolicking in that spinning-mill! Roxana was queen among those girls!

.   .   .   .

"I was made for action. The Lord drove me, but I was ready. I have always been going at full speed. The fifty years of my active life have been years of rapid development."

Mrs. Stowe said of her father: "He often expressed to

me great displeasure at the publication of private diaries of
good men, especially if they were of a melancholy cast, or
those recording great alternations of ecstasy and gloom.
Indeed, for no other thing did he become more celebrated than for his power of imparting hope to the de-
sponding; and it was those dark and doubting hours of his
own early life — painful as they were — which furnished
him with the necessary knowledge for the guidance of
hundreds of sensitive and troubled spirits to the firm
ground of a cheerful, intelligent religious hope." He never
preached without his eye on his audience. He noticed
every change of countenance, every indication of awakened
interest; and these he immediately followed up by seeking
private conversation. His ardor in this pursuit was singular and almost indescribable. He used to liken it to the
ardor of the chase.

Speaking of his wife Roxana, Dr. Beecher said: "There
were some things about your mother's religious character
peculiar, and very satisfactory in the retrospect. She
thought herself converted when five or six years old. She
could scarcely remember the time, but that, in all her
childish joys and sorrows, she went to God in prayer.
She experienced resignation, if any one ever did. I never
saw the like, — so entire, without reservation or shadow of
turning. In no exigency was she taken by surprise. She
was just there, quiet as an angel above. I never heard a
murmur; and if there ever was a perfect mind as respects
submission, it was hers. I never witnessed a movement of
the least degree of selfishness; and if there ever was any
such thing in the world as disinterestedness, she had it."

Dr. Beecher married Roxana Foote in 1799, as soon as
possible after his settlement in the town of East Hampton,
Long Island. He was then twenty-four years old, full of
youthful energy, not to be daunted by the strange conditions of his new island home.

The parish of East Hampton was still a wild and removed spot when Dr. Beecher carried thither his young wife. The place was first visited by white people under Hudson eleven years before the arrival of the Mayflower at Plymouth. "They found an interminable beach of snowy sand, on which the ocean never ceases to beat; dark forests, wild fowl in countless flocks, and throngs of admiring and astonished savages. . . . When Dr. Beecher went to this picturesque but wild spot a windmill stood at each end of the one long street. There were no trees except a line of poplars between two of the best houses, and a single enormous elm which had been trimmed up to a head."

East Hampton was early settled by intelligent men, and there was but one church, a large dignified building with bell and clock, the finest on the island. In these early days one fourth of the whales stranded on the beach were always presented to the minister as a portion of his salary.

The part of the parish first settled was Gardiner's Island, which was separated from the town by a bay four or five miles wide. This island has never passed out of the hands of the Gardiner family, and while Dr. Beecher was at East Hampton he found true pleasure and companionship with the seventh heir, John Lyon Gardiner, whose hospitable mansion was always ready to receive the young minister. Here it was that Dr. Beecher and his wife started in life. Here he planted an orchard, the first that had been seen in that land, behind a pleasant house on the grassy street very near to the tumbling sea. Here their life of tireless industry went on. Mrs. Beecher added to everything else a love of painting, and finished twenty-four fine miniatures upon ivory at this period. But as children came to them, the remoteness and the labor of their post were too great, and they removed to Litchfield, Connecticut, whither the minister had been "called."

Harriet Beecher was born in Litchfield, June 14, 1811.

This town was first settled in 1720 in a pleasant high country among hills, lakes, and valleys. Evidently intelligent men founded also this settlement, because they were stirring patriots during the war of the revolution, and were visited by Washington, Lafayette, Rochambeau, and many of the principal officers of the army. One of the chief heroes of that time lived to be a parishioner of Dr. Beecher. Also during his life in Litchfield and helping to make the town famous, were, among others, Governor Oliver Wolcott, Jr., a member of Washington's cabinet, John Pierpont the poet, and Judge Reeve. These men became intimate friends of Dr. Beecher; especially Judge Reeve, who had founded in Litchfield a celebrated law school, to which young men were sent from nearly every State in the union. The Reverend Mr. Huntington, who preceded Dr. Beecher, wrote of Litchfield: "It is a delightful village on a fruitful hill, richly endowed with schools, both professional and scientific, with its remarkable governors and judges, with its learned lawyers and senators, and representatives both in the National and State departments, and with a population enlightened and respectable. Litchfield was now in its glory."

The meeting-house, of course, made a great impression upon the child Harriet. She described it later in life in her first book, called "The Mayflower:" "To my childish eyes our old meeting-house was an awe-inspiring thing. To me it seemed fashioned very nearly on the model of Noah's Ark and Solomon's Temple, as set forth in the pictures in my Scripture Catechism. . . . Its double row of windows, of which I knew the number by heart, its doors, with great wooden quirls over them; its belfry, projecting out at the east end; its steeple and bell, all inspired as much sense of the sublime in me as Strasbourg Cathedral itself. . . . But the glory in the execution of those good old billowy compositions called fuguing tunes, where the four parts that compose the choir take up the song, and go racing around one after another, each singing a different set of words, till at length, by some inexplicable magic, they all come together again, and sail smoothly out into a rolling sea of harmony! I remember the wonder with which I used to look from side to side when treble, tenor, counter, and bass, were thus roaring and foaming, and it verily seemed to me as if the psalm were going to pieces among the breakers, and the delighted astonishment with which I found that each particular verse did emerge whole and uninjured from the storm."

Harriet Beecher was hardly four years old when her mother died, leaving eight little children weeping round her bed. Of these children two possessed what the world calls genius. They were all more or less distinguished, Catherine, the eldest, being a woman of remarkable character. Harriet and Henry Ward were next to the youngest, always inseparable companions, always inspired with the tenderest love and faith in each other to the end of life.

Mrs. Stowe says of her mother and of her touching departure from this world: "I was between three and four years of age when our mother died, and my own personal recollections of her are therefore but few. But the deep interest and veneration that she inspired in all who knew her was such that, during all my childhood, I was constantly hearing her spoken of, and, from one friend or another, some incident or anecdote of her life was constantly being impressed on me.

"Mother was one of those strong, restful, yet widely sympathetic natures, in whom all around seemed to find comfort and repose. She was of a temperament peculiarly restful and peace-giving. Her union of spirit with God, unruffled and unbroken even from early childhood, seemed to impart to her an equilibrium and healthful placidity that no earthly reverses ever disturbed. The communion between her and my father was a peculiar one. It was an intimacy throughout the whole range of their being. There was no human mind in whose decisions he had greater confidence. Both intellectually and morally he regarded her as the better and stronger portion of himself, and I remember hearing him say that, after her death, his first sensation was a sort of terror, like that of a child suddenly shut out alone in the dark.

"Her death occurred at a time when the New England ministry were in a peculiar crisis of political and moral trial, and the need of such a stay and support in his household was more than ever felt. . . . I asked him the question whether he ever had any reason to believe that the spirits of the blessed are ever permitted to minister to us in our earthly sorrows, and he said, after a moment of deep thought, 'I never but once had anything like it. It was a time of great trial and obloquy, and I had been visiting around in my parish, and heard many things here and there that distressed me. I came home to my house almost overwhelmed; it seemed as if I must sink under it. I went to sleep in the north bedroom, — the room where your mother died. I dreamed that I heard voices and footsteps in the next room, and that I knew immediately it was Roxana and Mary Hubbard coming to see me. The door opened, and Mary stayed without, but your mother came in and came toward me. She did not speak, but she smiled on me a smile of heaven, and with that smile all my sorrow passed away. I awoke joyful, and I was light-hearted for weeks after.'

"In my own early childhood only two incidents of my mother twinkle like rays through the darkness. One was of our all running and dancing out before her from the nursery to the sitting-room one Sabbath morning, and her pleasant voice saying after us, 'Remember the Sabbath day to keep it holy.'

"Another remembrance is this: Mother was an enthusiastic horticulturalist in all the small ways that limited means allowed. Her brother John, in New York, had just sent her a small parcel of fine tulip-bulbs. I remember rummaging these out of an obscure corner of the nursery one day when she was gone out, and being strongly seized with the idea that they were good to eat, and using all the little English I then possessed to persuade my brothers that these were onions such as grown people ate, and would be very nice for us. So we fell to and devoured the whole; and I recollect being somewhat disappointed in the odd, sweetish taste, and thinking that onions were not as nice as I had supposed. Then mother's serene face appeared at the nursery door, and we all ran toward her, and with one voice began to tell our discovery and achievement. We had found this bag of onions and had eaten them all up.

"Also I remember that there was not even a momentary expression of impatience, but that she sat down and said: 'My dear children, what you have done makes mamma very sorry; those were not onion-roots, but roots of beautiful flowers; and if you had let them alone, ma would have had next summer in the garden great beautiful red and yellow flowers such as you never saw.' I remember how drooping and dispirited we all grew at this picture, and how sadly we regarded the empty paper bag.

"Then I have a recollection of her reading to the children one evening aloud Miss Edgeworth's 'Frank,' which had just come out, I believe, and was exciting a good deal of attention among the educational circles of Litchfield. After that, I remember a time when every one said she was sick; when, if I went into the street, every one asked me how my mother was; when I saw the shelves of the closets crowded with delicacies which had been sent in for her, and how I used to be permitted to go once a day into

her room, where she sat bolstered up in bed, taking her
gruel. I have a vision of a very fair face, with a bright
red spot on each cheek, and a quiet smile as she offered
me a spoonful of her gruel; of our dreaming one night,
we little ones, that mamma had got well, and waking in
loud transports of joy, and being hushed down by some
one coming into the room.   Our dream was indeed a true
one. She was forever well; but they told us she was
dead, and took us in to see what seemed so cold, and so
unlike anything we had ever seen or known of her.

"Then came the funeral. Henry was too little to go.
I remember his golden curls and little black frock, as he
frolicked like a kitten in the sun in ignorant joy.

"I remember the mourning dresses, the tears of the
older children, the walking to the burial ground, and somebody's speaking at the grave, and the audible sobbing of
the family; and then all was closed, and we little ones, to
whom it was so confused, asked the question where she
was gone, and would she never come back?

"They told us at one time that she had been laid in the
ground, at another that she had gone to heaven; whereupon Henry, putting the two things together, resolved to
dig through the ground and go to heaven to find her; for,
being discovered under sister Catherine's window one
morning digging with great zeal and earnestness, she called
to him to know what he was doing, and, lifting his curly
head with great simplicity, he answered, 'Why, I'm going
to heaven to find ma.'

"Although mother's bodily presence disappeared from
our circle, I think that her memory and example had more
influence in moulding her family, in deterring from evil
and exciting to good, than the living presence of many
mothers. It was a memory that met us everywhere, for
every person in the town, from the highest to the lowest,
seemed to have been so impressed by her character and life

that they constantly reflected some portion of it back upon us.

"Even our portly old black washerwoman, Candace, who came once a week to help off the great family wash, would draw us aside, and, with tears in her eyes, tell us of the saintly virtues of our mother.

"I recollect that at first the house was full of little works of ingenuity, and taste, and skill, which had been wrought by her hand, — furniture adorned with painting; pictures of birds and flowers, done with minutest skill; fine embroidery, with every variety of lace and cobweb stitch; exquisite needle-work, which has almost passed out of memory in our day. I remember the bobbin and pillows with which she made black lace. Many little anecdotes were told me among her friends of her ceaseless activity and contrivance in these respects.

"One thing in her personal appearance every one spoke of, — that she never spoke in company or before strangers without blushing. She was of such great natural sensitiveness and even timidity that, in some respects, she never could conform to the standard of what was expected of a pastor's wife. In the weekly female prayer-meetings she could never lead the devotions. Yet it was not known that anybody ever expressed criticism or censure on this account. It somehow seemed to be felt that her silent presence had more power than the audible exercises of another. Such impression has been given me by those who have spoken of this peculiarity.

"There was one passage of Scripture always associated with her in our minds in childhood; it was this: ' Ye are come unto Mount Zion, the city of the living God, to the heavenly Jerusalem, and to an innumerable company of angels; to the general assembly and Church of the first born, and to the spirits of just men made perfect.'

"We all knew that this was what our father repeated to

her when she was dying, and we often repeated it to each other. It was to that we felt we *must* attain, though we scarcely knew how. In every scene of family joy or sorrow, or when father wished to make an appeal to our hearts which he knew we could not resist, he spoke of mother.

"I remember still the solemn impression produced on my mind when I was only about eight years old. I had been violently seized with malignant scarlet fever, and lain all day insensible, and father was in an agony of apprehension for my life. I remember waking up just as the beams of the setting sun were shining into the window, and hearing his voice in prayer by my bedside, and of his speaking of 'her blessed mother who is now a saint in heaven,' and wondering in my heart what that solemn appeal might mean.

"I think it will be the testimony of all her sons that her image stood between them and the temptations of youth as a sacred shield; that the hope of meeting her in heaven has sometimes been the last strand which did not part in hours of fierce temptation; and that the remembrance of her holy life and death was a solemn witness of the truth of religion, which repelled every assault of skepticism, and drew back the soul from every wandering to the faith in which she lived and died."

Of this sad year after her mother's death, Catherine Beecher wrote: "The experience of this year in our family history was similar to that of a landscape in sunshine suddenly overcast with heavy clouds. The gentle, contented, smiling, healthful mother was gone, and the sunlight of our home departed with her to return no more."

Dr. Beecher married twice again during his long life, but Roxana was the wife of his young heart and the true companion of his thought. His piety and purpose found support and development in her companionship.

The prayer of this mother's heart was, that all her sons should devote themselves to the ministry, and this wish was accomplished. What her prayer for her daughters may have been we cannot know, but her influence was such that she left, as Mrs. Stowe always believed, an indelible impression upon her own life.

Doubtless it was a recognition of Harriet's sensitive nature, and the harm which might be done by leaving her in the shadow of the family grief, which led her aunt to carry her away to Nutplains, after her mother's death, to make a long visit. It was good for her to be there, although the intellectual food seems to have been rather strong for her years. A love of wit and humor was as natural to her as to her grandmother, and, as we have seen, they enjoyed much together.

Mrs. Stowe writes of this visit: "Among my earliest recollections are those of a visit to Nutplains immediately after my mother's death. Aunt Harriet Foote, from whom I was named, who was with mother during all her last sickness, took me home to stay with her. I can now remember, at the close of what seemed to me a long day's ride, arriving after dark at a lonely little white farmhouse, and being brought into a large parlor where a cheerful wood fire was crackling, partly burned down into great heavy coals. I was placed in the arms of an old lady, who held me close and wept silently, a thing at which I marveled, for my great loss was already faded from my childish mind. But I could feel that this dear old grandmother received me with a heart full of love and sorrow. I recall still her bright white hair, the benign and tender expression of her venerable face, and the great gold ring she wore, which seemed so curious to my childish eyes. It was her wedding-ring, as she often told me afterward. There was a little tea-table set out before the fire, and Uncle George came in from his farm-work, and sat down with grandma and Aunt Harriet to tea.

"After supper I remember grandma's reading prayers, as was her custom, from a great prayer-book, which was her constant companion. To this day certain portions of the evening service never recur to me without bringing up her venerable image and the tremulous tones of her aged voice, which made that service have a different effect on me from any other prayers I heard in early life.

"Then I remember being put to bed by my aunt in a large room, on one side of which stood the bed appropriated to her and me, and on the other that of my grandmother. The beds were curtained with a printed India linen, which had been brought home by my seafaring uncle; and I recollect now the almost awe-struck delight with which I gazed on the strange mammoth plants, with great roots and endless convolutions of branches, in whose hollows appeared Chinese summer-houses, adorned with countless bells, and perched jauntily aloft, with sleepy-looking Mandarins smoking, and a Chinaman attendant just in the act of ringing some of the bells with a hammer. Also here and there were birds bigger than the mandarins, with wide-open beaks just about to seize strange-looking insects; and a constant wonder to my mind was why the man never struck the bells, nor the bird ever caught the insect.

"My Aunt Harriet was no common character. A more energetic human being never undertook the education of a child. Her ideas of education were those of a vigorous Englishwoman of the old school. She believed in the Church, and, had she been born under that régime, would have believed in the king stoutly, although, being of the generation following the Revolution, she was a not less stanch supporter of the Declaration of Independence.

"According to her views, little girls were to be taught to move very gently, to speak softly and prettily, to say ' Yes, ma'am ' and ' No, ma'am,' never to tear their clothes, to sew and to knit at regular hours, to go to church on Sunday and make all the responses, and to come home and be catechised.

"I remember those catechisings, when she used to place my little cousin Mary and myself bolt upright at her knee, while black Dinah and Harvey the bound-boy were ranged at a respectful distance behind us; for Aunt Harriet always impressed it upon her servants 'to order themselves lowly and reverently to all their betters,' — a portion of the Church Catechism which always pleased me, particularly when applied to *them*, as it insured their calling me 'Miss Harriet,' and treating me with a degree of consideration which I never enjoyed in the more democratic circle at home.

"I became a proficient in the Church Catechism, and gave my aunt great satisfaction by the old-fashioned gravity and steadiness with which I learned to repeat it.

"As my father was a Congregationalist minister, I believe Aunt Harriet, though the highest of High-Church women, felt some scruples of delicacy as to whether it was desirable my religious education should be entirely out of the sphere of my birth, and therefore, when the catechetical exercise was finished, and my cousin, who was a lamb of the true Church, dismissed, she would say to me, 'Niece, you have to learn another catechism, because your father is a Presbyterian minister,' and would therefore endeavor to make me commit to memory the Assembly's Catechism.

"At this lengthening of exercises I secretly murmured. I was rather pleased at the first question in the Church Catechism, which is certainly quite level to any child's capacity, 'What is your name?' It was such an easy, good start. I could say it so loud and clear; and I was accustomed to compare it with the first question in the Primer, 'What is the chief end of man?' as vastly more difficult for me to remember. In fact, between my aunt's secret unbelief and my own childish impatience of too much catechism, the matter was indefinitely postponed after a few ineffectual attempts, and I was overjoyed to hear her announce privately to grandmother that she thought it would be time enough for Harriet to learn the Presbyterian Catechism when she went home.

"In her own private heart my aunt did not consider my father an ordained minister; and, as she was a woman who always acted up to her beliefs, when on a visit to our family she would walk straight past his meeting-house, as she always called it, to the little Episcopal *church*, where the Gospel was dispensed in what she considered an orderly manner. It was a triumph of principle, for she was very fond and proud of father, and had a lively, acute mind peculiarly fitted to appreciate his preaching, which she would often have been very glad to hear.

"She generally contrived, in speaking of these subjects before me, to restrain herself, and probably was not aware of the sharpness with which little ears sometimes attend to conversations which are not meant for them to hear, and perhaps was entirely unaware that I pondered in my mind a declaration I once heard her make, that ' many persons out of the Episcopal Church would be saved at last, but that they were resting entirely on *uncovenanted mercy.*'

.   .   .   .

"I really think grandma stood a little in awe of Aunt Harriet. Occasionally she would give me privately her opinion of her when she was out of the room, — opinions always very charming in my eyes, because they took my part in every childish grief, and in all those disciplinary sorrows which Aunt Harriet often thought the wisest expression of love to little girls. When I broke my needles, tore my clothes, lost my thimble, slipped out of the house and sauntered by the river when I should have been sew-

ing, grandmother was always an accessory after the fact;
and when she could not save me from condign punishment,
would comfort me with the private assurance that 'I was
a poor child, and that Harriet needed punishing a great
deal more herself than I did.'

"It is said that such indulgences are dangerous to children, but I cannot remember that they ever did me any
harm. In the main, I thought that justice and right were
on Aunt Harriet's side; yet I loved grandma for the exces-
sive tenderness that blinded her to all my faults. I did
not really believe her sweet and comfortable sayings to be
exactly true; I only saw how much she must love, to be
so blind to all my faults.

"But grandmother was not by any means a weak woman.
Her mind was active and clear; her literary taste just, her
reading extensive. My image of her in later years is of
one always seated at a great round table covered with
books, among which nestled her work-basket. Among
these, chiefest, her large Bible and prayer-book; Lowth's
"Isaiah," which she knew almost by heart; Buchanan's
"Researches in Asia;" "Bishop Heber's Life;" and Dr.
Johnson's "Works," which were great favorites with
her. . . .

"We used to read much to her: first many chapters of
the Bible, in which she would often interpose most graphic
comments, especially in the Evangelists, where she seemed
to have formed an idea of each of the apostles so distinct
and dramatic that she would speak of them as acquaintances.
She would always smile indulgently at Peter's remarks.
'There he is again, now; that's just like Peter. He's always so ready to put in!' She was fond of having us read
Isaiah to her in Lowth's translation, of which she had read
with interest all the critical notes.

"Concerning Dr. Johnson's Christian character, she once
informed me, with some degree of trouble, that she had

had a discussion with my brother Edward, and that he thought that President Edwards was a better Christian than Dr. Johnson. 'He sent me his life to read,' she said, 'and I have read it, and he was a very good Christian; but, after all, I doubt if he could have written better prayers than these of Dr. Johnson's. Now just hear this,' she would say, and then she would read prayers which that great master of English, that deep and melancholy nature, certainly made wonderfully forcible and touching.

"Sometimes, in later years, after my brothers and I were grown up, we, being trained Congregationalists, would raise with our uncle and with Aunt Harriet the controverted questions of our respective faiths, which would be mooted with great vim. Grandma was always secretly uneasy lest these controversies should lead to any real disunion of feeling.

"On one occasion, after her hearing had become slightly impaired, a wordy battle had been raging round her for some time, which, as she could not understand what we said, and as we seemed to be getting more and more earnest, moved her solicitude very deeply. At last she called one of my brothers to her, and said, 'There, now, if you have talked long enough, I want you to read something to me,' and gave him that eloquent chapter in Isaiah which begins, 'Arise, shine, for thy light is come, and the glory of the Lord is risen upon thee;' and goes on to describe the day when the whole earth shall be full of the glory of the Lord. Her face, while he was reading, was like a transparency, luminous with internal light. At the close she said, 'Bishop Heber tells in his memoirs how, off in India, there were four ministers of Christ met together, all of different denominations, and they read this chapter together, and found then there was one thing they all agreed in exactly.'

"We all looked at each other and smiled, for we were

conscious that our discussion had been in the most perfect love and good will.

. . . .

"One other thing must be confessed: in her secret heart grandma was, and always remained, a Tory. In her this took no aggressive form. It was only the clinging of a loving and constant nature to that which in childhood and youth she had learned to love and venerate. On these points she always observed a discreet silence in the family circle, but made a confidante of me in my early childhood. When, after hearing King George abused roundly one day by some patriotic American, she took the first opportunity to tell me privately that 'she did n't believe that the king was to blame;' and then she opened her old English prayer-book, and read in a trembling voice the old prayers for the king and queen, and all the royal family, and told me how it grieved her when they stopped reading them in all the churches. She supposed it was all right, she said, but she could n't bear to give it up; they might have some other way to settle it.

"When afterward I ventured to say something to Aunt Harriet about it, she laughingly asserted that grandma was always an old Tory among them. I think, in the recollections of all the children, our hours spent at Nutplains were the golden hours of our life. Aunt Harriet had precisely the turn which made her treasure every scrap of a family relic and history. And even those of the family who had passed away forever seemed still to be living at Nutplains, so did she cherish every memorial, and recall every action and word. There was Aunt Catherine's embroidery; there were Aunt Mary's paintings and letters; there the things which Uncle Samuel had brought from foreign shores; frankincense from Spain, mats and baskets from Mogadore, and various other trophies locked in drawers, which Aunt Harriet displayed to us on every visit.

"At Nutplains our mother, lost to us, seemed to live
again. We saw her paintings, her needlework, and heard
a thousand little sayings and doings of her daily life. And
so dear was everything that belonged to grandmother and
our Nutplains home, that the Episcopal service, even
though not well read, was always chosen during our visits
there in preference to our own. It seemed a part of Nutplains and of the life there.

"There was also an interesting and well-selected library,
and a portfolio of fine engravings; and, though the place
was lonely, yet the cheerful hospitality that reigned there
left them scarcely ever without agreeable visitors.

.   .   .   .

"The earliest poetry that I ever heard were the ballads
of Walter Scott, which Uncle George repeated to Cousin
Mary and me the first winter that I was there. The story
of the black and white huntsman made an impression on
me that I shall never forget. His mind was so steeped in
poetical literature that he could at any time complete any
passage in Burns or Scott from memory. As for graver
reading, there was Rees's Cyclopedia, in which I suppose
he had read every article, and which was often taken down
when I became old enough to ask questions, and passages
pointed out in it for my reading.

"All these remembrances may explain why the lonely
little white farmhouse under the hill was such a Paradise
to us, and the sight of its chimneys after a day's ride was
like a vision of Eden. In later years, returning there, I
have been surprised to find that the hills around were so
bleak and the land so barren; that the little stream near
by had so few charms to uninitiated eyes. To us, every
juniper-bush, every wild sweetbrier, every barren sandy
hillside, every stony pasture, spoke of bright hours of love,
when we were welcomed back to Nutplains as to our mother's heart."

During this first long visit after her mother's death
Harriet distinguished herself by committing to memory
a wonderful assortment of hymns, poems, and scriptural
passages, which enabled her, possessed as she was of a
very retentive mind, to use and quote these valuable ad-
juncts of her writings during her mature life. She was
only five years old the following winter when she and
Henry, hand in hand, walked every day to Ma'am Kil-
bourne's school. He was a chubby little fellow, and the
weather appeared to make no difference to either of them.
With the ability to read, Mrs. Stowe said, in after years,
there seemed to germinate in herself the intense literary
longing that belonged to her from that time. The desire
for expression so early developed reminds us of her father
in his great age, when he exclaimed, "I am sick, because I
cannot reveal the feelings of my heart;" and again when
he took up his rusty fiddle, thrummed the strings, played
a note or two unsatisfied, and said, "If I could only play
what I hear inside of me, I'd beat Paganini." In those
days there were few books for children. Harriet used to
go searching hungrily through barrels of old sermons and
pamphlets stored in a corner of the garret, looking for
something "good to read." It seemed to her there were
thousands of the most unintelligible things. An appeal
"on the unlawfulness of a man marrying his wife's sister"
turned up as she investigated, "by twos, or threes, or
dozens, till her soul despaired of finding an end. At last
her patient search was rewarded, for at the very bottom of
a barrel of musty sermons she discovered an ancient volume of 'The Arabian Nights.' With this her fortune
was made, for in these most fascinating of fairy tales the
imaginative child discovered a well-spring of joy that was
all her own. When things went astray with her, when
her brothers started off on long excursions, refusing to
take her with them, or in any other childish sorrow, she

had only to curl herself up in some snug corner and sail forth on her bit of enchanted carpet into fairyland to forget all her griefs."

In this way the nature of the child developed itself, as the leaf quietly breaks away from the sheath that bound it, — as the fruit at last forms and ripens on the bough. She was not an easy child for the careful women of the household to deal with, but her father held her in his heart and watched her growth. Grandmother Foote, too, as we have seen, had her own ideas of Aunt Harriet's strict methods of government, and the dreaming child found shelter under her wing at Nutplains as well as in her father's study at Litchfield.

CHAPTER II

Two years after the death of his wife, Dr. Beecher married Miss Harriet Porter of Portland, Maine. He had the good fortune to meet this lady in Boston, whither he had gone to preach, and where she was visiting a married sister. Miss Porter belonged to the best society of the time. One of her brothers was first governor of the new State of Maine, one was twice appointed minister to Great Britain. Of herself it was said that "her facility, gracefulness, amenity, and dignity were proverbial, and were the same in all her relations. Her sense of rectitude, order, and propriety was exquisite." Mrs. Stowe describes the advent of the new mother: —

"I was about six years old, and slept in the nursery with my two younger brothers. We knew that father was gone away somewhere on a journey, and was expected home, and therefore the sound of a bustle or disturbance in the house more easily awoke us. We heard father's voice in the entry, and started up in our little beds, crying out as he entered our room, ' Why, here's pa!' A cheerful voice called out from behind him, 'And here's ma!'

"A beautiful lady, very fair, with bright blue eyes, and soft auburn hair bound round with a black velvet bandeau, came into the room smiling, eager, and happy-looking, and, coming up to our beds, kissed us, and told us that she loved little children, and that she would be our mother. We wanted forthwith to get up and be dressed, but she pacified us with the promise that we should find her in the morning.

"Never did stepmother make a prettier or sweeter impression. The next morning, I remember, we looked at her with awe. She seemed to us so fair, so delicate, so elegant, that we were almost afraid to go near her. We must have been rough, red-cheeked, hearty country children, honest, obedient, and bashful. She was peculiarly dainty and neat in all her ways and arrangements; and I remember I used to feel breezy, and rough, and rude in her presence. We felt a little in awe of her, as if she were a strange princess rather than our own mamma; but her voice was very sweet, her ways of moving and speaking very graceful, and she took us up in her lap and let us play with her beautiful hands, which seemed wonderful things, made of pearl, and ornamented with strange rings."

There is a letter from the second Mrs. Lyman Beecher describing each of the children of Roxana Foote. She characterizes every one with a discerning touch. Towards the last she says: "Harriet and Henry come next, and they are always hand in hand. They are as lovely children as I ever saw; amiable, affectionate, and very bright."

There is a fragment of a letter written two years later by one of the children, which gives a glimpse of the family:

"Mamma is well, and don't laugh any more than she used to. Catherine goes on just as she always did, making fun for everybody. George is as usual. Harriet makes just as many wry faces, is just as odd, and loves to be laughed at as much as ever. Henry does not improve much in talking, but speaks very thick. Charles is the most mischievous little fellow I ever knew. He seems to do it for the very love of it; he is punished and punished again, but it has no effect. He is the same honest little boy, and I love him dearly. Poor little Fred has been quite unwell, but has got better now; he grows more and more interesting every day. Now for the boarders. Miss M—— is just as amiable and lovely as when you was here.

Miss B—— loves fun still. Miss W—— and L—— same
as usual. Miss C—— the most obliging and useful of the
family. To conclude, the old cat has got the consumption."

Henry Ward Beecher, in later life, described the effect
upon his childish mind of the new mother: "My dear
mother—not one that gave me birth, for I do not remember to have ever seen her face, but she that brought
me up, she that did the office-work of a mother, if ever
a mother did; she that, according to her ability, performed
to the uttermost her duties—was a woman of profound
veneration, rather than of a warm and loving nature.
Therefore her prayer was invariably a prayer of deep yearning reverence. I remember well the impression which it
made on me. There was a mystic influence about it. A
sort of sympathetic hold it had upon me, but still I always
felt when I went to prayer, as though I were going into a
crypt, where the sun was not allowed to come; and I
shrunk from it."

In these days of continual oversight of the education of
children it is well to recall the long hours Harriet Beecher
was allowed to pass in her father's study. We recognize
the good to the developed man which comes from solitude
and opportunity to make his own discoveries; what then
shall we say of the value to a child, whose mind receives
impressions like that of a sensitive plate, when allowed to
range freely and seek the thing he loves.

"High above all the noise of the house," wrote Mrs.
Stowe, "this room had to me the air of a refuge and a
sanctuary. Its walls were set round from floor to ceiling
with the friendly, quiet faces of books, and there stood my
father's great writing-chair, on one arm of which lay open
always his Cruden's Concordance and his Bible. Here I
loved to retreat and niche myself down in a quiet corner
with my favorite books around me. I had a kind of shel-

tered feeling as I thus sat and watched my father writing, turning to his books and speaking from time to time to himself, in a loud earnest whisper. I vaguely felt that he was about some holy and mysterious work quite beyond my little comprehension, and I was careful never to disturb him by question or remark.

"The books ranged around filled me, too, with a solemn awe. On the lower shelves were enormous folios, on whose backs I spelled in black letters, 'Lightfoot Opera,' a title whereat I wondered, considering the bulk of the volumes. Above these, grouped along in friendly social rows, were books of all sorts, sizes, and bindings, the titles of which I had read so often that I knew them by heart. There were 'Bell's Sermons,' 'Bonnett's Inquiries,' 'Bogue's Essays,' 'Toplady on Predestination,' 'Boston's Four-fold State,' 'Law's Serious Call,' and other works of that kind. These I looked over wistfully day after day, without even a hope of getting something interesting out of them. The thought that father could read and understand things like these filled me with a vague awe, and I wondered if I should ever be old enough to know what it was all about.

"But there was one of my father's books that proved a mine of wealth to me. It was a happy hour when he brought home and set up in his bookcase Cotton Mather's 'Magnalia,' in a new edition of two volumes. What wonderful stories those! Stories, too, about my own country. Stories that made me feel the very ground I trod on to be consecrated by some special dealing of God's providence."

About this time, somebody seems to have read aloud the Declaration of Independence. "I had never heard it before," wrote Mrs. Stowe, "and even now had but a vague idea of what was meant by some parts of it. Still I gathered enough from the recital of the abuses and injuries that had driven my nation to this course to feel myself

swelling with indignation, and ready with all my little
mind and strength to applaud the concluding passage,
which Colonel Talmadge rendered with resounding majesty.
I was as ready as any of them to pledge my life, fortune,
and sacred honor for such a cause. The heroic element
was strong in me, having come down by ordinary generation from a long line of Puritan ancestry, and just now it
made me long to do something, I knew not what: to fight
for my country, or to make some declaration on my own
account."

When the little girl was ten or eleven years old, she
went to the Litchfield Academy, where the teachers appear
to have won her love and confidence.   Mrs. Stowe says of
this period, "Much of the training and inspiration of my
early days consisted not in the things I was supposed to
be studying, but in hearing, while seated unnoticed at my
desk, the conversation of Mr. Brace with the older classes.
There, from hour to hour, I listened with eager ears to
historical criticisms and discussions, or to recitations in
such works as 'Paley's Moral Philosophy,' 'Blair's Rhetoric,' 'Allison on Taste,' all full of most awakening suggestions to my thoughts.

"Mr. Brace exceeded all teachers I ever knew in the
faculty of teaching composition.   The constant excitement
in which he kept the minds of his pupils, the wide and
varied regions of thought into which he led them, formed
a preparation for composition, the main requisite for which
is to have something which one feels interested to say."

It was evidently one of Harriet's earliest joys at school
to be allowed to write compositions.   Her young soul was
already overflowing with thought and feeling.   She was
only twelve years old when a school exhibition took place,
whereat three of the best compositions were read aloud before "all the literati of Litchfield."

"When my turn came," said Mrs. Stowe in after years,

"I noticed that father, who was sitting on high by Mr. Brace, brightened and looked interested, and at the close I heard him ask, ' Who wrote that composition ? ' ' Your daughter, sir,' was the answer. It was the proudest moment of my life. There was no mistaking father's face when he was pleased, and to have interested him was past all juvenile triumphs."

The subject, "Can the Immortality of the Soul be proved by the Light of Nature," was indeed an extraordinary one to be treated by a child of twelve years, but the manner of the treatment is that of undeveloped genius. Her arguments, drawn from history, from Addison, and other writers, show no mental indigestion. At the end she says: "Never till the blessed light of the Gospel dawned on the borders of the pit, and the heralds of the Cross proclaimed 'Peace on earth and good will to men,' was it that bewildered and misled man was enabled to trace his celestial origin and glorious destiny."

The winter of her eleventh year Harriet passed at Nutplains, where Catherine wrote to her in February: —

"I suppose you will be very glad to hear you have a little sister at home. We have no name for her yet.

"We all want you at home very much, but hope you are now where you will learn to stand and sit straight, and hear what people say to you, and sit still in your chair, and learn to sew and knit well, and be a good girl in every particular; and if you don't learn while you are with Aunt Harriet, I am afraid you never will."

The time had now come when Harriet was to leave Litchfield, not permanently at first, but as it proved, she was there very little after her twelfth year. She loved the place! it made an indelible impression on her mind, and in later life she says of it: —

"My earliest recollections of Litchfield are those of its beautiful scenery, which impressed and formed my mind

long before I had words to give names to my emotions, or
could analyze my mental processes. I remember standing
often in the door of our house and looking over a distant
horizon, where Mount Tom reared its round blue head
against the sky, and the Great and Little Ponds, as they
were called, gleamed out amid a steel-blue sea of distant
pine groves. To the west of us rose a smooth-bosomed
hill called Prospect Hill; and many a pensive, wondering
hour have I sat at our play-room window, watching the
glory of the wonderful sunsets that used to burn themselves out, amid voluminous wreathings, or castellated
turrets of clouds, — vaporous pageantry proper to a moun-
tainous region.

"Litchfield sunsets were famous, because perhaps
watched by more appreciative and intelligent eyes than the
sunsets of other mountain towns around. The love and
notice of nature was a custom and habit of the Litchfield
people; and always of a summer evening the way to Prospect Hill was dotted with parties of strollers who went up
thither to enjoy the evening.

"On the east of us lay another upland, called Chestnut
Hills, whose sides were wooded with a rich growth of
forest-trees; whose changes of tint and verdure, from the
first misty tints of spring green, through the deepening
hues of summer, into the rainbow glories of autumn, was
a subject of constant remark and of pensive contemplation
to us children. We heard them spoken of by older people,
pointed out to visitors, and came to take pride in them as
a sort of birthright.

"Seated on the rough granite flag-steps of the east front
door with some favorite book, — if by chance we could find
such a treasure, — the book often fell from the hand while
the eyes wandered far off into those soft woody depths
with endless longings and dreams, — dreams of all those
wild fruits, and flowers, and sylvan treasures which some

Saturday afternoon's ramble had shown us lay sheltered in those enchanted depths. There were the crisp apples of the pink azalea, — honeysuckle apples we called them; there were scarlet wintergreen berries; there were pink shell blossoms of trailing arbutus, and feathers of ground pine; there were blue, and white, and yellow violets, and crowsfoot, and bloodroot, and wild anemone, and other quaint forest treasures.

"Between us and those woods lay the Bantam River, — a small, clear rocky stream, pursuing its way through groves of pine and birch, now so shallow that we could easily ford it by stepping from stone to stone, and again, in spots, so deep and wide as to afford bathing and swimming room for the young men and boys of the place. Many and many a happy hour we wandered up and down its tangled, rocky, and ever-changing banks, or sat under a thick pine bower, on a great granite slab called Solitary Rock, round which the clear brown waters gurgled.

"At the north of the house the horizon was closed in with distant groves of chestnut and hickory, whose waving tops seemed to have mysteries of invitation and promise to our childhood. I had read, in a chance volume of Gesner's 'Idyls,' of tufted groves, where were altars to Apollo, and where white-robed shepherds played on ivory flutes, and shepherdesses brought garlands to hang round the shrines, and for a long time I nourished a shadowy impression that, could I get into those distant northern groves, some of these dreams would be realized. These fairy visions were, alas! all dissolved by an actual permission to make a Saturday afternoon's excursion in these very groves, which were found to be used as goose-pastures, and to be destitute of the flowery treasures of the Chestnut Hills forests.

"My father was fond of excursions with his boys into the forests about for fishing and hunting. At first I remember these only as something pertaining to father and the older boys, they being the rewards given for good conduct. I remember the regretful interest with which I watched their joyful preparations for departure. They were going to the Great Pond — to Pine Island — to that wonderful blue pine forest which I could just see on the horizon, and who knew what adventures they might meet! Then the house all day was so still; no tramping of laughing, wrestling boys, — no singing and shouting; and perhaps only a long seam on a sheet to be oversewed as the sole means of beguiling the hours of absence. And then dark night would come down, and stars look out from the curtains, and innuendoes would be thrown out of children being sent to bed, and my heart would be rent with anguish at the idea of being sent off, before the eventful expedition had reported itself. And then what joy to hear at a distance the tramp of feet, the shouts and laughs of older brothers; and what glad triumph when the successful party burst into the kitchen with long strings of perch, roach, pickerel, and bullheads, with waving blades of sweet-flag, and high heads of cat-tail, and pockets full of young wintergreen, of which a generous portion was bestowed always upon me. These were the trophies, to my eyes, brought from the land of enchantment. And then what cheerful hurrying and scurrying to and fro, and waving of lights, and what cleaning of fish in the back shed, and what calling for frying-pan and gridiron, over which father solemnly presided; for to his latest day he held the opinion that no feminine hand could broil or fry fish with that perfection of skill which belonged to himself alone, as king of woodcraft and woodland cookery.

"I was always safe against being sent to bed for a happy hour or two, and patronized with many a morsel of the supper which followed, as father and brothers were generally too flushed with victory to regard very strictly dull household rules.

"Somewhat later, I remember, were the expeditions for chestnuts and walnuts in the autumn, to which all we youngsters were taken. I remember the indiscriminate levy which on such occasions was made on every basket the house contained, which, in the anticipated certainty of a great harvest to bring home, were thought to be only too few. I recollect the dismay with which our second mother, the most ladylike and orderly of housekeepers, once contemplated the results of these proceedings in her well arranged linen-room, where the contents of stocking baskets, patch baskets, linen baskets, yarn baskets, and thread baskets were all pitched into a promiscuous heap by that omnipotent marauder, Mr. Beecher, who had accomplished all this confusion with the simple promise to bring the baskets home full of, chestnuts.

"What fun it was, in those golden October days, when father dared William and Edward to climb higher than he could, and shake down the glossy chestnuts! To the very last of his life, he was fond of narrating an exploit of his climbing a chestnut-tree that grew up fifty feet without branches slantwise over a precipice, and then whirling himself over the abyss to beat down the chestnuts for the children below. 'That was a thing,' he said, 'that I would n't let any of the boys do.' And those chestnuts were had in everlasting remembrance. I verily believe that he valued himself more on some of these exploits than even his best sermons.

"My father was famous for his power of exciting family enthusiasm. Whenever he had a point to carry or work to be done, he would work the whole family up to a pitch of fervent zeal, in which the strength of each one seemed quadrupled. For instance: the wood of the family used to be brought in winter on sleds, and piled up in the yard, exactly over the spot where father wished in early spring to fix his cucumber and melon frames; for he always made it a point to have cucumbers as soon as Dr. Taylor, who lived in New Haven, and had much warmer and drier land; and he did it by dint of contrivance and cucumber frames, as aforesaid. Of course, as all this wood was to be cut, split, and carried into the wood-house before an early garden could be started, it required a miracle of generalship to get it done, considering the immense quantity required in that climate to keep an old windy castle of a house comfortable. How the axes rung, and the chips flew, and the jokes and stories flew faster; and when all was cut and split, then came the great work of wheeling in and piling; and then I, sole little girl among so many boys, was sucked into the vortex of enthusiasm by father's well-pointed declaration that he 'wished Harriet was a boy, she would do more than any of them.'

"I remember putting on a little black coat which I thought looked more like the boys, casting needle and thread to the wind, and working almost like one possessed for a day and a half, till in the afternoon the wood was all in and piled, and the chips swept up. Then father tackled the horse into the cart, and proclaimed a grand fishing party down to Little Pond. And how we all floated among the lily-pads in our boat, christened 'The Yellow Perch,' and every one of us caught a string of fish, which we displayed in triumph on our return.

"There were several occasions in course of the yearly housekeeping requiring every hand in the house, which would have lagged sadly had it not been for father's inspiring talent. One of these was the apple-cutting season, in the autumn, when a barrel of cider apple-sauce had to be made, which was to stand frozen in the milk-room and cut out from time to time in red glaciers, which, when duly thawed, supplied the table. The work was done in the kitchen, an immense brass kettle hanging over the deep fireplace, a bright fire blazing and snapping, and all

hands, children and servants, employed on the full baskets
of apples and quinces which stood around. I have the
image of my father still as he sat working the apple-peeler.
'Come, George,' he said, 'I'll tell you what we'll do to
make the evening go off. You and I'll take turns, and
we'll see who'll tell the most out of Scott's novels;' for
those were the days when the ' Tales of my Landlord' and
'Ivanhoe' had just appeared. And so they took them,
novel by novel, reciting scenes and incidents, which kept
the eyes of all the children wide open, and made the work
go on without flagging.

"Occasionally he would raise a point of theology on
some incident narrated, and ask the opinion of one of his
boys, and run a sort of tilt with him, taking up the wrong
side of the question for the sake of seeing how the young-
ster could practice his logic. If the party on the other
side did not make a fair hit at him, however, he would
stop and explain to him what he ought to have said.
'The argument lies so, my son; do that, and you'll trip
me up.' Much of his teaching to his children was in this
informal way.

"In regard to Scott's novels, it will be remembered
that, at the time they came out, novel writing stood at so
low an ebb that most serious-minded people regarded novel
reading as an evil. Such a thing as a novel was not to be
found in our house. And I well recollect the despairing
and hungry glances with which I used to search through
father's library, meeting only the same grim sentinels.
There, to be sure, was ' Harmer on Solomon's Song,' which
I read, and nearly got by heart, because it told about the
same sort of things I had once read of in the 'Arabian
Nights.' And there was the ' State of the Clergy during
the French Revolution,' which had horrible stories in it
stranger than fiction. Then there was a side-closet full
of documents, a weltering ocean of pamphlets, in which I

dug and toiled for hours to be repaid by disinterring a delicious morsel of a ‘ Don Quixote ’ that had once been a book, but was now lying in forty or fifty *disjecta membra*, amid Calls, Appeals, Sermons, Essays, Reviews, Replies, and Rejoinders. The turning up of such a fragment seemed like the rising of an enchanted island out of an ocean of mud.

“Great was the light and joy, therefore, when father spoke *ex cathedra :* ‘ George, you may read Scott’s novels. I have always disapproved of novels as trash, but in these is real genius and real culture, and you may read them.’ And we did read them; for in one summer we went through ‘ Ivanhoe ’ seven times, and were both of us able to recite many of its scenes, from beginning to end, verbatim.

“One of father’s favorite resorts was Aunt Esther’s room, about half a minute’s walk from our house. How well I remember that room! a low-studded parlor, looking out on one side into a front yard shaded with great elm-trees; on the other, down a green hillside, under the branches of a thick apple-orchard. The floor was covered with a neat red and green carpet; the fireplace resplendent with the brightest of brass andirons, small hanging book-shelves over an old-fashioned mahogany bureau; a cush-ioned rocking chair; a neat cherry tea-table; and an old-fashioned looking-glass, with a few chairs, completed the inventory. I must not forget to say that a bed was turned up against the wall, and concealed in the daytime by a decorous fall of chintz drapery.

.   .   .   .

“Aunt Esther herself, with her sparkling hazel eyes, her keen, ready wit, and never-failing flow of anecdote and information, interested us even more than the best things she could produce from her closet. She had read on all subjects — chemistry, philosophy, physiology, but especially on natural history, where her anecdotes were inexhaustible. If any child was confined to the house by sickness, her recounting powers were a wonderful solace. I once heard a little patient say, 'Only think! Aunt Esther has told me *nineteen rat stories* all in a string!' In fact we thought there was no question we could ask her that she could not answer.

"I remember once we said to her, 'Aunt Esther, how came you to know so much about every sort of thing?' 'Oh,' said she, 'you know the Bible says the works of the Lord are great, sought out of all them that have pleasure therein. Now I happened to have pleasure therein, and so I sought them out.'

"It was here that father came to read her his sermons, or the articles that he was preparing for the 'Christian Spectator;' for he was a man who never could be satisfied to keep anything he wrote to himself. First he would read it to mother, and then he would say, 'I think now I'll go over and read it to Esther.'

"It was in Aunt Esther's room that I first found a stray volume of Lord Byron's poetry, which she gave me one afternoon to appease my craving for something to read. It was the 'Corsair.' I shall never forget how it astonished and electrified me, and how I kept calling to Aunt Esther to hear the wonderful things that I found in it, and to ask what they could mean. 'Aunt Esther, what does it mean — "One I never loved enough to hate"?'

"'Oh, child, it's one of Byron's strong expressions.'

"I went home absorbed and wondering about Byron; and after that I listened to everything that father and mother said at the table about him. I remember hearing father relate the account of his separation from his wife; and one day, hearing him say, with a sorrowful countenance, as if announcing the death of some one very interesting to him, 'My dear, Byron is dead — *gone.*' After being awhile silent, he said, ' Oh, I 'm sorry that Byron is dead. I did hope he would live to do something for Christ. What a harp he might have swept!' The whole impression made upon me by the conversation was solemn and painful.

"I remember taking my basket for strawberries that afternoon, and going over to a strawberry field on Chestnut Hill. But I was too dispirited to do anything; so I lay down among the daisies, and looked up into the blue sky, and thought of that great eternity into which Byron had entered, and wondered how it might be with his soul.

"The next Sunday father preached a funeral sermon on this text: ' The name of the just is as brightness, but the memory of the wicked shall rot.' The main idea of the sermon was that goodness only is immortal, and that no degree of brilliancy and genius can redeem vice from perishing. He spoke of the different English classics, and said that the impurities of Sterne and Swift had already virtually consigned them almost to oblivion. Then after a brief sketch of Byron's career, and an estimate of his writings, he said that some things he had written would be as imperishable as brass; but that the impurities of other portions of his works, notwithstanding the beauty of the language, would in a few years sink them in oblivion. He closed with a most eloquent lamentation over the wasted life and misused powers of the great poet.

"I was eleven years old at the time, and did not generally understand father's sermons, but this I understood . perfectly, and it has made an impression on me that has never been effaced.

"If it be recollected that the audience to whom he preached was largely composed of the students of the law school, sons of the first families from all parts of the Union, and graduates of the first colleges, and the pupils of the female school, also from the first families in all parts of the nation, and that the Byronic fever was then at its height among the young people, it will be seen how valuable may have been the moral discriminations and suggestions of such a sermon.

"Father often said, in after years, that he wished he could have seen Byron, and presented to his mind his views of religious truth. He thought if Byron 'could only have talked with Taylor and me, it might have got him out of his troubles;' for never did men have more utter and complete faith in the absolute verity and power of what they regarded as Gospel doctrine than my father and the ministers with whom he acted. And though he firmly believed in total depravity, yet practically he never seemed to realize that people were unbelievers for any other reason than for want of light, and that clear and able arguments would not at once put an end to skepticism.

"With all that was truly great among men he felt a kindred sympathy. Genius and heroism would move him even to tears. I recollect hearing him read aloud Milton's account of Satan's marshaling his forces of fallen angels after his expulsion from heaven. The description of Satan's courage and fortitude was read with such evident sympathy as quite enlisted me in his favor, and in the passage, —

> 'Millions of spirits, for his fault amerced
> Of heaven, and from eternal splendors flung
> For his revolt, yet faithful how they stood,
> Their glory withered; as when heaven's fire
> Hath scathed the forest oaks or mountain pines,
> With singèd top, their stately growth, though bare,
> Stands on the blasted heath. He now prepared
> To speak; whereat their doubled ranks they bend
> From wing to wing, and half inclose him round
> With all his peers: attention held them mute.
> Thrice he essayed, and thrice, in spite of scorn,
> Tears, such as angels weep, burst forth,' —

On reaching this point father burst into tears himself, and the reading ended.

"He had always, perhaps on the same principle, au intense admiration for Napoleon Bonaparte, which he never
cared to disguise.   He was wont to say that he was a
glorious fellow, and ought to have succeeded.   The criticisms on his moral character, ambition, unscrupulousness,
etc., he used to meet by comparing him with the Bourbons
whom he supplanted, — 'not a whit better morally, and
imbecile to boot.'   Of the two, he thought it better that
a wise and able bad man should reign than a stupid and
weak bad man.   He never altogether liked Dr. Channing's
article on Napoleon.   'Why rein his character up,' he
said, 'by the strict rules of Christian perfection, when you
never think of applying it to the character of any other
ruler or general of the day?'

"The fact is, that his sympathy with genius was so intense, especially executive genius, that it created what
might almost be called a personal affection toward the great
leader, and with it was blent somewhat of the anxiety of
the pastor, the habitual bishop of souls, for a gifted but
erratic nature.   His mind was greatly exercised about the
condition of the emperor's soul, and he read every memoir
emanating from St. Helena with the earnest desire of
shaping out of those last conversations some hope for his
eternal future.

"Father was very fond of music, and very susceptible
to its influence; and one of the great eras of the family
in my childish recollection, is the triumphant bringing
home from New Haven a fine-toned upright piano, which
a fortunate accident had brought within the range of a
poor country minister's means.   The ark of the covenant
was not brought into the tabernacle with more gladness
than this magical instrument into our abode.

.   .   .   .

"Father soon learned to accompany the piano with his
violin in various psalm tunes and Scotch airs, and brothers

Edward and William to perform their part on the flute.
So we had often domestic concerts, which, if they did not
attain to the height of artistic perfection, filled the house
with gladness.

"One of my most decided impressions of the family as
it was in my childish days was of a great household inspired by a spirit of cheerfulness and hilarity, and of my
father, though pressed and driven with business, always
lending an attentive ear to anything in the way of life and
social fellowship. My oldest sister, whose life seemed a
constant stream of mirthfulness, was his favorite and companion, and he was always more than indulgent toward
her pranks and jokes."

In a letter to her son, written in 1886, speaking of this
period of her life, Mrs. Stowe says: "Somewhere between
my twelfth and thirteenth year I was placed under the
care of my elder sister Catherine, in the school that she
had just started in Hartford, Connecticut. When I entered the school there were not more than twenty-five
scholars in it, but it afterwards numbered its pupils by
the hundreds. The schoolroom was on Main Street,
nearly opposite Christ Church, over Sheldon & Colton's
harness store, at the sign of the two white horses. I
never shall forget the pleasure and surprise which these
two white horses produced in my mind when I first saw
them. One of the young men who worked in the rear of
the harness store had a most beautiful tenor voice, and it
was my delight to hear him singing in school hours: —

> 'When in cold oblivion's shade
> Beauty, wealth, and power are laid,
> When, around the sculptured shrine,
> Moss shall cling and ivy twine,
> Where immortal spirits reign,
> There shall we all meet again.'

"As my father's salary was inadequate to the wants of
his large family, the expense of my board in Hartford was

provided for by a species of exchange. Mr. Isaac D. Bull sent a daughter to Miss Pierce's seminary in Litchfield, and she boarded in my father's family in exchange for my board in her father's family. If my good, refined, neat, particular stepmother could have chosen, she could not have found a family more exactly suited to her desires. The very soul of neatness and order pervaded the whole establishment.

"The mother of the family gave me at once a child's place in her heart. A neat little hall chamber was allotted to me for my own, and a well made and kept single bed was given me, of which I took daily care with awful satisfaction. If I was sick nothing could exceed the watchful care and tender nursing of Mrs. Bull. In school my two most intimate friends were the leading scholars. They had written to me before I came and I had answered their letters, and on my arrival they gave me the warmest welcome. One was Catherine Ledyard Cogswell, daughter of the leading and best-loved of Hartford physicians. The other was Georgiana May, daughter of a most lovely Christian woman who was a widow.

.   .   .   .

"Catherine and Georgiana were reading Virgil when I came to the school. I began the study of Latin alone, and at the end of the first year made a translation of Ovid in verse, which was read at the final exhibition of the school, and regarded, I believe, as a very creditable performance. I was very much interested in poetry, and it was my dream to be a poet. I began a drama called 'Cleon.' The scene was laid in the court and time of the emperor Nero, and Cleon was a Greek lord residing at Nero's court, who, after much searching and doubting, at last comes to the knowledge of Christianity."

For a girl of her age this drama is indeed remarkable.

The little books in which the fragments of the play were
written are now before me, and I can seem to see the
young girl exciting herself over the scenes as they appeared
to her imagination.   The following extracts will give a
hint of her growing power.   The play is prefaced by a map
of the ground around Olympia, drawn by her own hand.
She indicates the situation of the city, the temple of Jupiter, the sacred olive-tree, whence victors were crowned,
the way of the processions, the treasurer's house, the
Hippodrome, the seats of the judges, Alphæus River, and
much beside.

The drama opens in a street of Rome.

Enter LENTULUS, LUCULLUS, *and others.*

Lentulus.   And so you missed the banquet — 't is a pity !
         You would have seen a new sight in those days.
Lucullus.   Why — was 't uncommon?
Len.   Jupiter, that it was ! why, this same Cleon,
         He is a perfect prince in entertainments.

         .   .   .   .

         Such show of plates and cups both gold and silver,
         Such flaming rainbows of all colored stones,
             Such wine, such music. . . .
Luc.   And so the emperor himself was there.

         .   .   .   .

         He takes to this young lord with special favor.

         .   .   .   .

         We shall live twice as fast while he is here.
Len.   By Bacchus then we shall be lived to death.
         I'm almost out of breath with living now.

         .   .   .   .

Luc.   Cleon seeks pleasure with a ravening thirst.

         .   .   .   .

         Diversion is his labor and he works
         With hand and foot and soul both night and day
         He throws out money with so flush a hand
         As makes e'en Nero's waste seem parsimony.

         .   .   .   .

SCENE. *Cleon's house. An apartment splendidly furnished. Cleon reclining on a couch.*

Enter SLAVE.

Slave. My lord, an aged man doth wait to see you.
Cleon. Well, have him up.   [*Exit Slave.*
      In nature's name what now!

Enter DIAGORAS.

Cleon. Ha! may I trust my eyes, Diagoras!
Dia. I am Diagoras if thou art Cleon.
Cleon. Why then thou art, but wherefore eye me so?
      Sit down and contemplate me at your leisure.
Dia. Thou dost not seem the same that once I knew.
Cleon. Why, that's the truth — for since that time, good
      sire
      Nature hath made me present of ten years,
      And much hath been rubbed off or out of me
      In the rough jostle of this worthy world.

      .   .   .   .

      I pray you to sit down.
Dia.   There is no seat.
Cleon. Why, thou hast lost thy eyes, good sire, I think;
      Thou'st a fair choice between some thirty couches,
      Phrygian and Græcian and of every name.
Dia. Oh, then these beds adorned with pearls and gold
      Are made to sit on. Pray you pardon me;
      I am a simple man, used to plain things.

      .   .   .   .

Cleon. Ah, I divine thou art displeased, good master.

      .   .   .   .

      As it is there is no choice between two evils:
      Either to rest thy philosophic feet
      Upon this most profanely glittering floor
      Which as thou seest is all inlaid with gems,
      Or rest thyself on these aforesaid beds.
      Nay, I but jested; look not sad, good father,
      Thou knowest Cleon's reckless tongue of old;
      I do assure thee of a hearty welcome.
      And pray you sit that I may see thee longer.
                    .   [*Seats him on a couch.*
Dia. But I am sad for what I see and hear.

I hear thou art the common talk for waste,
And that in riot and loose luxury
Thou dost outstrip even these degenerate days.

. . . .

And thou companion of the very scum,
The very dross and dregs of all mankind;
Cleon. Which is the Emperor!
Dia. Be that as it may, such is the tale of thee;
Which I discredited until I came
To look upon thee with my personal eyes;
And I have questioned much . . .
Is this the Athenian Cleon? Is this he
Who drank philosophy and worshiped virtue?
This he who triumphed in the Olympic race
Followed by wondering eyes? . . .
Rememberest thou the glory of those days?

. . . .

Cleon. Good master! I am even as you see,
A most degenerate and apostate thing
Convicted utterly. . . .
Dia. But canst thou tamely sink into a brute?

. . . .

Cleon. 'T is but anticipating transmigration.
And then, if ever I am called to that
I shall behave the more respectably
For having practiced somewhat in this world.

. . . .

Dia. I do not wish to hear thy mockery.

. . . .

Oh, could thy noble brother from the dead
Look up, how would his high-born spirit burn
To see thee groveling in this filthy sty.
Cleon [*much moved*].
'T is well! 'T is well! Thou shouldst have spoke
of him
My brother . . .
You find me, it is true, embedded here,
Sunk as you say in this luxurious slough.

. . . .

Would that there were no vestige of high hopes,
No ghosts of happier moments to return,

. . . .

No need to labor in such desperate case.

.   .   .   .

It is my curse that I have had all things.

.   .   .   .

The things that satisfy the common crowd
I have possessed and desperately striven
To bend my soul to satisfaction with them.

.   .   .   .

Scene changes.

And what said Cleon? Steady as Heaven
He answered with a decorous majesty
Declaring in so many words his purpose,
And willing to abide whate'er should come.
Why, Nero could have stood a fiery answer,
But this severe composure madded him.

.   .   .   .

His face grew livid and he stamped his foot

.   .   .   .

And bade the slaves bring in the torture.

.   .   .   .

The worst of us were scarce prepared for that.

.   .   .   .

SCENE: CLEON, NERO.
Cleon, weak and faint, led in by two soldiers.

Nero. Sit down, Lord Cleon.
Cleon. I can stand.
Nero. My lord, we have bethought us since last night,
Regretting much that reverence for the gods
By thee attacked so fired our mind with zeal
As to outstep the limits of our mercy.
We would that gentler measures had been tried
Or thine avowal in less open day,
Less in the very teeth of our commands.

.   .   .   .

Cleon. Grieve not, my liege, for you have scarcely wronged
        me.
Nero. There have been few frequenters of our court
On whom our eye hath borne such kind regard.
Thyself doth know how we have chosen thee
To be the prime companion of our revels,

From which hath grown a friendship of whose strength
We knew not till of late; for when last night,
The fumes of wine dispelled and ourselves cool,
Our very heart was shaken with remorse.

. . . .

Nero will ask thee pardon of his wrong;
Thy friend and not thy prince behold in him.

. . . .

Cleon. My sovereign, Cleon hath no way complained.

. . . .

Nero. But here, my lord, our mind is much perplexed.
We have forbid and interdict this faith
As what we have good cause to know is ill,
Infecting men with pestilential fumes,
Transforming them to haters of the Gods.

. . . .

We would give tolerance to the freest thought
Wert not that we have lately given to justice
The sect and faith which thou canst not embrace
Save 'gainst our face — against our very laws.

. . . .

We are thy friend and not disposed to hear
That which might chafe us to severity,
Of which the gods do know we 've had enough.

. . . .

My lord, we cannot think that you will hold it.
We are persuaded of your better reason
To be a follower of a crazy Jew.

Cleon [*starting up*].

. . . .

I could sit still to hear myself reviled,
But not my sovereign . . . .
I will not hold the right of drawing breath
Unless —

Nero. These are most decorous fruits of holy faith!

. . . .

Cleon. I stand rebuked, my lord, both before thee
And Him who is thy King no less than mine,
For whose sake I would reverence all forms.

. . . .

Nero. Thou art resolved to trespass on forbearance,
Yet we will still forbear and seek to conquer

By mildness more than force. . . .
Since this name moves you, we will say no more.
What need we say. Suppose you be a Christian,
Why need all nature know it; be you quiet,
You shall have private tolerance; hold your peace
And worship what you will out of my sight.

.   .   .   .

Cleon. But then, if I am questioned of my faith?
Nero. Art thou so versed in smooth decoying phrase

.   .   .   .

And cannot turn off blank enquiry?

.   .   .   .

But we can put you in a post of honor
So that all men shall wink upon thy will.

.   .   .   .

Cleon. My lord, I scarce can trust myself to answer,

.   .   .   .

Since I have heard such degradation named.
In place of open bold apostasy,

.   .   .   .

Thou dost propose an hourly, daily lie.

.   .   .   .

· It is my settled purpose while I live
To leave no word or argument untried
To win all men to reverence Him.

.   .   .   .

"I filled blank book after blank book," Mrs. Stowe
says, "with this drama. It filled my thoughts sleeping
and waking. One day sister Catherine pounced down
upon me, and said that I must not waste my time writing
poetry, but discipline my mind by the study of Butler's
'Analogy.' So after this I wrote out abstracts from the
'Analogy,' and instructed a class of girls as old as myself,
being compelled to master each chapter just ahead of the
class I was teaching. About this time I read Baxter's
'Saint's Rest.' I do not think any book affected me more
powerfully. As I walked the pavements I used to wish
that they might sink beneath me if only I might find myself in heaven. I was at the same time very much inter-

ested in Butler's 'Analogy,' for Mr. Brace used to lecture
on such themes when I was at Miss Pierce's school at
Litchfield. I also began the study of French and Italian
with a Miss Degan, who was born in Italy.

"It was about this time that I first believed myself to
be a Christian. I was spending my summer vacation at
home, in Litchfield. I shall ever remember that dewy,
fresh summer morning. I knew that it was a sacramental
Sunday, and thought with sadness that when all the good
people should take the sacrificial bread and wine I should
be left out. I tried hard to feel my sins and count them
up; but what with the birds, the daisies, and the brooks
that rippled by the way, it was impossible. I came into
church quite dissatisfied with myself, and as I looked upon
the pure white cloth, the snowy bread and shining cups
of the communion table, thought with a sigh: 'There
won't be anything for me to-day; it is all for these grown-
up Christians.' Nevertheless, when father began to speak,
I was drawn to listen by a certain pathetic earnestness in
his voice. Most of father's sermons were as unintelligible
to me as if he had spoken in Choctaw. But sometimes he
preached what he was accustomed to call a ' frame sermon;'
that is, a sermon that sprung out of the deep feeling of the
occasion, and which consequently could be neither premed-
itated nor repeated. His text was taken from the Gospel
of John, the declaration of Jesus: ' Behold, I call you no
longer servants, but friends.' His theme was Jesus as a
soul friend offered to every human being.

"Forgetting all his hair-splitting distinctions and dialectic
subtleties, he spoke in direct, simple, and tender language
of the great love of Christ and his care for the soul. He
pictured Him as patient with our errors, compassionate
with our weaknesses, and sympathetic for our sorrows.
He went on to say how He was ever near us, enlightening
our ignorance, guiding our wanderings, comforting our

sorrows with a love unwearied by faults, unchilled by in-
gratitude, till at last He should present us faultless before
the throne of his glory with exceeding joy.

"I sat intent and absorbed.   Oh! how much I needed
just such a friend, I thought to myself.   Then the awful
fact came over me that I had never had any conviction
of my sins, and consequently could not come to Him.   I
longed to cry out 'I will,' when father made his passionate
appeal, 'Come, then, and trust your soul to this faithful
friend.'   Like a flash it came over me that if I needed
conviction of sin, He was able to give me even this also.
I would trust Him for the whole.   My whole soul was
illumined with joy, and as I left the church to walk home,
it seemed to me as if Nature herself were hushing her
breath to hear the music of heaven.

"As soon as father came home and was seated in his
study, I went up to him and fell in his arms, saying,
'Father, I have given myself to Jesus, and He has taken
me.'   I never shall forget the expression of his face as he
looked down into my earnest, childish eyes; it was so
sweet, so gentle, and like sunlight breaking out upon a
landscape.   'Is it so?' he said, holding me silently to his
heart, as I felt the hot tears fall on my head.   'Then has
a new flower blossomed in the kingdom this day.'"

If she could have been let alone, her son says in his
valuable compilation of Mrs. Stowe's Letters and Journals, and taught "to look up and not down, forward and
not back, out and not in," this religious experience might
have gone on as sweetly and naturally as the opening of
a flower in the gentle rays of the sun.   But unfortunately
this was not possible at that time, when self-examination
was carried to an extreme that was calculated to drive a
nervous and sensitive mind well-nigh distracted.   First,
even her sister Catherine was afraid that there might be
something wrong in the case of a lamb that had come into

the fold without being first chased all over the lot by the
shepherd; great stress being laid, in those days, on what
was called "being under conviction." Then also the
pastor of the First Church in Hartford, a bosom friend of
Dr. Beecher, looked with melancholy and suspicious eyes
on this unusual and doubtful path to heaven, — but more
of this hereafter. Harriet's conversion took place in the
summer of 1825, when she was fourteen, and the following
year, April, 1826, Dr. Beecher resigned his pastorate in
Litchfield to accept a call to the Hanover Street Church,
in Boston. In a letter to her grandmother Foote at Guilford, dated Hartford, March 4, Harriet writes: —

"You have probably heard that our home in Litchfield
is broken up. Papa has received a call to Boston, and
concluded to accept, because he could not support his
family in Litchfield. He was dismissed last week Tuesday, and will be here (Hartford) next Tuesday with
mamma and Isabel. Aunt Esther will take Charles and
Thomas to her house for the present. Papa's salary is to
be $2,000 and $500 settlement.

"I attend school constantly and am making some progress in my studies. I devote most of my attention to
Latin and to arithmetic, and hope soon to prepare myself
to assist Catherine in the school."

This breaking up of the Litchfield home led Harriet,
under her father's advice, to seek to connect herself with
the First Church of Hartford. Accordingly, accompanied
by two of her school friends, she went one day to the
pastor's study to consult with him concerning the contemplated step. The good man listened attentively to the
child's simple and modest statement of Christian experience, and then with an awful, though kindly solemnity
of speech and manner said, "Harriet, do you feel that if
the universe should be destroyed (awful pause) you could
be happy with God alone?" After struggling in vain, in

her mental bewilderment, to fix in her mind some definite conception of the meaning of the sounds which fell on her ear like the measured strokes of a bell, the child of fourteen stammered out, "Yes, sir."

"You realize, I trust," continued the doctor, "in some measure at least, the deceitfulness of your heart, and that in punishment for your sins God might justly leave you to make yourself as miserable as you have made yourself sinful?"

"Yes, sir," again stammered Harriet.

Having thus effectually, and to his own satisfaction, fixed the child's attention on the morbid and over-sensitive workings of her own heart, the good and truly kind-hearted man dismissed her with a fatherly benediction. But where was the joyous ecstasy of that beautiful Sabbath morning of a year ago? Where was that heavenly friend? Yet was not this as it should be, and might not God leave her "to make herself as miserable as she had made herself sinful"?

In a letter addressed to her brother Edward, about this time, she writes: "My whole life is one continued struggle: I do nothing right. I yield to temptation almost as soon as it assails me. My deepest feelings are very evanescent. I am beset behind and before, and my sins take away all my happiness. But that which most constantly besets me is pride, — I can trace almost all my sins back to it."

At this period the influence of her sister Catherine, the eldest of Dr. Beecher's children, may be clearly seen.

Miss Beecher was a woman of singular and original power, and from her earliest years exercised strong sway over the excitable poetic nature of this younger sister. Her own character had been strengthened by much sorrow. At the age of twenty-two, having become engaged to Professor Fisher of Yale College, her lover was lost at sea, the ship which was to have borne him to England being wrecked on the Irish coast.

"Without this incident," writes the Rev. C. E. Stowe, "'The Minister's Wooing' never would have been written, for both Mrs. Marvyn's terrible soul struggles and old Candace's direct and effective solution of all religious difficulties find their origin in this stranded, storm-beaten ship on the coast of Ireland, and the terrible mental conflicts through which her sister afterward passed, for she believed Professor Fisher eternally lost. No mind more directly and powerfully influenced Harriet's than that of her sister Catherine, unless it was her brother Edward's, and that which acted with such overwhelming power on the strong, unyielding mind of the older sister must have, in time, a permanent and abiding influence on the mind of the younger."

Catherine's bravery was only equalled by her family affection; she lent herself to her younger sister's interests with peculiar zeal, and took her into the school she had founded, where as pupil and teacher Harriet passed the early years of her young womanhood.

CHAPTER III

FOR several years Dr. Beecher had seen himself running aground in Litchfield financially. Therefore when an invitation came from Boston, urging his presence in that city as a last and saving hope for orthodoxy, he made up his mind to leave the pleasant places which had become dear to him and turn to other fields. His letter of " request for dismission " gives a wonderfully frank description of his household affairs. He read it in full to his congregation. He begins : " When I gave myself to God in the Gospel of his Son, it was done with the following views : That all expectation of accumulating property for myself and family be relinquished, leaving it to God in his own way to take care of me when sickness or age should supersede active labor. . . . I never expected or desired to give my children anything but their own minds and faculties, properly cultivated and prepared for active usefulness. . . . With these views I gave myself to the ministry, first at East Hampton, on Long Island, with a salary of three hundred dollars and my firewood, which, after five years, was raised to four hundred dollars ; and then, as my family increased, proving incompetent, at the end of another five years I obtained a dismission, and settled in this place, May 29, 1810, upon a salary of eight hundred dollars, with an understanding that I might calculate upon a voluntary supply of wood. Early after my settlement, my wife (of beloved memory) informed me from year to year that my income did not meet the unavoidable expenses of the family, and advised me to communicate the fact to the society."

Dr. Beecher continues : " I replied that I had come

hither with the determination of removing no more, and
that in my judgment the condition of the society forbade
a request for the increase of my salary." He then gives
in detail the efforts made by his wife, who used all her
little fortune in the attempt to take boarders. This venture was a total loss. The two elder children were then
teaching, and were able to turn their earnings into the
family coffer, but the sons were all to be educated for the
ministry, as they showed no talent for anything but study.
The utmost economy was of no avail, and after much suffering, when they were at the lowest ebb of their fortunes,
a letter came from Boston, urging Dr. Beecher to become
the pastor of the Hanover Street Church.

"For several days and nights, while agitated by this
subject, I endured what I shall not attempt to describe.
. . . I hope you will do me the justice to believe that I
have endeavored to conduct uprightly, and in the fear of
God, and that the friendship between us, which has been
confirmed by the joys and the sorrows of fifteen years, may
not all in a moment be sacrificed, but that you will extend
to me in this heart-breaking moment the consolation of
believing that I have not forfeited your confidence, your
affection, and an interest in your prayers."

In after life, Mrs. Stowe said of this Boston era: "It
was the high noon of my father's manhood, the flood-tide
of his powers; and a combination of circumstances in the
history of Massachusetts brought him in to labor there just
as a whole generation were on the return-wave of a great
moral reaction. The strict theocracy founded by the
Puritans in the State of Massachusetts had striven by all
the ingenuity of legislation and institution to impress the
Calvinistic seal indelibly on all the future generations of
Massachusetts, so that no man of other opinions should
minister in the church, or bear office in the State. As in
Connecticut, so in Massachusetts, a reaction had come in
and forced open the doors of the State, and rent the sole

power from the clergy; but the revolution had gone deeper
and farther and extended to ideas and theologies. . . .
The party, called for convenience Unitarian, . . . consisted of persons of the most diverse and opposite shades
of opinion, united only in the profession of not believing
Calvinism as taught by the original founders of Massachusetts. . . .

"Calvinism or Orthodoxy was the despised and perse-
cuted form of faith. It was the dethroned royal family
wandering like a permitted mendicant in the city where it
once had held court, and Unitarianism reigned in its stead.

"All the literary men of Massachusetts were Unitarian.
All the trustees and professors of Harvard College were
Unitarians. All the élite of wealth and fashion crowded
Unitarian churches. The judges on the bench were Unitarian, giving decisions by which the peculiar features of
church organization, so carefully ordained by the Pilgrim
Fathers, had been nullified. The church, as consisting,
according to their belief, in regenerate people, had been
ignored, and all the power had passed into the hands of
the congregation. This power had been used by the
majorities to settle ministers of the fashionable and reign-
ing type in many of the towns of Eastern Massachusetts.
The dominant majority entered at once into possession of
churches and church property, leaving the orthodox minority to go out into schoolhouses or town halls, and build
their churches as best they could. Old foundations established by the Pilgrim Fathers for the perpetuation and
teaching of their own views in theology were seized upon
and appropriated to the support of opposing views. A
fund given for preaching an annual lecture on the Trinity
was employed for preaching an annual attack upon it, and
the Hollis professorship of divinity at Cambridge was employed for the furnishing of a class of ministers whose sole
distinctive idea was declared warfare with the ideas and
intentions of the donor.

"So bitter and so strong had been the reaction of a
whole generation against the too stringent bands of their
fathers, — such the impulse with which they broke from
the cords with which their ancestors sought to bind them
forever.   But in every such surge of society, however
confident and overbearing, there lies the element of a
counter reaction, and when Dr. Beecher came to Boston
this element had already begun to assert itself.

.   .   .   .

"He had not been in Boston many weeks before every
leisure hour was beset by people who came with earnest
intention to express to him those various phases of weary,
restless, wandering desire and aspiration proper to an earnest people whose traditional faith has been broken up,
but who have not outlived the necessity of definite and
settled belief.   From minds of every class, in every circle
of society, the most fashionable and the most obscure, these
inquirers were constantly coming with every imaginable
theological problem, from the inspiration of the Bible out
through all the minutest ramifications of doctrinal opinion
or personal religious experience. . . .

"The effect of all this on my father's mind was to keep
him at a white heat of enthusiasm.   Within a stone's
throw of our door was the old Copp's Hill burying-ground,
where rested the bones of the Puritan founders; and,
though not a man ordinarily given to sentiment or to visiting of graves, we were never left to forget in any prayer
of his that the bones of our fathers were before our door.

"His family prayers at this period, departing from the
customary forms of unexcited hours, became often upheav-
ings of passionate emotion such as I shall never forget.
' Come, Lord Jesus,' he would say, ' here where the bones
of the fathers rest, here where the crown has been torn
from thy brow, come and recall thy wandering children.
Behold thy flock scattered on the mountain — these sheep,

what have they done?   Gather them, gather them, O good
Shepherd, for their feet stumble upon the dark mountains.'

. . . .

"Dr. Beecher kept a load of sand in his cellar, to which
he would run at odd intervals and shovel vigorously, throwing it from one side the cellar to the other, on his favorite theory of working off nervous excitement through the
muscles, and his woodpile and woodsaw were inestimable
means to the same end.   He had, also, in the back yard,
parallel bars, a single bar, ladder, and other simple gym-
nastic apparatus, where he would sometimes astonish his
ministerial visitors by climbing ropes hand over hand,
whirling over on the single bar.

. . . .

"The time that he spent in actual preparation for a
public effort was generally not long.   If he was to preach
in the evening he was to be seen all day talking with
whoever would talk, accessible to all, full of everybody's
affairs, business, and burdens, till an hour or two before
the time, when he would rush up into his study (which he
always preferred should be the topmost room of the house),
and, throwing off his coat, after a swing or two with the
dumb-bells to settle the balance of his muscles, he would
sit down and dash ahead, making quantities of hieroglyphic
notes on small, stubbed bits of paper, about as big as the
palm of his hand.   The bells would begin to ring and still
he would write.   They would toll loud and long, and his
wife would say, 'He will certainly be late,' and then would
be running up and down stairs of messengers to see that
he was finished, till, just as the last stroke of the bell was
dying away, he would emerge from the study with his coat
very much awry, come down the stairs like a hurricane,
stand impatiently protesting while female hands that ever
lay in wait adjusted his cravat and settled his coat collar,
calling loudly the while for a pin to fasten together the

stubbed little bits of paper aforesaid, which being duly
dropped into the crown of his hat, and hooking wife or
daughter like a satchel on his arm, away he would start
on such a race through the streets as left neither brain nor
breath till the church was gained. Then came the pro-
cess of getting in through crowded aisles wedged up with
heads, the bustle, and stir, and hush to look at him, as,
with a matter-of-fact, business-like push, he elbowed his
way through them and up the pulpit stairs."

This period in Boston was the time when Harriet felt
she drew nearer to her father than at any other period of
her life; yet she did not go with the family in the first
instance, but continued her stay at the school in Hartford,
where she became a teacher long before she ceased to be
a pupil.

There are many letters written to her brother Edward,
begun about this time, which show the unnatural vein into
which a delicate sympathetic girl could easily fall when
exposed to influences such as have been described.

Her brain had already wearied her body in the double
race for development. The sincerity of her nature is
beautifully apparent in these letters. The habit of confession is not one that suited a human soul like hers, accustomed to seek the Divine throne alone, hand in hand with
the Divine Son. To her mind there was no earthly intermediary necessary, nor was there a barrier of eighteen
hundred years between her life and the life of Christ; she
only saw a marvelous sequence of time, every day laden
with new proofs of the necessity and the verity of this
presence in her world. But the atmosphere of that period
and the terrible arguments of her father and of her sister
Catherine were sometimes more than she could endure.
She says to Edward: —

"Many of my objections you did remove that afternoon
we spent together. After that I was not as unhappy as I

had been.   I felt, nevertheless, that my views were very
indistinct and contradictory, and feared that if you left me
thus I might return to the same dark, desolate state in
which I had been all summer.   I felt that my immortal
interest, my happiness for both worlds, was depending on
the turn my feelings might take.   In my disappointment
and distress I called upon God, and it seemed as if I was
heard.   I felt that He could supply the loss of all earthly
love.   All misery and darkness were over.   I felt as if
restored, nevermore to fall.   Such sober certainty of waking bliss had long been a stranger to me.   But even then
I had doubts as to whether these feelings were right, because I felt love to God alone without that ardent love for
my fellow-creatures which Christians have often felt. . . .
I cannot say exactly what it is makes me reluctant to
speak of my feelings.   It costs me an effort to express
feeling of any kind, but more particularly to speak of my
private religious feelings."

   This difficulty in expressing the deepest feelings of
her heart to another shows already the gathering wave
which was to break by and by, not in lamentations over
her own lot, but into a *Miserere* which was to become a
Magnificat for the sufferings of the down-trodden of the
earth, and for their regeneration.   Delivered from herself,
she became a deliverer.   Again she writes to her brother: —

   "I wish I could describe to you how I feel when I pray.
I feel that I love God, — that is, that I love Christ, —
that I find comfort and happiness in it, and yet it is not
that kind of comfort which would arise from free communication of my wants and sorrows to a friend.   I sometimes wish that the Saviour were visibly present in this
world, that I might go to Him for a solution of some of
my difficulties. . . . Do you think, my dear brother,
that there is such a thing as so realizing the presence and

character of God that He can supply the place of earthly friends? I really wish to know what you think of this. . . . Do you suppose that God really loves sinners before they come to Him? Some say that we ought to tell them that God hates them, that He looks on them with utter abhorrence, and that they must love Him before He will look on them otherwise. Is it right to say to those who are in deep distress, ' God is interested in you; He feels for and loves you '?"

At last came the vacation days when Harriet went to Boston to see her family. She writes to Georgiana May: —

"In the first place, on my arrival, I was obliged to spend two days in talking and telling news. Then after that came calling, visiting, etc., and then I came off to Groton to see my poor brother George, who was quite out of spirits and in very trying circumstances. To-morrow I return to Boston and spend four or five days, and then go to Franklin, where I spend the rest of my vacation.

"I found the folks all well on my coming to Boston, and as to my new brother, James, he has nothing to distinguish him from forty other babies, except a very large pair of blue eyes and an uncommonly fair complexion, a thing which is of no sort of use or advantage to a man or boy.

"I am thinking very seriously of remaining in Groton and taking care of the female school, and at the same time being of assistance and company for George. On some accounts it would not be so pleasant as returning to Hartford, for I should be among strangers. Nothing upon this point can be definitely decided till I have returned to Boston, and talked to papa and Catherine."

"Harriet reads everything," Edward wrote of his sister, "that she can lay hands on, and sews and knits vigorously." Doubtless a memory of these over-working days lingered with Mrs. Stowe in after life, when she said: "Women have no idea how much vitality runs off from the ends of their fingers when they should be resting." Neither was she a friend of the kindergarten system. "I can't bear to see these little animals (for children are hardly more in the earliest years) drawing all the vitality out of these sweet, delicate young girls just coming into womanhood." Of course Froebel and his followers stood aghast, but the improvement in method since those early days goes to prove that Mrs. Stowe's common sense was not altogether at fault.

Catherine's affection for Harriet did not allow any symptoms of ill to escape her observation. While the latter was at home, Catherine wrote to Dr. Beecher: —

"I have received some letters from Harriet to-day which make me feel uneasy. She says, ' I don't know as I am fit for anything, and I have thought that I could wish to die young, and let the remembrance of me and my faults perish in the grave, rather than live, as I fear I do, a trouble to every one. You don't know how perfectly wretched I often feel: so useless, so weak, so destitute of all energy. Mamma often tells me that I am a strange, inconsistent being. Sometimes I could not sleep, and have groaned and cried till midnight, while in the daytime I tried to appear cheerful, and succeeded so well that papa reproved me for laughing so much. I was so absent sometimes that I made strange mistakes, and then they all laughed at me, and I laughed, too, though I felt as though I should go distracted. I wrote rules; made out a regular system for dividing my time; but my feelings vary so much that it is almost impossible for me to be regular.' "

"But let Harriet ' take courage in her dark sorrows and melancholies,' as Carlyle says; Samuel Johnson, too, had hypochondrias; all great souls are apt to have, and to be in thick darkness generally till the eternal ways and the celestial guiding stars disclose themselves, and the vague abyss of life knits itself up into firmaments for them."

"At the same time (the winter of 1827)," continues her son, "Catherine writes to Edward concerning Harriet: 'If she could come here (Hartford) it might be the best thing for her, for she can talk freely to me. I can get her books, and Catherine Cogswell, Georgiana May, and her friends here could do more for her than any one in Boston, for they love her, and she loves them very much. Georgiana's difficulties are different from Harriet's — she is speculating about doctrines, etc. Harriet will have young society here all the time, which she cannot have at home, and I think cheerful and amusing friends will do much for her. I can do better in preparing her to teach drawing than any one else, for I best know what is needed.'"

Catherine seems to have had a sublime confidence in herself which goes more than half way to fight the battles of life. This confidence does not come without foundation. A distinguished theologian of New England said to a German professor, concerning one of her publications: —

"The ablest refutation of Edwards on 'The Will' which was ever written is the work of a woman, the daughter of Dr. Lyman Beecher." The worthy Teuton raised both hands in undisguised astonishment. "You have a woman that can write an able refutation of Edwards on 'The Will?' God forgive Christopher Columbus for discovering America!"

It does not appear at this juncture that the forces worked together for returning Harriet immediately to the school. She went instead with her friend Miss May to visit her grandmother again, where she seems in some degree to have recovered the tone of her spirits.

In the autumn, however, she returned, and in January wrote to her grandmother, Mrs. Foote: "I have been constantly employed from nine in the morning until after dark at night, in taking lessons of a painting and drawing master, with only an intermission long enough to swallow a little dinner which was sent to me in the schoolroom.

"You may easily believe that after spending the day in this manner, I did not feel in a very epistolary humor in the evening, and if I had been, I could not have written, for when I did not go immediately to bed I was obliged to get a long French lesson.

"The seminary is finished, and the school going on nicely. Miss Clarissa Brown is assisting Catherine in the school. Besides her, Catherine, and myself, there are two other teachers who both board in the family with us: one is Miss Degan, an Italian lady who teaches French and Italian; she rooms with me, and is very interesting and agreeable. Miss Hawks is rooming with Catherine. In some respects she reminds me very much of my mother. She is gentle, affectionate, modest, and retiring, and much beloved by all the scholars. . . . I am still going on with my French, and carrying two young ladies through Virgil, and if I have time, shall commence Italian.

"I am very comfortable and happy.

"I propose, my dear grandmamma, to send you by the first opportunity a dish of fruit of my own painting. Pray do not now devour it in anticipation, for I cannot promise that you will not find it sadly tasteless in reality. If so, please excuse it, for the sake of the poor young artist. I admire to cultivate a taste for painting, and I wish to improve it; it was what my dear mother admired and loved, and I cherish it for her sake. I have thought more of this dearest of all earthly friends these late years, since I have been old enough to know her character and appreciate her worth. I sometimes think that, had she lived, I might have been both better and happier than I now am, but God is good and wise in all His ways."

When we consider the somewhat stern character of "Sister Catherine," and remember how this young girl worked without intermission day in and day out, we see that she was quite right; "happier," if not "better," indeed she might have been.

In the spring of the same year Harriet writes again to Edward: —

"It is only to the most perfect Being in the universe that imperfection can look and hope for patience. How strange! . . . You do not know how harsh and forbidding everything seems, compared with His character. All through the day in my intercourse with others, everything has a tendency to destroy the calmness of mind gained by communion with Him. One flatters me, another is angry with me, another is unjust to me.

"You speak of your predilections for literature having been a snare to you. I have found it so myself. I can scarcely think, without tears and indignation, that all that is beautiful and lovely and poetical has been laid on other altars. Oh! will there never be a poet with a heart enlarged and purified by the Holy Spirit, who shall throw all the graces of harmony, all the enchantments of feeling, pathos, and poetry, around sentiments worthy of. them? . . . It matters little what service He has for me. . . . I do not mean to live in vain. He has given me talents, and I will lay them at his feet, well satisfied if He will accept them. All my powers He can enlarge. He made my mind, and He can teach me to cultivate and exert its faculties."

Her schemes for going to Groton to help George did not meet with approval. In February, 1829, she writes again to Edward, as usual, from the school in Hartford: —

"My situation this winter is in many respects pleasant. I room with three other teachers, Miss Fisher, Miss Mary Dutton, and Miss Brigham. Ann Fisher you know.

Miss Dutton is about twenty, has a fine mathematical
mind, and has gone as far into that science, perhaps, as
most students at college. She is also, as I am told, quite
learned in the languages. . . . Miss Brigham is somewhat
older; is possessed of a fine mind and most unconquerable
energy and perseverance of character. From early childhood she has been determined to obtain an education, and
to attain to a certain standard. Where persons are determined to be anything, they will be. I think, for this
reason, she will make a first-rate character. Such are my
companions. We spend our time in school during the
day, and in studying in the evening. My plan of study
is to read rhetoric and prepare exercises for my class the
first half hour in the evening; after that the rest of the
evening is divided between French and Italian. Thus you
see the plan of my employment and the character of my
immediate companions. Besides these, there are others
among the teachers and scholars who must exert an influence over my character. Miss Degan, whose constant
occupation it is to make others laugh; Mrs. Gamage, her
room-mate, a steady, devoted, sincere Christian. . . . Little things have great power over me, and if I meet with
the least thing that crosses my feelings, I am often rendered unhappy for days and weeks. . . . I wish I could
bring myself to feel perfectly indifferent to the opinions of
others. I believe that there never was a person more
dependent on the good and evil opinions of those around
than I am. This desire to be loved forms, I fear, the great
motive for all my actions. . . . I have been reading carefully the book of Job, and I do not think that it contains
the views of God which you presented to me. God seems to
have stripped a dependent creature of all that renders life
desirable, and then to have answered his complaints from
the whirlwind; and instead of showing mercy and pity, to
have overwhelmed him by a display of his power and jus-

tice. . . . With the view I received from you, I should
have expected that a being who sympathizes with his
guilty, afflicted creatures would not have spoken thus.
Yet, after all, I do believe that God is such a being as you
represent Him to be, and in the New Testament I find in
the character of Jesus Christ a revelation of God as merciful and compassionate; in fact, just such a God as I need.

"Somehow or another you have such a reasonable sort
of way of saying things that, when I come to reflect, I
almost always go over to your side. . . . My mind is
often perplexed, and such thoughts arise in it that I cannot pray, and I become bewildered. The wonder to me
is, how all ministers and all Christians can feel themselves
so inexcusably sinful, when it seems to me we all come
into the world in such a way that it would be miraculous
if we did not sin. Mr. Hawes always says in prayer, 'We
have nothing to offer in extenuation of any of our sins,'
and I always think when he says it, that we have everything to offer in extenuation. The case seems to me exactly as if I had been brought into the world with such a
thirst for ardent spirits that there was just a possibility,
though no hope, that I should resist, and then my eternal
happiness made dependent on my being temperate. Sometimes when I try to confess my sins, I feel that after all
I am more to be pitied than blamed, for I have never
known the time when I have not had a temptation within
me so strong that it was certain I should not overcome it.
This thought shocks me, but it comes with such force, and
so appealingly, to all my consciousness, that it stifles all
sense of sin."

The following summer, in July, she writes to Edward:
"I have never been so happy as this summer. I began it
in more suffering than I ever before have felt, but there is
One whom I daily thank for all that suffering, since I hope
that it has brought me at last to rest entirely in Him."

"So, after four years of struggling and suffering," writes her son, "she returns to the place where she started from as a child of thirteen. It has been like watching a ship with straining masts and storm-beaten sails, buffeted by the waves, making for the harbor, and coming at last to quiet anchorage. There have been, of course, times of darkness and depression, but never any permanent loss of the religious trustfulness and peace of mind indicated by this letter."

Happily, also, those striving years, when learning and imparting were accomplished almost with the same breath, at last were ended. Yet a change had been wrought in herself, which must not be overlooked; a change wholly disregarded in the intensified atmosphere of her life. She had not grown to be a strong woman; the apparently "healthy and hearty" child had been suffered to think and feel, to study and starve (as we may say), starve for relaxation, until she became a woman subject to much suffering and many inadequacies of physical life. If we seem to be brought by a contemplation of this subject to a lower level, it is because Mrs. Stowe, by physical weakness, was often unable to bear the stress and strain of her experience, and was brought to a lower level herself. She loved more, and consequently suffered more than others, and the weight of her suffering was heavier because she had grown up, apparently, almost without care either from herself or others in behalf of her body. Yet Dr. Beecher had already discovered that his own life of intellectual storm and stress required a physical balance. The wood that he sawed, the land that he redeemed, the trees that he planted and nourished, all attest to his faith in these matters; but, for women, life in the open air was not thought to be necessary; the same canons were not brought to bear in their behalf. They were always tired from the ceaseless round of indoor duties and lack of true relaxation which should draw neither too much upon the brain nor the body. Now every child is regarded from the physical point of view as well as the mental.

As to the spiritual life, perhaps, she was better off than the larger number of children of our day. With all our boasted education, it is only here and there when some holy man or woman appears as an educator for the people that Christ is born anew and the principles of his teaching are again made to live before us.

From this period of Harriet Beecher's life we must look upon her as a woman far from vigorous, yet laying upon herself every burden within her reach. She was twenty-one years old when we find her writing to her friend Miss May: —

"After the disquisition on myself above cited, you will be prepared to understand the changes through which this wonderful *ego et me ipse* has passed.

"The amount of the matter has been, as this inner world of mine has become worn out and untenable, I have at last concluded to come out of it and live in the eternal one, and, as F—— S—— once advised me, to give up the pernicious habit of meditation to the first Methodist minister that would take it, and try to mix in society somewhat as another person would.

"'*Horas non numero nisi serenas.*' Uncle Samuel, who sits by me, has just been reading the above motto, the inscription on a sun-dial in Venice. It strikes me as having a distant relationship to what I was going to say. I have come to a firm resolution to count no hours but unclouded ones, and to let all others slip out of my memory and reckoning as quickly as possible. . . .

"I am trying to cultivate a general spirit of kindliness towards everybody. Instead of shrinking into a corner to notice how other people behave, I am holding out my hand to the right and to the left, and forming casual or inci-

dental acquaintances with all who will be acquainted with
me. In this way I find society full of interest and pleasure, — a pleasure which pleaseth me more because it is not
old and worn out. From these friendships I expect little;
therefore generally receive more than I expect. From
past friendships I have expected everything, and must of
necessity have been disappointed. The kind words and
looks and smiles I call forth by looking and smiling are
not much by themselves, but they form a very pretty
flower border to the way of life. They embellish the day
or the hour as it passes, and when they fade they only do
just as you expected they would. This kind of pleasure
in acquaintanceship is new to me. I never tried it before.
When I used to meet persons, the first inquiry was, ' Have
they such and such a character, or have they anything
that might possibly be of use or harm to me ? '

  . . . .

"Your long letter came this morning. It revived much
in my heart. Just think how glad I must have been this
morning to hear from you. I was glad. . . . I thought
of it through all the vexations of school — I have a letter
at home; and when I came home from school, I went
leisurely over it.

"This evening I have spent in a little social party, —
a dozen or so, — and I have been zealously talking all the
evening. When I came to my cold, lonely room, there
was your letter lying on the dressing-table. It touched
me with a sort of painful pleasure, for it seems to me uncertain, improbable, that I shall ever return and find you
as I have found your letter. Oh, my dear G——, it is
scarcely well to love friends thus. The greater part that
I see cannot move me deeply. They are present, and I
enjoy them; they pass, and I forget them. But those that
I love differently; those that I *love ;* and oh, how much
that word means! I feel sadly about them. They may

change; they must die; they are separated from me, and I ask myself why should I wish to love with all the pains and penalties of such conditions? I check myself when expressing feelings like this, so much has been said of it by the sentimental, who talk what they could not have felt. But it is so deeply, sincerely so in me, that sometimes it will overflow. Well, there is a heaven, — a heaven, — a world of love, and love after all is the life-blood, the existence, the all in all of mind."

CHAPTER IV

IT was a momentous affair to the family when Dr.
Beecher decided to leave Boston after six years of service
and go to Cincinnati. There was a project on foot of
founding the Lane Theological Seminary at that place,
but the whole idea was to be given up unless Dr. Beecher
would become its president.

"With Dr. Beecher and his wife," writes his grandson,
"were to go Miss Catherine Beecher, who had conceived
the scheme of founding in Cincinnati, then considered the
capital of the West, a female college, and Harriet, who
was to act as her principal assistant. In the party were
also George, who was to enter Lane as a student, Isabella,
James, the youngest son, and Miss Esther Beecher, the
'Aunt Esther' of the children."

In the autumn they started upon their long journey,
and Harriet writes to one of her friends in Hartford: —

"Well, my dear, the great sheet is out, and the letter
is begun. All our family are here (in New York), and
in good health.

"Father is to perform to-night in the Chatham Theatre!
'positively for the *last* time this season!' I don't know,
I'm sure, as we shall ever get to Pittsburgh. Father is
staying here begging money for the Biblical Literature
professorship; the incumbent is to be C. Stowe. Father
begged two thousand dollars yesterday, and now the good
people are praying him to abide certain days, as he suc-
ceeds so well. They are talking of sending us off and

keeping him here. I really dare not go and see Aunt
Esther and mother now; they were in the depths of tribulation before at staying so long, and now, 'in the lowest
depths, *another* deep'! Father is in high spirits. He is
all in his own element, — dipping into books; consulting
authorities for his oration; going round here, there, everywhere; begging, borrowing, and spoiling the Egyptians;
delighted with past success and confident for the future.

"Wednesday. Still in New York. I believe it would
kill me dead to live long in the way I have been doing
since I have been here. It is a sort of agreeable delirium.
There's only one thing about it, it is too *scattering*. I
begin to be athirst for the waters of quietness."

Writing from Philadelphia, she adds: —

"Well, we did get away from New York at last, but it
was through much tribulation. The truckman carried all
the family baggage to the wrong wharf, and, after waiting
and waiting on board the boat, we were obliged to start
without it, George remaining to look it up. Arrived here
late Saturday evening, — dull, drizzling weather; poor
Aunt Esther in dismay, — not a clean cap to put on, —
mother in like state; all of us destitute. We went, half
to Dr. Skinner's and half to Mrs. Elmes's: mother, Aunt
Esther, father, and James to the former; Kate, Bella, and
myself to Mr. Elmes's. They are rich, hospitable folks,
and act the part of Gaius in apostolic times. . . . Our
trunks came this morning. Father stood and saw them
all brought into Dr. Skinner's entry, and then he swung
his hat and gave a ' hurrah,' as any man would whose wife
had not had a clean cap or ruffle for a week. Father does
not succeed very well in opening purses here. Mr. East-
man says, however, that this is not of much consequence.
I saw to-day a notice in the ' Philadelphian ' about father,
setting forth how ' this distinguished brother, with his large
family, having torn themselves from the endearing scenes

of their home,' etc., etc., 'were going, like Jacob,' etc., —
a very scriptural and appropriate flourish. It is too much
after the manner of men, or, as Paul says, speaking 'as a
fool.' A number of the pious people of this city are coming
here this evening to hold a prayer-meeting with reference
to the journey and its object. For *this* I thank them."

From Downington she writes: —

"Here we all are, — Noah and his wife and his sons
and his daughters, with the cattle and creeping things, all
dropped down in the front parlor of this tavern, about
thirty miles from Philadelphia. If to-day is a fair specimen of our journey, we shall find a very pleasant, obliging
driver, good roads, good spirits, good dinner, fine scenery,
and now and then some 'psalms and hymns and spiritual
songs;' for with George on board you may be sure of
music of some kind. Moreover, George has provided
himself with a quantity of tracts, and he and the children
have kept up a regular discharge at all the wayfaring
people we encountered. I tell him he is *peppering* the
land with moral influence.

"We are all well; all in good spirits. Just let me give
you a peep into our traveling household. Behold us,
then, in the front parlor of this country inn, all as much
at home as if we were in Boston. Father is sitting opposite to me at this table, reading; Kate is writing a billet-
doux to Mary on a sheet like this; Thomas is opposite,
writing in a little journal that he keeps; Sister Bell, too,
has her little record; George is waiting for a seat that
he may produce his paper and write. As for me, among
the multitude of my present friends, my heart still makes
occasional visits to absent ones, — visits full of pleasure,
and full of cause of gratitude to Him who gives us friends.
I have thought of you often to-day, my G. We stopped
this noon at a substantial Pennsylvania tavern, and among
the flowers in the garden was a late monthly honeysuckle

like the one at North Guilford. I made a spring for it, but George secured the finest bunch, which he wore in his button-hole the rest of the noon.

"This afternoon, as we were traveling, we struck up and sang ' Jubilee.' It put me in mind of the time when we used to ride along the rough North Guilford roads and make the air vocal as we went along. Pleasant times those. Those were blue skies, and that was a beautiful lake, and noble pine-trees and rocks they were that hung over it. But those we shall look upon ' na mair.'

"Well, my dear, there is a land where we shall not *love* and *leave*. Those skies shall never cease to shine, the waters of life we shall *never* be called upon *to leave*. We have here no continuing city, but we seek one to come. In such thoughts as these I desire ever to rest, and with such words as these let us ' comfort one another and edify one another.' "

"Harrisburg, Sunday evening. Mother, Aunt Esther, George, and the little folks have just gathered into Kate's room, and we have just been singing. Father has gone to preach for Mr. De Witt. To-morrow we expect to travel sixty-two miles, and in two more days shall reach Wheeling; there we shall take the steamboat to Cincinnati."

As soon as the first letters from Hartford were received, Harriet responded to her sister Mary: —

"My DEAR SISTER, — The Hartford letter from all and sundry has just arrived, and after cutting all manner of capers expressive of thankfulness, I have skipped three stairs at a time up to the study to begin an answer. My notions of answering letters are according to the literal sense of the word, — not waiting six months and then scrawling a lazy reply, but sitting down the moment you have read a letter, and telling, as Dr. Woods says, ' how the subject strikes you.' I wish I could be clear that the

path of duty lay in talking to you this afternoon, but as
I find a loud call to consider the heels of George's stockings, I must only write a word or two, and then resume
my darning-needle. You don't know how anxiously we
all have watched for some intelligence from Hartford.
Not a day has passed when I have not been the efficient
agent in getting somebody to the post-office, and every
day my heart has sunk at the sound of 'No letters.' I
felt a tremor quite sufficient for a lover when I saw your
handwriting once more, so you see that in your old age
you can excite quite as much emotion as did the admirable Miss Byron in her adoring Sir Charles. I hope the
consideration and digestion of this fact will have its due
weight in encouraging you to proceed.

"The fact of our having received said letter is as yet
a state secret, not to be made known till all our family
circle 'in full assembly meet' at the tea-table. Then
what an illumination! ' How we shall be edified and
fructified,' as that old Methodist said. It seems too bad
to keep it from mother and Aunt Esther a whole afternoon, but then I have the comfort of thinking that we are
consulting for their greatest happiness 'on the whole,'
which is metaphysical benevolence.

"So kind Mrs. Parsons stopped in the very midst of her
pumpkin pies to think of us? Seems to me I can see her
bright, cheerful face now! And then those well-known
handwritings! We *do* love our Hartford friends dearly;
there can be, I think, no controverting that fact. Kate
says that the word *love* is used in *six senses*, and I am
sure in some one of them they will all come in. Well,
good-by for the present.

"Evening. Having finished the last hole on George's
black vest, I stick in my needle and sit down to be sociable. You don't know how coming away from New
England has sentimentalized us all! Never was there

such an abundance of meditation on our native land, on the joys of friendship, the pains of separation. Catherine had an alarming paroxysm in Philadelphia which expended itself in 'The Emigrant's Farewell.' After this was sent off she felt considerably relieved. My symptoms have been of a less acute kind, but, I fear, more enduring. There! the tea-bell rings. Too bad! I was just going to say something bright. Now to take your letter and run! How they will stare when I produce it!

"After tea. Well, we have had a fine time. When supper was about half over, Catherine began: 'We have a dessert that we have been saving all the afternoon,' and then I held up my letter. 'See here, this is from Hartford!' I wish you could have seen Aunt Esther's eyes brighten, and mother's pale face all in a smile, and father, as I unfolded the letter and began. Mrs. Parsons's notice of her Thanksgiving predicament caused just a laugh, and then one or two sighs (I told you we were growing sentimental!). We did talk some of keeping it (Thanksgiving), but perhaps we should all have felt something of the text, 'How shall we sing the Lord's song in a strange land?' Your praises of Aunt Esther I read twice in an audible voice, as the children made some noise the first time. I think I detected a visible blush, though she found at that time a great deal to do in spreading bread and butter for James, and shuffling his plate; and, indeed, it was rather a vehement attack on her humility, since it gave her at least 'angelic perfection,' if not 'Adamic' (to use Methodist technics). Jamie began his Sunday-school career yesterday. The superintendent asked him how old he was. 'I'm four years old now, and when *it snows very hard* I shall be five,' he answered. I have just been trying to make him interpret his meaning; but he says, 'Oh, I said so because I could not think of anything else to say.' By the by, Mary, speaking of the temptations

of cities, I have much solicitude on Jamie's account lest
he should form improper intimacies, for yesterday or day
before we saw him parading by the house with his arm
over the neck of a great hog, apparently on the most ami-
cable terms possible; and the other day he actually got
upon the back of one, and rode some distance. So much
for allowing these animals to promenade the streets, a
particular. in which Mrs. Cincinnati has imitated the
domestic arrangements of some of her elder sisters, and a
very disgusting one it is.

"Our family physician is one Dr. Drake, a man of a
good deal of science, theory, and reputed skill, but a sort
of general mark for the opposition of all the medical cloth
of the city. He is a tall, rectangular, perpendicular sort of
a body, as stiff as a poker, and enunciates his prescriptions
very much as though he were delivering a discourse on the
doctrine of election. The other evening he was detained
from visiting Kate, and he sent a very polite, ceremonious
note containing a prescription, with Dr. D.'s compliments
to Miss Beecher, requesting that she would take the inclosed in a little molasses at nine o'clock precisely.

"The house we are at present inhabiting is the most
inconvenient, ill-arranged, good-for-nothing, and altogether
to be execrated affair that ever was put together. It was
evidently built without a thought of a winter season.
The kitchen is so disposed that it cannot be reached from
any part of the house without going out into the air.
Mother is actually obliged to put on a bonnet and cloak
every time she goes into it. In the house are two parlors
with folding doors between them. The back parlor has
but one window, which opens on a veranda, and has its
lower half painted to keep out what little light there is.
I need scarcely add that our landlord is an old bachelor,
and of course acted up to the light he had, though he left
little enough of it for his tenants."

The story continues in her letters to Georgiana May: —

"Bishop Purcell visited our school to-day, and expressed himself as greatly pleased that we had opened such an one here. He spoke of my poor little geography,[1] and thanked me for the unprejudiced manner in which I had handled the Catholic question in it. I was of course flattered that he should have known anything of the book.

"How I wish you could see Walnut Hills. It is about two miles from the city, and the road to it is as picturesque as you can imagine a road to be without 'springs that run among the hills.' Every possible variety of hill and vale of beautiful slope, and undulations of land set off by velvet richness of turf and broken up by groves and forests of every outline of foliage, make the scene Arcadian. You might ride over the same road a dozen times a day untired, for the constant variation of view caused by ascending and descending hills relieves you from all tedium. Much of the wooding is beech of a noble growth. The straight, beautiful shafts of these trees as one looks up the cool green recesses of the woods seem as though they might form very proper columns for a Dryad temple. There! Catherine is growling at me for sitting up so late; so 'adieu to music, moonlight, and you.' I meant to tell you an abundance of classical things that I have been thinking to-night, but 'woe 's me.'

"Since writing the above my whole time has been taken up in the labor of our new school, or wasted in the fatigue and lassitude following such labor. To-day is Sunday, and I am staying at home because I think it is time to take some efficient means to dissipate the illness and bad feelings of divers kinds that have for some time been

___

[1] This geography was begun by Mrs. Stowe during the summer of 1832, while visiting her brother William at Newport, R. I. It was completed during the winter of 1833, and published by the firm of Corey, Fairbank & Webster, of Cincinnati.

growing upon me. At present there is and can be very
little system or regularity about me. About half of my
time I am scarcely alive, and a great part of the rest the
slave and sport of morbid feeling and unreasonable prejudice. I have everything but good health.

"I still rejoice that this letter will find you in good old
Connecticut — thrice blessed — 'oh, had I the wings of a
dove' I would be there too. Give my love to Mary H.
I remember well how gently she used to speak to and smile
on that forlorn old daddy that boarded at your house one
summer. It was associating with her that first put into
my head the idea of saying something to people who were
not agreeable, and of saying something when I had nothing
to say, as is generally the case on such occasions."

Again she writes to the same friend: "Your letter, my
dear G., I have just received, and read through three
times. Now for my meditations upon it. What a woman
of the world you are grown. How good it would be for
me to be put into a place which so breaks up and precludes
thought. Thought, intense emotional thought, has been
my disease. How much good it might do me to be where
I could not but be thoughtless. . . .

"Now, Georgiana, let me copy for your delectation a
list of matters that I have jotted down for consideration
at a teachers' meeting to be held to-morrow night. It
runneth as follows. Just hear! 'About quills and paper
on the floor; forming classes; drinking in the entry (cold
water, mind you); giving leave to speak; recess-bell, etc.,
etc.' 'You are tired, I see,' says Gilpin, 'so am I,' and
I spare you.

"I have just been hearing a class of little girls recite,
and telling them a fairy story which I had to spin out as
it went along, beginning with 'Once upon a time there
was,' etc., in the good old-fashioned way of stories.

"Recently I have been reading the life of Madame de

Staël and 'Corinne.' I have felt an intense sympathy
with many parts of that book, with many parts of her
character. But in America feelings vehement and absorbing like hers become still more deep, morbid, and impassioned by the constant habits of self-government which the
rigid forms of our society demand. They are repressed,
and they burn inward till they burn the very soul, leaving
only dust and ashes. It seems to me the intensity with
which my mind has thought and felt on every subject presented to it has had this effect. It has withered and exhausted it, and though young, I have no sympathy with
the feelings of youth. All that is enthusiastic, all that
is impassioned in admiration of nature, of writing, of character, in devotional thought and emotion, or in the emotions of affection, I have felt with vehement and absorbing
intensity, — felt till my mind is exhausted, and seems to
be sinking into deadness. Half of my time I am glad to
remain in a listless vacancy, to busy myself with trifles,
since thought is pain, and emotion is pain."

It was at this time that Harriet first tried her wings
before the public of letters. An award of fifty dollars being offered by the editor of "The Western Magazine" for
a story, she entered into competition, and easily took the
prize. From this moment she devoted herself to an occupation more congenial to her nature than any other. She
also joined a social and literary club, which counted among
its members nearly all the distinguished men and women
of Cincinnati.

She writes of this club to Miss May: —

"I am wondering as to what I shall do next. I have
been writing a piece to be read next Monday evening at
Uncle Sam's *soirée* (the Semi-Colon). It is a letter purporting to be from Dr. Johnson. I have been stilting
about in his style so long that it is a relief to me to come
down to the jog of common English. Now I think of it,

I will just give you a history of my campaign in this circle.

"My first piece was a letter from Bishop Butler, written in his outrageous style of parentheses and foggification. My second a satirical essay on the modern uses of languages. This I shall send to you, as some of the gentlemen, it seems, took a fancy to it and requested leave to put it in the ' Western Magazine,' and so it is in print. It is ascribed to *Catherine*, or I don't know that I should have let it go. I have no notion of appearing *in propria persona*.

"The next piece was a satire on certain members who were getting very much into the way of joking on the worn-out subjects of matrimony and old maid and old bachelorism. I therefore wrote a set of legislative enactments purporting to be from the ladies of the society, forbidding all such allusions in future. It made some sport at the time. I try not to be personal, and to be courteous, even in satire.

"But I have written a piece this week that is making me some disquiet. I did not like it that there was so little that was serious and rational about the reading. So I conceived the design of writing a *set of letters*, and throwing them in, as being the letters of a friend. I wrote a letter this week for the first of the set, — easy, not very sprightly, — describing an imaginary situation, a house in the country, a gentleman and lady, Mr. and Mrs. Howard, as being pious, literary, and agreeable. I threw into the letter a number of little particulars and incidental allusions to give it the air of having been really a letter. I meant thus to give myself an opportunity for the introduction of different subjects and the discussion of different characters in future letters.

"I meant to write on a great number of subjects in future. Cousin Elisabeth, only, was in the secret; Uncle Samuel and Sarah Elliot were not to know.

"Yesterday morning I finished my letter, smoked it to make it look yellow, tore it to make it look old, directed it and scratched out the direction, postmarked it with red ink, sealed it and broke the seal, all this to give credibility to the fact of its being a real letter. Then I inclosed it in an envelope, stating that it was a part of a *set* which had incidentally fallen into my hands. This envelope was written in a scrawny, scrawly gentleman's hand.

"I put it into the office in the morning, directed to ' Mrs. Samuel E. Foote,' and then sent word to Sis that it was coming, so that she might be ready to enact the part.

"Well, the deception took. Uncle Sam examined it and pronounced, *ex cathedra*, that it must have been a real letter. Mr. Greene (the gentleman who reads) declared that it must have come from Mrs. Hall, and elucidated the theory by spelling out the names and dates which I had erased, which, of course, he accommodated to his own tastes. But then, what makes me feel uneasy is that Elisabeth, after reading it, did not seem to be exactly satisfied. She thought it had too much sentiment, too much particularity of incident, — she did not exactly know what. She was afraid that it would be criticised unmercifully. Now Elisabeth has a tact and quickness of perception that I trust to, and her remarks have made me uneasy enough. I am unused to being criticised, and don't know how I shall bear it."

About a year after the arrival of Dr. Beecher's family in Cincinnati, the subject of slavery was first brought under Harriet's personal observation during a visit in Kentucky. Miss Dutton, one of the teachers in Miss Beecher's Institute, was her companion. Harriet found herself on the estate which was later known as Colonel Shelby's in "Uncle Tom's Cabin." Many years after, Miss Dutton said, in speaking of this visit: —

"Harriet did not seem to notice anything in particular that happened, but sat much of the time as though abstracted in thought. When the negroes did funny things and cut up capers, she did not seem to pay the slightest attention to them. Afterwards, however, in reading 'Uncle Tom,' I recognized scene after scene of that visit portrayed with the most minute fidelity, and knew at once where the material for that portion of the story had been gathered."

But the great subject of slavery was not yet the ruling thought of her existence. She continues to write to Miss May on the subject of education: —

"We mean to turn over the West by means of *model schools* in this, its capital. We mean to have a young ladies' school of about fifty or sixty, a primary school of little girls to the same amount, and then a primary school for *boys*. We have come to the conclusion that the work of teaching will never be rightly done till it passes into *female* hands. This is especially true with regard to boys. To govern boys by moral influences requires tact and talent and versatility; it requires also the same division of labor that female education does. But men of tact, versatility, talent, and piety will not devote their lives to teaching. They must be ministers and missionaries, and all that, and while there is such a thrilling call for action in this way, every man who is merely teaching feels as if he were a Hercules with a distaff, ready to spring to the first trumpet that calls him away. As for division of labor, men must have salaries that can support wife and family, and, of course, a revenue would be required to support a requisite number of teachers if they could be found.

"Then, if men have more knowledge they have less talent at communicating it, nor have they the patience, the long-suffering, and gentleness necessary to superintend the formation of character. We intend to make these principles understood, and ourselves to set the example of what females can do in this way. You see that first-rate talent is necessary for all that we mean to do, especially for the last, because here we must face down the prejudices of society, and we must have exemplary success to be believed. We want original, planning minds, and you do not know how few there are among females, and how few we can command of those that exist."

In after years Mrs. Stowe wrote of their home in Cincinnati: —

"Dr. Beecher's residence on Walnut Hills was in many respects peculiarly pleasant. It was a two-story brick edifice of moderate dimensions, fronting the west, with a long L running back into the primeval forest, or grove, as it was familiarly called, which here came up to the very door. Immense trees — beech, black oak, and others — spread their broad arms over the back yard, affording in summer an almost impenetrable shade.

"An airy veranda was built in the angle formed by the L along the entire inner surface of the house, from which, during the fierce gales of autumn and winter, we used to watch the tossing of the spectral branches, and listen to the roaring of the wind through the forest. Two or three large beeches and elms had been with difficulty saved from the inexorable woodman's axe, and though often menaced as endangering the safety of the house from their great height, they still flourish in beauty. Through that beautiful grove the doctor and two of his sons, during the three years 1834-37, passed daily to and from the seminary buildings. A rustic gate was hung between the back yard and the grove, and the path crossed a *run*, or gully, where for a season an old carpenter's bench supplied the place of bridge. In that grove was a delightful resort of the young people from the city, of Dr. Beecher's flock, who often came out to spend a social hour or enjoy a picnic in the woods.

"During the first year of Dr. Beecher's Walnut Hills life, the care of the family was shared between Mrs. Beecher and Aunt Esther, though, as the health of the former declined, the burden of responsibility fell more and more upon the latter. The family was large, comprising, including servants, thirteen in all, besides occasional visitors.

"The house was full. There was a continual high tide of life and animation. The old carryall was constantly vibrating between home and the city, and the excitement of going and coming rendered anything like stagnation an impossibility. And if we take into account the constant occurrence of matters for consultation respecting the seminary and the students, or respecting the Church and congregation in the city, or respecting Presbytery, Synod, and General Assembly, as well as the numberless details of shopping, marketing, which must be done in the city, it will be seen that at no period of his life was Dr. Beecher's mind more constantly on the stretch, exerted to the utmost tension of every fibre, and never, to use an expressive figure of Professor Stowe, did he wheel a greater number of heavily laden wheelbarrows all at one and the same time. Had he husbanded his energies and turned them in a single channel, the mental fire might have burned steadily on till long after threescore years and ten. But this was an impossibility. Circumstances and his own constitutional temperament united to spur him on, and for more than twenty of his best years he worked under a high pressure, to use his favorite expression, to the *ne plus*, — that is, to the utmost limit of physical and moral endurance.

"It was an exuberant and glorious life while it lasted. The atmosphere of his household was replete with moral oxygen, — full charged with intellectual electricity. Nowhere else have we felt anything resembling or equaling it. It was a kind of moral heaven, the purity, vivacity, inspiration, and enthusiasm of which only those can appreciate who have lost it, and feel that in this world there is, there can be, ' no place like home.' "

"During the summer of 1834," writes her son, "the young teacher and writer made her first visit East since leaving New England two years before. Its object was mainly to be present at the graduation of her favorite brother, Henry Ward, from Amherst College. The earlier part of this journey was performed by means of stage to Toledo, and thence by steamer to Buffalo. A pleasant bit of personal description, and also of impressions of Niagara, seen for the first time on this journey, are given in a letter sent back to Cincinnati during its progress. In it she says of her fellow-travelers: —

"'Then there was a portly, rosy, clever Mr. Smith, or Jones, or something the like; and a New Orleans girl looking like distraction, as far as dress is concerned, but with the prettiest language and softest intonations in the world, and one of those faces which, while you say it is n't handsome, keeps you looking all the time to see what it can be that is so pretty about it. Then there was Miss B., an independent, good-natured, do-as-I-please sort of a body, who seemed of perpetual motion from morning till night. Poor Miss D. said, when we stopped at night, "Oh, dear! I suppose Lydia will be fiddling about our room till morning, and we shall not one of us sleep." Then, by way of contrast, there was a Mr. Mitchell, the most gentlemanly, obliging man that ever changed his seat forty times a day to please a lady. Oh, yes, he could ride outside, — or, oh, certainly, he could ride inside, — he had no objection to this, or that, or the other. Indeed, it was difficult to say what could come amiss to him. He speaks in a soft, quiet manner, with something of a drawl, using very correct, well-chosen language, and pronouncing

all his words with carefulness; has everything in his dress
and traveling appointments *comme il faut ;* and seems to
think there is abundant time for everything that is to be
done in this world, without, as he says, "any unnecessary
excitement." Before the party had fully discovered his
name he was usually designated as "the obliging gentleman," or "that gentleman who is so accommodating." Yet
our friend, withal, is of Irish extraction, and I have seen
him roused to talk with both hands and a dozen words in
a breath. He fell into a little talk about abolition and
slavery with our good Mr. Jones, a man whose mode of
reasoning consists in repeating the same sentence at regular
intervals as long as you choose to answer it. This man,
who was finally convinced that negroes were black, used it
as an irrefragable argument to all that could be said, and
at last began to deduce from it that they might just as
well be slaves as anything else, and so he proceeded till all
the philanthropy of our friend was roused, and he sprung
up all lively and oratorical and gesticulatory and indignant
to my heart's content. I like to see a quiet man that can
be roused.' "

In this same letter she describes Niagara. Her style
is of the very fibre of her own being, and she lives again
for us as we read: —

"Let me tell, if I can, what is unutterable. I did not
once think whether it was high or low; whether it roared
or did n't roar; whether it equaled my expectations or not.
My mind whirled off, it seemed to me, in a new, strange
world. It seemed unearthly, like the strange, dim images
in the Revelation. I thought of the great white throne;
the rainbow around it; the throne in sight like unto an
emerald; and oh! that beautiful water rising like moonlight, falling as the soul sinks when it dies, to rise refined, spiritualized, and pure; that rainbow, breaking out,
trembling, fading, and again coming like a beautiful spirit

walking the waters. Oh, it is lovelier than it is great; it
is like the Mind that made it: great, but so veiled in
beauty that we gaze without terror. I felt as if I could
have *gone over* with the waters; it would be so beautiful
a death; there would be no fear in it. I felt the rock
tremble under me with a sort of joy. I was so maddened
that I could have gone too, if it had gone.''

It was during Harriet's absence in the East that the
news reached her of the death of a dear friend, Eliza Tyler,
the young wife of Professor Stowe. Calvin E. Stowe and
his wife Eliza Tyler had been among the most valued members of the social club of which Harriet Beecher has already
given us a picture. Eliza Tyler was about the same age as
Harriet. They became very close friends, and the news of
her death was a true sorrow. There were not many women
of her character and tastes anywhere, but Cincinnati was
robbed of its dearest joy to Harriet when Eliza Tyler died.
Professor Stowe was born in Natick, Massachusetts, in 1802,
early enough to be cognizant of all the theological warfare
of the period. The battle was hotly fought out in Connecticut between the factions of the Doctors Taylor and
Tyler, the latter representing the radical branch of the
argument. Professor Stowe was sensitive to impressions,
eager for learning, with an extraordinary memory, reading
German and Hebrew with absolute ease, with a keen sense
of humor, and a still keener power of suffering from depression of spirits. His quick insight and unusual, almost exceptional, learning doubtless caused him early to espouse
the Tyler views in theology, and ultimately led him to find
his first wife.

When Harriet Beecher returned from her visit to the
East, she found Mr. Stowe plunged in the deepest woe. He
was always very dependent upon cheerful surroundings, and
now she saw him suffering from grief, utterly lonely and
forlorn. When he could be aroused from his sorrow his

mind reasserted itself and made him a very witty and delightful companion; but left to himself he easily relapsed
into the darkness of grief. For two years, while busily
occupied as usual with matters of education, with ever
closer observation of the South, and the condition of the
slaves, with theological discussions and the social life
around her, she spent herself in endeavoring to soothe
this sad and solitary man.

The distance was not great between the sympathy and
loving care she gave to Professor Stowe during this period,
and the love which by and by declared itself. At the end
of the two years she became his wife. She writes to Miss
May : —

January 6, 1836.

"Well, my dear G., about half an hour more and your
old friend, companion, schoolmate, sister, etc., will cease
to be Hatty Beecher, and change to nobody knows who.
My dear, you are engaged, and pledged in a year or two
to encounter a similar fate, and do you wish to know how
you shall feel? Well, my dear, I have been dreading and
dreading the time, and lying awake all last week wondering how I should live through this overwhelming crisis,
and lo! it has come, and I feel *nothing at all.*"

This letter was interrupted by the arrival of Professor
Stowe upon the scene, and was left in her desk unfinished
until three weeks after the wedding, when she added : —

"My husband and self are now quietly seated by our
own fireside, as domestic as any pair of tame fowl you
ever saw; he writing to his mother, and I to you. Two
days after our marriage we took a wedding excursion, so
called, though we would most gladly have been excused this
conformity to ordinary custom had not necessity required
Mr. Stowe to visit Columbus, and I had too much adhesive-
ness not to go too. Ohio roads at this season are no joke,
I can tell you, though we were, on the whole, wonderfully

taken care of, and our expedition included as many pleasures as an expedition at this time of the year *ever* could.

"And now, my dear, perhaps the wonder to you, as to
me, is how this momentous crisis in the life of such a wisp
of nerve as myself has been transacted so quietly.   My
dear, it is a wonder to myself.   I am tranquil, quiet, and
happy.   I look *only* on the present, and leave the future
with Him who has hitherto been so kind to me.   'Take
no thought for the morrow' is my motto, and my comfort
is to rest on Him in whose house there are many mansions
provided when these fleeting earthly ones pass away.

"Dear Georgy, naughty girl that I am, it is a month
that I have let the above lie by, because I got into a strain
of emotion in it that I dreaded to return to.   Well, so it
shall be no longer.   In about five weeks Mr. Stowe and
myself start for New England.   He sails the first of May.
I am going with him to Boston, New York, and other
places, and shall stop finally at Hartford, whence, as soon
as he is gone, it is my intention to return westward."

Thus, at the very threshold of their new life, Harriet and
her husband discovered that, great as their love for each
other might be, it was ever to be enlarged and made more
beautiful by their devotion to the common welfare.   The
condition of the public schools of Cincinnati was then far
behind the best intelligence of the age.   Harriet had devoted herself, up to the time of her marriage, to bringing
about some reformation in education, private as well as
public, and Professor Stowe had been one of the founders
of "The College for Teachers," an institution which exercised much influence in elevating the standard of teaching.
It was natural, under the circumstances, that Professor
Stowe should have been selected by the state legislature as
the right man to send abroad and report upon the common
schools of Europe, especially those of Prussia.   There was
great need also of foreign books for Lane Seminary, and

who was so well fitted as Professor Stowe to select these ? It was decided, therefore, that he should leave home on this double mission. Mrs. Stowe could hardly have been a child of her father without a feeling of being born to serve the world as well as to live and love in her own little round. Professor Stowe was of the same mind, and lived in the same atmosphere as his wife in this respect. There seems to have been no question between them as to the acceptance of this call. The need was clear to them both ; also it must have been quite evident that he was the only man capable of fulfilling such errands, with intelligence, for Cincinnati. His knowledge of Greek and Hebrew, German and Italian, was remarkable for any period, but was exceptional at a time when German dictionaries were so rare and inaccessible that Theodore Parker was obliged to walk from Watertown to Professor Ticknor's house in Boston to consult one. Professor Stowe's scholarship was not always, we have heard, of the most accurate kind, but he read with absolute ease the most recondite books in many languages. To the end of his life he carried a small Greek Testament and a copy of the Divina Commedia in his pocket, and died with them under his pillow ; when one copy of either of his favorites was worn out he would buy a new one; they were his inseparable companions.

This long parting of the newly married lovers was not easy. Evidently Mrs. Stowe found it difficult to keep up her husband's spirits. She was already unable to go with him, but she went to watch his departure from New York, and to cheer him on his way by a letter, to be opened on the voyage, sparkling with her wit and wisdom.

"Now, my dear, that you are gone where you are out of the reach of my care, advice, and good management, it is fitting that you should have something under my hand and seal for your comfort and furtherance in the new world you are going to. Firstly, I must caution you to set your face as a flint against the 'cultivation of indigo,' as Elisabeth calls it, in any way or shape. . . . But seriously, dear one, you must give more way to hope than to memory. You are going to a new scene now, and one that I hope will be full of enjoyment to you. I want you to take the good of it.

"Only think of all you expect to see: the great libraries and beautiful paintings, fine churches, and, above all, think of seeing Tholuck, your great Apollo. My dear, I wish I were a man in your place; if I wouldn't have a grand time!"

During the long summer and autumn of her husband's absence Mrs. Stowe lived at her father's home in Cincinnati, writing busily for a local paper, of which Henry Ward had accepted the temporary editorship, as well as for other journals in New York and at the West; beside these engagements, she wrote a daily journal to her husband, wherein we see, as in a glass, the crumbling and upheaving here and there of the great earthquake of war for slavery which was still to wait a quarter of a century for its awful development.

Mrs. Stowe was not yet altogether an abolitionist. Theodore D. Weld was a young student in the Seminary, who by lecturing in the South had earned the money for his education. He also earned what he had not foreseen, a knowledge of slavery, which made him a strong advocate for its abolition. He had won several slaveholders over to his faith, some of whom had freed their slaves. One of these gentlemen, Mr. Birney, came to Cincinnati and joined with Dr. Bailey in editing an anti-slavery newspaper there. Kentucky slave owners, getting wind of this, came to Cincinnati, and destroyed the Press. Mobocracy reigned; the people took sides hotly. Mrs. Stowe wrote to her husband: —

"For my part, I can easily see how such proceedings

may make converts to abolitionism, for already my sympathies are strongly enlisted for Mr. Birney, and I hope that
he will stand his ground and assert his rights.   The office
is fire-proof, and inclosed by high walls.   I wish he would
man it with armed men, and see what can be done.   If I
were a man I would go, for one, and take good care of at
least one window.   Henry sits opposite me writing a most
valiant editorial, and tells me to tell you he is waxing
mighty in battle.

.   .   .   .

"I told you in my last that the mob broke into Birney's
Press, where, however, the mischief done was but slight.
The object appeared to be principally to terrify.   Immediately there followed a general excitement in which even
good men in their panic and prejudice about abolitionism forgot that mobs were worse evils than these, talked
against Birney, and winked at the outrage; N. Wright
and Judge Burnet, for example.   Meanwhile the turbulent
spirits went beyond this and talked of revolution and of
righting things without law that could not be righted by
it.   At the head of these were Morgan, Neville, Long-
worth, Joseph Graham, and Judge Burke.   A meeting
was convoked at Lower Market Street to decide whether
they would permit the publishing of an abolition paper,
and to this meeting all the most respectable citizens were
by name summoned.

.   .   .   .

"For a day or two we did not know but there would
actually be war to the knife, as was threatened by the
mob, and we really saw Henry depart with his pistols with
daily alarm, only we were all too full of patriotism not to
have sent every brother we had rather than not have had
the principles of freedom and order defended.

"But here the tide turned.   The mob, unsupported by
a now frightened community, slunk into their dens and
were still."

The sense of obedience to law still holds her: "Pray what is there in Cincinnati to satisfy one whose mind is awakened on this subject?" she continues. "No one can have the system of slavery brought before him without an irrepressible desire to *do* something; and what is there to be done?"

In the early autumn, before Professor Stowe could return to his wife, she gave birth to twin daughters, who were named by her Eliza and Isabella; but the moment he reached New York, in mid-winter, after a two months' voyage home from London, and heard the news, he insisted they should be called Eliza Tyler and Harriet Beecher.

During the following summer, Mrs. Stowe's health became very delicate, and she went to make a long visit at the house of the Rev. William Beecher in Putnam, Ohio. Professor Stowe wrote to her: —

"This alliance between the old school (Presbyterians) and slaveholders will make more abolitionists than anything that has been done yet."

In January, Mrs. Stowe's third child, Henry, was born. She wrote in June to Georgiana May: —

"MY DEAR, DEAR GEORGIANA, — Only think how long it is since I have written to you, and how changed I am since then, — the mother of three children! Well, if I have not kept the reckoning of old times, let this last circumstance prove my apology, for I have been hand, heart, and head full since I saw you.

"Now, to-day, for example, I'll tell you what I had on my mind from dawn to dewy eve. In the first place I waked about half after four and thought, 'Bless me, how light it is! I must get out of bed and rap to wake up Mina, for breakfast must be had at six o'clock this morning.' So out of bed I jump and seize the tongs and pound, pound, pound over poor Mina's sleepy head, charitably allowing her about half an hour to get waked up in, — that being the quantum of time that it takes me, — or used to. Well, then baby wakes — quâ, quâ, quâ, so I give him his breakfast, dozing meanwhile and soliloquizing as follows: ' Now I must not forget to tell Mr. Stowe about the starch and dried apples ' — doze — ' ah, um, dear me! why does n't Mina get up? I don't hear her,' — doze — ' a, um, — I wonder if Mina has soap enough! I think there were two bars left on Saturday ' — doze again — I wake again. ' Dear me, broad daylight! I must get up and go down and see if Mina is getting breakfast.' Up I jump and up wakes baby. ' Now, little boy, be good and let mother dress, because she is in a hurry.' I get my frock half on, and baby by that time has kicked himself down off his pillow, and is crying and fisting the bedclothes in great order. I stop with one sleeve off and one on to settle matters with him. Having planted him bolt upright and gone all up and down the chamber barefoot to get pillows and blankets to prop him up, I finish putting my frock on and hurry down to satisfy myself by actual observation that the breakfast is in progress. Then back I come into the nursery, where, remembering that it is washing day, and that there is a great deal of work to be done, I apply myself vigorously to sweeping, dusting, and the setting to rights so necessary where there are three little mischiefs always pulling down as fast as one can put up.

.   .   .   .

" Well, Georgy, this marriage is — yes, I will speak well of it, after all; for when I can stop and think long enough to discriminate my head from my heels, I must say that I think myself a fortunate woman both in husband and children. My children I would not change for all the ease, leisure, and pleasure that I could have without them. They are money on interest whose value will be constantly increasing."

One of her friends at this time was anxious to get her to finish a story she had partly written, and for the conclusion of which the editor was waiting. This friend's account of difficulties is amusing, because both the ladies chose to be amused, and carried the matter off in such a humorous vein; but it easily has another side, when we consider Mrs. Stowe's health, and the work which lay before her.

"'Come, Harriet,' said I," wrote her friend, "as I found her tending one baby and watching two others just able to walk, 'where is that piece for the "Souvenir" which I promised the editor I would get from you and send on next week? You have only this one day left to finish it, and have it I must.'

"'And how will you get it, friend of mine?' said Harriet. 'You will at least have to wait till I get housecleaning over and baby's teeth through.'

"'As to house-cleaning, you can defer it one day longer; and as to baby's teeth, there is to be no end to them, as I can see. No, no; to-day that story must be ended. There Frederick has been sitting by Ellen and saying all those pretty things for more than a month now, and she has been turning and blushing till I am sure it is time to go to her relief. Come, it would not take you three hours at the rate you can write to finish the courtship, marriage, catastrophe, éclaircissement, and all; and this three hours' labor of your brains will earn enough to pay for all the sewing your fingers could do for a year to come. Two dollars a page, my dear, and you can write a page in fifteen minutes! Come, then, my lady housekeeper, economy is a cardinal virtue; consider the economy of the thing.'

"'But, my dear, here is a baby in my arms and two little pussies by my side, and there is a great baking down in the kitchen, and there is a "new girl" for "help," besides preparations to be made for housecleaning next week. It is really out of the question, you see.'

"'I see no such thing. I do not know what genius is given for, if it is not to help a woman out of a scrape. Come, set your wits to work, let me have my way, and you shall have all the work done and finish the story, too.'

"'Well, but kitchen affairs?'

"'We can manage them, too. You know you can write anywhere and anyhow. Just take your seat at the kitchen table with your writing weapons, and while you superintend Mina, fill up the odd snatches of time with the labors of your pen.'

"I carried my point. In ten minutes she was seated; a table with flour, rolling-pin, ginger, and lard on one side, a dresser with eggs, pork, and beans, and various cooking utensils on the other, near her an oven heating, and beside her a dark-skinned nymph, waiting orders.

"'Here, Harriet,' said I, 'you can write on this atlas in your lap; no matter how the writing looks, I will copy it.'

"'Well, well,' said she, with a resigned sort of amused look. 'Mina, you may do what I told you, while I write a few minutes, till it is time to mould up the bread. Where is the inkstand?'

"'Here it is, close by, on the top of the tea-kettle,' said I.

"At this Mina giggled, and we both laughed to see her merriment at our literary proceedings.

"I began to overhaul the portfolio to find the right sheet.

"'Here it is,' said I. 'Here is Frederick sitting by Ellen, glancing at her brilliant face, and saying something about "guardian angel," and all that — you remember?'

"'Yes, yes,' said she, falling into a muse, as she attempted to recover the thread of her story.

"'Ma'am, shall I put the pork on the top of the beans?' asked Mina.

"'Come, come,' said Harriet, laughing.   'You see how it is.   Mina is a new hand and cannot do anything without me to direct her.   We must give up the writing for to-day.'

"'No, no; let us have another trial.   You can dictate as easily as you can write.   Come, I can set the baby in this clothes-basket and give him some mischief or other to keep him quiet; you shall dictate and I will write.   Now, this is the place where you left off: you were describing the scene between Ellen and her lover; the last sentence was, "Borne down by the tide of agony, she leaned her head on her hands, the tears streamed through her fingers, and her whole frame shook with convulsive sobs."   What shall I write next?'

"'Mina, pour a little milk into this pearlash,' said Harriet.

.   .   .   .

"'Here,' said I, 'let me direct Mina about these matters, and write a while yourself.'

"Harriet took the pen and patiently set herself to the work.   For a while my culinary knowledge and skill were proof to all Mina's investigating inquiries, and they did not fail till I saw two pages completed.

"'You have done bravely,' said I, as I read over the manuscript; 'now you must direct Mina a while.   Meanwhile dictate and I will write.'

"Never was there a more docile literary lady than my friend.   Without a word of objection she followed my request.

"'I am ready to write,' said I.   'The last sentence was: "What is this life to one who has suffered as I have?"   What next?'

"'Shall I put in the brown or the white bread first?' said Mina.

"'The brown first,' said Harriet.

"'What is this life to one who has suffered as I have?"' said I.

"Harriet brushed the flour off her apron and sat down for a moment in a muse.   Then she dictated as follows: —

"'"Under the breaking of my heart I have borne up. I have borne up under all that tries a woman, — but this thought, — oh, Henry!"'

"'Ma'am, shall I put ginger into this pumpkin?' queried Mina.

"'No, you may let that alone just now,' replied Harriet.   She then proceeded: —

"'"I know my duty to my children.   I see the hour must come.   You must take them, Henry; they are my last earthly comfort."'

"'Ma'am, what shall I do with these egg-shells and all this truck here?' interrupted Mina.

"'Put them in the pail by you,' answered Harriet.

"'"They are my last earthly comfort,"' said I.   'What next?'

"She continued to dictate: —

"'"You must take them away.   It may be — perhaps it *must* be — that I shall soon follow, but the breaking heart of a wife still pleads, 'a little longer, a little longer.'"'

"'How much longer must the gingerbread stay in?' inquired Mina.

"'Five minutes,' said Harriet.

"'"A little longer, a little longer,"' I repeated in a dolorous tone, and we burst into a laugh.

"Thus we went on, cooking, writing, nursing, and laughing, till I finally accomplished my object.   The piece was finished, copied, and the next day sent to the editor."

It is not wonderful, certainly, to find the following letter written to Georgiana May in December, 1840.   In the previous month of May, another boy, Frederick William, had been brought into the world. Mrs. Stowe says: —

"For a year I have held the pen only to write an occasional business letter such as could not be neglected. This was primarily owing to a severe neuralgic complaint that settled in my eyes, and for two months not only made it impossible for me to use them in writing, but to fix them with attention on anything. I could not even bear the least light of day in my room. Then my dear little Frederick was born, and for two months more I was confined to my bed. Besides all this, we have had an unusual amount of sickness in our family. . . .

"For all that my history of the past year records so many troubles, I cannot, on the whole, regard it as a very troublous one. I have had so many counterbalancing mercies that I must regard myself as a person greatly blessed. It is true that about six months out of the twelve I have been laid up with sickness, but then I have had every comfort and the kindest of nurses in my faithful Anna. My children have thriven, and on the whole 'come to more,' as the Yankees say, than the care of them. Thus you see my troubles have been but enough to keep me from loving earth too well."

During this hard time the navigation of the Ohio had been impeded for several months. Cincinnati was like a besieged city; no supplies could reach the people. Flour and pork, which happily could be had at reasonable prices, kept them from starving, but in Mrs. Stowe's delicate condition it was especially difficult to bear. She was singularly uncomplaining, and the only mention we find of this state of public affairs is in a letter from Professor Stowe to his mother. A few months earlier there had been a meeting of all the Beecher family in Cincinnati, a very exciting affair to old Dr. Beecher as well as to the eleven children. Two of them had never met before!

The Doctor's pulpit was filled that Sunday, in the morning by his son Edward, by William in the afternoon, and by George in the evening. All these things drew upon Mrs. Stowe's nervous energy, already at a low ebb. She was obliged to leave home. Taking her six-year-old daughter Hattie with her she went first to Hartford, where the following letter reached her from her husband. She had confided to him in a previous letter some of her literary plans and aspirations; Professor Stowe replies: —

"My dear, you must be a literary woman. It is so written in the book of fate. Make all your calculations accordingly. Get a good stock of health and brush up your mind. Drop the E. out of your name. It only incumbers it and interferes with the flow and euphony. Write yourself fully and always Harriet Beecher Stowe, which is a name euphonious, flowing, and full of meaning. Then my word for it, your husband will lift up his head in the gate, and your children will rise up and call you blessed.

"Our humble dwelling has to-day received a distinguished honor of which I must give you an account. It was a visit from his excellency the Baron de Roenne, ambassador of his majesty the King of Prussia to the United States. He was pleased to assure me of the great satisfaction my report on Prussian schools had afforded the king and members of his court, with much more to the same effect. Of course, having a real live lord to exhibit, I was anxious for some one to exhibit him to; but neither Aunt Esther nor Anna dared venture near the study, though they both contrived to get a peep at his lordship from the little chamber window as he was leaving.

"And now, my dear wife, I want you to come home as quick as you can. The fact is I cannot live without you, and if we were not so prodigious poor I would come for you at once. There is no woman like you in this wide world. Who else has so much talent with so little self-conceit; so much reputation with so little affectation; so much literature with so little nonsense; so much enterprise with so little extravagance; so much tongue with so little scold; so much sweetness with so little softness; so much of so many things and so little of so many other things?"

In answer to this letter, Mrs. Stowe writes from Hartford: —

"I have seen Johnson of the 'Evangelist.' He is very liberally disposed, and I may safely reckon on being paid for all I do there. Who is that Hale, Jr., that sent me the 'Boston Miscellany,' and will he keep his word with me? His offers are very liberal, — twenty dollars for three pages, not very close print. Is he to be depended on? If so, it is the best offer I have received yet. I shall get something from the Harpers some time this winter or spring. Robertson, the publisher here, says the book ('The Mayflower') will sell, and though the terms they offer me are very low, that I shall make something on it. For a second volume I shall be able to make better terms. On the whole, my dear, if I choose to be a literary lady, I have, I think, as good a chance of making profit by it as any one I know of. But with all this, I have my doubts whether I shall be able to do so.

"Our children are just coming to the age when everything depends on my efforts. They are delicate in health, and nervous and excitable, and need a mother's whole attention. Can I lawfully divide my attention by literary efforts?

"There is one thing I must suggest. If I am to write, I must have a room to myself, which shall be *my* room. I have in my own mind pitched on Mrs. Whipple's room. I can put the stove in it. I have bought a cheap carpet for it, and I have furniture enough at home to furnish it comfortably, and I only beg in addition that you will let me change the glass door from the nursery into that room and keep my plants there, and then I shall be quite happy.

"All last winter I felt the need of some place where I could go and be quiet and satisfied. I could not there, for there was all the setting of tables, and clearing up of tables, and dressing and washing of children, and everything else going on, and the continual falling of soot and coal dust on everything in the room was a constant annoyance to me, and I never felt comfortable there, though I tried hard. Then if I came into the parlor where you were, I felt as if I were interrupting you, and you know you sometimes thought so, too.

"Now this winter let the cooking-stove be put into that room, and let the pipe run up through the floor into the room above. The children can be washed and dressed and keep their playthings in the upper room and play there when we don't want them below. You can study by the parlor fire, and I and my plants, etc., will take the other room. I shall keep my work and all my things there, and feel settled and quiet. I intend to have a regular part of each day devoted to the children, and then I shall take them in there."

In his reply to this letter Professor Stowe says: —

"The little magazine ('The Souvenir') goes ahead finely. Fisher sent down to Fulton the other day and got sixty subscribers. He will make the June number as handsome as possible, as a specimen number for the students, several of whom will take agencies for it during the coming vacation. You have it in your power by means of this little magazine to form the mind of the West for the coming generation. It is just as I told you in my last letter. God has written it in his book that you must be a literary woman, and who are we that we should contend against God? You must therefore make all your calculations to spend the rest of your life with your pen.

"If you only could come home to-day how happy should I be. I am daily finding out more and more (what I knew very well before) that you are the most intelligent and agreeable woman in the whole circle of my acquaintance."

"That Professor Stowe's devoted admiration for his wife was reciprocated," writes their son Charles, "and that a most perfect sympathy of feeling existed between the husband and wife, is shown by a line in one of Mrs. Stowe's letters from Hartford in which she says: 'I was telling Belle yesterday that I did not know till I came away how much I was dependent upon you for information. There are a thousand favorite subjects on which I could talk with you better than with any one else. If you were not already my dearly loved husband I should certainly fall in love with you.'"

In this same letter she writes of herself: —

"One thing more in regard to myself. The absence and wandering of mind and forgetfulness that so often vexes you is a physical infirmity with me. It is the failing of a mind not calculated to endure a great pressure of care, and so much do I feel the pressure I am under, so much is my mind often darkened and troubled by care, that life seriously considered holds out few allurements, — only my children.

"In returning to my family, from whom I have been so long separated, I am impressed with a new and solemn feeling of responsibility. It appears to me that I am not probably destined for long life; at all events, the feeling is strongly impressed upon my mind that a work is put into my hands which I must be earnest to finish shortly. It is nothing great or brilliant in the world's eye; it lies in one small family circle, of which I am called to be the central point."

We find in a journal of this period: "For many weeks past my mind has been oppressed with a strong sense of the importance of the early education of my children, and with an ever agonizing sense of incompetence to undertake it. Where so many of the wisest and best *fail*, how can *I* hope to succeed. My only hope is in prayer. God is all powerful. . . .

"The most fearful thing about this education matter is, that it is example more than word. Talk as you will, the child follows what he *sees*, not what he hears. The prevailing tone of the parent's character will make the temper of the household; the spirit of the parent will form the spirit of the child."

On the way home from her visit to the East, Mrs. Stowe traveled for the first time by rail, and of this novel experience she writes to Miss Georgiana May: —

BATAVIA, August 29.

"Here I am at Brother William's, and our passage along this railroad reminds me of the verse of the psalm: —

    'Tho' lions roar and tempests blow,
    And rocks and dangers fill the way.'

"Such confusion of tongues, such shouting and swearing, such want of all sort of system and decency in arrangements, I never desire to see again. I was literally almost trodden down and torn to pieces in the Rochester depot when I went to help my poor, near-sighted spouse in sorting out the baggage. You see there was an accident which happened to the cars leaving Rochester that morning, which kept us two hours and a half at the passing place this side of Auburn, waiting for them to come up and go by us. The consequence was that we got into this Rochester depot aforesaid after dark, and the steamboat, the canal boat, and the Western train of cars had all been kept waiting three hours beyond their usual time, and they all broke loose upon us the moment we put our heads out of the cars, and such a jerking, and elbowing, and scuffling, and swearing, and protesting, and scolding you never heard, while the great locomotive sailed up and down in the midst thereof, spitting fire and smoke like some great fiend monster diverting himself with our commotions. I do think these steam concerns border a little too much on the supernatural to be agreeable, especially when you are shut up in a great dark depot after sundown.

"Well, after all, we had to ride till twelve o'clock at night to get to Batavia, and I 've been sick abed, so to speak, ever since."

The winter was one of peculiar trial to the family at Walnut Hills; as Mrs. Stowe writes, "It was a season of sickness and gloom." Typhoid fever raged among the students of the seminary, and the house of the president was converted into a hospital, while the members of his family were obliged to devote themselves to nursing the sick and dying.

In July, a few weeks before the birth of her third daughter, Georgiana May, a most terrible and overwhelming sorrow came on Mrs. Stowe, in common with all the family, in the sudden death of her brother, the Rev. George Beecher.

In October she writes to one of her brothers: —

"Our straits for money this year are unparalleled even in our annals. Even our bright and cheery neighbor Allen begins to look blue, and says six hundred dollars is the very most we can hope to collect of our salary, once twelve hundred dollars. We have a flock of entirely destitute young men in the seminary, as poor in money as they are rich in mental and spiritual resources. They promise to

be as fine a band as those we have just sent off. We have
two from Iowa and Wisconsin who were actually crowded
from secular pursuits into the ministry by the wants of
the people about them. Revivals began, and the people
came to them saying, ' We have no minister, and you must
preach to us, for you know more than we do.' "

Professor Stowe was obliged to go to the East in order
to raise money for the struggling seminary. His wife
wrote to him: —

"I am already half sick with confinement to the house
and overwork. If I should sew every day for a month to
come I should not be able to accomplish a half of what is
to be done, and should be only more unfit for my other
duties."

Exception has been taken to the idea that Mrs. Stowe
suffered from poverty. Her children were always made
comfortable. She had a devoted young woman, Anna, who
was her friend, companion, nurse for her children, and a
second self in household labors, such as only a loving, sympathetic heart like Mrs. Stowe's could draw to her side and
hold by her affection through a long series of years; also
there was a colored woman in the kitchen for the simple
cooking and the rougher work of the household. Nevertheless, for Mrs. Stowe it was indeed "suffering from poverty." Professor Stowe's salary was very uncertain, as we
have seen. They were both pledged to Christ's work in
the world, and did not count the dollars and cents before
undertaking any labor which was required of them. Even
if a salary generous for a professor in those days had been
regularly paid, it would not have been more than sufficient
for seven children and an invalid wife! Her husband was
not lacking in affection nor in constant endeavor, but they
were neither of them far-sighted from a worldly point of
view. For nearly two years at this period the trouble
continued which bore so hardly upon the wife and mother.

Professor Stowe having been called away to a ministerial convention at Detroit, his wife wrote to him: —

June 16.

"My dear Husband, — It is a dark, sloppy, rainy, muddy, disagreeable day, and I have been working hard (for me) all day in the kitchen, washing dishes, looking into closets, and seeing a great deal of that dark side of domestic life which a housekeeper may who will investigate too curiously into minutiæ in warm, damp weather, especially after a girl who keeps all clean on the *outside* of cup and platter, and is very apt to make good the rest of the text in the *inside* of things.

"I am sick of the smell of sour milk, and sour meat, and sour everything, and then the clothes *will* not dry, and no wet thing does, and everything smells mouldy; and altogether I feel as if I never wanted to eat again.

"Your letter, which was neither sour nor mouldy, formed a very agreeable contrast to all these things; the more so for being unexpected. I am much obliged to you for it. As to my health, it gives me very little solicitude, although it is bad enough and daily growing worse. I feel no life, no energy, no appetite, or rather a growing distaste for food; in fact, I am becoming quite ethereal. Upon reflection I perceive that it pleases my Father to keep me in the fire, for my whole situation is excessively harassing and painful. I suffer with sensible distress in the brain, as I have done more or less since my sickness last winter, a distress which some days takes from me all power of planning or executing anything; and you know that, except this poor head, my unfortunate household has no mainspring, for nobody feels any kind of responsibility to do a thing in time, place, or manner, except as I oversee it.

"Georgiana is so excessively weak, nervous, cross, and fretful, night and day, that she takes all Anna's strength

and time with her; and then the children are, like other
little sons and daughters of Adam, full of all kinds of
absurdity and folly.

"When the brain gives out, as mine often does, and one
cannot think or remember anything, then what is to be
done? All common fatigue, sickness, and exhaustion is
nothing to this distress. Yet do I rejoice in my God,
and know in whom I believe, and only pray that the fire
may consume the dross; as to the gold, that is imperishable. No real evil can happen to me, so I fear nothing
for the future, and only suffer in the present tense.

"God, the mighty God, is mine, of that I am sure, and
I know He knows that though flesh and heart fail, I am
all the while desiring and trying for his will alone. As
to a journey, I need not ask a physician to see that it is
needful to me as far as health is concerned, that is to say,
all human appearances are that way, but I feel no particular choice about it. If God wills I go. He can easily
find means. Money, I suppose, is as plenty with Him
now as it always has been, and if He sees it is really best
He will doubtless help me."

Professor Stowe was doubtless much moved by this
letter. We find he was able to get the means for sending
his wife eastward to her friends in Hartford and Boston during the summer, but her condition was such that he was
not greatly relieved. In March she writes: —

"For all I have had trouble I can think of nothing but
the greatness and richness of God's mercy to me in giving
me such friends, and in always caring for us in every strait.
There has been no day this winter when I have not had
abundant reason to see this. Some friend has always
stepped in to cheer and help, so that I have wanted for
nothing. My husband has developed wonderfully as house-
father and nurse. You would laugh to see him in his

spectacles gravely marching the little troop in their night-
gowns up to bed, tagging after them, as he says, like an
old hen after a flock of ducks.   The money for my journey has been sent in from an unknown hand in a wonderful manner.   All this shows the care of our Father, and
encourages me to rejoice and to hope in Him."

It was decided that she must try Dr. Wesselhoeft's
water-cure at Brattleboro', Vermont, her increasing debility
giving cause for anxiety.   On her journey she sends a
line back from Pittsburgh to her husband, to which he
replies, giving her the names of two ladies, strangers, who
have sent him money, hearing of illness in the family.   He
continues: —

"Henry and I have been living in a Robinson Crusoe
and man Friday sort of style, greatly to our satisfaction,
ever since you went away."

Happily, two of Mrs. Stowe's sisters, Catherine and
Mary, were able to be with her during a part of her absence, but she was obliged to be away from her husband
and children eleven months!   It was a weary interval.

BRATTLEBORO', September.

"MY DEAR HUSBAND, — I have been thinking of all
your trials, and I really pity you in having such a wife.
I feel as if I had been only a hindrance to you instead of
a help, and most earnestly and daily do I pray to God to
restore my health that I may do something for you and
my family.   I think if I were only at home I could at
least sweep and dust, and wash potatoes, and cook a little,
and talk to my children, and should be doing something
for my family.   But the hope of getting better buoys me
up.   I go through these tedious and wearisome baths and
bear that terrible douche thinking of my children.   They
never will know how I love them. . . .

"There is great truth and good sense in your analysis

of the cause of our past failures. We have now come to
a sort of crisis. If you and I do as we should for *five
years* to come the character of our three oldest children
will be established. This is why I am willing to spend so
much time and make such efforts to have health. Oh,
that God would give me these five years in full possession
of mind and body, that I may train my children as they
should be trained. I am fully aware of the importance of
system and order in a family. I know that nothing can
be done without it; it is the keystone, the *sine quâ non*,
and in regard to my children I place it next to piety. At
the same time it is true that both Anna and I labor under
serious natural disadvantages on this subject. It is not
all that is necessary to feel the importance of order and
system, but it requires a particular kind of talent to carry
it through a family. Very much the same kind of talent,
as Uncle Samuel said, which is necessary to make a good
prime minister. . . .

"I think you might make an excellent sermon to Christians on the care of health, in consideration of the various
infirmities and impediments to the developing the results
of religion, that result from bodily ill health, and I wish
you would make one, that your own mind may be more
vividly impressed with it. The world is too much in a
hurry. Ministers think there is no way to serve Christ
but to overdraw on their physical capital for four or five
years for Christ, and then have nothing to give, but become a mere burden on his hands for the next five. . . .

November 18. "The daily course I go through presup-
poses a degree of vigor beyond anything I ever had before.
For this week, I have gone before breakfast to the wave-
bath and let all the waves and billows roll over me till
every limb ached with cold, and my hands would scarcely
have feeling enough to dress me. After that I have walked
till I was warm, and come home to breakfast with such an

appetite! Brown bread and milk are luxuries indeed, and the only fear is that I may eat too much. At eleven comes my douche, to which I have walked in a driving rain for the last two days, and after it walked in the rain again till I was warm. (The umbrella you gave me at Natick answers finely, as well as if it were a silk one.) After dinner I roll ninepins or walk till four, then sitz-bath, and another walk till six.

"I am anxious for your health; do be persuaded to try a long walk before breakfast. You don't know how much good it will do you. Don't sit in your hot study without any ventilation, a stove burning up all the vitality of the air and weakening your nerves, and above all, do *amuse* yourself. Go to Dr. Mussey's and spend an evening, and to father's and Professor Allen's. When you feel worried go off somewhere and forget and throw it off. I should really rejoice to hear that you and father and mother, with Professor and Mrs. Allen, Mrs. K., and a few others of the same calibre would agree to meet together for dancing cotillons. It would do you all good, and if you took Mr. K.'s wife and poor Miss Much-Afraid, her daughter, into the alliance, it would do them good. Bless me! what a profane set everybody would think you were, and yet you are the people of all the world most solemnly in need of it. I wish you could be with me in Brattleboro' and coast down hill on a sled, go sliding and snowballing by moonlight! I would snowball every bit of the *hypo* out of you! Now, my dear, if you are going to get sick, I am going to come home. There is no use in my trying to get well if you, in the meantime, are going to run yourself down."

January, 1847.

"MY DEAR SOUL,—I received your most melancholy effusion, and I am sorry to find it's just so. I entirely agree and sympathize. Why did n't you engage the two tombstones — one for you and one for me?

.   .   .   .

"But, seriously, my dear husband, you must try and be patient, for this cannot last forever. Be patient and bear it like the toothache, or a driving rain, or anything else that you cannot escape. To see things as through a glass darkly is your infirmity, you know; but the Lord will yet deliver you from this trial. I know how to pity you, for the last three weeks I have suffered from an over-whelming mental depression, a perfect heartsickness. All I wanted was to get home and die. Die I was very sure I should, at any rate, but I suppose I was never less pre-pared to do so."

Happily the long exile was ended at last, and Mrs. Stowe returned to her rejoicing family. In the following January her son, Samuel Charles, was born. Shortly after, Professor Stowe became ill and was sent in turn to Brattle-boro', where he remained alone for fifteen months. Mrs. Stowe writes to Miss May: —

"My beloved Georgy, — For six months after my return from Brattleboro' my eyes were so affected that I wrote scarce any, and my health was in so strange a state that I felt no disposition to write. After the birth of little Charley my health improved, but my husband was sick, and I have been so loaded and burdened with cares as to drain me dry of all capacity of thought, feeling, memory, or emotion.

"Well, Georgy, I am thirty-seven years old! I am glad of it. I like to grow old and have six children and cares endless. I wish you could see me with my flock all around me. They sum up my cares, and were they gone

I should ask myself, What now remains to be done?
They are my work, over which I fear and tremble."

Cholera was rife this year in Cincinnati. Professor
Stowe was anxious to return, and be with his family, but
his wife would not hear of it.

Her journal letter says, June 29th : —

"MY DEAR HUSBAND, — This week has been unusually
fatal. The disease in the city has been malignant and
virulent. Hearse drivers have scarce been allowed to
unharness their horses, while furniture carts and common
vehicles are often employed for the removal of the dead.
The sable trains which pass our windows, the frequent
indications of crowding haste, and the absence of reverent
decency have, in many cases, been most painful. Of
course all these things, whether we will or no, bring very
doleful images to the mind.

"On Tuesday one hundred and sixteen deaths from
cholera were reported, and that night the air was of that
peculiarly oppressive, deathly kind that seems to lie like
lead on the brain and soul.

"As regards your coming home, I am decidedly opposed
to it. First, because the chance of your being taken ill is
just as great as the chance of your being able to render us
any help. To exchange the salubrious air of Brattleboro'
for the pestilent atmosphere of this place with your system
rendered sensitive by water-cure treatment would be extremely dangerous. It is a source of constant gratitude to
me that neither you nor father are exposed to the dangers
here. Second, none of us are sick, and it is very uncertain whether we shall be.

.　　.　　.　　.　　.　　.　　.　　.　　.　　.

"July 4. All well. The meeting yesterday was very
solemn and interesting. There is more or less sickness

about us, but no very dangerous cases. One hundred and
twenty burials from cholera alone yesterday, yet to-day we
see parties bent on pleasure or senseless carousing, while
to-morrow and next day will witness a fresh harvest of
death from them. How we can become accustomed to
anything! A while ago ten a day dying of cholera struck
terror to all hearts; but now the tide has surged up gradually until the deaths average over a hundred daily, and
everybody is getting accustomed to it. Gentlemen make
themselves agreeable to ladies by reciting the number of
deaths in this house or that. This, together with talk of
funerals, cholera medicines, cholera dietetics, and chloride
of lime, form the ordinary staple of conversation. Serious
persons, of course, throw in moral reflections to their taste.

"July 10. Yesterday little Charley was taken ill, not
seriously, and at any other season I should not be alarmed.
Now, however, a slight illness seems like a death sentence,
and I will not dissemble that I feel from the outset very
little hope. I still think it best that you should not return. By so doing you might lose all you have gained.
You might expose yourself to a fatal incursion of disease.
It is decidedly not your duty to do so.

"July 12. Yesterday I carried Charley to Dr. Pulte,
who spoke in such a manner as discouraged and frightened
me. He mentioned dropsy on the brain as a possible
result. I came home with a heavy heart, sorrowing, desolate, and wishing my husband and father were here.

"About one o'clock this morning Miss Stewart suddenly
opened my door, crying, ' Mrs. Stowe, Henry is vomiting.'
I was on my feet in an instant, and lifted up my heart for
help. He was, however, in a few minutes relieved. Then
I turned my attention to Charley, who was also suffering,
put him into a wet sheet, and kept him there until he was
in a profuse perspiration. He is evidently getting better,
and is auspiciously cross. Never was crossness in a baby

more admired.   Anna and I have said to each other exult-
ingly a score of times, 'How cross the little fellow is!
How he does scold!'

"July 15.   Since I last wrote, our house has been a
perfect hospital, — Charley apparently recovering, but still
weak and feeble, unable to walk or play, and so miserably
fretful and unhappy.   Sunday Anna and I were fairly
stricken down, as many others are, with no particular
illness, but with such miserable prostration.   I lay on the
bed all day reading my hymn-book and thinking over passages of Scripture.

"July 17.   To-day we have been attending poor old
Aunt Frankie's[1] funeral.   She died yesterday morning,
taken sick the day before while washing.   Good, honest,
trustful old soul!   She was truly one who hungered and
thirsted for righteousness.

"Yesterday morning our poor little dog, Daisy, who
had been ailing the day before, was suddenly seized with
frightful spasms, and died in half an hour.   Poor little
affectionate thing!   If I were half as good for my nature
as she for hers I should be much better than I am.   While
we were all mourning over her the news came that Aunt
Frankie was breathing her last.   Hatty, Eliza, Anna, and
I made her shroud yesterday, and this morning I made
her cap.   We have just come from her grave.

"July 23.   At last, my dear, the hand of the Lord
hath touched us.   We have been watching all day by the
dying bed of little Charley, who is gradually sinking.
After a partial recovery from the attack I described in my
last letter he continued for some days very feeble, but still
we hoped for recovery.   About four days ago he was taken
with decided cholera, and now there is no hope of his sur-
viving this night.

"Every kindness is shown us by the neighbors.   Do

[1] An old colored woman.

not return. All will be over before you could possibly get here, and the epidemic is now said by the physicians to prove fatal to every new case. Bear up. Let us not faint when we are rebuked of Him. I dare not trust myself to say more, but shall write again soon.

July 26.

"My dear Husband, — At last it is over, and our dear little one is gone from us. He is now among the blessed. My Charley — my beautiful, loving, gladsome baby, so loving, so sweet, so full of life and hope and strength — now lies shrouded, pale and cold, in the room below. Never was he anything to me but a comfort. He has been my pride and joy. Many a heartache has he cured for me. Many an anxious night have I held him to my bosom and felt the sorrow and loneliness pass out of me with the touch of his little warm hands. Yet I have just seen him in his death agony, looked on his imploring face when I could not help nor soothe nor do one thing, not one, to mitigate his cruel suffering, do nothing but pray in my anguish that he might die soon. I write as though there were no sorrow like my sorrow, yet there has been in this city, as in the land of Egypt, scarce a house without its dead. This heart-break, this anguish, has been everywhere, and when it will end God alone knows."

Professor Stowe returned to Cincinnati with a new purpose in his mind. He had struggled through seventeen of the best years of his life serving Lane Seminary and the people of Cincinnati as far as in him lay. Now, two or three invitations had been received from the East, one of which (from Bowdoin College) he accepted with peculiar pleasure, because he graduated there, and passed in Brunswick his happy early years. He could not leave Lane Seminary until he should find some one to fill his place, but it was decided that Mrs. Stowe, with three of the children,

should leave Cincinnati in April and establish herself in a
house in Brunswick, ready to receive the rest of the family.

Of this journey Mrs. Stowe writes: —

"The boat got into Pittsburgh between four and five
on Wednesday. The agent for the Pennsylvania Canal
came on board and soon filled out our tickets, calling my
three chicks one and a half. We had a quiet and agreeable passage, and crossed the slides at five o'clock in the
morning, amid exclamations of unbounded delight from all
the children, to whom the mountain scenery was a new
and amazing thing. We reached Hollidaysburg about
eleven o'clock, and at two o'clock in the night were called
up to get into the cars at Jacktown. Arriving at Philadelphia about three o'clock in the afternoon, we took the
boat and railroad line for New York.

"At Lancaster we telegraphed to Brooklyn, and when
we arrived in New York, between ten and eleven at night,
Cousin Augustus met us and took us over to Brooklyn.
We had ridden three hundred miles since two o'clock that
morning, and were very tired. . . . I am glad we came
that way, for the children have seen some of the finest
scenery in our country. . . . Henry's people are more
than ever in love with him, and have raised his salary to
$3300, and given him a beautiful horse and carriage
worth $600. . . . My health is already improved by the
journey, and I was able to walk a good deal between the
locks on the canal. As to furniture, I think that we may
safely afford an outlay of $150, and that will purchase all
that may be necessary to set us up, and then we can get
more as we have means and opportunity. . . . If I got
anything for those pieces I wrote before coming away, I
would like to be advised thereof by you. . . . My plan
is to spend this week in Brooklyn, the next in Hartford,
the next in Boston, and go on to Brunswick some time in
May or June."

May 18, we find her writing from Boston, where she is staying with her brother, Rev. Edward Beecher : —

"MY DEAR HUSBAND, — I came here from Hartford on Monday, and have since then been busily engaged in the business of buying and packing furniture.

"I expect to go to Brunswick next Tuesday night by the Bath steamer, which way I take as the cheaper. My traveling expenses, when I get to Brunswick, including everything, will have been seventy-six dollars. . . . And now, lastly, my dear husband, you have never been wanting . . . in kindness, consideration, and justice, and I want you to reflect calmly how great a work has been imposed upon me at a time when my situation particularly calls for rest, repose, and quiet.

"To come alone such a distance with the whole charge of children, accounts, and baggage; to push my way through hurrying crowds, looking out for trunks, and bargaining with hackmen, has been a very severe trial of my strength, to say nothing of the usual fatigues of traveling."

"It was at this time," continues her son, "and as a result of the experiences of this trying period, that Mrs. Stowe wrote that little tract dear to so many Christian hearts, 'Earthly Care a Heavenly Discipline.'"

Few women have known greater earthly cares. That she saw her way through them, even while in the valley of darkness, and was able to guide others to the light, giving them the help and support by which she learned to live and to rejoice, this was her mission to the world.

CHAPTER V

On the eve of sailing for Brunswick, Mrs. Stowe writes to Mrs. Sykes (Miss May): "I am wearied and worn out with seeing to bedsteads, tables, chairs, mattresses, with thinking about shipping my goods and making out accounts, and I have my trunk yet to pack, as I go on board the Bath steamer this evening. I beg you to look up Brunswick on the map; it is about half a day's ride in the cars from Boston. I expect to reach there by the way of Bath by to-morrow forenoon. There I have a house engaged and kind friends who offer every hospitable assistance. Come, therefore, to see me, and we will have a long talk in the pine woods, and knit up the whole history from the place where we left it."

Before leaving Boston she had written to her husband in Cincinnati: "You are not able just now to bear anything, my dear husband, therefore trust all to me; I never doubt or despair. I am already making arrangements with editors to raise money.

"I have sent some overtures to Wright. If he accepts my pieces and pays you for them, take the money and use it as you see necessary; if not, be sure and bring the pieces back to me. I am strong in spirit, and God who has been with me in so many straits will not forsake me now. I know Him well; He is my Father, and though I may be a blind and erring child, He will help me for all that. My trust through all errors and sins is in Him. He who helped poor timid Jacob through all his fears and appre-

hensions, who helped Abraham even when he sinned, who
was with David in his wanderings, and who held up the
too confident Peter when he began to sink, — He will help
us, and his arms are about us, so that we shall not sink,
my dear husband."

She writes from Brunswick the last of May: "After a
week of most incessant northeast storm, most discouraging
and forlorn to the children, the sun has at length come
out. . . . There is a fair wind blowing, and every prospect, therefore, that our goods will arrive promptly from
Boston, and that we shall be in our own house by next
week. Mrs. Upham [1] has done everything for me, giving
up time and strength and taking charge of my affairs in
a way without which we could not have got along at all in
a strange place and in my present helpless condition. This
family is delightful, there is such a perfect sweetness and
quietude in all its movements. Not a harsh word or
hasty expression is ever heard. It is a beautiful pattern
of a Christian family, a beautiful exemplification of religion." . . .

The events of the first summer in Brunswick are graphi-
cally described by Mrs. Stowe in a letter written to her
sister in-law, Mrs. George Beecher, in December.

"MY DEAR SISTER, — Is it really true that snow is on
the ground and Christmas coming, and I have not written
unto thee, most dear sister? No, I don't believe it! I
have n't been so naughty — it 's all a mistake — yes, written I must have — and written I have, too — in the night-
watches as I lay on my bed — such beautiful letters — I wish
you had only received them; but by day it has been hurry,
hurry, hurry, and drive, drive, drive! or else the calm of
a sick-room, ever since last spring.

"I put off writing when your letter first came, because

[1] Wife of Professor Upham of Bowdoin College.

I meant to write you a long letter, — a full and complete
one; and so days slid by, — and became weeks, — and my
little Charley came . . . etc. and etc. !!! Sarah, when
I look back, I wonder at myself, not that I forget any one
thing that I should remember, but that I have remembered
anything. From the time that I left Cincinnati with my
children to come forth to a country that I knew not of
almost to the present time, it has seemed as if I could
scarcely breathe, I was so pressed with care. My head
dizzy with the whirl of railroads and steamboats; then ten
days' sojourn in Boston, and a constant toil and hurry in
buying my furniture and equipments; and then landing in
Brunswick in the midst of a drizzly, inexorable northeast storm, and beginning the work of getting in order a
deserted, dreary, damp old house. All day long running
from one thing to another, as, for example, thus: —

"'Mrs. Stowe, how shall I make this lounge, and what
shall I cover the back with first?'

"*Mrs. Stowe.* 'With the coarse cotton in the closet.'

"*Woman.* 'Mrs. Stowe, there isn't any more soap to
clean the windows.'

"*Mrs. Stowe.* 'Where shall I get soap?'

"'Here, H., run up to the store and get two bars.'

"'There is a man below wants to see Mrs. Stowe about
the cistern. Before you go down, Mrs. Stowe, just show
me how to cover this round end of the lounge.'

"'There's a man up from the depot, and he says that
a box has come for Mrs. Stowe, and it's coming up to the
house; will you come down and see about it?'

"'Mrs. Stowe, don't go till you have shown the man
how to nail that carpet in the corner. He's nailed it all
crooked; what shall he do? The black thread is all used up,
and what shall I do about putting gimp on the back of that
sofa? Mrs. Stowe, there is a man come with a lot of pails
and tinware from Furbish; will you settle the bill now?'

"'Mrs. Stowe, here is a letter just come from Boston inclosing that bill of lading; the man wants to know what he shall do with the goods. If you will tell me what to say, I will answer the letter for you.'

"'Mrs. Stowe, the meat-man is at the door. Hadn't we better get a little beefsteak, or something, for dinner?'

"'Shall Hatty go to Boardman's for some more black thread?'

"'Mrs. Stowe, this cushion is an inch too wide for the frame. What shall we do now?'

"'Mrs. Stowe, where are the screws of the black walnut bedstead?'

"'Here's a man has brought in these bills for freight. Will you settle them now?'

"'Mrs. Stowe, I don't understand using this great needle. I can't make it go through the cushion; it sticks in the cotton.'

"Then comes a letter from my husband, saying he is sick abed, and all but dead; don't ever expect to see his family again; wants to know how I shall manage, in case I am left a widow; knows we shall get in debt and never get out; wonders at my courage; thinks I am very sanguine; warns me to be prudent, as there won't be much to live on in case of his death, etc., etc., etc. I read the letter and poke it into the stove, and proceed. . . .

"Some of my adventures were quite funny; as for example: I had in my kitchen-elect no sink, cistern, or any other water privileges, so I bought at the cotton factory two of the great hogsheads they bring oil in, which here in Brunswick are often used for cisterns, and had them brought up in triumph to my yard, and was congratulating myself on my energy, when lo and behold! it was discovered that there was no cellar door except one in the kitchen, which was truly a strait and narrow way, down a long pair of stairs. Hereupon, as saith John Bunyan,

I fell into a muse, — how to get my cisterns into my cellar. In days of chivalry I might have got a knight to make me a breach through the foundation walls, but that was not to be thought of now, and my oil hogsheads, standing disconsolately in the yard, seemed to reflect no great credit on my foresight. In this strait I fell upon a real honest Yankee cooper, whom I besought, for the reputation of his craft and mine, to take my hogsheads to pieces, carry them down in staves, and set them up again, which the worthy man actually accomplished one fair summer forenoon, to the great astonishment of 'us Yankees.' When my man came to put up the pump, he stared very hard to see my hogsheads thus translated and standing as innocent and quiet as could be in the cellar, and then I told him, in a very mild, quiet way, that I got 'em taken to pieces and put together, — just as if I had been always in the habit of doing such things. Professor Smith came down and looked very hard at them and then said, 'Well, nothing can beat a willful woman.' Then followed divers negotiations with a very clever, but (with reverence) somewhat lazy gentleman of jobs, who occupieth a carpenter's shop opposite to mine. This same John Titcomb, my very good friend, is a character peculiar to Yankeedom. He is part owner and landlord of the house I rent, and connected by birth with all the best families in town; a man of real intelligence, and good education, a great reader, and quite a thinker. Being of an ingenious turn, he does painting, gilding, staining, upholstery jobs, varnishing, all in addition to his primary trade of carpentry. But he is a man studious of ease, and fully possessed with the idea that man wants but little here below; so he boards himself in his workshop on crackers and herring, washed down with cold water, and spends his time working, musing, reading new publications, and taking his comfort. In his shop you shall see a joiner's bench, hammers, planes, saws,

gimlets, varnish, paint, picture frames, fence posts, rare
old china, one or two fine portraits of his ancestry, a bookcase full of books, the tooth of a whale, an old spinning-
wheel and spindle, a lady's parasol frame, a church lamp
to be mended, in short, Henry says Mr. Titcomb's shop is
like the ocean; there is no end to the curiosities in it.

"In all my moving and fussing Mr. Titcomb has been
my right-hand man. Whenever a screw was loose, a nail
to be driven, a lock mended, a pane of glass set, — and these
cases were manifold, — he was always on hand. But my
sink was no fancy job, and I believe nothing but a very
particular friendship would have moved him to undertake
it. So this same sink lingered in a precarious state for
some weeks, and when I had *nothing else to do*, I used
to call and do what I could in the way of enlisting the
good man's sympathies in its behalf.

"How many times I have been in and seated myself in
one of the old rocking-chairs, and talked first of the news
of the day, the railroad, the last proceedings in Congress,
the probabilities about the millennium, and thus brought
the conversation by little and little round to my sink! . . .
because, till the sink was done, the pump could not be
put up, and we couldn't have any rain-water. Sometimes
my courage would quite fail me to introduce the subject,
and I would talk of everything else, turn and get out of
the shop, and then turn back as if a thought had just
struck my mind, and say: —

"'Oh, Mr. Titcomb! about that sink?'

"'Yes, ma'am, I was thinking about going down street
this afternoon to look out stuff for it.'

"'Yes, sir, if you would be good enough to get it done
as soon as possible; we are in great need of it.'

"'I think there's no hurry. I believe we are going
to have a dry time now, so that you could not catch any
water, and you won't need a pump at present.'

"These negotiations extended from the first of June to the first of July, and at last my sink was completed, and so also was a new house spout, concerning which I had had divers communings with Deacon Dunning of the Baptist church. Also during this time good Mrs. Mitchell and myself made two sofas, or lounges, a barrel chair, divers bedspreads, pillow cases, pillows, bolsters, mattresses; we painted rooms; we revarnished furniture; we — what *did* n't we do?

"Then came on Mr. Stowe; and then came the eighth of July and my little Charley. I was really glad for an excuse to lie in bed, for I was full tired, I can assure you. Well, I was what folks call very comfortable for two weeks, when my nurse had to leave me. . . .

"During this time I have employed my leisure hours in making up my engagements with newspaper editors. I have written more than anybody, or I myself, would have thought. I have taught an hour a day in our school, and I have read two hours every evening to the children. The children study English history in school, and I am reading Scott's historic novels in their order. To-night I finish the 'Abbot;' shall begin 'Kenilworth' next week; yet I am constantly pursued and haunted by the idea that I don't do anything. Since I began this note I have been called off at least a dozen times; once for the fish-man, to buy a codfish; once to see a man who had brought me some barrels of apples; once to see a book-man; then to Mrs. Upham, to see about a drawing I promised to make for her; then to nurse the baby; then into the kitchen to make a chowder for dinner; and now I am at it again, for nothing but deadly determination enables me ever to write; it is rowing against wind and tide.

"I suppose you think now I have begun, I am never going to stop, and, in truth, it looks like it; but the spirit moves now and I must obey.

"Christmas is coming, and our little household is all alive with preparations; every one collecting their little gifts with wonderful mystery and secrecy. . . .

"To tell the truth, dear, I am getting tired; my neck and back ache, and I must come to a close.

"Your ready kindness to me in the spring I felt very much; and *why* I did not have the sense to have sent you one line just by way of acknowledgment, I'm sure I don't know; I felt just as if I had, till I awoke, and behold! I had not. But, my dear, if my wits are somewhat wool-gathering and unsettled, my heart is as true as a star. I love you, and have thought of you often.

"This fall I have felt often *sad*, lonesome, both very unusual feelings with me in these busy days; but the breaking away from my old home, and leaving father and mother, and coming to a strange place affected me naturally. In those sad hours my thoughts have often turned to George; I have thought with encouragement of his blessed state, and hoped that I should soon be there, too. I have many warm and kind friends here, and have been treated with great attention and kindness. Brunswick is a delightful residence, and if you come East next summer, you must come to my new home. George[1] would delight to go a-fishing with the children, and see the ships, and sail in the sailboats, and all that.

"Give Aunt Harriet's love to him, and tell him when he gets to be a painter to send me a picture.

"Affectionately yours,
"H. Stowe."

Her spirit was still unsatisfied. In spite of striving and incessant devotion, there was yet a deeper cry in her for humanity, which had not found expression. Few women had suffered more or had enjoyed more than she;

---

[1] Her brother George's only child.

her experience was ripe for others, and her joy was large enough to give hope to the down-trodden.

Upon her way to Brunswick she stopped, as we have said, at the house of her brother in Boston, Dr. Edward Beecher. Daniel Webster's seventh of March speech was still ringing in the ears of the people. The hated Compromise had been defended by their idol, and he was cast into the dust. "Ichabod," Whittier cried, "so fallen, so lost! ' When honor dies the man is dead.' "

The hearts of men were aflame at the Fugitive Slave Act, which was then being debated and finally passed by the Congress of that year. The conversation turned upon this topic, and heart-rending scenes were described of families broken up, men frozen by flight in winter through rivers and pathless forests on their way to Canada. After Mrs. Stowe reached Brunswick Mrs. Edward Beecher wrote to her sister: "Hattie, if I could use a pen as you can, I would write something to make this whole nation feel what an accursed thing slavery is."

One of Mrs. Stowe's children remembers well the scene in the little parlor in Brunswick when the letter alluded to was received. Mrs. Stowe herself read it aloud to the assembled family, and when she came to the passage, "I would write something that would make this whole nation feel what an accursed thing slavery is," Mrs. Stowe rose up from her chair, crushing the letter in her hand, and with an expression on her face that stamped itself on the mind of her child, said: "I will write something. I will if I live."

In December, Mrs. Stowe sent a message to her sister: "Tell Katy I thank her for her letter and will answer it. As long as the baby sleeps with me nights I can't do much at anything, but I will do it at last. I will write that thing if I live.

"What are folks in general saying about the slave law,

and the stand taken by Boston ministers universally, except Edward?

"To me it is incredible, amazing, mournful!! I feel as if I should be willing to sink with it, were all this sin and misery to sink in the sea. . . . I wish father would come on to Boston, and preach on the Fugitive Slave Law, as he once preached on the slave-trade, when I was a little girl in Litchfield. I sobbed aloud in one pew and Mrs. Judge Reeves in another. I wish some Martin Luther would arise to set this community right."

She also writes to Professor Stowe at Christmas time and cheers him up by telling him of stories she had been writing for the "Era," and other papers, in which he figures as a farmer, the facts being drawn from life!! But the New Year had not arrived when she records days of terrible cold, which made it almost impossible to hold a pen.

December 29. "We have had terrible weather here. I remember such a storm when I was a child in Litchfield. Father and mother went to Warren, and were almost lost in the snowdrifts.

"Sunday night I rather watched than slept. The wind howled, and the house rocked just as our old Litchfield house used to. The cold has been so intense that the children have kept begging to get up from table at mealtimes to warm feet and fingers. Our air-tight stoves warm all but the floor, — heat your head and keep your feet freezing. If I sit by the open fire in the parlor my back freezes; if I sit in my bedroom and try to write my head aches and my feet are cold. I am projecting a sketch for the 'Era' on the capabilities of liberated blacks to take care of themselves. Can't you find out for me how much Willie Watson has paid for the redemption of his friends, and get any items in figures of that kind that you can pick up in Cincinnati? . . . When I have a headache and feel

sick, as I do to-day, there is actually not a place in the
house where I can lie down and take a nap without being
disturbed.   Overhead is the school-room, next door is the
dining-room, and the girls practice there two hours a day.
If I lock my door and lie down, some one is sure to be
rattling the latch before fifteen minutes have passed. . . .
There is no doubt in my mind that our expenses this year
will come two hundred dollars, if not three, beyond our
salary.   We shall be able to come through, notwithstanding, but I don't want to feel obliged to work as hard
every year as I have this.   I can earn four hundred dollars
a year by writing, but I don't want to feel that I must,
and when weary with teaching the children, and tending
the baby, and buying provisions, and mending dresses,
and darning stockings, sit down and write a piece for some
paper.

.   .   .   .

"Ever since we left Cincinnati to come here the good
hand of God has been visibly guiding our way.   Through
what difficulties have we been brought!   Though we knew
not where means were to come from, yet means have been
furnished every step of the way, and in every time of need.
I was just in some discouragement with regard to my writing; thinking that the editor of the 'Era' was overstocked
with contributors, and would not want my services another
year, and lo! he sends me one hundred dollars, and ever
so many good words with it.   Our income this year will
be seventeen hundred dollars in all, and I hope to bring
our expenses within thirteen hundred."

Twenty-five years afterwards Mrs. Stowe wrote to her
son Charles of this period of her life: "I well remember
the winter you were a baby and I was writing 'Uncle
Tom's Cabin.'   My heart was bursting with the anguish
excited by the cruelty and injustice our nation was showing to the slave, and praying God to let me do a little,

and to cause my cry for them to be heard. I remember many a night weeping over you as you lay sleeping beside me, and I thought of the slave mothers whose babes were torn from them."

In April the first chapter of "Uncle Tom's Cabin" was dispatched to Dr. Gamaliel Bailey, the editor of the "National Era" in Washington. In July, Mrs. Stowe wrote as follows: —

BRUNSWICK, July 9, 1851.

FREDERICK DOUGLASS, ESQ.:

Sir, — You may perhaps have noticed in your editorial readings a series of articles that I am furnishing for the "Era" under the title of "Uncle Tom's Cabin, or Life among the Lowly."

In the course of my story the scene will fall upon a cotton plantation. I am very desirous, therefore, to gain information from one who has been an actual laborer on one, and it occurred to me that in the circle of your acquaintance there might be one who would be able to communicate to me some such information as I desire. I have before me an able paper written by a Southern planter, in which the details and *modus operandi* are given from his point of sight. I am anxious to have something more from another standpoint. I wish to be able to make a picture that shall be graphic and true to nature in its details. Such a person as Henry Bibb, if in the country, might give me just the kind of information I desire. You may possibly know of some other person. I will subjoin to this letter a list of questions, which in that case you will do me a favor by inclosing to the individual, with the request that he will at earliest convenience answer them.

For some few weeks past I have received your paper through the mail, and have read it with great interest, and desire to return my acknowledgments for it. It will be a pleasure to me at some time when less occupied to contribute something to its columns. I have noticed with regret your sentiments on two subjects, — the church and African colonization, . . . with the more regret because I think you have a considerable share of reason for your feelings on both these subjects; but I would willingly, if I could, modify your views on both points.

In the first place you say the church is "pro-slavery." There is a sense in which this may be true. The American church of all denominations, taken as a body, comprises the best and most conscientious people in the country. I do not say it comprises none but these, or that none such are found out of it, but only if a census were taken of the purest and most high-principled men and women of the country, the majority of them would be found to be professors of religion in some of the various Christian denominations. This fact has given to the church great weight in this country, — the general and predominant spirit of intelligence and probity and piety of its majority has given it that degree of weight that it has the power to decide the great moral questions of the day. Whatever it unitedly and decidedly sets itself against as moral evil it can put down. In this sense the church is responsible for the sin of slavery. Dr. Barnes has beautifully and briefly expressed this on the last page of his work on slavery, when he says: "Not all the force out of the church could sustain slavery an hour if it were not sustained in it." It then appears that the church has the power to put an end to this evil and does not do it. In this sense she may be said to be pro-slavery. But the church has the same power over intemperance, and Sabbath-breaking, and sin of all kinds. There is not a doubt that if the moral power of the church were brought up to the New Testament standpoint it is sufficient to put an end to all these as well as to slavery. But I would ask you, Would you consider it a fair representation of the Christian church in this country to say that it is pro-intemperance, pro-Sabbath-breaking, and pro everything that it might put down if it were in a higher state of moral feeling? If you should make a list of all the abolitionists of the country, I think that you would find a majority of them in the church, — certainly some of the most influential and efficient ones are ministers.

I am a minister's daughter, and a minister's wife, and I have had six brothers in the ministry (one is in heaven); I certainly ought to know something of the feelings of ministers on this subject. I was a child in 1820 when the Missouri question was agitated, and one of the strongest and deepest impressions on my mind was that made by my father's sermons and prayers, and the anguish of his soul for the poor slave at that time. I remember his preaching drawing tears down the hardest faces of the old farmers in his congregation.

I well remember his prayers morning and evening in the family for "poor, oppressed, bleeding Africa," that the time of her deliverance might come; prayers offered with strong crying and tears, and which indelibly impressed my heart and made me what I am from my very soul, the enemy of all slavery. Every brother I have has been in his sphere a leading anti-slavery man. One of them was to the last the bosom friend and counselor of Lovejoy. As for myself and husband, we have for the last seventeen years lived on the border of a slave State, and we have never shrunk from the fugitives, and we have helped them with all we had to give. I have received the children of liberated slaves into a family school, and taught them with my own children, and it has been the influence that we found in the church and by the altar that has made us do all this. Gather up all the sermons that have been published on this offensive and unchristian Fugitive Slave Law, and you will find that those against it are numerically more than those in its favor, and yet some of the strongest opponents have not published their sermons. Out of thirteen ministers who meet with my husband weekly for discussion of moral subjects, only three are found who will acknowledge or obey this law in any shape.

After all, my brother, the strength and hope of your oppressed race does lie in the church, — in hearts united to Him of whom it is said, "He shall spare the souls of the needy, and precious shall their blood be in his sight." Everything is against you, but Jesus Christ is for you, and He has not forgotten his church, misguided and erring though it be. I have looked all the field over with despairing eyes; I see no hope but in Him. This movement must and will become a purely religious one. The light will spread in churches, the tone of feeling will rise, Christians North and South will give up all connection with, and take up their testimony against, slavery, and thus the work will be done.

The great story was at last finished in "The National Era," April, 1852. She had put her life-blood, her prayers, and her tears into the work; yet she had no reason to know that her labors were to find response in the world.

"After sending the last proof-sheet to the office," she says, "I sat alone reading Horace Mann's eloquent plea for the young men and women, then about to be consigned to the slave warehouse of Bruin & Hill in Alexandria, Virginia, — a plea impassioned, eloquent, but vain, as all other pleas on that side had ever proved in all courts hitherto. It seemed that there was no hope, that nobody would hear, nobody would read, nobody pity; that this frightful system, that had already pursued its victims into the free States, might at last even threaten them in Canada."

She began to reflect if she had done all in her power, and sitting down again at her desk, she wrote letters to Prince Albert, to the Duke of Argyll, to the Earls of Carlisle and Shaftesbury, to Macaulay, Dickens, and others whom she knew to be interested in the cause of anti-slavery. These she ordered to be sent to their several addresses, accompanied by the very earliest copies of her book that should be printed.

Very soon she was assured of the success of her sketches in book form. The whole year's work in "The National Era" brought her only three hundred dollars; but Mr. Jewett, a Boston publisher, having offered to bring it out immediately in one volume, three thousand copies were sold the first day of publication.

She began to reflect how the subject had lain dormant in her mind since she was a child, how she had been led step by step to do her work, and a sense of detachment grew upon her daily.

The modesty of Mrs. Stowe's demeanor throughout the altogether extraordinary experience which came to her after the publication of "Uncle Tom's Cabin" is to be understood only by looking upon her life from her own standpoint. She was pursued by the thought that the freedom of the slaves was not yet accomplished, and although the hearts of good men were hot with desire to achieve this end, no one could see how the great result was to be won. She had done something, she said to herself; God had stirred the hearts of men through her, but what more could be done! This was her constant cry, her ever present thought. Letters of congratulation poured in upon her and were gratefully received. The well known men and women, both of Europe and America, responded to her appeal, but she was entirely spent, and could not see the

way.   Soon after the appearance of her book, she felt the
need of change, and left home, going to stop for a while
with her brother Henry, where she could rest, and at
the same time watch the progress of events.   She soon
wrote to her husband: —

"The mother of the Edmondson girls [two slave girls
formerly, redeemed by the Plymouth Church at the instance
of Henry Ward Beecher], now aged and feeble, is in the
city.   I did not actually know when I wrote ' Uncle Tom '
of a living example in which Christianity had reached its
fullest development under the crushing wrongs of slavery,
but in this woman I see it.   I never knew before what I
could feel till, with her sorrowful, patient eyes upon me,
she told me her history and begged my aid.   The expression
of her face as she spoke, and the depth of patient sorrow
in her eyes, was beyond anything I ever saw.

" ' Well,' said I, when she had finished, ' set your heart
at rest; you and your children shall be redeemed.   If I
can't raise the money otherwise, I will pay it myself.'
You should have seen the wonderfully sweet, solemn look
she gave me as she said, ' The Lord bless you, my child! '

"I have received a sweet note from Jenny Lind,
with her name and her husband's with which to head my
subscription list.   They give a hundred dollars.   Another
hundred is subscribed by Mr. Bowen in his wife's name,
and I have put my own name down for an equal amount.
A lady has given me twenty-five dollars, and Mr. Storrs
has pledged me fifty dollars.   Milly and I are to meet the
ladies of Henry's and Dr. Cox's churches to-morrow, and
she is to tell them her story.   I have written to Drs.
Bacon and Dutton in New Haven to secure a similar meeting of ladies there.   I mean to have one in Boston, and
another in Portland.   It will do good to the givers as
well as to the receivers.

"But all this time I have been so longing to get your

letter from New Haven, for I heard it was there. It is
not fame nor praise that contents me. I seem never to
have needed love so much as now. I long to hear you
say how much you love me. Dear one, if this effort im-
pedes my journey home, and wastes some of my strength,
you will not murmur. When I see this Christlike soul
standing so patiently bleeding, yet forgiving, I feel a
sacred call to be the helper of the helpless, and it is better
that my own family do without me for a while longer than
that this mother lose all. *I must redeem her.*

"New Haven, June 2. My old woman's case pro-
gresses gloriously. I am to see the ladies of this place
to-morrow. Four hundred dollars were contributed by
individuals in Brooklyn, and the ladies who took subscription papers at the meeting will undoubtedly raise two
hundred dollars more."

Before leaving New York, Mrs. Stowe gave Milly Edmondson her check for the entire sum necessary to pur-
chase her own freedom and that of her children, and sent
her home rejoicing. That this sum was made up to her
by the generous contributions of those to whom she ap-
pealed is shown by a note written to her husband in July.
She says: —

"Had a very kind note from A. Lawrence inclosing a
twenty dollar gold piece for the Edmondsons. Isabella's
ladies gave me twenty-five dollars, so you see our check is
more than paid already."

Although during her visit in New York, Mrs. Stowe
made many new friends, and was overwhelmed with con-
gratulations and praise of her book, the most pleasing incident of this time seems to have been an epistolatory interview with Jenny Lind (Goldschmidt). In writing of it
to her husband she says: —

"Well, we have heard Jenny Lind, and the affair was
a bewildering dream of sweetness and beauty. Her face

and movements are full of poetry and feeling. She has the artless grace of a little child, the poetic effect of a wood-nymph, is airy, light, and graceful.

"We had first-rate seats, and how do you think we got them? When Mr. Howard went early in the morning for tickets, Mr. Goldschmidt told him it was impossible to get any good ones, as they were all sold. Mr. Howard said he regretted that, on Mrs. Stowe's account, as she was very desirous of hearing Jenny Lind. 'Mrs. Stowe!' exclaimed Mr. Goldschmidt, 'the author of "Uncle Tom's Cabin?"' Indeed, she shall have a seat, whatever happens!' Thereupon he took his hat and went out, returning shortly with tickets for two of the best seats in the house, inclosed in an envelope directed to me in his wife's hand-writing. To-day I sent a note of acknowledgment with a copy of my book. I am most happy to have seen her, for she is a noble creature."

In the "History of the United States" by Mr. J. F. Rhodes there is a brief critical review of Mrs. Stowe's work which may be received as the ultimate view of posterity. The historian says: "There was a correct picture of the essential features of slavery in 'Uncle Tom's Cabin,' the book which everybody read. The author of it had 'but one purpose, to show the institution of slavery truly just as it existed. While she had not the facts which a critical historian would have collected, — for the 'Key to Uncle Tom's Cabin' was not compiled until after the novel was written, — she used with the intuition of genius the materials gained through personal observation, and the result was what she desired." Again he continues: "One of the finest touches in 'Uncle Tom' is his joyful expression when told by his good and indulgent master that he should be set free and sent back to his old home in Kentucky. In attributing the common desire of humanity to the negro, the author was as true as she was effective."

A perfect history of the writing of "Uncle Tom" and of the effect produced by its appearance is given by Mrs. Stowe in the form of an introduction to the illustrated edition published many years later. We cannot do better than to repeat exactly this eloquent story of her success. The account she gives is unvarnished and unexaggerated. We can study in this paper the wonderful change which has taken place in her style when we compare these pages with her early letters.

"The author of 'Uncle Tom' had for many years lived in Ohio on the confines of a slave state, and had thus been made familiar with facts and occurrences in relation to the institution of American slavery. Some of the most harrowing incidents related in the story had from time to time come to her knowledge in conversation with former slaves now free in Ohio. The cruel sale and separation of a married woman from her husband, narrated in Chapter XII., 'Select Incidents of Lawful Trade,' had passed under her own eye while passenger on a steamboat on the Ohio River. Her husband and brother had once been obliged to flee with a fugitive slave woman by night, as described in Chapter IX., and she herself had been called to write the letters for a former slave woman, servant in her own family, to a slave husband in Kentucky, who, trusted with unlimited liberty, free to come and go on business between Kentucky and Ohio, still refused to break his pledge of honor to his master, though that master from year to year deferred the keeping of his promise of freedom to the slave. It was the simple honor and loyalty of this Christian black man, who remained in slavery rather than violate a trust, that first impressed her with the possibility of such a character as, years after, was delineated in Uncle Tom.

"From time to time incidents were brought to her knowledge which deepened her horror of slavery. In her own family she had a private school for her children, and as there was no provision for the education of colored children in her vicinity, she allowed them the privilege of attending. One day she was suddenly surprised by a visit from the mother of one of the brightest and most amusing of these children. It appeared that the child had never been emancipated, and was one of the assets of an estate in Kentucky, and had been seized and carried off by one of the executors, and was to be sold by the sheriff at auction to settle the estate. The sum for the little one's ransom was made up by subscription in the neighborhood, but the incident left a deep mark in Mrs. Stowe's mind as to the practical workings of the institution of slavery.

"But it was not for many years that she felt any call to make use of the materials thus accumulating. In fact, it was a sort of general impression upon her mind, as upon that of many humane people in those days, that the subject was so dark and painful a one, so involved in difficulty and obscurity, so utterly beyond human hope or help, that it was of no use to read, or think, or distress one's self about it. There was a class of professed Abolitionists in Cincinnati and the neighboring regions, but they were unfashionable persons and few in number. Like all asserters of pure abstract right as applied to human affairs, they were regarded as a species of moral monomaniacs, who, in the consideration of one class of interests and wrongs, had lost sight of all proportion and all good judgment. Both in church and in state they were looked upon as ' those that troubled Israel.'

"It was a general saying among conservative and sagacious people that this subject was a dangerous one to investigate, and that nobody could begin to read and think upon it without becoming practically insane; moreover, that it was a subject of such delicacy that no discussion of it could be held in the free States without impinging upon the sensibilities of the slave States, to whom alone the management of the matter belonged.

"So when Dr. Bailey — a wise, temperate, and just man, a model of courtesy in speech and writing — came to Cincinnati and set up an anti-slavery paper, proposing a fair discussion of the subject, there was an immediate excitement. On two occasions a mob led by slaveholders from Kentucky attacked his office, destroyed his printing-press, and threw his types into the Ohio River. The most of the Cincinnati respectability, in church and state, contented themselves on this occasion with reprobating the imprudence of Dr. Bailey in thus ' arousing the passions of our fellow-citizens of Kentucky.' In these mobs and riots the free colored people were threatened, maltreated, abused, and often had to flee for their lives. Even the servants of good families were often chased to the very houses of their employers, who rescued them with difficulty; and the story was current in those days of a brave little woman who defended her black waiter, standing, pistol in hand, on her own doorstep, and telling the mob face to face that they should not enter except over her dead body.

"Professor Stowe's house was more than once a refuge for frightened fugitives on whom the very terrors of death had fallen, and the inmates slept with arms in the house and a large bell ready to call the young men of the adjoining Institution, in case the mob should come up to search the house. Nor was this a vain or improbable suggestion, for the mob in their fury had more than once threatened to go up and set fire to Lane Seminary, where a large body of the students were known to be abolitionists. Only the fact that the Institution was two miles from the city, with a rough and muddy road up a long high hill, proved its salvation. Cincinnati mud, far known for its depth and tenacity, had sometimes its advantages.

"The general policy of the leaders of society, in cases of such disturbances, was after the good old pattern in Judæa, where a higher One had appeared, who disturbed the traders in swine; 'they besought him that he would depart out of their coasts.' Dr. Bailey at last was induced to remove his paper to Washington, and to conduct his investigation under the protection of the national Capitol, — and there for years he demonstrated the fact that the truth may be spoken plainly yet courteously, and with all honorable and Christian fairness, on the most exciting of subjects. In justice to the South it must be said that his honesty, courage, and dignity of character won for him friends even among the most determined slaveholders. Manly men have a sort of friendship for an open, honest opponent, like that of Richard Cœur de Lion for Saladin.

"Far otherwise was the fate of Lovejoy, who essayed an anti-slavery paper at Alton, Illinois. A mob from Missouri besieged the office, set the house on fire, and shot him at the door. It was for some days reported that Dr. Beecher's son, Rev. Edward Beecher, known to have been associated with Lovejoy at this period, had been killed at the same time. Such remembrances show how well grounded were the fears which attended every effort to agitate this subject. People who took the side of justice and humanity in those days had to count the cost and pay the price of their devotion. In those times, when John G. Fee, a young Kentucky student in Lane Seminary, liberated his slaves, and undertook to preach the gospel of emancipation in Kentucky, he was chased from the State, and disinherited by his own father. Berea College, for the education of colored and white, stands to-day a triumphant monument of his persistence in well-doing. Mr. Van Zandt, a Kentucky farmer, set free his slaves and came over and bought a farm in Ohio. Subsequently, from an impulse of humanity, he received and protected fugitive slaves in the manner narrated in Chapter IX. of 'Uncle Tom's Cabin.' For this he was seized, imprisoned, his property attached, and he was threatened with utter ruin. Salmon P. Chase, then a rising young lawyer in Cincinnati, had the bravery to appear as his lawyer. As he was leaving the court-room, after making his plea, one of the judges remarked, 'There goes a young man who has *ruined* himself to-day,' and the sentiment was echoed by the general voice of society. The case went against Van Zandt, and Mr. Chase carried it up to the Supreme Court of the United States, which, utterly ignoring argument and justice, decided it against him. But a few years more, and Salmon P. Chase was himself Chief Justice of the United States. It was one of those rare dramatic instances in which courage and justice sometimes bring a reward even in this life.

"After many years' residence in Ohio, Mrs. Stowe returned to make her abode in New England, just in the height of the excitement produced by the Fugitive Slave Law. Settled in Brunswick, Maine, she was in constant communication with friends in Boston, who wrote to her from day to day of the terror and despair which that law had occasioned to industrious, worthy colored people who had from time to time escaped to Boston, and were living in peace and security. She heard of families broken up and fleeing in the dead of winter to the frozen shores of Canada. But what seemed to her more inexplicable, more dreadful, was the apparent apathy of the Christian world of the free North to these proceedings. The pulpits that denounced them were exceptions; the voices raised to remonstrate few and far between.

"In New England, as at the West, professed abolitionists were a small, despised, unfashionable band, whose constant remonstrances from year to year had been disregarded as the voices of impracticable fanatics. It seemed now as if the system once confined to the Southern States was rousing itself to new efforts to extend itself all over the North, and to overgrow the institutions of free society.

"With astonishment and distress Mrs. Stowe heard on all sides, from humane and Christian people, that the slavery of the blacks was a guaranteed constitutional right, and that all opposition to it endangered the national Union. With this conviction she saw that even earnest and tender-hearted Christian people seemed to feel it a duty to close their eyes, ears, and hearts to the harrowing details of slavery, to put down all discussion of the subject, and even to assist slave owners to recover fugitives in Northern States. She said to herself, these people cannot know what slavery is; they do not see what they are defending; and hence arose a purpose to write some sketches which should show to the world slavery as she had herself seen it. Pondering this subject, she was one day turning over a little bound volume of an anti-slavery magazine, edited by Mrs. Dr. Bailey, of Washington, and there she read the account of the escape of a woman with her child on the ice of the Ohio River from Kentucky. The incident was given by an eye-witness, one who had helped the woman to the Ohio shore. This formed the first salient point of the story. She began to meditate. The faithful slave husband in Kentucky occurred to her as a pattern of Uncle Tom, and the scenes of the story began gradually to form themselves in her mind.

"The first part of the book ever committed to writing was the death of Uncle Tom. This scene presented itself almost as a tangible vision to her mind while sitting at the communion table in the little church in Brunswick. She was perfectly overcome by it, and could scarcely restrain the convulsion of tears and sobbings that shook her frame.

She hastened home and wrote it, and her husband being away she read it to her two sons of ten and twelve years of age. The little fellows broke out into convulsions of weeping, one of them saying, through his sobs, 'Oh! mamma, slavery is the most cursed thing in the world!' From that time the story can less be said to have been composed by her than imposed upon her. Scenes, incidents, conversations rushed upon her with a vividness and importunity that would not be denied. The book insisted upon getting itself into being, and would take no denial. After the two or three first chapters were written, she wrote to Dr. Bailey of the 'National Era' that she was planning a story that might probably run through several numbers of the 'Era.' In reply she received an instant application for it, and began immediately to send off weekly installments. She was then in the midst of heavy domestic cares, with a young infant, with a party of pupils in her family to whom she was imparting daily lessons with her own children, and with untrained servants requiring constant supervision, but the story was so much more intense a reality to her than any other earthly thing that the weekly installment never failed. It was there in her mind day and night waiting to be written, and requiring but a few moments to bring it into visible characters.

"The weekly number was always read to the family circle before it was sent away, and all the household kept up an intense interest in the progress of the story.

"As the narrative appeared in the 'Era,' sympathetic words began to come to her from old workers who had long been struggling in the anti-slavery cause. She visited Boston, went to the Anti-Slavery rooms, and reinforced her répertoire of facts by such documents as Theodore D. Weld's 'Slavery As It Is,' the Lives of Josiah Henson and Lewis Clarke, particulars from both whose lives were inwoven with the story in the characters of Uncle Tom and George Harris.

"In shaping her material the author had but one purpose, to show the institution of slavery truly, just as it
existed. She had visited in Kentucky, had formed the
acquaintance of people who were just, upright, and generous, and yet slaveholders. She had heard their views and
appreciated their situation; she felt that justice required
that their difficulties should be recognized and their virtues
acknowledged. It was her object to show that the evils
of slavery were the inherent evils of a bad *system*, and
not always the fault of those who had become involved in
it and were its actual administrators.

"Then she was convinced that the presentation of slavery
alone, in its most dreadful forms, would be a picture of
such unrelieved horror and darkness as nobody could be
induced to look at. Of set purpose, she sought to light up
the darkness by humorous and grotesque episodes, and the
presentation of the milder and more amusing phases of
slavery, for which her recollection of the never-failing wit
and drollery of her former colored friends in Ohio gave
her abundant material. As the story progressed, a young
publisher, J. P. Jewett, of Boston, set his eye upon it,
and made overtures for the publication of it in book form,
to which she consented. After a while she had a letter
from him expressing his fears that she was making the
story too long for a one-volume publication. He reminded
her that it was an unpopular subject, and that people
would not willingly hear much about it; that one short
volume might possibly sell, but if it grew to two it might
prove a fatal obstacle to its success. Mrs. Stowe replied
that she did not make the story, that the story made itself,
and that she could not stop it till it was done. The feeling that pursued her increased in intensity to the last, till
with the death of Uncle Tom it seemed as if the whole
vital force had left her. A feeling of profound discouragement came over her. Would anybody read it? Would

anybody listen? Would this appeal, into which she had
put heart, soul, mind, and strength, which she had written
with her heart's blood, — would it, too, go for nothing, as
so many prayers and groans and entreaties of these poor
suffering souls had already gone? There had just been
a party of slaves who had been seized and thrown into
prison in Washington for a vain effort to escape. They
were, many of them, partially educated, cultivated young
men and women, to whom slavery was intolerable. When
they were retaken and marched through the streets of
Washington, followed by a jeering crowd, one of them,
named Emily Edmonson, answered one man who cried
shame upon her, that she was not ashamed, — that she
was proud that she and all the rest of them had made an
effort for liberty! It was the sentiment of a heroine, but
she and her sisters were condemned no less to the auction-
block.

"'Uncle Tom's Cabin' was published March 20, 1852.
The despondency of the author as to the question whether
anybody would read or attend to her appeal was soon dispelled. Ten thousand copies were sold in a few days, and
over three hundred thousand within a year, and eight
power-presses, running day and night, were barely able to
keep pace with the demand for it. It was read everywhere, apparently, and by everybody, and she soon began
to hear echoes of sympathy all over the land. The indignation, the pity, the distress, that had long weighed upon
her soul seemed to pass off from her, and into the readers
of the book.

"The following note from a lady, an intimate friend, was
a specimen of many which the post daily brought her: —

"'My DEAR MRS. STOWE, — I sat up last night until
long after one o'clock, reading and finishing "Uncle Tom's
Cabin." I *could not* leave it any more than I could have

left a dying child; nor could I restrain an almost hysterical
sobbing for an hour after I laid my head upon my pillow.
I thought I was a thoroughgoing abolitionist before, but
your book has awakened so strong a feeling of indignation
and of compassion, that I seem never to have had *any*
feeling on this subject till now.   But what can we do?
Alas! alas! what *can* we do?   This storm of feeling has
been raging, burning like a very fire in my bones all the
livelong night, and through all my duties this morning it
haunts me, — I *cannot* away with it.   Gladly would I
have gone out in the midnight storm last night, and, like
the blessed martyr of old, been stoned to death, if that
could have rescued these oppressed and afflicted ones.   But
that would avail nothing.   And now what am I doing?
Just the most foolish thing in the world.   Writing to you,
who need no incitement; to you, who have spun from
your very vitals this tissue of agony and truths; for I
know, I feel, that there are burning drops of your heart's
best blood here concentrated.   To *you*, who need no encouragement or sympathy of mine, and whom I would not
insult by praise, — oh, no, you stand on too high an emi-
nence for praise; but methinks I see the prayers of the
poor, the blessings of those who are ready to perish, gathering in clouds about you, and forming a halo round your
beloved head.   And surely the tears of gentle, sympathiz-
ing childhood, that are dropping about many a Christian
hearthstone over the wrongs and cruelties depicted by you
so touchingly, will water the sod and spring up in bright
flowers at your feet.   And better still, I *know*, — I see,
in the flushing cheek, the clenched hand and indignant
eye of the young man, as he dashes down the book and
paces the room to hide the tears that he is too proud to
show, too powerless to restrain, that you are sowing seed
which shall yet spring up to the glory of God, to the good
of the poor slave, to the enfranchisement of our beloved
though guilty country.'

" In one respect, Mrs. Stowe's expectations were strikingly different from fact. She had painted slaveholders as amiable, generous, and just. She had shown examples among them of the noblest and most beautiful traits of character; had admitted fully their temptations, their perplexities, and their difficulties, so that a friend of hers who had many relatives in the South wrote to her in exultation : ' Your book is going to be the great pacificator; it will unite both North and South.' Her expectation was that the professed abolitionists would denounce it as altogether too mild in its dealings with slaveholders. To her astonishment it was the extreme abolitionists who received, and the entire South who rose up against it.

" The most valuable of the letters referred to were from Lord Carlisle, the Rev. Charles Kingsley, the Earl of Shaftesbury, Archbishop Whately, Hon. Arthur Helps, Frederika Bremer, and George Sand. The latter thus introduced ' Uncle Tom's Cabin ' to the literary world of France : —

To review a book, the very morrow after its appearance, in the very journal where it has just been published, is doubtless contrary to usage, but in this case it is the most disinterested homage that can be rendered, since the immense success attained by this work at its publication does not need to be set forth.

This book is in all hands and in all journals. It has, and will have, editions in every form; people devour it, they cover it with tears. It is no longer permissible to those who can read not to have read it, and one mourns that there are so many souls condemned never to read it, — helots of poverty, slaves through ignorance, for whom society has been unable as yet to solve the double problem of uniting the food of the body with the food of the soul.

It is not, then, it cannot be, an officious and needless

task to review this book of Mrs. Stowe. We repeat, it is a homage, and never did a generous and pure work merit one more tender and spontaneous. She is far from us; we do not know her who has penetrated our hearts with emotions so sad and yet so sweet. Let us thank her the more. Let the gentle voice of woman, the generous voice of man, with the voices of little children, so adorably glorified in this book, and those of the oppressed of this old world, let them cross the seas and hasten to say to her that she is esteemed and beloved!

If the best eulogy which one can make of the author is to love her, the truest that one can make of the book is to love its very faults. It has faults, — we need not pass them in silence, we need not evade the discussion of them, — but you need not be disturbed about them, you who are rallied on the tears you have shed over the fortunes of the poor victims in a narrative so simple and true.

These defects exist only in relation to the conventional rules of art, which never have been and never will be absolute. If its judges, possessed with the love of what they call "artistic work," find unskillful treatment in the book, look well at them to see if their eyes are dry when they are reading this or that chapter.

They will recall to your mind that Ohio senator, who, having sagely demonstrated to his little wife that it is a political duty to refuse asylum and help to the fugitive slave, ends by taking two in his own carriage, in a dark night, over fearful roads, where he must from time to time plunge into mud to his waist to push on the vehicle. This charming episode in "Uncle Tom" (a digression, if you will) paints well the situation of most men placed between their prejudices and established modes of thought and the spontaneous and generous intuitions of their hearts.

It is the history, at the same time affecting and pleasing, of many independent critics. Whatever they may be in the matter of social or literary questions, those who pretend always to judge by strict rules are often vanquished by their own feelings, and sometimes vanquished when unwilling to avow it.

I have always been charmed by the anecdote of Voltaire, ridiculing and despising the fables of La Fontaine, seizing the book and saying, "Look here, now, you will see in the very first one" — he reads one. "Well, that is passable, but see how stupid this is!" — he reads a second, and finds after all that it is quite pretty; a third disarms him again, and at last he throws down the volume, saying, with ingenuous spite, "It's nothing but a collection of masterpieces." Great souls may be bilious and vindictive, but it is impossible for them to remain unjust and insensible.

It, however, should be said to people of culture, who profess to be able to give correct judgments, that if their culture is of the truest kind it will never resist a just and right emotion. Therefore it is that this book, defective according to the rules of the modern French romance, intensely interests everybody and triumphs over all criticisms in the discussions it causes in domestic circles.

For this book is essentially domestic and of the family, — this book, with its long discussions, its minute details, its portraits carefully studied. Mothers of families, young girls, little children, servants even, can read and understand them, and men themselves, even the most superior, cannot disdain them. We do not say that the success of the book is because its great merits redeem its faults; we say its success is because of these very alleged faults.

For a long time we have striven in France against the prolix explanations of Walter Scott. We have cried out against those of Balzac, but on consideration have perceived that the painter of manners and character has never done too much, that every stroke of the pencil was needed for the general effect. Let us learn then to appreciate all kinds of treatment, when the effect is good, and when they bear the seal of a master hand.

Mrs. Stowe is all instinct; it is the very reason that she appears to some not to have talent. Has she not talent? What is talent? Nothing, doubtless, compared to genius; but has she genius? I cannot say that she has talent as one understands it in the world of letters, but she has genius, as humanity feels the need of genius, — the genius of goodness, not that of the man of letters, but of the saint. Yes, — a saint! Thrice holy the soul which thus loves, blesses, and consoles the martyrs. Pure, penetrating, and profound the spirit which thus fathoms the recesses of the human soul. Noble, generous, and great the heart which embraces in her pity, in her love, an entire race, trodden down in blood and mire under the whip of ruffians and the maledictions of the impious.

Thus should it be, thus should we value things ourselves. We should feel that genius is heart, that power is *faith*, that talent is *sincerity*, and, finally, *success is sympathy*, since this book overcomes us, since it penetrates the breast, pervades the spirit, and fills us with a strange sentiment of mingled tenderness and admiration for a poor negro lacerated by blows, prostrate in the dust, there gasping on a miserable pallet, his last sigh exhaled towards God.

In matters of art there is but one rule, to paint and to move. And where shall we find creations more complete, types more vivid, situations more touching, more original, than in "Uncle Tom," — those beautiful relations of the slave with the child of his master, indicating a state of things unknown among us; the protest of the master himself against slavery during that innocent part of life when his soul belongs to God alone? Afterwards, when society takes him, the law chases away God, and interest deposes conscience. In coming to mature years the infant ceases to be *man* and becomes master. God dies in his soul.

What hand has ever drawn a type more fascinating and admirable than St. Clair, — this exceptional nature, noble, generous, and loving, but too soft and too nonchalant to be really great? Is it not man himself, human nature itself, with its innate virtues, its good aspirations, and its deplorable failures? — this charming master who loves and is beloved, who thinks and reasons, but concludes nothing and does nothing! He spends in his day treasures of indulgence, of consideration, of goodness; he dies without having accomplished anything. The story of his precious life is all told in a word, — "to aspire and to regret." He has never learned to *will*. Alas! is there not something of this even among the bravest and best of men?

The life and death of a little child and of a negro slave! — that is the whole book! This negro and this child are two saints of heaven! The affection that unites them, the respect of these two perfect ones for each other, is the only love-story, the only passion of the drama. I know not what other genius but that of sanctity itself could shed over this affection and this situation a charm so powerful and so sustained. The child reading the Bible on the knees of the slave, dreaming over its mysteries and enjoying them in her exceptional maturity; now covering him with flowers like a doll, and now looking to him as something sacred, passing from tender playfulness to tender veneration, and then fading away through a mysterious malady which seems to be nothing but the wearing of pity in a nature too pure, too divine, to accept earthly law; dying finally in the arms of the slave, and calling him after her to the bosom of God, — all this is so new, so beautiful, that one asks one's self in thinking of it whether the success which has attended the work is after all equal to the height of the conception.

Children are the true heroes of Mrs. Stowe's works. Her soul, the most motherly that could be, has conceived of these little creatures in a halo of grace. George Shelby, the little Harry, the cousin of Eva, the regretted babe of the little wife of the Senator, and Topsy, the poor, diabolic, excellent Topsy, — all the children that one sees, and even those that one does not see in this romance, but of whom one has only a few words from their desolate mothers, seem to us a world of little angels, white and black, where any mother may recognize some darling of her own, source of her joys and tears. In taking form in the spirit of Mrs. Stowe, these children, without ceasing to be children, assume ideal graces, and come at last to interest us more than the personages of an ordinary love-story.

Women, too, are here judged and painted with a master hand; not merely mothers who are sublime, but women who are not mothers either in heart or in fact, and whose infirmities are treated with indulgence or with rigor. By the side of the methodical Miss Ophelia, who ends by learning that duty is good for nothing without love, Marie St. Clair is a frightfully truthful portrait. One shudders in thinking that she exists, that she is everywhere, that each of us has met her and seen her, perhaps, not far from us, for it is only necessary that this charming creature should have slaves to torture, and we should see her revealed complete through her vapors and her nervous complaints.

The saints also have their claw! it is that of the lion. She buries it deep in the conscience, and a little of burning indignation and of terrible sarcasm does not, after all, misbecome this Harriet Stowe, this woman so gentle, so humane, so religious, and full of evangelical unction. Ah! yes, she is a very good woman, but not what we derisively call "goody good." Hers is a heart strong and courageous, which in blessing the unhappy and applauding the faithful, tending the feeble and succoring the irresolute, does not hesitate to bind to the pillory the hardened tyrant, to show to the world his deformity.

She is, in the true spirit of the word, consecrated. Her fervent Christianity sings the praise of the martyr, but permits no man the right to perpetuate the wrong. She denounces that strange perversion of Scripture which tolerates the iniquity of the oppressor because it gives opportunity for the virtues of the victims. She calls on God himself, and threatens in his name; she shows us human law on one side, and God on the other!

Let no one say that, because she exhorts to patient endurance of wrong, she justifies those who do the wrong. Read the beautiful page where George Harris, the white slave, embraces for the first time the shores of a free territory, and presses to his heart wife and child, who at last are *his own*. What a beautiful picture, that! What a large heart-throb! what a triumphant protest of the eternal and inalienable right of man to liberty!

Honor and respect to you, Mrs. Stowe! Some day your recompense, which is already recorded in heaven, will come also in this world.   GEORGE SAND.

NOHANT, December 17, 1852.

" Madame L. S. Belloc, also a well-known and distinguished writer, the translator of Miss Edgeworth's and of other English works into French, says : —

" ' When the first translation of " Uncle Tom " was published in Paris there was a general hallelujah for the author and for the cause. A few weeks after, M. Charpentier, one of our best publishers, called on me to ask a new translation. I objected that there were already so many it might prove a failure. He insisted, saying, " Il n'y aura jamais assez de lecteurs pour un tel livre," and he particularly desired a special translation for his own collection, " Bibliothèque Charpentier," where it is catalogued, and where it continues now to sell daily. " La Case de l'Oncle Tom " was the fifth, if I recollect rightly, and a sixth illustrated edition appeared some months after. It was read by high and low, by grown persons and children. A great enthusiasm for the anti-slavery cause was the result. The popularity of the work in France was immense, and no doubt influenced the public mind in favor of the North during the war of secession.'

"The next step in the history of 'Uncle Tom' was a meeting at Stafford House, when Lord Shaftesbury recommended to the women of England the sending of an 'affectionate and Christian address to the women of America.'

"This address, composed by Lord Shaftesbury, was taken in hand for signatures by energetic canvassers in all parts of England, and also among resident English on the Continent. The demand for signatures went as far forth as the city of Jerusalem. When all the signatures were collected, the document was forwarded to the care of Mrs. Stowe in America, with a letter from Lord Carlisle, recommending it to her, to be presented to the ladies of America in such way as she should see fit.

"It was exhibited first at the Boston anti-slavery fair, and now remains in its solid oak case, a lasting monument of the feeling called forth by 'Uncle Tom's Cabin.'

"It is in twenty-six thick folio volumes, solidly bound in morocco, with the American eagle on the back of each. On the first page of the first volume is the address beautifully illuminated on vellum, and following are the subscribers' names, filling the volumes. There are 562,448 names of women of every rank of life, from the nearest in rank to the throne of England to the wives and daughters of the humblest artisan and laborer. Among all who signed it is fair to presume there was not one who had not read the book, and did not, at the time of signing, feel a sympathy for the cause of the oppressed people whose wrongs formed its subject. The address, with its many signatures, was simply a relief to that impulsive desire to *do* something for the cause of the slave, which the reading of 'Uncle Tom's Cabin' appeared to inspire.

"Of the wisdom of this step there have been many opinions. Nobody, however, can doubt that Lord Shaftesbury, who had spent a long life in labors to lift burdens from the working-classes of England, and who had redeemed from slavery and degradation English women and children in its mines and collieries, had thereby acquired a certain right to plead for the cause of oppressed working-classes in all countries.

"The address was received as a welcome word of cheer and encouragement by that small band of faithful workers who for years had stood in an unfashionable minority; but so far as the feeling expressed in it was one of real Christian kindliness and humility, it was like a flower thrown into the white heat of a furnace. It added intensity, if that were possible, to that terrific conflict of forces which was destined never to cease till slavery was finally abolished.

"It was a year after the publication of 'Uncle Tom' that Mrs. Stowe visited England, and was received at Stafford House, there meeting all the best known and best worth knowing of the higher circles of England.

.   .   .   .

"A series of addresses presented to Mrs. Stowe at this time by public meetings in different towns of England, Scotland, and Ireland, still remain among the literary curiosities relating to this book. The titles of these are somewhat curious: 'Address from the Inhabitants of Berwick-upon-Tweed;' 'Address from the Inhabitants of Dalkeith;' 'Address from the Committee of the Glasgow Female Anti-Slavery Society;' 'Address from the Glasgow University Abstainers' Society;' 'Address from a Public Meeting in Belfast, Ireland;' 'Address from the Committee of the Ladies' Anti-Slavery Society, Edinburgh;' 'Address from the City of Leeds.'

"All these public meetings, addresses, and demonstrations of sympathy were, in their time and way, doubtless of perfect sincerity. But when the United States went into a state of civil war, these demonstrations ceased.

"But it is due to the brave true working-classes of England to say that in this conflict, whenever they thought the war was one of justice to the slave, they gave it their sympathy, and even when it brought hardship and want to their very doors, refused to lend themselves to any popular movement which would go to crusht he oppressed in America.

"It is but justice also to the Duchess of Sutherland to say that although by the time our war was initiated she had retired from her place as leader of society to the chamber of the invalid, yet her sympathies expressed in private letters ever remained true to the cause of freedom.

"Her son-in-law, the Duke of Argyll, stood almost alone in the House of Lords in defending the cause of the Northern States. It is, moreover, a significant fact that the Queen of England, in concurrence with Prince Albert, steadily resisted every attempt to enlist the warlike power of England against the Northern States.

"But Almighty God had decreed the liberation of the African race, and though Presidents, Senators, and Representatives united in declaring that such were not *their* intentions, yet by great signs and mighty wonders was this nation compelled to listen to the voice that spoke from heaven, — 'Let my people go.'

"'Uncle Tom's Cabin,' in the fervor which conceived it, in the feeling which it inspired through the world, was only one of a line of ripples marking the commencement of mighty rapids, moving by forces which no human power could stay to an irresistible termination, — towards human freedom.

"Now the war is over, slavery is a thing of the past;

slave-pens, blood-hounds, slave-whips, and slave-coffles are only bad dreams of the night; and now the humane reader can afford to read 'Uncle Tom's Cabin' without an expenditure of torture and tears."

Nothing need be added to this story respecting the growth, development, and reception of "Uncle Tom."

It only remains for us to follow her, now suddenly launched upon an ocean of new experiences; experiences such as are known in this world to the few men and women whose sympathies have led them to give their lives indeed for others. We look back upon the dreaming child, we follow the eager girl, unconscious of incessant labor, conscious only of aspiration and endeavor; we watch the tender mother; and then we see her, forever the same, a tiny figure standing forgetful of herself against the dark vast background of her country's life.

CHAPTER VI

In the autumn of the same year that "Uncle Tom"
was published, Mrs. Stowe returned to Brooklyn, where
she cemented her friendship with her brother's parishioner, Mrs. John T. Howard. Mr. Howard was one
of the earliest promoters of Plymouth Church, and from
their first acquaintance to the end of his life Mr. and
Mrs. Howard and their children were Mr. Beecher's unwavering supporters and faithful friends. By this time
Mrs. Stowe's foreign correspondence had increased. The
letters exchanged across the water were the beginning of
some of her most valued friendships. Her brother Henry
said, many years after leaving Indianapolis for Brooklyn:
"I have no opportunity to tell my friends there how dearly
I love them, but pearls and diamonds do not change when
laid away in a bag, neither do such friendships." It was
the same with Mrs. Stowe. Her genius for friendship was
only another phase of her intimate life which the world
could not see. Her love once given was not subject to any
"wind of doctrine." Days, weeks, and months could pass
without communication, but her heart was always remembering and alive.

Mrs. Howard has written a delightful account of the
beginning of her lifelong intimacy with Mrs. Stowe.

"The newspapers were then filled with accounts of the
wonderful success of the book at home and abroad," writes
Mrs. Howard. "When ready to return to her home in

Andover, she urged my going with her, an invitation that I gladly accepted. To lessen the fatigue of the long railroad journey, we spent one night in Hartford with Mrs. Stowe's sister, Mrs. Perkins. After a pleasant evening with the family, we retired, sharing the same room at Mrs. Stowe's request. I soon disrobed and lay upon the bed, looking at her little childish figure gathered in a heap upon the floor as she sat brushing out her long curls with a thoughtful look upon her face, which I did not disturb by words.

"At last she spoke, and said, 'I have just received a letter from my brother Edward from Galesburg, Illinois. He is greatly disturbed lest all this praise and notoriety should induce pride and vanity, and work harm to my Christian character.' She dropped her brush from her hand and exclaimed with earnestness, 'Dear soul, he need not be troubled. He does n't know that I did not write that book.' ' What!' said I, 'you did not write "Uncle Tom"?' 'No,' she said, 'I only put down what I saw.' 'But you have never been at the South, have you?' I asked. 'No,' she said, 'but it all came before me in visions, one after another, and I put them down in words.' But being still skeptical, I said, 'Still you must have arranged the events.' 'No,' said she, 'your Annie reproached me for letting Eva die. Why! I could not help it. I felt as badly as any one could! It was like a death in my own family, and it affected me so deeply that I could not write a word for two weeks after her death.' 'And did you know,' I asked, 'that Uncle Tom would die?' 'Oh yes,' she answered, 'I knew that he must die from the first, but I did not know *how*. When I got to that part of the story, I saw no more for some time. I was physically exhausted, too. Mr. Stowe had then accepted a call to Andover, and had to go there to find a house for the family.

" ' He urged my going with him for the change, and I went. No available home could be found, and the Faculty gave us permission to occupy a large stone building which had been built for a gymnasium. I had always longed to plan a house for myself, and we entered into the work with great interest. We consulted an architect, and had been with him arranging the plan for rooms, pantries, and other household conveniences, all the morning.

" ' I was very tired when we returned to our boarding-house to the early midday dinner. After dinner we went to our room for rest. Mr. Stowe threw himself upon the bed; I was to use the lounge; but suddenly arose before me the death scene of Uncle Tom with what led to it — and George's visit to him. I sat down at the table and wrote nine pages of foolscap paper without pausing, except long enough to dip my pen into the inkstand. Just as I had finished, Mr. Stowe awoke. "Wife," said he, "have not you lain down yet?" "No," I answered. "I have been writing, and I want you to listen to this, and see if it will do." I read aloud to him with the tears flowing fast. He wept, too, and before I had finished, his sobs shook the bed upon which he was lying. He sprang up, saying, "Do! I should think it would do!" and folding the sheets he immediately directed and sent them to the publisher, without one word of correction or revision of any kind. I have often thought,' she continued, ' that if anything had happened to that package in going, it would not have been possible for me to have reproduced it.'

"As I lay there and listened to this wonderful account, how could I help believing that God inspires his children, and that mighty works do still show forth themselves in those who are prepared to be his mediums. If I had only possessed the limner's power, how gladly would I have put upon canvas that face, lit with a light divine, as though remembering those angel visits, and still saying,

'Behold the handmaid of the Lord. Let it be unto me as Thou wilt.'

"Many years after this occurrence," continues Mrs. Howard, "a new edition of 'Uncle Tom' was brought out by her publishers. In the preface was a paper by Mrs. Stowe, giving an account of the writing of the book. In this account she speaks of having *many years before* written a sketch of the death of an old slave, and of her reading it to her children, who were very much affected by it, this being the original idea (in part) of 'Uncle Tom.' The next time I saw her I spoke of it, and reminded her of what she had told me just after 'Uncle Tom' was published. There seemed to me a serious inconsistency between the two accounts. 'No,' said she, 'both are true, for I had entirely forgotten that I had ever written that sketch, and I suppose that I had unconsciously woven it in with the other.'"

There is still another discrepancy in this narration. Professor Stowe did not accept the appointment to Andover until after the publication of "Uncle Tom." A letter from his wife in Boston, while he is still in Brunswick at his post, considers the subject of acceptance, and puts before him what Professor Park has to say on the subject. They did not go to the boarding-house, it appears, until the summer, when "Uncle Tom" had been published three or four months. There is a letter from the Committee of Trustees written in June of this year suggesting the "old stone house" as a possible resort if they feel inclined to fit it up. Therefore the subject had not been considered before "Uncle Tom" was printed, and Mrs. Stowe must have written the chapter as described after a busy day either in Brunswick or in Boston. It is true that neither of these slips disturbs in the least the true value of the story. The work which she was to do lay upon her heart, and the first available instant, even one which seemed necessary for repose, was seized upon and dedicated to this service. The almost incredible swiftness of the writing proves the rapt condition of her mind. Surely it is not wonderful that some of the details of the occasion were forgotten.

Mrs. Howard was a generous intermediary between Henry Ward Beecher and his sister. Harriet was always anxious to know how it was with her brother, and he found little time for correspondence. His daring in those exciting days laid him open to the attacks of the enemy.

"Has the pressure really affected Henry's health?" Mrs. Stowe writes. "I have been so sheltered and hemmed in in my retirement that I have not read the articles in the 'Observer.' . . . I am reminded of one of Aunt Esther's stories. A man, when very drunk, had the habit of using very abusive language to his wife, to which she paid no attention, but went about her affairs as usual. At last he fell to praying about her, saying all manner of horrid things against her in his prayers. Still she gave no heed.

"'Why, do you hear,' said a neighbor, 'how that man goes on?'

"'Oh, poh!' said his wife, 'he'll get over it by and by.'

"'But do just hear him praying.'

"'Oh, let him pray, nobody minds his prayers.'

"So it has struck me that both the secular and the pious abuse of the 'Observer' are equally unworthy of attention. All we have to do is to *live on*."

The year following the publication of "Uncle Tom" was a very hard one. Mrs. Stowe was necessarily much away from home. Her visits at Brooklyn, which were a necessity after her writing was done, were followed by the news that Professor Stowe had accepted the call received from the Andover Theological Seminary to become Professor of Sacred Literature there. She was disinclined to leave

Brunswick, where she found herself surrounded with loving friends from the moment of her arrival, but she wrote: "For my part, if I *must* leave Brunswick I would rather leave at once. I can tear away with a sudden pull more easily than to linger there knowing that I am to leave at last. I shall never find people whom I shall like better than those of Brunswick."

Again Professor Stowe was called away to Cincinnati, and again his wife set herself to the task of making a new home. The house decided upon for their abode in Andover was known at this time as the old stone work-shop, but it was soon transformed by her care and ingenuity into a pleasant residence, and called "The Stone Cabin." I can well remember the cosy aspect of the house in winter, the windows full of flowering plants, and a general air of comfort pervading it. Here many interesting persons, drawn by her great fame, came to visit her, and here she continued her public and private labors. During the first summer, before the house was ready, she wrote to her husband: —

"What a beautiful place it is! There is everything here that there is at Brunswick except the sea, — a great exception. Yesterday I was out all the forenoon sketching elms. There is no end to the beauty of these trees. I shall fill my book with them before I get through. We had a levee at Professor Park's last week, — quite a brilliant affair. To-day there is to be a fishing party to go to Salem beach and have a chowder.

"It seems almost too good to be true that we are going to have such a house in such a beautiful place, and to live here among all these agreeable people, where everybody seems to love you so much and to think so much of you. I am almost afraid to accept it, and should not, did I not see the Hand that gives it all and know that it is both firm and true. He knows if it is best for us, and his blessing addeth no sorrow therewith. I cannot describe to you the constant undercurrent of love and joy and peace ever flowing through my soul. I am so happy — so blessed!"

And again: —

"I seem to have so much to fill my time, and yet there is my Maine story waiting. However, I am composing it every day, only I greatly need living studies for the filling in of my sketches. There is 'old Jonas,' my 'fish father,' a sturdy, independent fisherman farmer, who in his youth sailed all over the world and made up his mind about everything. In his old age he attends prayer-meetings and reads the 'Missionary Herald.' He also has plenty of money in an old brown sea-chest. He is a great heart with an inflexible will and iron muscles. I must go to Orr's Island and see him again. I am now writing an article for the 'Era' on Maine and its scenery, which I think is even better than the 'Independent' letter. In it I took up Longfellow. Next I shall write one on Hawthorne and his surroundings.

"To-day Mr. Jewett sent out a most solemnly savage attack upon me from the 'Alabama Planter.' Among other things it says: 'The plan for assaulting the best institutions in the world may be made just as rational as it is by the wicked (perhaps unconsciously so) authoress of this book. The woman who wrote it must be either a very bad or a very fanatical person. For her own domestic peace we trust no enemy will ever penetrate into her household to pervert the scenes he may find there with as little logic or kindness as she has used in her "Uncle Tom's Cabin."' There's for you!"

Her absence from home and children for the long time required to go to Andover and start things afresh there filled her mind with cares and anxieties.

She wrote to her husband: —

1853]   ATTACKS AND ANXIETIES   169

"A day or two ago, my mind lay clear as glass, and I
thought I had no will but God's, and could have none.
Lo! his hand touches a spring, and I see what poor trash
I am. But I am his chosen one for all that, and I shall
reign with Him when all the stars have done blossoming,
and if I am so poor I am betrothed to One who is Heir of
all things. I read Chaucer a great deal yesterday, and am
charmed at the reverential Christian spirit in which he
viewed all things. He thought of marriage as 'a most
dread sacrament,' just as I do; and surely, if our catechism
says truly, a sacrament is an outward and visible sign of
an inward and spiritual grace."

Professor Stowe was often greatly agitated by the difficulties which surrounded them. At such times, no matter
what her occupation was, she would drop everything to
write and try to soothe him. The large square sheets of
old-fashioned paper covered with her fine script would
make many a book beside those which belong to the public.
In one of these letters, she says: —

"I grieve to see how much you suffer; but God, I am
persuaded, has better things in store for you. I trust you
will be of good cheer."

One would hardly guess that it was she who was bearing
the burden of the family to such an extent if she did not
occasionally recount the details, in order, as it appears, to
divert his mind from the painful channels of his own despair. The attacks made upon his wife after the publication of "Uncle Tom" oppressed him. "For myself," she
said, "I have not an anxiety, but am only *vulnerable*
through you. That you should be exposed to this annoyance on my account is the real and only trouble I have
had. For me, what harm can —— or anybody else do
to me? 'Who is he that can harm you if ye be followers
of that which is good?' In this belief I have tried to
keep near to Him who only is good. . . . Let me recom-

mend to you what my good mother Edmondson says has been her relief: 'Oh, many a time,' she says, 'my heart has been *so heavy* — and I've been to the throne of Grace and when I've poured out my sorrows to the Lord, I've come away and felt that *I can live a little longer.*'

"So God lays on you a heavy burden in the internal structure of your mind; but how blessed is this baptism of sorrow. Would you part with what you have gained by your peculiar suffering? *I* can see that you have acquired by it much that gives you power over other minds. There is not one sorrow that I have had that I would part with, — nay, I bear with joy all that falls on my heart from day to day. I say 'Welcome, cross of Christ!'"

Mr. J. R. Howard says that his father was making a brief visit to Mrs. Stowe at this period, when "one afternoon she told him that she often arose in the morning at half past four and went out to enjoy the birds and the dawn, and she challenged him to join her. The next morning they went out, and in that rare, sweet atmosphere they talked, and were silent, together. And she read to him some verses which she had written at such an hour. Since then they have been read and sung by many, to whom they have brought the very peace of Christ." I give the first stanza of the well-known beautiful hymn: —

> "Still, still with Thee when purple morning breaketh,
>   When the bird waketh and the shadows flee;
>   Fairer than morning, lovelier than the daylight,
>   Dawns the sweet consciousness, I am with thee!"

Even in the heat and hurry of that time the "central peace" of which Wordsworth speaks was ever at her heart.

The Maine story to which Mrs. Stowe has already referred was begun before she left Brunswick, but she was obliged to lay it aside on account of the numberless attacks made upon "Uncle Tom," which must finally be answered. Unhappily the beautiful beginning of "The

Pearl of Orr's Island," one of her best pieces of writing, was never followed out in the same vein.

Mrs. Stowe had scarcely set herself to the task of writing what she calls "A key to unlock 'Uncle Tom's Cabin,'" when she discovered it to be a far greater labor than she anticipated. She had spoken, in writing to Mrs. Howard, of an additional twenty-five pages which she was to add to the next edition of "Uncle Tom," but she soon found herself launched upon a work which was to occupy her for many months and make an entirely new book.

Late in the winter, she wrote to her husband: —

"I am now very much driven. I am preparing a Key to unlock 'Uncle Tom's Cabin.' It will contain all the original facts, anecdotes, and documents on which the story is founded, with some very interesting and affecting stories parallel to those told of Uncle Tom. Now I want you to write for me just what you heard that slave-buyer say, exactly as he said it, that people may compare it with what I have written. My Key will be stronger than the Cabin."

In regard to this "Key" Mrs. Stowe also wrote to the Duchess of Sutherland upon hearing that she had headed an address from the women of England to those of America: —

It is made up of the facts, the documents, the things which my own eyes have looked upon and my hands have handled, that attest this awful indictment upon my country. I write it in the anguish of my soul, with tears and prayer, with sleepless nights and weary days. I bear my testimony with a heavy heart, as one who in court is forced by an awful oath to disclose the sins of those dearest.

So I am called to draw up this fearful witness against my country and send it into all countries, that the general voice of humanity may quicken our paralyzed vitality, that all Christians may pray for us, and that shame, honor, love of country, and love of Christ may be roused to give us strength to cast out this mighty evil. Yours for the oppressed,   H. B. STOWE.

She continued the exhausting labor of preparing this book until the spring, when an invitation came from the friends of emancipation in England urging her to come over to them. It was a great opportunity which Professor Stowe and his wife accepted gladly. Meanwhile a letter had been received from Mrs. Follen, who was then in London, asking for information about the writer of "Uncle Tom." Mrs. Stowe replied: —

ANDOVER, February 16.

MY DEAR MADAM, — I hasten to reply to your letter, to me the more interesting that I have long been acquainted with you, and during all the nursery part of my life made daily use of your poems for children.

I used to think sometimes in those days that I would write to you, and tell you how much I was obliged to you for the pleasure which they gave us all.

So you want to know something about what sort of a woman I am! Well, if this is any object, you shall have statistics free of charge. To begin, then, I am a little bit of a woman, — somewhat more than forty, about as thin and dry as a pinch of snuff; never very much to look at in my best days, and looking like a used-up article now.

I was married when I was twenty-five years old to a man rich in Greek and Hebrew, Latin and Arabic, and, alas! rich in nothing else. When I went to housekeeping, my entire stock of china for parlor and kitchen was bought for eleven dollars. That lasted very well for two years, till my brother was married and brought his bride to visit me. I then found, on review, that I had neither plates

nor teacups to set a table for my father's family; wherefore I thought it best to reinforce the establishment by
getting me a tea-set that cost ten dollars more, and this, I
believe, formed my whole stock in trade for some years.

But then I was abundantly enriched with wealth of
another sort.

I had two little curly-headed twin daughters to begin
with, and my stock in this line has gradually increased,
till I have been the mother of seven children, the most
beautiful and the most loved of whom lies buried near my
Cincinnati residence.   It was at his dying bed and at his
grave that I learned what a poor slave mother may feel
when her child is torn away from her.   In those depths
of sorrow which seemed to me immeasurable, it was my
only prayer to God that such anguish might not be suffered
in vain.   There were circumstances about his death of
such peculiar bitterness, of what seemed almost cruel suffering, that I felt that I could never be consoled for it
unless this crushing of my own heart might enable me to
work out some great good to others. . . .

I allude to this here because I have often felt that
much that is in that book ("Uncle Tom") had its root in
the awful scenes and bitter sorrows of that summer.   It
has left now, I trust, no trace on my mind except a deep
compassion for the sorrowful, especially for mothers who
are separated from their children.

During long years of struggling with poverty and sickness, and a hot, debilitating climate, my children grew up
around me.   The nursery and the kitchen were my principal fields of labor.   Some of my friends, pitying my
trials, copied and sent a number of little sketches from my
pen to certain liberally paying "Annuals" with my name.
With the first money that I earned in this way I bought
a feather-bed! for as I had married into poverty and without a dowry, and as my husband had only a large library

of books and a great deal of learning, the bed and pillows were thought the most profitable investment. After this I thought that I had discovered the philosopher's stone. So when a new carpet or mattress was going to be needed, or when, at the close of the year, it began to be evident that my family accounts, like poor Dora's, "wouldn't add up," then I used to say to my faithful friend and factotum Anna, who shared all my joys and sorrows, "Now, if you will keep the babies and attend to the things in the house for one day, I'll write a piece, and then we shall be out of the scrape." So I became an author, — very modest at first, I do assure you, and remonstrating very seriously with the friends who had thought it best to put my name to the pieces by way of getting up a reputation; and if you ever see a woodcut of me, with an immoderately long nose, on the cover of all the U. S. Almanacs, I wish you to take notice that I have been forced into it contrary to my natural modesty by the imperative solicitations of my dear five thousand friends and the public generally. One thing I must say with regard to my life at the West, which you will understand better than many English women could.

I lived two miles from the city of Cincinnati, in the country, and domestic service, not always you know to be found in the city, is next to an impossibility to obtain in the country, even by those who are willing to give the highest wages; so what was to be expected for poor me, who had very little of this world's goods to offer?

Had it not been for my inseparable friend Anna, a noble-hearted English girl, who landed on our shores in destitution and sorrow, and clave to me as Ruth to Naomi, I had never lived through all the trials which this uncertainty and want of domestic service imposed on both; you may imagine, therefore, how glad I was when, our seminary property being divided out into small lots which were rented at a low price, a number of poor families settled in

our vicinity, from whom we could occasionally obtain domestic service. About a dozen families of liberated slaves
were among the number, and they became my favorite
resort in cases of emergency. If anybody wishes to have
a black face look handsome, let them be left, as I have
been, in feeble health in oppressive hot weather, with a
sick baby in arms, and two or three other little ones in the
nursery, and not a servant in the whole house to do a
single turn. Then, if they could see my good old Aunt
Frankie coming with her honest, bluff, black face, her
long, strong arms, her chest as big and stout as a barrel,
and her hilarious, hearty laugh, perfectly delighted to take
one's washing and do it at a fair price, they would appreciate the beauty of black people.

My cook, poor Eliza Buck, — how she would stare to
think of her name going to England! — was a regular epi-
tome of slave life in herself; fat, gentle, easy, loving and
lovable, always calling my very modest house and door-
yard "The Place," as if it had been a plantation with seven
hundred hands on it. She had lived through the whole
sad story of a Virginia-raised slave's life. In her youth
she must have been a very handsome mulatto girl. Her
voice was sweet, and her manners refined and agreeable.
She was raised in a good family as a nurse and seamstress.
When the family became embarrassed, she was suddenly
sold on to a plantation in Louisiana. She has often told
me how, without any warning, she was suddenly forced
into a carriage, and saw her little mistress screaming and
stretching her arms from the window towards her as she
was driven away. She has told me of scenes on the Louisiana plantation, and she has often been out at night by
stealth ministering to poor slaves who had been mangled
and lacerated by the lash. Hence she was sold into Kentucky, and her last master was the father of all her children. On this point she ever maintained a delicacy and

reserve that always appeared to me remarkable. She always called him her husband; and it was not till after she had lived with me some years that I discovered the real nature of the connection. I shall never forget how sorry I felt for her, nor my feelings at her humble apology, "You know, Mrs. Stowe, slave women cannot help themselves." She had two very pretty quadroon daughters, with her beautiful hair and eyes, interesting children, whom I had instructed in the family school with my children. Time would fail to tell you all that I learned incidentally of the slave system in the history of various slaves who came into my family, and of the underground railroad which, I may say, ran through our house. But the letter is already too long.

You ask with regard to the remuneration which I have received for my work here in America. Having been poor all my life and expecting to be poor the rest of it, the idea of making money by a book which I wrote just because I could not help it never occurred to me. It was therefore an agreeable surprise to receive ten thousand dollars as the first-fruits of three months' sale. I presume as much more is now due. Mr. Bosworth in England, the firm of Clarke & Co., and Mr. Bentley, have all offered me an interest in the sales of their editions in London. I am very glad of it, both on account of the value of what they offer, and the value of the example they set in this matter, wherein I think that justice has been too little regarded.

I have been invited to visit Scotland, and shall probably spend the summer there and in England.

I have very much at heart a design to erect in some of the Northern States a normal school for the education of colored teachers in the United States and in Canada. I have very much wished that some permanent memorial of good to the colored race might be created out of the proceeds of a work which promises to have so unprecedented

a sale. My own share of the profits will be less than that
of the publishers, either English or American; but I am
willing to give largely for this purpose, and I have no
doubt that the publishers, both American and English,
will unite with me; for nothing tends more immediately
to the emancipation of the slave than the education and
elevation of the free.

I am now writing a work which will contain, perhaps,
an equal amount of matter with "Uncle Tom's Cabin." It
will contain all the facts and documents on which that
story was founded, and an immense body of facts, reports
of trials, legal documents, and testimony of people now
living South, which will more than confirm every statement in "Uncle Tom's Cabin."

I must confess that till I began the examination of
facts in order to write this book, much as I thought I knew
before, I had not begun to measure the depth of the abyss.
The law records of courts and judicial proceedings are so
incredible as to fill me with amazement whenever I think
of them. It seems to me that the book cannot but be
felt, and, coming upon the sensibility awaked by the
other, do something.

I suffer exquisitely in writing these things. It may
be truly said that I write with my heart's blood. Many
times in writing "Uncle Tom's Cabin" I thought my health
would fail utterly; but I prayed earnestly that God would
help me till I got through, and still I am pressed beyond
measure and above strength.

This horror, this nightmare abomination! can it be in
my country! It lies like lead on my heart, it shadows my
life with sorrow; the more so that I feel, as for my own
brothers, for the South, and am pained by every horror I
am obliged to write, as one who is forced by some awful
oath to disclose in court some family disgrace. Many
times I have thought that I must die, and yet I pray God

that I may live to see something done. I shall in all probability be in London in May: shall I see you?

It seems to me so odd and dream-like that so many persons desire to see me, and now I cannot help thinking that they will think, when they do, that God hath chosen "the weak things of this world."

If I live till spring I shall hope to see Shakespeare's grave, and Milton's mulberry-tree, and the good land of my fathers, — old, old England! May that day come!

    Yours affectionately,   H. B. STOWE.

A sequel to the statements in this letter regarding the profits received from the sales of "Uncle Tom's Cabin" is given by Charles Dudley Warner in an admirable history of the book published in "The Atlantic Monthly." Mr. Warner says : —

"The story was dramatized in the United States in August, 1852, without the consent or knowledge of the author, and was played most successfully in the leading cities, and subsequently was acted in every capital in Europe. Mrs. Stowe had neglected to secure the dramatic rights, and she derived no benefit from the great popularity of a drama which still holds the stage. From the phenomenal sale of a book which was literally read by the whole world, the author received only the ten per cent. on the American editions, and by the laws of her own country her copyright expired before her death."

Professor and Mrs. Stowe sailed from New York in April for Liverpool to see Europe for the first time. In spite of all the delightful recognition she had received from England, through letters, she could not fail to be surprised at the universal respect and affection which followed her footsteps everywhere.

Mrs. Stowe not only wrote long letters home to her children and family describing the almost unspeakable pleasures of this summer tour, but before another year two volumes of "Sunny Memories" were given to the public. Her industry never slackened. On arriving at Liverpool, she tells her children that they were considering the subject of which hotel they should find most convenient, "when we found the son of Mr. Cropper, of Dingle Bank, waiting in the cabin to take us with him to their hospitable abode. In a few moments after the baggage had been examined, we all bade adieu to the old ship, and went on board the little steam tender which carries passengers up to the city.

. . . .

"I had an early opportunity of making acquaintance with my English brethren; for, much to my astonishment, I found quite a crowd on the wharf, and we walked up to our carriage through a long lane of people, bowing, and looking very glad to see us.

"When I came to get into the hack it was surrounded by more faces than I could count. They stood very quietly, and looked very kindly, though evidently very much determined to look. Something prevented the hack from moving on; so the interview was prolonged for some time.

"Our carriage at last drove on, taking us through Liverpool and a mile or two out, and at length wound its way along the gravel paths of a beautiful little retreat, on the banks of the Mersey, called the 'Dingle.' It opened to my eyes like a paradise, all wearied as I was with the tossing of the sea.

"The next morning we slept late and hurried to dress, remembering our engagement to breakfast with the brother of our host, whose cottage stands on the same ground, within a few steps of our own. I had not the slightest idea of what the English mean by a breakfast, and therefore went in all innocence, supposing I should see nobody but the family circle of my acquaintances. Quite to my astonishment, I found a party of between thirty and forty people; ladies sitting with their bonnets on, as in a morning call. It was impossible, however, to feel more than a momentary embarrassment in the friendly warmth and cordiality of the circle by whom we were surrounded.

"In the evening I went into Liverpool to attend a party of friends of the anti-slavery cause. When I was going away, the lady of the house said that the servants were anxious to see me; so I came into the dressing-room to give them an opportunity.

"The next day was appointed to leave Liverpool. A great number of friends accompanied us to the cars, and a beautiful bouquet of flowers was sent with a very affecting message from a sick gentleman, who, from the retirement of his chamber, felt a desire to testify his sympathy. We left Liverpool with hearts a little tremulous and excited by the vibration of an atmosphere of universal sympathy and kindness, and found ourselves, at length, shut from the warm adieu of our friends, in a snug compartment of the railroad car.

"Well, we are in Scotland at last," she continues, "and now our pulse rises as the sun declines in the west. We catch glimpses of Solway Frith and talk about Redgauntlet. The sun went down and night drew on; still we were in Scotland. Scotch ballads, Scotch tunes, and Scotch literature were in the ascendant. We sang ' Auld Lang Syne,' ' Scots wha hae,' and ' Bonnie Doon,' and then, changing the key, sang ' Dundee,' ' Elgin,' and ' Martyr.'

"' Take care,' said Mr. Stowe; ' don't get too much excited.'

"' Ah,' said I, ' this is a thing that comes only once in a lifetime; do let us have the comfort of it. We shall never come into Scotland for the *first time* again.'

"While we were thus at the fusion point of enthusiasm, the cars stopped at Lockerbie, where the real Old Mortality is buried. All was dim and dark outside, but we soon became conscious that there was quite a number of people collected, peering into the window; and with a strange kind of thrill, I heard my name inquired for in the Scottish accent. I went to the window; there were men, women, and children gathered, and hand after hand was presented, with the words, ' Ye 're welcome to Scotland! '

"Then they inquired for and shook hands with all the party, having in some mysterious manner got the knowledge of who they were, even down to little G., whom they took to be my son. Was it not pleasant, when I had a heart so warm for this old country? I shall never forget the thrill of those words, ' Ye 're welcome to Scotland,' nor the ' Gude-night.'

" After that we found similar welcomes in many succeeding stopping-places; and though I did wave a towel out of the window, instead of a pocket-handkerchief, and commit other awkwardnesses, from not knowing how to play my part, yet I fancied, after all, that Scotland and we were coming on well together. Who the good souls were that were thus watching for us through the night, I am sure I do not know; but that they were of the ' one blood ' which unites all the families of the earth, I felt.

"At Glasgow, friends were waiting in the station-house. Earnest, eager, friendly faces, ever so many. Warm greetings, kindly words. A crowd parting in the middle, through which we were conducted into a carriage, and loud cheers of welcome sent a throb, as the voice of living Scotland.

"I looked out of the carriage, as we drove on, and saw, by the light of a lantern, Argyll Street. It was past twelve o'clock when I found myself in a warm, cosy parlor, with friends whom I have ever since been glad to remember. In a little time we were all safely housed in our hospitable apartments, and sleep fell on me for the first time in Scotland.

"The next morning I awoke worn and weary, and scarce could the charms of the social Scotch breakfast restore me.

. . . .

"All this day is a confused dream to me of a dizzy and overwhelming kind. So many letters that it took brother Charles from nine in the morning till two in the afternoon to read and answer them in the shortest manner; letters from all classes of people, high and low, rich and poor, in all shades and styles of composition, poetry and prose; some mere outbursts of feeling ; some invitations; some advice and suggestions; some requests and inquiries; some presenting books, or flowers, or fruit.

"Then came, in their turn, deputations from Paisley, Greenock, Dundee, Aberdeen, Edinburgh, and Belfast in Ireland; calls of friendship, invitations of all descriptions to go everywhere, and to see everything, and to stay in so many places. One kind, venerable minister, with his lovely daughter, offered me a retreat in his quiet manse on the beautiful shores of the Clyde.

"For all these kindnesses, what could I give in return? There was scarce time for even a grateful thought on each. People have often said to me that it must have been an exceeding bore. For my part, I could not think of regarding it so. It only oppressed me with an unutterable sadness.

"In the afternoon I rode out with the lord provost to see the cathedral. The lord provost answers to the lord mayor in England. His title and office in both countries continue only a year, except in case of reëlection.

"As I saw the way to the cathedral blocked up by a throng of people who had come out to see me, I could not help saying, ' What went ye out for to see? a reed shaken with the wind?' In fact, I was so worn out that I could hardly walk through the building. The next morning I was so ill as to need a physician, unable to see any one that called, or to hear any of the letters. I passed most of the day in bed, but in the evening I had to get up, as I had engaged to drink tea with two thousand people."

Speaking of one of the gatherings of the working people which she especially enjoyed in Glasgow at this time, she says: "I was struck this night with the resemblance between the Scotchman and the New Englander. One sees the distinctive nationality of a country more in the middle and laboring classes than in the higher, and accordingly at this meeting there was more nationality, I thought, than at the other."

Writing from Scotland to her Aunt Esther, Mrs. Stowe says: "The views of Scotland, which lay on my mother's table, even while I was a little child, and in poring over which I spent so many happy dreamy hours, — the Scotch ballads which were the delight of our evening fireside, and which seemed almost to melt the soul out of me, before I was old enough to understand their words, — the songs of Burns, which had been a household treasure among us, — the enchantments of Scott, — all these dimly returned upon me. It was the result of them all which I felt in nerve and brain.

"And that reminds me how much of our pleasure in literature results from its reflection on us from other minds.

"So in coming to Scotland I seem to feel not only my own individuality, but all that my friends would have felt, had they been with me. For sometimes we seem to be encompassed, as by a cloud, with a sense of the sympathy of the absent and the dead."

She continues to their children: —

"Somewhere near Roseneath I was presented, by his own request, to a broad-shouldered Scotch farmer, who stood some six feet two, and who paid me the compliment to say that he had read my book, and that he would walk six miles to see me any day. Such a flattering evidence

of discriminating taste, of course, disposed my heart towards him; but when I went up and put my hand into his
great prairie of a palm, I was as a grasshopper in my own
eyes.   I inquired who he was and was told he was one of
the Duke of Argyll's farmers.   I thought to myself if all
the duke's farmers were of this pattern, that he might be
able to speak to the enemy in the gates to some purpose.

"It was concluded after we left Roseneath that, instead
of returning by the boat, we should take carriage and ride
home along the banks of the river.   In our carriage were
Mr. S. and myself, Dr. Robson, and Lady Anderson.
About this time I commenced my first essay towards giving
titles, and made, as you may suppose, rather an odd piece
of work of it, generally saying ' Mrs.' first, and ' Lady '
afterwards, and then begging pardon.   Lady Anderson
laughed and said she would give me a general absolution.
She is a truly genial, hearty Scotchwoman, and seemed to
enter happily into the spirit of the hour.

"As we rode on, we found that the news of our coming
had spread through the village.   People came and stood in
their doors, beckoning, bowing, smiling, and waving their
handkerchiefs, and the carriage was several times stopped
by persons who came to offer flowers.   I remember, in
particular, a group of young girls bringing to the carriage
two of the most beautiful children I ever saw, whose little
hands literally deluged us with flowers.

"At the village of Helensburgh we stopped a little
while to call upon Mrs. Bell, the wife of Mr. Bell, the
inventor of the steamboat.   His invention in this country
was at about the same time as that of Fulton in America.
Mrs. Bell came to the carriage to speak to us.   She is a
venerable woman, far advanced in years.   They had prepared a lunch for us, and quite a number of people had
come together to meet us, but our friends said there was
not time for us to stop.

"We rode through several villages after this, and met everywhere a warm welcome. What pleased me was, that it was not mainly from the literary, nor the rich, nor the great, but the plain, common people. The butcher came out of his stall and the baker from his shop, the miller dusty with flour, the blooming, comely young mother, with her baby in her arms, all smiling and bowing, with that hearty, intelligent, friendly look, as if they knew we should be glad to see them.

"Once, while we stopped to change horses, I, for the sake of seeing something more of the country, walked on. It seems the honest landlord and his wife were greatly disappointed at this; however, they got into the carriage and rode on to see me, and I shook hands with them with a right good will.

"We saw several of the clergymen, who came out to meet us; and I remember stopping just to be introduced, one by one, to a most delightful family, a gray-headed father and mother, with comely brothers and fair sisters, all looking so kindly and homelike that I should have been glad to accept the invitation they gave me to their dwelling.

"This day has been a strange phenomenon to me. In the first place, I have seen in all these villages how universally the people read. I have seen how capable they are of a generous excitement and enthusiasm, and how much may be done by a work of fiction so written as to enlist those sympathies which are common to all classes. Certainly a great deal may be effected in this way, if God gives to any one the power, as I hope He will to many. The power of fictitious writing, for good as well as evil, is a thing which ought most seriously to be reflected on. No one can fail to see that in our day it is becoming a very great agency.

"We came home quite tired, as you may well suppose.

You will not be surprised that the next day I found myself more disposed to keep my bed than go out.

"Two days later: We bade farewell to Glasgow, overwhelmed with kindness to the last, and only oppressed by the thought of how little that was satisfactory we were able to give in return. Again we were in the railroad car on our way to Edinburgh. A pleasant two hours' trip is this from Glasgow to Edinburgh. When the cars stopped at Linlithgow station, the name started us as out of a dream. Here was born that woman whose beauty and whose name are set in the strong rough Scotch heart, as a diamond in granite!

"In Edinburgh the cars stopped amid a crowd of people who had assembled to meet us. The lord provost met us at the door of the car, and presented us to the magistracy of the city and the committees of the Edinburgh Anti-Slavery Societies. The drab dresses and pure white bonnets of many Friends were conspicuous among the dense moving crowd, as white doves seen against a dark cloud. Mr. S. and myself, and our future hostess, Mrs. Wigham, entered the carriage with the lord provost, and away we drove, the crowd following with their shouts and cheers. I was inexpressibly touched and affected by this. While we were passing the monument of Scott, I felt an oppressive melancholy. What a moment life seems in the presence of the noble dead! What a momentary thing is art, in all its beauty! Where are all those great souls that have created such an atmosphere of light about Edinburgh? and how little a space was given them to live and enjoy!

"We drove all over Edinburgh, up to the castle, to the university, to Holyrood, to the hospitals, and through many of the principal streets, amid shouts, and smiles, and greetings. Some boys amused me very much by their pertinacious attempts to keep up with the carriage.

"'Heck,' says one of them, 'that's her; see the *courls!*'

"The various engravers who have amused themselves by diversifying my face for the public, having all, with great unanimity, agreed in giving prominence to this point, I suppose the urchins thought they were on safe ground there. I certainly think I answered one good purpose that day, and that is of giving the much-oppressed and calumniated class called boys an opportunity to develop all the noise that was in them, — a thing for which I think they must bless me in their remembrances.

"At last the carriage drove into a deep-graveled yard, and we alighted at a porch covered with green ivy, and found ourselves once more at home.

"You may spare your anxieties about me, for I do assure you that if I were an old Sèvres china jar I could not have more careful handling than I do. Everybody is considerate; a great deal to say when there appears to be so much excitement. Everybody seems to understand how good-for-nothing I am; and yet, with all this consideration, I have been obliged to keep my room and bed for a good part of the time. Of the multitudes who have called, I have seen scarcely any.

"To-morrow evening is to be the great tea-party here. How in the world I am ever to live through it I don't know.

"April 26. Last night came off the *soirée*. The hall was handsomely decorated with flags in front. We went with the lord provost in his carriage. We went up as before into a dressing-room, where I was presented to many gentlemen and ladies. When we go in, the cheering, clapping, and stamping at first strike one with a strange sensation; but then everybody looks so heartily pleased and delighted, and there is such an all-pervading atmosphere of geniality and sympathy, as makes me in a few moments feel quite at home. After all, I consider that these cheers and applauses are Scotland's voice to

America, a recognition of the brotherhood of the countries.

"The national penny offering, consisting of a thousand golden sovereigns on a magnificent silver salver, stood conspicuously in view of the audience. It has been an unsolicited offering, given in the smallest sums, often from the extreme poverty of the giver. The committee who collected it in Edinburgh and Glasgow bore witness to the willingness with which the very poorest contributed the offering of their sympathy. In one cottage they found a blind woman, and said, 'Here, at least, is one who will feel no interest, as she cannot have read the book.'

"'Indeed,' said the old lady, 'if I cannot read, my son has read it to me, and I've got my penny saved to give.'

"It is to my mind extremely touching to see how the poor, in their poverty, can be moved to a generosity surpassing that of the rich. Nor do I mourn that they took it from their slender store, because I know that a penny given from a kindly impulse is a greater comfort and blessing to the poorest giver than even a penny received.

"As in the case of the other meeting, we came out long before the speeches were ended. Well, of course I did not sleep all night, and the next day I felt quite miserable.

"As to all engagements, however, I am in a state of happy acquiescence, having resigned myself, as a very tame lion, into the hands of my keepers. Whenever the time comes for me to do anything, I try to behave as well as I can, which, as Dr. Young says, is all that an angel could do in the same circumstances.

"As to the letters I receive, many of them are mere outbursts of feeling; yet they are interesting as showing the state of the public mind. Many of them are on kindred topics of moral reform, in which they seem to have an intuitive sense that we should be interested. I am not, of course, able to answer them all, but brother Charles does,

and it takes a good part of every day. One was from a shoe-
maker's wife in one of the islands, with a copy of very
fair verses. Many have come accompanying little keepsakes
and gifts. It seems to me rather touching and sad, that
people should want to give me things when I am not able
to give an interview or even a note in return. Charles
wrote from six to twelve o'clock, steadily, answering letters.

"The meeting in Dundee was in a large church, densely
crowded, and conducted much as the others had been.
When they came to sing the closing hymn, I hoped they
would sing Dundee; but they did not, and I fear in Scotland, as elsewhere, the characteristic national melodies are
giving way before more modern ones."

It is very interesting in following Mrs. Stowe's footsteps
through Scotland to see how her minute knowledge of the
history and literature of the country made every spot alive
with spirits of the past or figures of the fancy. As they
passed Glamis Castle she says: "We could see but a
glimpse of it from the road, but the very sound of the
name was enough to stimulate our imagination. Scott says
in his 'Demonology' that he never came anywhere near to
being overcome with a superstitious feeling, except twice
in his life, and one was on the night he slept in Glamis
Castle. . . . Scarcely ever a man had so much relish for
the supernatural and so little faith in it.

"I enjoyed my ride to Aberdeen more than anything we
had seen, the country is so wild and singular. . . . The
architecture of the cathedrals of Glasgow and Aberdeen
reminds me of what Walter Scott says of the Scotch people,
whom he compares to the native sycamore of their hills,
'which scorns to be biased in its mode of growth, even by
the influence of the prevailing wind, but, shooting its
branches with equal boldness in every direction, shows no
weather side to the storm, and may be broken, but can
never be bended.'

"We lingered a long time about Aberdeen Cathedral, and could scarcely tear ourselves away. We paced up and down under the old trees, looking off on the waters of the Don, listening to the waving branches, and, falling into a dreamy state of mind, thought what if it were six hundred years ago, and we were pious, simple-hearted old abbots! What a fine place that would be to walk up and down at eventide or on a Sabbath morning, reciting penitential psalms or reading St. Augustine.

"I cannot get over the feeling that the souls of the dead do somehow connect themselves with the places of their former habitation, and that the hush and thrill of spirit which we feel in them may be owing to the overshadowing presence of the invisible."

Of Abbotsford she says: "I observe that it is quite customary to speak as if it were a pity he ever undertook it; but viewed as a development of his inner life, as a working out in wood and stone of favorite fancies and cherished ideas, the building has to me a deep interest. . . . Wrought out in this way it has grown up like a bank of coral; . . . we should look at it as the poet's endeavor to render outward and visible the dreamland of his thoughts, and to create for himself a refuge from the cold dull realities of life in an architectural romance."

Nothing escaped her eye that was connected with the memory of Scott. She notes that the porch was copied from one at Linlithgow Palace; that the black and white marbles were from the Hebrides; the carved oak for one room from Dunfermline Abbey; the ceiling of another copied from Roslin; and a fireplace copied from a niche at Melrose. There also she marked the ancient pulpit of Erskine, wrought into a wall, the old door of Tolbooth prison, and many other delightful things which Scott appropriated to make his home unique and interesting to readers and scholars, if not to the eye of the ordinary tourist.

Her account of Melrose, too, is as fresh as if a large half-century of devotees of Scott had not walked through it, — and her devotion at Dryburgh that of a friend to Scott as well as a lover of his genius.

"It was a rainy, misty morning," she continued, "when I left my kind retreat and friends in Edinburgh. Considerate as everybody had been about imposing on my time or strength, still you may well believe that I was much exhausted. We left Edinburgh, therefore, with the determination to plunge at once into some hidden and unknown spot, where we might spend two or three days quietly by ourselves; remembering your Sunday at Stratford-on-Avon, I proposed that we should go there. As Stratford, however, is off the railroad line, we determined to accept the invitation, which was lying by us, from our friend, Joseph Sturge, of Birmingham, and take sanctuary with him. So we wrote on, intrusting him with the secret, and charging him on no account to let any one know of our arrival."

Of course the secret could not be kept.

"As we were drinking tea that evening, Elihu Burritt came in. It was the first time I had ever seen him, though I had heard a great deal of him from our friends in Edinburgh. He is a man in middle life, tall and slender, with fair complexion, blue eyes, an air of delicacy and refinement, and manners of great gentleness. My ideas of the 'learned blacksmith' had been of something altogether more ponderous and peremptory. Elihu has been for some years operating, in England and on the Continent, in a movement which many in our half-Christianized times regard with as much incredulity as the grim old warlike barons did the suspicious imbecilities of reading and writing. The sword now, as then, seems so much more direct a way to terminate controversies, that many Christian men, even, cannot conceive how the world is to get along without it.

"Before we left, we had agreed to meet a circle of friends from Birmingham, consisting of the Abolition Society there, which is of long standing, extending back in its memories to the very commencement of the agitation under Clarkson and Wilberforce. The windows of the parlor were opened to the ground; and the company invited filled not only the room, but stood in a crowd on the grass around the window. Among the peaceable company present was an admiral in the navy, a fine, cheerful old gentleman, who entered with hearty interest into the scene.

"A throng of friends accompanied us to the depot, while from Birmingham we had the pleasure of the company of Elihu Burritt, and enjoyed a delightful run to London, where we arrived towards evening."

The evening of her arrival in London, she went to a dinner at the lord mayor's, where she saw many distinguished persons.

"A very dignified gentleman, dressed in black velvet, with a fine head, made his way through the throng, and sat down by me, introducing himself as Lord Chief Baron Pollock. He told me he had just been reading the legal part of the 'Key to Uncle Tom's Cabin,' and remarked especially on the opinion of Judge Ruffin, in the case of *State* v. *Mann*, as having made a deep impression on his mind.

"Dinner was announced between nine and ten o'clock, and we were conducted into a splendid hall, where the tables were laid.

"Directly opposite me was Mr. Dickens, whom I now beheld for the first time, and was surprised to see looking so young. Mr. Justice Talfourd, known as the author of 'Ion,' was also there with his lady. She had a beautiful, antique cast of head. The lord mayor was simply dressed in black, without any other adornment than a massive gold chain. We rose from table between eleven and twelve o'clock — that is, we ladies — and went into the drawing-room, where I was presented to Mrs. Dickens and several other ladies. Mrs. Dickens is a good specimen of a truly English woman; tall, large, and well developed, with fine, healthy color, and an air of frankness, cheerfulness, and reliability. A friend whispered to me that she was as observing and fond of humor as her husband.

"After a while the gentlemen came back to the drawing-room, and I had a few moments of very pleasant, friendly conversation with Mr. Dickens. They are both people that one could not know a little of without desiring to know more."

The following day the American party dined with Lord Carlisle, of whom Mrs. Stowe says: —

"Lord Carlisle is a great friend to America, and so is his sister, the Duchess of Sutherland. He is the only English traveler who ever wrote notes on our country in a real spirit of appreciation.

"We went about seven o'clock, the dinner hour being here somewhere between eight and nine. We were shown into an ante-room adjoining the entrance hall, and from that into an adjacent apartment, where we met Lord Carlisle. The room had a pleasant, social air, warmed and enlivened by the blaze of a coal fire and wax candles.

"We had never, any of us, met Lord Carlisle before; but the considerateness and cordiality of our reception obviated whatever embarrassment there might have been in this circumstance. In a few moments after we were all seated, a servant announced the Duchess of Sutherland, and Lord Carlisle presented me. She is tall and stately, with a most noble bearing. Her fair complexion, blonde hair, and full lips speak of Saxon blood.

"The only person present not of the family connection was my quondam correspondent in America, Arthur Helps. Somehow or other I had formed the impression from his

writings that he was a venerable sage of very advanced
years, who contemplated life as an aged hermit from the
door of his cell. Conceive my surprise to find a genial
young gentleman of about twenty-five, who looked as if he
might enjoy a joke as well as another man.

"After the ladies left the table, the conversation turned
on the Maine law, which seems to be considered over here
as a phenomenon in legislation, and many of the gentlemen present inquired about it with great curiosity.

"After the gentlemen rejoined us, the Duke and Duchess
of Argyll came in, and Lord and Lady Blantyre. These
ladies are the daughters of the Duchess of Sutherland.
The Duchess of Argyll is of slight and fairy-like figure,
with flaxen hair and blue eyes, answering well enough to
the description of Annot Lyle in the 'Legend of Montrose.'
Lady Blantyre was somewhat taller, of fuller figure, with a
very brilliant bloom. Lord Blantyre is of the Stuart blood,
a tall and slender young man with very graceful manners.

"As to the Duke of Argyll, we found that the picture
drawn of him by his countrymen in Scotland was in every
way correct. Though slight of figure, with fair complexion and blue eyes, his whole appearance is indicative of
energy and vivacity. His talents and efficiency have made
him a member of the British Cabinet at a much earlier age
than is usual; and he has distinguished himself not only
in political life, but as a writer, having given to the world
a work on Presbyterianism, embracing an analysis of the
ecclesiastical history of Scotland since the Reformation,
which is spoken of as written with great ability, and in a
most liberal spirit. He made many inquiries about our
distinguished men, particularly of Emerson, Longfellow,
and Hawthorne; also of Prescott, who appears to be a
general favorite here. I felt at the moment that we never
value our own literary men so much as when we are placed
in a circle of intelligent foreigners."

Of another entertainment she writes: —

"Before the evening was through I was talked out and
worn out; there was hardly a chip of me left. To-morrow
at eleven o'clock comes the meeting at Stafford House.
What it will amount to I do not know; but I take no
thought for the morrow."

May 8.

MY DEAR C., — In fulfillment of my agreement I will
tell you, as nearly as I can remember, all the details of the
meeting at Stafford House. At about eleven o'clock we
drove under the arched carriage-way of a mansion exter-
nally not very showy in appearance.

When the duchess appeared, I thought she looked
handsomer by daylight than in the evening. She received
us with the same warm and simple kindness which she had
shown before. We were presented to the Duke of Sutherland. He is a tall, slender man, with rather a thin face,
light-brown hair, and a mild blue eye, with an air of gentleness and dignity.

Among the first that entered were the members of the
family, the Duke and Duchess of Argyll, Lord and Lady
Blantyre, the Marquis and Marchioness of Stafford, and
Lady Emma Campbell. Then followed Lord Shaftesbury
with his beautiful lady, and her father and mother, Lord
and Lady Palmerston. Lord Palmerston is of middle
height, with a keen dark eye and black hair streaked with
gray. There is something peculiarly alert and vivacious
about all his movements; in short, his appearance perfectly
answers to what we know of him from his public life.
One has a strange, mythological feeling about the existence
of people of whom one hears for many years without ever
seeing them. While talking with Lord Palmerston I
could but remember how often I had heard father and Mr.
S. exulting over his foreign dispatches by our own fireside. There were present, also, Lord John Russell, Mr.

Gladstone, and Lord Granville. The latter we all thought very strikingly resembled in his appearance the poet Longfellow.

After lunch the whole party ascended to the picture-gallery, passing on our way the grand staircase and hall, said to be the most magnificent in Europe. The company now began to assemble and throng the gallery, and very soon the vast room was crowded. Among the throng I remember many presentations, but of course must have forgotten many more. Archbishop Whately was there, with Mrs. and Miss Whately; Macaulay, with two of his sisters; Milman, the poet and historian; the Bishop of Oxford, Chevalier Bunsen and lady, and many more.

When all the company were together, Lord Shaftesbury read a very short, kind, and considerate address in behalf of the ladies of England, expressive of their cordial welcome.

This Stafford House meeting, in any view of it, is a most remarkable fact. Kind and gratifying as its arrangements have been to me, I am far from appropriating it to myself individually as a personal honor. I rather regard it as the most public expression possible of the feelings of the women of England on one of the most important questions of our day, that of individual liberty considered in its religious bearings.

On this occasion the Duchess of Sutherland presented Mrs. Stowe with a superb gold bracelet, made in the form of a slave's shackle, bearing the inscription: "We trust it is a memorial of a chain that is soon to be broken." On two of the links were inscribed the dates of the abolition of the slave-trade and of slavery in English territory. Years after its presentation to her, Mrs. Stowe was able to have engraved on the clasp of this bracelet, "Constitutional Amendment (forever abolishing slavery in the United States)."

Of a breakfast at Sir Charles Trevelyan's, she tells her
daughter: —

"We were set down at Westbourne Terrace, somewhere,
I believe, about eleven o'clock, and found quite a number
already in the drawing-room. I had met Macaulay before,
but being seated between him and Dean Milman, I must
confess I was a little embarrassed at times, because I
wanted to hear what they were both saying at the same
time. However, by the use of the faculty by which you
play a piano with both hands, I got on very comfortably.

"There were several other persons of note present at
this breakfast, whose conversation I had not an opportunity of hearing, as they sat at a distance from me. There
was Lord Glenelg, brother of Sir Robert Grant, governor
of Bombay, whose beautiful hymns have rendered him
familiar in America. The favorite one, commencing

'When gathering clouds around I view,'

was from his pen.

"The historian Hallam was also present, and I think it
very likely there may have been other celebrities whom I
did not know. I am always finding out, a day or two
after, that I have been with somebody very remarkable
and did not know it at the time."

She continues to her sister: —

"Like Miss Edgeworth's philosophic little Frank, we
are obliged to make out a list of what man *must* want and
of what he *may* want; and in our list of the former we
set down, in large and decisive characters, one quiet day for
the exploration and enjoyment of Windsor.

.   .   .   .

"One of the first objects that attracted my attention
upon entering the vestibule was a baby's wicker wagon,
standing in one corner. It was much such a carriage as all
mothers are familiar with; such as figures largely in the

history of almost every family. It had neat curtains and cushions of green merino, and was not royal, only maternal. I mused over the little thing with a good deal of interest.

"We went for our dinner to the White Hart, the very inn which Shakespeare celebrates in his 'Merry Wives,' and had a most overflowing merry time of it. After dinner we had a beautiful drive.

"We were bent upon looking up the church which gave rise to Gray's 'Elegy in a Country Churchyard,' intending when we got there to have a little scene over it; Mr. S., in all the conscious importance of having been there before, assuring us that he knew exactly where it was. So, after some difficulty with our coachman, and being stopped at one church which would not answer our purpose in any respect, we were at last set down by one which looked authentic; embowered in mossy elms, with a most ancient and goblin yew-tree, an ivy-mantled tower, all perfect as could be. Here, leaning on the old fence, we repeated the Elegy, which certainly applies here as beautifully as language could apply.

"Imagine our chagrin, on returning to London, at being informed that we had not been to the genuine churchyard after all. The gentleman who wept over the scenes of his early days on the wrong doorstep was not more grievously disappointed. However, he and we could both console ourselves with the reflection that the emotion was admirable, and wanted only the right place to make it the most appropriate in the world.

"The evening after our return from Windsor was spent with our kind friends, Mr. and Mrs. Gurney. After breakfast the next day, Mr. S., C., and I drove out to call upon Kossuth. We found him in an obscure lodging on the outskirts of London. I would that some of the editors in America, who have thrown out insinuations about his living in luxury, could have seen the utter bareness and plainness of the reception room, which had nothing in it beyond the simplest necessaries. He entered into conversation with us with cheerfulness, speaking English well, though with the idioms of foreign languages. When we parted he took my hand kindly and said, ' God bless you, my child! '

"I have been quite amused with something which has happened lately. This week the ' Times ' has informed the United Kingdom that Mrs. Stowe is getting a new dress made! It wants to know if Mrs. Stowe is aware what sort of a place her dress is being made in; and there is a letter from a dressmaker's apprentice stating that it is being made up piecemeal, in the most shockingly distressed dens of London, by poor, miserable white slaves, worse treated than the plantation slaves of America!

"Now Mrs. Stowe did not know anything of this, but simply gave the silk into the hands of a friend, and was in due time waited on in her own apartment by a very re-spectable-appearing woman, who offered to make the dress, and lo, this is the result! Since the publication of this piece, I have received earnest missives, from various parts of the country, begging me to interfere, hoping that I was not going to patronize the white slavery of England, and that I would employ my talents equally against oppression in every form. Could these people only know in what sweet simplicity I had been living in the State of Maine, where the only dressmaker of our circle was an intelligent, refined, well-educated woman who was considered as the equal of us all, and whose spring and fall ministrations to our wardrobe were regarded a double pleasure, — a friendly visit as well as a domestic assistance, — I say, could they know all this, they would see how guiltless I was in the matter. I verily never thought but that the nice, pleasant person who came to measure me for my silk dress was going to take it home and make it herself; it never occurred to me that she was the head of an establishment."

May 22, she writes to her husband, whose duties had obliged him to return to America: "To-day we went to hear a sermon in behalf of the ragged schools by the Archbishop of Canterbury. My thoughts have been much saddened by the news which I received of the death of Mary Edmondson."

"May 30. The next day from my last letter came off Miss Greenfield's concert, of which I send a card. You see in what company they have put your poor little wife. Funny! — isn't it? Well, the Hons. and Right Hons. all were there. I sat by Lord Carlisle.

"After the concert the duchess asked Lady Hatherton and me to come round to Stafford House and take tea, which was not a thing to be despised, either on account of the tea or the duchess. A lovelier time we never had, — present, the Duchess of Argyll, Lady Caroline Campbell, Lady Hatherton, and myself. We had the nicest cup of tea, with such cream, and grapes and apricots, with some Italian bread, etc.

"When we were going the duchess got me, on some pretext, into another room, and came up and put her arms round me, with her noble face all full of feeling.

"'Oh, Mrs. Stowe, I have been reading that last chapter in the "Key;" Argyll read it aloud to us. Oh, surely, surely, you will succeed, — God surely will bless you!'

"I said then that I thanked her for all her love and feeling for us, told her how earnestly all the women of England sympathized with her, and many in America. She looked really radiant and inspired. Had those who hang back from our cause seen her face, it might have put a soul into them as she said again, 'It will be done — it will be done — oh, I trust and pray it may!'

"So we kissed each other, and vowed friendship and fidelity — so I came away.

"To-day I am going with Lord Shaftesbury to St.

Paul's to see the charity children, after which lunch with
Dean Milman.

"May 31.   We went to lunch with Miss R. at Oxford
Terrace, where, among a number of distinguished guests,
was Lady Byron, with whom I had a few moments of
deeply interesting conversation.   No engravings that ever
have been circulated in America do any justice to her appearance.   She is of slight figure, formed with exceeding
delicacy, and her whole form, face, dress, and air unite to
make an impression of a character singularly dignified,
gentle, pure, and yet strong.   No words addressed to me
in any conversation hitherto have made their way to my
inner soul with such force as a few remarks dropped by her
on the present religious aspect of England, — remarks of
such quality as one seldom hears.

"We have borne in mind your advice to hasten away to
the Continent.   Charles wrote, a day or two since, to Mrs.
C. at Paris to secure very private lodgings, and by no
means let any one know that we were coming.   She has
replied, urging us to come to her house, and promising entire seclusion and rest.   So, since you departed, we have
been passing with a kind of comprehensive skip and jump
over remaining engagements.   And just the evening after
you left came off the presentation of the inkstand by the
ladies of Surrey Chapel.

"It is a beautiful specimen of silver-work, eighteen
inches long, with a group of silver figures on it representing
Religion, with the Bible in her hand, giving liberty to the
slave.   The slave is a masterly piece of work.   He stands
with his hands clasped, looking up to Heaven, while a
white man is knocking the shackles from his feet.   But
the prettiest part of the scene was the presentation of a
gold pen by a band of beautiful children, one of whom
made a very pretty speech.   I called the little things
to come and stand around me, and talked with them a

few minutes, and this was all the speaking that fell to my share.

"To-morrow we go — go to quiet, to obscurity, to peace — to Paris, to Switzerland; there we shall find the loveliest glen, and, as the Bible says, 'fall on sleep.'"

"Monday, June 13. We went this morning to the studio of M. Belloc, who is to paint my portrait. The first question which he proposed, with a genuine French air, was the question of 'pose' or position. It was concluded that, as other pictures had taken me looking at the spectator, this should take me looking away. M. Belloc remarked that M. Charpentier said I appeared always with the air of an observer, — was always looking around on everything. Hence M. Belloc would take me 'en observatrice, mais pas en curieuse.'

"Saturday, June 25. Lyons to Genève. As this was our first experience in the diligence line, we noticed particularly every peculiarity. I had had the idea that a diligence was a rickety, slow-moulded, antediluvian nondescript, toiling patiently along over impassable roads at a snail's pace. Judge of my astonishment at finding it a full-blooded, vigorous monster, of unscrupulous railway momentum and imperturbable equipose of mind. Down the macadamized slopes we thundered at a prodigious pace; up the hills we trotted, with six horses, three abreast; madly through the little towns we burst, like a whirlwind, crashing across the pebbled streets, and out upon the broad, smooth road again. Before we had well considered the fact that we were out of Lyons we stopped to change horses. Done in a jiffy; and whoop, crick, crack, whack, rumble, bump, whir, whisk, away we blazed, till, ere we knew it, another change and another.

"As evening drew on, a wind sprang up and a storm seemed gathering on the Jura. The rain dashed against the panes of the berlin as we rode past the grim-faced monarch of the 'misty shroud.' It was night as we drove into Geneva and stopped at the Messagerie. I heard with joy a voice demanding if this were *Madame Besshare*. I replied, not without some scruples of conscience, 'Oui, Monsieur, c'est moi,' though the name did not sound exactly like the one to which I had been wont to respond. In half an hour we were at home in the mansion of Monsieur Fazy."

Of their Swiss retreat her brother says: —

"The people of the neighborhood, having discovered who Harriet was, were very kind, and full of delight at seeing her. It was Scotland over again. We have had to be unflinching to prevent her being overwhelmed, both in Paris and Geneva, by the same demonstrations of regard. To this we were driven, as a matter of life and death. It was touching to listen to the talk of these secluded mountaineers. The good hostess, even the servant-maids, hung about Harriet, expressing such tender interest for the slave. All had read 'Uncle Tom;' and it had apparently been an era in their life's monotony, for they said, 'Oh, madame, do write another! Remember, our winter nights here are very long!'

"Here, then, I am, writing these notes in the *salle à manger* of the inn, where other voyagers are eating and drinking, and there is H. feeding on the green moonshine of an emerald ice cave. One would almost think her incapable of fatigue. How she skips up and down high places and steep places, to the manifest perplexity of the honest guide Kienholz *père*, who tries to take care of her, but does not exactly know how! She gets on a pyramid of débris, which the edge of the glacier is ploughing and grinding up, sits down, and falls — not asleep exactly, but into a trance. W. and I are ready to go on: we shout; our voice is lost in the roar of the torrent. We send the guide. He goes down, and stands doubtfully. He does

not know exactly what to do. She hears him, and starts
to her feet, pointing with one hand to yonder peak, and
with the other to that knife-like edge that seems cleaving
heaven with its keen and glistening scimitar of snow, reminding one of Isaiah's sublime imagery, ' For my sword is
bathed in heaven.' She points at the grisly rocks, with
their jags and spear-points. Evidently she is beside herself, and thinks she can remember the names of those
monsters, born of earthquake and storm, which cannot be
named nor known but by sight, and then are known at
once perfectly and forever."

In the month of September Mrs. Stowe returned to
America; "almost sadly," she writes, "as a child might
leave its home, I left the shores of kind, strong old England — the mother of us all." She hastened to throw herself with renewed energy into work for the slaves. She had
brought with her from England a good deal of money which
had been given her for the purpose of pressing the anti-
slavery cause. "She supported anti-slavery lectures wherever they were most needed, aided in establishing and maintaining anti-slavery publications, founded and assisted in
supporting schools in which colored people might be taught
how to avail themselves of the blessings of freedom. She
arranged public meetings, and prepared many of the addresses that should be delivered at them. She carried on
such an extensive correspondence with persons of all shades
of opinion in all parts of the world, that the letters received
and answered by her between 1853 and 1856 would fill
volumes. With all these multifarious interests, her children received a full share of her attention, nor were her
literary activities relaxed." In addition to the volumes
commemorating her enjoyment during the summer in England, she revised and enlarged her first book called "The
May-Flower" in the following winter.

CHAPTER VII

MRS. STOWE said at the moment of her first triumphal
tour through England: "The general topic of remark on
meeting me seems to be, that I am not so bad-looking as
they were afraid I was; and I do assure you when I have
seen the things that are put up in the shop-windows here
with my name under them, I have been lost in wondering
admiration at the boundless loving-kindness of my English
and Scottish friends in keeping up such a warm heart for
such a Gorgon. I should think that the Sphinx in the
London Museum might have sat for most of them. I am
going to make a collection of these portraits to bring home
to you. There is a great variety of them, and they will
be useful, like the Irishman's guide-board, which showed
where the road did not go."

I remember once accompanying Mrs. Stowe to a reception at a well-known house in Boston where before the evening was over the hostess drew me aside saying: "Why did
you never tell me that Mrs. Stowe was beautiful?" and
indeed when I observed her, in the full ardor of conversation, with her heightened color, her eyes shining and
awake but filled with great softness, her abundant curling
hair rippling naturally about her head and falling a little
at the sides (as in the portrait by Richmond), I quite
agreed with my hostess. Nor was that the first time her
beauty had been revealed to me; but she was seldom seen

to be beautiful by the great world, and the pleasure of this recognition was very great to those who loved her.

In personal appearance there was a strange similarity of character, not of likeness, between the three women of genius of that era, George Sand, George Eliot, and Mrs. Stowe. All three have been agreeably portrayed, while one of the pictures of Mrs. Stowe and one bust convey some idea of the beauty in her face. The similarity appeared when their minds were absorbed, or their spirits elsewhere; when they were sharing the daily round of life of which that other current of existence hardly took heed, although they wrought, and talked, and were present in the body, apparently, like those who surrounded them.

At such times a strange heaviness, a lack-lustre visage, was common to the three, and the portraits taken in such moments (the photographs seem especially possessed by this demon of absence) are painful, untrue, plain sometimes beyond words. Their faces become almost like stone masks, not etherealized as in death, but weighted with the heavier tasks of life.

The wonderful contrast produced by the reawakening in society when animated by conversation made them appear like different persons, and when true artists took these subjects in hand they presented them, of course, with the light of life in their faces. Nothing can be more striking than the contrast between certain photographs of George Sand and her portrait by Couture.[1] The same may be said also of the photographs of George Eliot and a charming drawing once made of her face in colored chalk. Mrs. Stowe's portrait by Richmond is not quite so close a likeness, but it resembles her much more nearly than those who have only known her photographs are willing to believe. The

---

[1] Of this portrait Gustave Flaubert says in a letter to George Sand " Celui que j'aime le mieux, c'est le dessin de Couture . . . moi, qui suis *un vieux romantique,* je retrouve là 'la tête de l'auteur' qui m'a fait tant rêver dans ma jeunesse."

bust also, done by Miss Durant in the studio of Baron de Triqueti, has preserved this sweet living expression of her countenance.[1] Of this work Mrs. Stowe's daughter wrote: "I well remember going with my mother for her sittings at the studio. The dim light, the marble dust and chippings covering the floor, the clink, clink of the chisels, and Miss Durant, tall, handsome, and animated before the mound of clay which day by day grew into a resemblance to my mother, and the Baron de Triqueti coming and going with kindly smiling face and friendly words, and my gentle little mother smiling, happy, and unconscious as a child. It all comes back to me like a dream — those far away, pleasant, happy days. . . . The bust, after it was finished, was taken to London, where I saw it, and thought it very beautiful and an excellent likeness of my mother at forty-six, — her age when it was taken." This bust was finally placed in the New York University, the gift of Dr. Wallace Wood.

Upon this subject of her personal appearance one of her old friends says: "Mrs. Stowe's face, like that of all her mother's children, showed the delicate refinement of the Foote mask overlaid by the stronger and more sanguine Beecher integument. Her curling, crispy hair, more or less freeing itself from the velvet bands with which she was accustomed to confine it, gave an informal grace to her head. Her eyes, whether twinkling with merriment or subdued to thoughtfulness, were always kind and pleasant. Her slender frame, with something of the ' Scholar's stoop ' of the shoulders, although so faithful a mother and housekeeper might claim other reasons besides study for that, was neatly but not stylishly dressed. Her manner was ever self-possessed, gentle, considerate; without the graces of one habituated to society, she was evidently a gentlewoman born and bred."

[1] A reproduction from the bust forms the frontispiece of this book.

Mrs. Stowe's first duty upon her return from this eventful journey to Europe was to write to the friends she had left behind. She sent an open letter to Scotland, fearing, as she said, that her delicate health had made her a very unsatisfactory guest. She begins with an introduction referring to her state of physical exhaustion after finishing the "Key to Uncle Tom's Cabin" and continues: —

The question will probably arise in your minds, Have the recent demonstrations in Great Britain done good to the Anti-slavery cause in America?

The first result of those demonstrations, as might have been expected, was an intense reaction. Every kind of false, evil, and malignant report has been circulated by malicious and partisan papers; and if there is any blessing in having all manner of evil said against us falsely, we have seemed to be in a fair way to come in possession of it.

The sanction which was given in this matter to the voice of the people, by the nobility of England and Scotland, has been regarded and treated with special rancor; and yet, in its place, it has been particularly important. Without it great advantages would have been taken to depreciate the value of the national testimony. The value of this testimony in particular will appear from the fact that the anti-slavery cause has been treated with especial contempt by the leaders of society in this country, and every attempt made to brand it with ridicule.

The effect of making a cause generally unfashionable is much greater in this world than it ought to be. It operates very powerfully with the young and impressible portion of the community; therefore Cassius M. Clay very well said with regard to the demonstration at Stafford House: "It will help our cause by rendering it fashionable."

With regard to the present state of the anti-slavery cause in America, I think, for many reasons, that it has never been more encouraging.   It is encouraging in this respect, that the subject is now fairly up for inquiry before the public mind, and that systematic effort which has been made for years to prevent its being discussed is proving wholly ineffectual.

The "Key to Uncle Tom's Cabin" has sold extensively at the South, following in the wake of "Uncle Tom." Not one fact or statement in it has been disproved as yet. I have yet to learn of even an *attempt* to disprove.

The "North American Review," a periodical which has never been favorable to the discussion of the slavery question, has come out with a review of "Uncle Tom's Cabin," in which, while rating the book very low as a work of art, they account for its great circulation and success by the fact of its being a true picture of slavery.   They go on to say that the system is one so inherently abominable that, unless slaveholders shall rouse themselves and abolish the principle of chattel ownership, they can no longer sustain themselves under the contempt and indignation of the whole civilized world.   What are the slaveholders to do when this is the best their friends and supporters can say for them?

I regret to say that the movements of Christian denominations on this subject are yet greatly behind what they should be.   Some movements have been made by religious bodies, of which I will not now speak; but as a general thing the professed Christian church is pushed up to its duty by the world, rather than the world urged on by the church.

The colored people in this country are rapidly rising in every respect.   I shall request Frederick Douglass to send you the printed account of the recent colored convention. It would do credit to any set of men whatever, and I hope you will get some notice taken of it in the papers of the United Kingdom.   It is time that the slanders against

this unhappy race should be refuted, and it should be seen
how, in spite of every social and political oppression, they
are rising in the scale of humanity. In my opinion they
advance quite as fast as any of the foreign races which have
found an asylum among us.

.   .   .   .

Yours in all sympathy,   H. B. Stowe.

Almost simultaneously she sent broadcast an appeal to
the women of America. The Kansas and Nebraska agitation was going on and she was in constant correspondence
with Charles Sumner and others who could keep her informed as to the condition of the struggle.

"I cannot believe," she wrote in her appeal, "that there
is a woman so unchristian as to think it right to inflict
upon her neighbor's child what she would consider worse
than death were it inflicted upon her own. I do not believe there is a wife who would think it right that *her*
husband should be sold to a trader to be worked all his life
without wages or a recognition of rights. I do not believe
there is a husband who would consider it right that his
wife should be regarded by law the property of another
man. I do not believe there is a father or mother who
would consider it right were they forbidden by law to teach
their children to read. I do not believe there is a brother
who would think it right to have his sister held as property, with no legal defense for her personal honor, by any
man living.

"The question is not now, Shall the wrongs of slavery
exist as they have within their own territories, but Shall
we permit them to be extended all over the free territories
of the United States? Shall the woes and the miseries
of slavery be extended over a region of fair, free, unoccu-
pied territory nearly equal in extent to the whole of the
free States?

"Women of the free States! the question is not Shall we remonstrate with slavery on its own soil, but Are we willing to receive slavery into the free States and Territories of this Union? Shall the whole power of these United States go into the hands of slavery? Shall every State in the Union be thrown open to slavery? This is the possible result and issue of the question now pending. This is the fearful crisis at which we stand.

"And now you ask, What can the *women* of a country do?

"O women of the free States! what did your brave mothers do in the days of our Revolution? Did not liberty in those days feel the strong impulse of woman's heart?

.   .   .   .

"The first duty of every American woman at this time is to thoroughly understand the subject for herself and to feel that she is bound to use her influence for the right. Then they can obtain signatures to petitions to our national legislature. They can spread information upon this vital topic throughout their neighborhoods. They can employ lecturers to lay the subject before the people. They can circulate the speeches of their members of Congress that bear upon the subject, and in many other ways they can secure to all a full understanding of the present position of our country.

"Above all, it seems to be necessary and desirable that we should make this subject a matter of earnest prayer. A conflict is now begun between the forces of liberty and despotism throughout the whole world. We who are Christians, and believe in the sure word of prophecy, know that fearful convulsions and overturnings are predicted before the coming of Him who is to rule the earth in righteousness. How important, then, in this crisis, that all who believe in prayer should retreat beneath the shadow of the Almighty!

"It is a melancholy but unavoidable result of such great encounters of principle that they tend to degenerate into sectional and personal bitterness. It is this liability that forms one of the most solemn and affecting features of the crisis now presented. We are on the eve of a conflict which will try men's souls, and strain to the utmost the bonds of brotherly union that bind this nation together.

. . . .

"For the sake, then, of our dear children, for the sake of our common country, for the sake of outraged and struggling liberty throughout the world, let every woman of America now do her duty."

Beside these public letters she dispatched, of course, many private ones. To a lady in Scotland, Mrs. Wigham, she writes in October: "I hear that the pro-slavery papers have been busy in fabricating every strange, odd, improbable combination of evil against me. When ' Uncle Tom ' came out first there was such a universal praising of it that I began to think ' Woe unto you when all men speak well of you.' I have been quite relieved of my fears on that score; if there is any blessing in all manner of evil said falsely against one I am likely to have it. But these things I never read; they cannot change my friends; they cannot change the truth, and above all, they cannot change God. . . . Meanwhile let me say that every anti-slavery person and paper speaks in one way, that of hope. They say that they are greatly encouraged."

A new series of difficulties for the anti-slavery cause now developed themselves. Mr. Garrison, being a friend of Theodore Parker and on the radical side of religious thought, gave Mrs. Stowe much uneasiness. "What I fear," she wrote him, "is that ' The Liberator ' [of which Mr. Garrison was the brave editor] will take from poor Uncle Tom his Bible and give him nothing in its place."

"Surely," replied Mr. Garrison, "you would not have

me disloyal to my conscience. How do you prove that you are not trammeled by educational or traditional notions as to the entire sanctity of the Bible ? "

Mrs. Stowe replied: " I would not attack the faith of a heathen without being sure that I had a better one to put in its place, because such at it is, it is better than nothing." The church took up the argument, Dr. Bacon and Dr. Kirk writing bravely on one side and Theodore Parker and Mr. Garrison on the other; Mrs. Stowe and her brothers adding their weight on the side of the old church. Happily the great struggle against slavery united even those who differed upon the methods to be employed for the education of the negro, and they still stood side by side in brotherly love.

In his "History of the United States from the Compromise of 1850 " Mr. James F. Rhodes gives a hint of the critical and dissenting spirit of this stormy period: —

"The graphic pen of Harriet Beecher Stowe has given a description of Douglas as he appeared this winter, and she has vividly characterized his manner of argument. . . . The author of ' Uncle Tom's Cabin,' and the society in which she moved, scorned Douglas. Her soul was bound up in the anti-slavery cause, and one might have expected from her a diatribe, only differing in force from those that other New England writers were publishing on every opportunity. But she was almost as much artist as abolitionist; and from the Senate gallery she looked upon the scene with the eye of an observer and student of character. In her description there is much of penetration. Serene as it is, one detects the striking impression made on the sensitive woman of genius by the man who was an intellectual giant."

Mr. Rhodes has reference to the Illinois senator, Stephen A. Douglas, whose course on the slavery question deserved all the reprobation it received. Of another and better

Douglass — Frederick, the eminent fugitive from slavery — we have a glimpse in the following letter to Mr. Garrison, touching the latter's criticism of Douglass's course in allying himself with the political abolitionists: —

CABIN, December 19, 1853.

MR. GARRISON.

Dear Sir, — After seeing you, I enjoyed the pleasure of a personal interview with Mr. Douglass, and I feel bound in justice to say that the impression was far more satisfactory than I had anticipated.

There did not appear to be any deep underlying stratum of bitterness; he did not seem to me malignant or revengeful. I think it was only a temporary excitement and one which he will outgrow.

I was much gratified with the growth and development both of his mind and heart. I am satisfied that his change of sentiment was not a mere political one but a genuine growth of his own conviction. A vigorous reflective mind like his cast among those who nourish these new sentiments is naturally led to modified views.

At all events, he holds no opinion which he cannot defend, with a variety of richness of thought and expression and an aptness of illustration which shows it to be a growth from the soil of his own mind with a living root, and not a twig broken off other men's thoughts and stuck down to subserve a temporary purpose.

His plans for the elevation of his own race are manly, sensible, comprehensive; he has evidently observed closely and thought deeply and will, I trust, act efficiently.

You speak of him as an apostate. I cannot but regard this language as unjustly severe. Why is he any more to be called an apostate for having spoken ill-tempered things of former friends than they for having spoken severely and cruelly as they have of him? Where is this work of ex-

communication to end? Is there but one true anti-slavery
church and all others infidels? Who shall declare which
it is? I feel bound to remonstrate with this — for the
same reason that I do with slavery — because I think it an
injustice. I must say still farther, that if the first allusion
to his family concerns was unfortunate this last one is more
unjustifiable still. I am utterly surprised at it. As a
friend to you and to him, I view it with the deepest concern and regret.

What Douglass *is* really, time will show. I trust that
he will make no farther additions to the already unfortunate controversial literature of the cause. *Silence* in this
case will be eminently — *golden.*

I must indulge the hope you will see reason at some
future time to alter your opinion and that what you now
cast aside as worthless shall yet appear to be a treasure.
There is abundant room in the anti-slavery field for him to
perform a work without crossing the track or impeding the
movements of his old friends, and perhaps in some future
time, meeting each other from opposite quarters of a victo-
rious field, you may yet shake hands together.

I write this note, because in the conversation I had with
you, and also with Miss Weston, I admitted so much that
was unfavorable to Mr. Douglass that I felt bound in justice to state the more favorable views which had arisen to
my mind.

Very sincerely your friend,   H. B. STOWE.

Again Mrs. Stowe set herself to the writing of a new
book. In preparing the "Key to Uncle Tom's Cabin" she
had collected much fresh material which she proceeded to
use for a story to be called "Dred." She was anxious to
show the general effect of slavery on society ; the demoraliza-
tion of all classes, and the corruption of Christianity which
follows in its trail.

All the summer and winter were absorbed in her labors for this book, which is one of her finest pieces of work. Harriet Martineau said of it, that in her opinion it was a greater story than "Uncle Tom;" and other tributes to the same effect were paid to her in England.

With the completion of her story, Mrs. Stowe again decided to find rest if possible, and certainly pleasure and diversion, in a second journey to Europe.

She set sail about the first of August, accompanied by her husband, her two eldest daughters, her son Henry, and her sister, Mrs. Perkins. The secondary object of her journey (only secondary to her own health) was that of securing a copyright to her new book. She had failed in getting one on "Uncle Tom." Sampson Low & Company were her publishers, who looked after her interests with personal good will.

Professor Stowe being obliged to return to his work in Andover after a brief absence, his wife wrote to him: "If 'Dred' has as good a sale in America as it is likely to have in England, we shall do well. There is such a demand that they had to placard the shop windows in Glasgow with,—

'To prevent disappointment,
"DRED"
Not to be had till,' etc.

"Everybody is after it, and the prospect is of an enormous sale.

"God, to whom I prayed night and day while I was writing the book, has heard me, and given us of worldly goods *more* than I asked. I feel, therefore, a desire to 'walk softly,' and inquire, For what has He so trusted us?

"Every day I am more charmed with the Duke and Duchess of Sutherland; they are simple-hearted, frank, natural, full of feeling, of piety, and good sense. They certainly are, apart from any considerations of rank or position, most interesting and noble people. The duke laughed heartily at many things I told him of our Andover theological tactics, of your preaching, etc.; but I think he is a sincere, earnest Christian.

"Our American politics form the daily topic of interest. The late movements in Congress are discussed with great warmth, and every morning the papers are watched for new details.

"I must stop now, as it is late and we are to leave here early to-morrow morning. We are going to Staffa, Iona, the Pass of Glencoe, and finally through the Caledonian Canal up to Dunrobin Castle, where a large party of all sorts of interesting people are gathered around the Duchess of Sutherland.   Affectionately yours,   HARRIET."

At Dunrobin, Mrs. Stowe found awaiting her the following note from her friend, Lady Byron:—

LONDON, September 10, 1856.

Your book, dear Mrs. Stowe, is of the "little leaven" kind, and must prove a great moral force, — perhaps not manifestly so much as secretly, and yet I can hardly conceive so much power without immediate and sensible effects; only there will be a strong disposition to resist on the part of all the hollow-hearted professors of religion, whose heathenisms you so unsparingly expose. They have a class feeling like others. To the young, and to those who do not reflect much on what is offered to their belief, you will do great good by showing how spiritual food is adulterated. The Bread from Heaven is in the same case as baker's bread. I feel that one perusal is not enough. It is a "mine," to use your own simile. If there is truth in what I heard Lord Byron say, that works of fiction *lived* only by the amount of *truth* which they contained, your story is sure of long life. . . .

I know now, more than before, how to value communion with you.

With kind regards to your family,
Yours affectionately,   A. T. NOEL BYRON.

From this pleasant abiding-place Mrs. Stowe writes to her husband: —

DUNROBIN CASTLE, September 15.

MY DEAR HUSBAND, — Everything here is like a fairy story.   The place is beautiful.   It is the most perfect combination of architectural and poetic romance with home comfort.   The people, too, are charming.   We have here Mr. Labouchere, a cabinet minister, and Lady Mary his wife, — I like him very much, and her, too, — Kingsley's brother, a very entertaining man, and to-morrow Lord Ellsmere is expected.   I wish you could be here, for I am sure you would like it.   Life is so quiet and sincere and friendly, that you would feel more as if you had come at the hearts of these people than in London.

The Sutherland estate looks like a garden.   We stopped at the town of Frain, four miles before we reached Sutherlandshire, where a crowd of well-to-do, nice-looking people gathered around the carriage, and as we drove off gave three cheers.   This was better than I expected, and looks well for their opinion of my views.

"Dred" is selling over here wonderfully.   Low says, with all the means at his command, he has not been able to meet the demand.   He sold fifty thousand in two weeks, and probably will sell as many more.

I am showered with letters, private and printed, in which the only difficulty is to know what the writers would be at.   I see evidently happiness and prosperity all through the line of this estate.   I see the duke giving his thought and time, and spending the whole income of this

estate in improvements upon it. I see the duke and duchess evidently beloved wherever they move. I see them
most amiable, most Christian, most considerate to everybody. The writers of the letters admit the goodness of the
duke, but denounce the system, and beg me to observe its
effects for myself. I do observe that, compared with any
other part of the Highlands, Sutherland is a garden. I
observe well-clothed people, thriving lands, healthy children, fine school-houses, and all that.

Henry was invited to the tenants' dinner, where he excited much amusement by pledging every toast in fair
water, as he has done invariably on all occasions since he
has been here.

The duchess, last night, showed me her copy of "Dred,"
in which she has marked what most struck or pleased her.
I begged it, and am going to send it to you. She said to
me this morning at breakfast, "The Queen says that she
began ' Dred ' the very minute she got it, and is deeply
interested in it."

She bought a copy of Lowell's poems, and begged me to
mark the best ones for her; so if you see him, tell him
that we have been reading him together. She is, taking
her all in all, one of the noblest-appointed women I ever
saw; real old genuine English, such as one reads of in
history; full of nobility, courage, tenderness, and zeal. It
does me good to hear her read prayers daily, as she does,
in the midst of her servants and guests, with a manner full
of grand and noble feeling.

Mrs. Stowe wrote to her friend, Mrs. Howard, at twelve
o'clock at night: —

"DEAR SUSY, — . . . The people here are such as
Henry " [Mr. Beecher] "would be delighted to know, and
how glad they would be to see him. The duchess since I

saw her has passed through a great sorrow in the loss of her son, and it seems to have only widened her heart and filled it with a deeper feeling for all suffering humanity. The news from America is eagerly watched by them, and the Duchess said: 'I only wish Fremont could be elected while you are here. I would have the castle illuminated.' You have no idea of the feelings of good people here about America. They say it is a ship freighted with the world's future; and they watch its struggle in the breakers with the deepest emotion. The old duke has been perfectly delighted with the hymns quoted in 'Dred,' and asked me where he could find such hymns. I have promised him a Plymouth hymn-book as soon as I can get one from America. He is unfortunately quite deaf, and being thus precluded from society spends all his time doing good. His estate has been changed from a desert to a garden. He has been to-day showing me his improvements. . . . When one sees money and station employed in this way, in raising up and educating a country, it seems something worth having. Susy dear, my paper and brain give out; but not my heart, which loves you all just as ever."

She continues in her journal to her husband: "Thursday Morning, September 25. We were obliged to get up at half past five the morning we left Dunrobin, an effort when one does n't go to bed till one o'clock. We found breakfast laid for us in the library, and before we had quite finished the duchess came in. Our starting off was quite an imposing sight. First came the duke's landau, in which were Mary, the duke, and myself; then a carriage in which were Eliza and Hatty, and finally the carriage which we had hired, with Henry, our baggage, and Mr. Jackson (the duke's secretary). The gardener sent a fresh bouquet for each of us, and there was such a leave-taking, as if we were old and dear friends. We did really love them, and had no doubt of their love for us.

"The duke rode with us as far as Dornach, where he showed us the cathedral beneath which his ancestors are buried, and where is a statue of his father, similar to one the tenants have erected on top of the highest hill in the neighborhood.

"We also saw the prison, which had but two inmates, and the old castle. Here the duke took leave of us, and taking our own carriage, we crossed the ferry and continued on our way. After a very bad night's rest at Inverness, in consequence of the town's being so full of people attending some Highland games that we could have no places at the hotel, and after a weary ride in the rain, we came into Aberdeen Friday night.

"To-morrow we go on to Edinburgh, where I hope to meet a letter from you. The last I heard from Low, he had sold sixty thousand of 'Dred,' and it was still selling well. I have not yet heard from America how it goes. The critics scold, and whiffle, and dispute about it, but on the whole it is a success, so the 'Times' says, with much coughing, hemming, and standing first on one foot and then on the other. If the 'Times' were sure we should beat in the next election, 'Dred' would go up in the scale; but as long as there is that uncertainty, it has first one line of praise, and then one of blame."

Henry Stowe returned to America in October, says the Rev. C. E. Stowe, to whom I am indebted for this sequence, to enter Dartmouth College, while the rest of the party pursued their way southward, as will be seen by the following letters: —

CITY OF YORK, October 10.

DEAR HUSBAND, — Henry will tell you all about our journey, and at present I have but little time for details.

I received your first letter with great joy, relief, and

gratitude, first to God for restoring your health and strength, and then to you, for so good, long, and refreshing a letter.

Henry, I hope, comes home with a serious determination to do well and be a comfort. Seldom has a young man seen what he has in this journey, or made more valuable friends.

Since we left Aberdeen, from which place my last was mailed, we have visited in Edinburgh with abounding delight; thence yesterday to Newcastle. Last night attended service in Durham Cathedral, and after that came to York, whence we send Henry to Liverpool.

I send you letters, etc., by him. One hundred thousand copies of "Dred" sold in four weeks! After that who cares what critics say? Its success in England has been complete, so far as sale is concerned. It is very bitterly attacked, both from a literary and a religious point of view. The "Record" is down upon it with a cartload of solemnity; the "Athenæum" with waspish spite; the "Edinburgh" goes out of its way to say that the author knows nothing of the society she describes; but yet it goes everywhere, is read everywhere, and Mr. Low says that he puts the hundred and twenty-fifth thousand to press confidently. The fact that so many good judges like it better than "Uncle Tom" is success enough.

In my journal to Henry, which you may look for next week, you will learn how I have been very near the Queen, and formed acquaintance with divers of her lords and ladies, and heard all she has said about "Dred;" how she prefers it to "Uncle Tom," how she inquired for you, and other matters.

Till then, I am, as ever, your affectionate wife,

H. B. STOWE.

Upon Mrs. Stowe's return to London she found a letter from Lady Byron, who wrote: —

OXFORD HOUSE, October 15.

DEAR MRS. STOWE, — The newspapers represent you as returning to London, but I cannot wait for the chance, slender I fear, of seeing you there, for I wish to consult you on a point admitting but of little delay. Feeling that the sufferers in Kansas have a claim not only to sympathy, but to the expression of it, I wish to send them a donation. It is, however, necessary to know what is the best application of money and what the safest channel. Presuming that you will approve the object, I ask you to tell me. Perhaps you would undertake the transmission of my £50. My present residence, two miles beyond Richmond, is opposite. I have watched for instructions of your course with warm interest. The sale of your book will go on increasing. It is beginning to be understood.

Believe me, with kind regards to your daughters,

Your faithful and affectionate   A. T. NOEL BYRON.

To this note the following answer was promptly returned: —

GROVE TERRACE, KENTISH TOWN, October 16.

DEAR LADY BYRON, — How glad I was to see your handwriting once more! how more than glad I should be to see *you!* I do long to see you. I have so much to say, — so much to ask, and need to be refreshed with a sense of a congenial and sympathetic soul.

Thank you, my dear friend, for your sympathy with our poor sufferers in Kansas. May God bless you for it! By doing this you will step to my side; perhaps you may share something of that abuse which they who "know not what they do" heap upon all who so feel for the right. I assure you, dear friend, I am *not* insensible to the fiery darts which thus fly around me.

One of the very pleasant experiences during this second journey to England was a visit to Lady Mary and Mr. Labouchere at Stoke Park. At the last moment the family luggage was detained, and all the party were prevented from going except Mrs. Stowe herself, who by chance had left certain dresses in London.

"I arrived alone," she wrote, "at the Slough Station, and found Lady Mary's carriage waiting. Away we drove through a beautiful park full of deer, who were so tame as to stand and look at us as we passed. The house is in the Italian style, with a dome on top, and wide terraces with stone balustrades around it.

"Lady Mary met me at the door, and seemed quite concerned to learn of our ill-fortune. We went through a splendid suite of rooms to a drawing-room, where a little tea-table was standing.

"After tea Lady Mary showed me my room. It had that delightful, homelike air of repose and comfort they succeed so well in giving to rooms here. There was a cheerful fire burning, an arm-chair drawn up beside it, a sofa on the other side with a neatly arranged sofa-table on which were writing materials. One of the little girls had put a pot of pretty greenhouse moss in a silver basket on this table, and my toilet cushion was made with a place in the centre to hold a little vase of flowers. Here Lady Mary left me to rest before dressing for dinner. I sat down in an easy-chair before the fire, and formed hospitable resolutions as to how I would try to make rooms always look homelike and pleasant to tired guests. Then came the maid to know if I wanted hot water, — if I wanted anything, — and by and by it was time for dinner. Going down into the parlor I met Mr. Labouchere, and we all went in to dinner. It was not quite as large a party as at Dunrobin, but much in the same way. No company, but several ladies who were all family connections.

"The following morning Lord Dufferin and Lord Alfred Paget, two gentlemen of the Queen's household, rode over from Windsor to lunch with us. They brought news of the goings-on there. Do you remember one night the Duchess of S. read us a letter from Lady Dufferin, describing the exploits of her son, who went yachting with Prince Napoleon up by Spitzbergen, and when Prince Napoleon and all the rest gave up and went back, still persevered and discovered a new island? Well, this was the same man. A thin, slender person, not at all the man you would fancy as a Mr. Great Heart, — lively, cheery, and conversational.

"Lord Alfred is also very pleasant.

"Lady Mary prevailed on Lord Dufferin to stay and drive with us after lunch, and we went over to Clifden, the duchess's villa, of which we saw the photograph at Dunrobin. For grace and beauty some of the rooms in this place exceed any I have yet seen in England.

"When we came back my first thought was whether Aunt Mary and the girls had come. Just as we were all going up to dress for dinner they appeared. Meanwhile, the Queen had sent over from Windsor for Lady Mary and her husband to dine with her that evening, and such invitations are understood as commands.

"So, although they themselves had invited four or five people to dinner, they had to go and leave us to entertain ourselves. Lady Mary was dressed very prettily in a flounced white silk dress with a pattern of roses woven round the bottom of each flounce, and looked very elegant. Mr. Labouchere wore breeches, with knee and shoe buckles sparkling with diamonds.

"They got home soon after we had left the drawing-room, as the Queen always retires at eleven. No late hours for her.

"The next day Lady Mary told me that the Queen had talked to her all about 'Dred,' and how she preferred it to 'Uncle Tom's Cabin,' how interested she was in Nina, how provoked when she died, and how she was angry that something dreadful did not happen to Tom Gordon. She inquired for papa, and the rest of the family, all of whom she seemed to be well informed about.

"The next morning we had Lord Dufferin again to breakfast. He is one of the most entertaining young men I have seen in England, full of real thought and noble feeling, and has a wide range of reading. He had read all our American literature, and was very flattering in his remarks on Hawthorne, Poe, and Longfellow. I find J. R. Lowell less known, however, than he deserves to be.

"Lord Dufferin says that his mother wrote him some verses on his coming of age, and that he built a tower for them and inscribed them on a brass plate. I recommend the example to you, Henry; make yourself the tower and your memory the brass plate.

"This morning came also, to call, Lady Augusta Bruce, Lord Elgin's daughter, one of the Duchess of Kent's ladies-in-waiting; a very excellent, sensible girl, who is a strong anti-slavery body.

"After lunch we drove over to Eton, and went in to see the provost's house. After this, as we were passing by Windsor the coachman suddenly stopped and said, 'The Queen is coming, my lady.' We stood still and the royal cortége passed. I only saw the Queen, who bowed graciously.

"Lady Mary stayed at our car door till it left the station, and handed in a beautiful bouquet as we parted. This is one of the loveliest visits I have made."

After filling a number of other pleasant engagements in

England, among which was a visit to Charles Kingsley and
his family, Mrs. Stowe and her party crossed the Channel.
She settled down for some months in Paris for the express
purpose of studying French.   From the French capital she
writes to her husband in Andover as follows: —

PARIS, November 7.

MY DEAR HUSBAND, — On the 28th, when your last
was written, I was at Charles Kingsley's.   It seemed odd
enough to Mary and me to find ourselves, long after dark,
alone in a hack, driving towards the house of a man whom
we never had seen (nor his wife either).

My heart fluttered as, after rumbling a long way through
the dark, we turned into a yard.   We knocked at a door
and were met in the hall by a man who stammers a little
in his speech, and whose inquiry, "Is this Mrs. Stowe?"
was our first positive introduction.   Ushered into a large,
pleasant parlor lighted by a coal fire, which flickered on
comfortable chairs, lounges, pictures, statuettes, and book-
cases, we took a good view of him.   He is tall, slender,
with blue eyes, brown hair, and a hale, well-browned face,
and somewhat loose-jointed withal.   His wife is a real
Spanish beauty.

How we did talk and go on for three days!   I guess he
is tired.   I'm sure we were.   He is a nervous, excitable
being, and talks with head, shoulders, arms, and hands,
while his hesitance makes it the harder.   Of his theology
I will say more some other time.   He, also, has been
through the great distress, the "Conflict of Ages," but has
come out at a different end from Edward, and stands with
John Foster, though with more positiveness than he.

He laughed a good deal at many stories I told him of
father, and seemed delighted to hear about him.   But he
is, what I did not expect, a zealous Churchman; insists
that the Church of England is the finest and broadest

platform a man can stand on, and that the thirty-nine articles are the only ones he could subscribe to. I told him
you thought them the best summary (of doctrine) you
knew, which pleased him greatly.

In writing from Paris, Mrs. Stowe tells her husband: —

"As usual, my horrid pictures do me a service, and people
seem relieved when they see me; think me even handsome
'in a manner.' Kingsley, in his relief, expressed as much
to his wife, and as beauty has never been one of my strong
points I am open to flattery upon it.

"We had a most agreeable call from Arthur Helps before
we left London. He, Kingsley, and all the good people
are full of the deepest anxiety for our American affairs.
They really do feel very deeply, seeing the peril so much
plainer than we do in America.

"November 30. This is Sunday evening, and a Sunday
in Paris always puts me in mind of your story about somebody who said, 'Bless you! they make such a noise that
the Devil could n't meditate.' All the extra work and
odd jobs of life are put into Sunday. Your washerwoman
comes Sunday, with her innocent, good-humored face, and
would be infinitely at a loss to know why she should n't.
Your bonnet, cloak, shoes, and everything are sent home
Sunday morning, and all the way to church there is such
whirligiging and pirouetting along the boulevards as almost
takes one's breath away. To-day we went to the Oratoire
to hear M. Grand Pierre. I could not understand much;
my French ear is not quick enough to follow. I could
only perceive that the subject was 'La Charité,' and that
the speaker was fluent, graceful, and earnest, the audience
serious and attentive.

"Last night we were at Baron de Triqueti's again, with
a party invited to celebrate the birthday of their eldest
daughter, Blanche, a lovely girl of nineteen. There were

some good ladies there who had come eighty leagues to
meet me, and who were so delighted with my miserable
French that it was quite encouraging. I believe I am getting over the sandbar at last, and conversation is beginning
to come easy to me.

"There were three French gentlemen who had just been
reading 'Dred' in English, and who were as excited and
full of it as could be, and I talked with them to a degree
that astonished myself. There is a review of 'Dred' in
the 'Revue des Deux Mondes' which has long extracts
from the book, and is written in a very appreciative and
favorable spirit. Generally speaking, French critics seem
to have a finer appreciation of my subtle shades of meaning
than English. I am curious to hear what Professor Park
has to say about it. There has been another review in
'La Presse' equally favorable. All seem to see the truth
about American slavery much plainer than people can who
are in it. If American ministers and Christians could see
through their sophistical spider-webs, with what wonder,
pity, and contempt they would regard their own vacillating
condition!

"We visit once a week at Madame Mohl's, where we meet
all sorts of agreeable people. Lady Elgin does n't go into
society now, having been struck with paralysis, but sits at
home and receives her friends as usual. This notion of
sitting always in the open air is one of her peculiarities.

"I must say, life in Paris is arranged more sensibly than
with us. Visiting involves no trouble in the feeding line.
People don't go to eat. A cup of tea and plate of biscuit
is all, — just enough to break up the stiffness.

"It is wonderful that the people here do not seem to have
got over 'Uncle Tom' a bit. The impression seems fresh
as if just published. How often have they said, That book
has revived the Gospel among the poor of France; it has
done more than all the books we have published put to-

gether. It has gone among *les ouvriers*, among the poor of Faubourg St. Antoine, and nobody knows how many have been led to Christ by it. Is not this blessed, my dear husband? Is it not worth all the suffering of writing it?

"January 25, Paris. Here is a story for Charley. The boys in the Faubourg St. Antoine are the children of *ouvriers*, and every day their mothers give them two sous to buy a luncheon. When they heard I was coming to the school, of their own accord they subscribed half their luncheon money to give to me for the poor slaves. This five-franc piece I have now; I have bought it of the cause for five dollars, and am going to make a hole in it and hang it round Charley's neck as a medal.

"I have just completed arrangements for leaving the girls at a Protestant boarding-school, while I go to Rome.

"We expect to start the 1st of February."

The party did not reach Rome without accident. The steamer ran ashore and broke a paddle wheel, and the miserable carriage which came to convey them from Civita Vecchia broke down also, but after every possible misadventure of travel, which she and her sister, Mrs. Perkins, bore with cheerfulness, they found a spot to rest their weary heads in the Eternal City.

It seemed at first as if they must pass the night in the streets, every hotel being too crowded to receive them. The next day they learned that a friend had been watching the "diligence" office for over a week and that delightful apartments were waiting for them into which they moved the following day with all possible expedition.

"One sees everybody here at Rome," she wrote presently,— "John Bright, Mrs. Hemans' son, Mrs. Gaskell, etc., etc. Over five thousand English travelers are said to be here. Jacob Abbot and wife are coming. Rome is a world! Rome is an astonishment! Papal Rome is an enchantress!"

From Naples she wrote to Professor Stowe: —

"The whole place recalled to my mind so vividly Milton's description of the infernal regions, that I could not but believe that he had drawn the imagery from this source. Milton, as we all know, was some time in Italy, and, although I do not recollect any account of his visiting Vesuvius, I cannot think how he should have shaped his language so coincidently to the phenomena if he had not.

"On the way down the mountain our ladies astonished the natives by making an express stipulation that our donkeys were not to be beaten, — why, they could not conjecture. The idea of any feeling of compassion for an animal is so foreign to a Neapolitan's thoughts that they supposed it must be some want of courage on our part. When, once in a while, the old habit so prevailed that the boy felt that he must strike the donkey, and when I forbade him, he would say, ' Courage, signora, courage.' "

Of Venice she says: —

"The great trouble of traveling in Europe, or indeed of traveling anywhere, is that you can never *catch* romance. No sooner are you in any place than being there seems the most natural, matter-of-fact occurrence in the world. Nothing looks foreign or strange to you. You take your tea and your dinner, eat, drink, and sleep as aforetime, and scarcely realize where you are or what you are seeing. But Venice is an exception to this state of things; it is all romance from beginning to end, and never ceases to seem strange and picturesque."

Mrs. Stowe returned to Rome for Holy Week. The ceremonies filled her heart with awe.

"Whatever dispute there may be about the other commemorative feasts of Christendom, the time of this epoch is fixed unerringly by the Jews' Passover. That great and solemn feast, therefore, stands as an historical monument to mark the date of the most important and thrilling events which this world ever witnessed."

As the spring approached Mrs. Stowe turned her face homeward. In Paris, she made up her mind to leave her daughters a few months longer at the excellent school where they had made good progress. She writes to her husband: —

"I have some business affairs to settle in England, and shall sail from Liverpool in the Europa on the sixth of June. I am *so* homesick to-day, and long with a great longing to be with you once more. I am impatient to go, and yet dread the voyage. Still, to reach you I must commit myself once more to the ocean, of which at times I have a nervous horror, as to the arms of my Father. 'The sea is his, and He made it.' It is a rude, noisy old servant, but it is always obedient to his will, and cannot carry me beyond his power and love, wherever or to whatever it bears me."

Upon her arrival in London she received a characteristic letter from Harriet Martineau, who says: —

AMBLESIDE, June 1.

DEAR MRS. STOWE, — I have been at my wits' end to learn how to reach you, as your note bore no direction but "London." Arnolds, Croppers, and others could give no light, and the newspapers tell only where you *had* been. So I commit this to your publishers, trusting that it will find you somewhere, and in time, perhaps, bring you here. *Can't* you come? You are aware that we shall never meet if you don't come soon. I see no strangers at all, but I hope to have breath and strength enough for a little talk with you, if you could come. You could have perfect freedom at the times when I am laid up, and we could seize my "capability seasons" for our talk.

The weather and scenery are usually splendid just now.

Did I see you (in white frock and black silk apron) when I was in Ohio in 1835? Your sister I knew well, and I have a clear recollection of your father. I believe and hope you were the young lady in the black silk apron.

Do you know I rather dreaded reading your book! Sick people *are* weak: and one of my chief weaknesses is dislike of novels (except some old ones which I almost know by heart). I knew that with you I should be safe from the cobweb-spinning of our modern subjective novelists and the jaunty vulgarity of our "funny philosophers" — the Dickens sort, who have tired us out. But I dreaded the alternative, — the too strong interest. But oh! the delight I have had in "Dred"! The genius carries all before it, and drowns everything in glorious pleasure. So marked a work of genius claims exemption from every sort of comparison ; but, *as you ask for my opinion of the book*, you may like to know that I think it far superior to "Uncle Tom." I have no doubt that a multitude of people will say it is a falling off, because they made up their minds that any new book of yours must be inferior to that, and because it is so rare a thing for a prodigious fame to be sustained by a second book; but in my own mind I am entirely convinced that the second book is by far the best. Such faults as you have are in the artistic department, and there is less defect in "Dred" than in "Uncle Tom," and the whole material and treatment seem to me richer and more substantial. I have had critiques of "Dred" from the two very wisest people I know, — perfectly unlike each other (the critics, I mean), and they delight me by thinking exactly like each other and like me. They distinctly prefer it to "Uncle Tom." To say the plain truth, it seems to me so splendid a work of genius that nothing that I can say can give you an idea of the intensity of admiration with which I read it. It seemed to me, as I told my nieces, that our English fiction writers had better shut up altogether and have done with it, for one will have no patience with any but didactic writing after yours. My nieces (and you may have heard that Maria, my nurse, is very, very clever) are thoroughly possessed with the book, and Maria says she feels as if a fresh department of human life had been opened to her since this day week. I feel the freshness no less, while, from my travels, I can be even more assured of the truthfulness of your wonderful representation. I see no limit to the good it may do by suddenly splitting open Southern life, for everybody to look into. It is precisely the thing that is most wanted, — just as "Uncle Tom" was wanted, three years since, to show what negro slavery in your republic was like. It is plantation-life, particularly in the present case, that I mean. As for your exposure of the weakness and helplessness of the churches, I deeply honor you for the courage with which you have made the exposure; but I don't suppose that any amendment is to be looked for in that direction. You have unburdened your own soul in that matter, and if they had been corrigible, you would have helped a good many more. But I don't expect that result. The Southern railing at you will be something unequaled, I suppose. I hear that three of us have the honor of being abused from day to day already, as most portentous and shocking women, you, Mrs. Chapman, and myself (as the traveler of twenty years ago). Not only newspapers, but pamphlets of such denunciation are circulated, I'm told. I'm afraid now I, and even Mrs. Chapman, must lose our fame, and all the railing will be engrossed by you. My little function is to keep English people tolerably right, by means of a London daily paper, while the danger of misinformation and misreading from the "Times" continues. I can't conceive how such a paper as the "Times" can fail to be *better informed* than it is. At times it seems as if its New York correspondent was making game of it. The able and excellent editor of the "Daily News" gives me complete liberty on American subjects, and Mrs. Chapman's and other friends' constant supply of information enables me to use this liberty for making the cause better understood. I hope I shall hear that you are coming. It is like a great impertinence — my having written so freely about your book; but you asked my opinion, — that is all I can say. Thank you much for sending the book to me. If you come you will write our names in it, and this will make it a valuable legacy to a nephew or niece.

Believe me gratefully and affectionately yours,

HARRIET MARTINEAU.

At Liverpool, on the eve of her departure for home, Mrs. Stowe dispatched a note to her daughters in Paris, telling them of her latest experiences.

"I spent the day before leaving London with Lady Byron. She is lovelier than ever, and inquired kindly about you both. I left London to go to Manchester, and reaching there found the Rev. Mr. Gaskell waiting to welcome me in the station. Mrs. Gaskell seems lovely at home, where besides being a writer she proves herself to be a first-class housekeeper, and performs all the duties of a minister's wife. After spending a delightful day with her I came here to the beautiful 'Dingle,' which is more enchanting than ever. I am staying with Mrs. Edward Cropper, Lord Denman's daughter.

"I want you to tell Aunt Mary that Mr. Ruskin lives with his father at a place called Denmark Hill, Camberwell. He has told me that the gallery of Turner pictures there is open to me or my friends at any time of the day or night. Both young and old Mr. Ruskin are fine fellows, sociable and hearty, and will cordially welcome any of my friends who desire to look at their pictures.

"I write in haste, as I must be aboard the ship to-morrow at eight o'clock. So good-by, my dear girls, from your ever affectionate mother."

Her last letter written before sailing was to Lady Byron, and serves to show how warm an intimacy had sprung up between them. It was as follows: —

June 5.

DEAR FRIEND, — I left you with a strange sort of yearning, throbbing feeling; you make me feel quite as I did years ago, a sort of girlishness quite odd for me. I have felt a strange longing to send you something. Don't smile when you see what it turns out to be. I have a weakness for your pretty Parian things; it is one of my own home peculiarities to have strong passions for pretty tea-cups and other little matters for my own quiet meals, when, as often happens, I am too unwell to join the family. So I send you a cup made of primroses, a funny little pitcher, quite large enough for cream, and a little vase for violets and primroses, — which will be lovely together; and when you use it think of me and that I love you more than I can say.

I often think how strange it is that I should *know* you — you who were a sort of legend of my early days; that I should love you is only a natural result. You seem to me to stand on the confines of that land where the poor formalities which separate hearts here pass like mist before the sun, and therefore it is that I feel the language of love must not startle you as strange or unfamiliar. You are so nearly there in spirit that I fear with every adieu that it may be the last; yet did you pass within the veil I should not feel you lost.

I have got past the time when I feel that my heavenly friends are *lost* by going there. I feel them *nearer*, rather than farther off.

So good-by, dear, dear friend, and if you see morning in our Father's house before I do, carry my love to those that wait for me, and if I pass first, you will find me there, and we shall love each other *forever*.

Ever yours,

H. B. STOWE.

CHAPTER VIII

MRS. STOWE left England full of renewed health, of joy in her larger love and larger faith, of comfort in knowing that those nearest to her were able to enjoy life by the rich reward, as she considered it, obtained through her books, and above all, that she was evidently a means by which freedom to the slaves would finally be secured.

But in the Divine sight there was chastening still in store for her. On the ninth of July, her eldest boy, Henry, was drowned while bathing in the Connecticut River at Hanover, where he was pursuing his studies as Freshman in Dartmouth College. In order to understand Mrs. Stowe's character more fully, we must hear of this sorrow from her own lips. She wrote to the Duchess of Sutherland, August 3d: —

DEAR FRIEND, — Before this reaches you you will have perhaps learned from other sources of the sad blow which has fallen upon us, — our darling, our good, beautiful boy, snatched away in the moment of health and happiness. Alas! could I know that when I parted from my Henry on English shores that I should never see him more? I returned to my home, and, amid the jubilee of meeting the rest, was fain to be satisfied with only a letter from him, saying that his college examinations were coming on, and he must defer seeing me a week or two till they were over. I thought then of taking his younger brother and going up to visit him; but the health of the latter seeming unfavorably affected by the seacoast air, I turned back with him to a water-cure establishment. Before I had been two weeks absent, a fatal telegram hurried me home, and when I arrived there, it was to find the house filled with his weeping classmates, who had just come, bringing his remains. There he lay so calm, so placid, so peaceful, that I could not believe that he would not smile upon me, and that my voice, which always had such power over him, could not recall him. There had always been such a peculiar union, such a tenderness between us. I had had such power always to call up answering feelings to my own, that it seemed impossible that he could be silent and unmoved at my grief. But yet, dear friend, I am sensible that in this last sad scene I had an alleviation that was not granted to you. I recollect, in the mournful letter you wrote me about that time, you said that you mourned that you had never told your own dear one how much you loved him. That sentence touched me at the time. I laid it to heart, and from that time lost no occasion of expressing to my children those feelings that we too often defer to express to our dearest friends till it is forever too late.

He did fully know how I loved him, and some of the last loving words he spoke were of me. The very day that he was taken from us, and when he was just rising from the table of his boarding-house to go whence he never returned, some one noticed the seal ring which you may remember to have seen on his finger, and said, "How beautiful that ring is!" "Yes," he said, "and best of all, it was my mother's gift to me." That ring, taken from the lifeless hand a few hours later, was sent to me. Singularly enough, it is broken right across the name from a fall a little time previous. . . .

It is a great comfort to me, dear friend, that I took Henry with me to Dunrobin. I hesitated about keeping him so long from his studies, but still I thought a mind so observing and appreciative might learn from such a tour more than through books, and so it was. He returned from England full of high resolves and manly purposes. "I may not be what the world calls a Christian," he wrote, "but I will live such a life as a Christian ought to live, such a life as every true man ought to live." Henceforth he became remarkable for a strict order and energy, and a vigilant temperance and care of his bodily health, docility and deference to his parents and teachers, and perseverance in every duty. . . . Well, from the hard battle of this life he is excused, and the will is taken for the deed, and whatever comes his heart will not be pierced as mine is. But I am glad that I can connect him with all my choicest remembrances of the Old World.

Dunrobin will always be dearer to me now, and I have felt towards you and the duke a turning of spirit, because I remember how kindly you always looked on and spoke to him. I knew then it was the angel of your lost one that stirred your hearts with tenderness when you looked on another so near his age. The plaid that the duke gave him, and which he valued as one of the chief of his boyish treasures, will hang in his room, — for still we have a room that we call his.

You will understand, you will feel, this sorrow with us as few can. My poor husband is much prostrated. I need not say more: you know what this must be to a father's heart. But still I repeat what I said when I saw you last. Our dead are ministering angels; they teach us to love, they fill us with tenderness for all that can suffer. These weary hours when sorrow makes us for the time blind and deaf and dumb, have their promise. These hours come in answer to our prayers for nearness to God. It is always our treasure that the lightning strikes. . . . I have poured out my heart to you because you can understand. While I was visiting in Hanover, where Henry died, a poor, deaf old slave woman, who has still five children in bondage, came to comfort me. "Bear up, dear soul," she said; "you must bear it, for the Lord loves ye." She said further, "Sunday is a heavy day to me, 'cause I can't work, and can't hear preaching, and can't read, so I can't keep my mind off my poor children. Some on 'em the blessed Master's got, and they's safe; but, oh, there are five that I don't know where they are."

What are our mother-sorrows to this! I shall try to search out and redeem these children, though, from the ill success of efforts already made, I fear it will be hopeless. Every sorrow I have, every lesson on the sacredness of family love, makes me the more determined to resist to the last this dreadful evil that makes so many mothers so much deeper mourners than I ever can be.

Affectionately yours,   H. B. STOWE.

About this same time she writes to her daughters in Paris: "Can anybody tell what sorrows are locked up with our best affections, or what pain may be associated with every pleasure? As I walk the house, the pictures he used to love, the presents I brought him, and the photographs I meant to show him, all pierce my heart. I have had a dreadful faintness of sorrow come over me at times. I have felt so crushed, so bleeding, so helpless, that I could only call on my Saviour with groanings that could not be uttered. Your papa justly said, 'Every child that dies is for the time being an only one; yes — his individuality no time, no change, can ever replace.'

"Two days after the funeral your father and I went to Hanover. We saw Henry's friends, and his room, which was just as it was the day he left it.

"'There is not another such room in the college as his,' said one of his classmates with tears. I could not help loving the dear boys as they would come and look sadly in, and tell us one thing and another that they remembered of him. 'He was always talking of his home and his sisters,' said one. The very day he died he was so happy because I had returned, and he was expecting soon to go home and meet me. He died with that dear thought in his heart.

"There was a beautiful lane leading down through a charming glen to the river. It had been for years the bathing-place of the students, and into the pure, clear water he plunged, little dreaming that he was never to come out alive.

"In the evening we went down to see the boating club, of which he was a member. He was so happy in this boating club. They had a beautiful boat called the Una, and a uniform, and he enjoyed it so much.

"This evening all the different crews were out; but Henry's had their flag furled, and tied with black crape. I felt such love to the dear boys, all of them, because they loved Henry, that it did not pain me as it otherwise would. They were glad to see us there, and I was glad that we could be there. Yet right above where their boats were gliding in the evening light lay the bend in the river, clear, still, beautiful, fringed with overhanging pines, from whence our boy went upward to heaven. To heaven — if earnest, manly purpose, if sincere, deliberate strife with besetting sin is accepted of God, as I firmly believe it is. Our dear boy was but a beginner in the right way. Had he lived, we had hoped to see all wrong gradually fall from his soul as the worn-out calyx drops from the perfected flower. But Christ has taken him into his own teaching.

"'And one view of Jesus as He is
Will strike all sin forever dead.'

"Since I wrote to you last we have had anniversary meetings, and with all the usual bustle and care, our house full of company. Tuesday we received a beautiful portrait

of our dear Henry, life-size, and as perfect almost as life.
It has just that half-roguish, half-loving expression with
which he would look at me sometimes, when I would come
and brush back his hair and look into his eyes. Every
time I go in or out of the room, it seems to give so bright
a smile that I almost think that a spirit dwells within it.

"When I am so heavy, so weary, and go about as if I
were wearing an arrow that had pierced my heart, I sometimes look up, and this smile seems to say, ' Mother, patience, I am happy. In our Father's house are many
mansions.' Sometimes I think I am like a gardener who
has planted the seed of some rare exotic. He watches as
the two little points of green leaf first spring above the
soil. He shifts it from soil to soil, from pot to pot. He
watches it, waters it, saves it through thousands of mischiefs and accidents. He counts every leaf, and marks the
strengthening of the stem, till at last the blossom bud was
fully formed. What curiosity, what eagerness, what expectation, — what longing now to see the mystery unfold
in the new flower.

"Just as the calyx begins to divide, and a faint streak
of color becomes visible, — lo! in one night the owner of
the greenhouse sends and takes it away. He does not consult me, he gives me no warning; he silently takes it, and
I look, but it is no more. What, then? Do I suppose he
has destroyed the flower? Far from it; I know that he
has taken it to his own garden. What Henry might have
been I could guess better than any one. What Henry is,
is known to Jesus only."

Shortly after this time, Mrs. Stowe wrote to her sister
Catherine : —

"If ever I was conscious of an attack of the Devil trying
to separate me from the love of Christ, it was for some
days after the terrible news came. I was in a state of
great physical weakness, most agonizing, and unable to

control my thoughts. Distressing doubts as to Henry's spiritual state were rudely thrust upon my soul. It was as if a voice had said to me: 'You trusted in God, did you? You believed that He loved you! You had perfect confidence that He would never take your child till the work of grace was mature! Now He has hurried him into eternity without a moment's warning, without preparation, and where is he?'

"I saw at last that these thoughts were irrational, and contradicted the calm, settled belief of my better moments, and that they were dishonorable to God, and that it was my duty to resist them, and to assume and steadily maintain that Jesus in love had taken my dear one to his bosom. Since then the Enemy has left me in peace. . . .

"God who made me capable of such an absorbing, unselfish devotion for my children, so that I would sacrifice my eternal salvation for them, — He certainly did not make me capable of more love, more disinterestedness than He has himself. He invented mothers' hearts, and He certainly has the pattern in his own, and my poor, weak rushlight of love is enough to show me that some things can and some things cannot be done. Mr. Stowe said in his sermon last Sunday that the mysteries of God's ways with us must be swallowed up by the greater mystery of the love of Christ, even as Aaron's rod swallowed up the rods of the magicians."

ANDOVER, September 1.

MY DARLING CHILDREN, — I must not allow a week to pass without sending a line to you. . . . Our home never looked lovelier. I never saw Andover look so beautiful; the trees so green, the foliage so rich. Papa and I are just starting to spend a week in Brunswick, for I am so miserable — so weak — the least exertion fatigues me, and much of my time I feel a heavy languor, indifferent to

everything. I know nothing is so likely to bring me up
as the air of the seaside. . . . I have set many flowers
around Henry's grave, which are blossoming; pansies,
white immortelle, white petunia, and verbenas. Papa
walks there every day, often twice or three times. The
lot has been rolled and planted with fine grass, which is
already up and looks green and soft as velvet, and the
little birds gather about it. To-night as I sat there the
sky was so beautiful, all rosy, with the silver moon looking
out of it. Papa said with a deep sigh, "I am submissive,
but not reconciled."

BRUNSWICK, September 6.

MY DEAR GIRLS, — Papa and I have been here for
four or five days past. We both of us felt so unwell that
we thought we would try the sea air and the dear old
scenes of Brunswick. Everything here is just as we left
it. We are staying with Mrs. Upham, whose house is as
wide, cool, and hospitable as ever. The trees in the yard
have grown finely, and Mrs. Upham has cultivated flowers
so successfully that the house is all surrounded by them.
Everything about the town is the same, even to Miss Gid-
ding's old shop, which is as disorderly as ever, presenting
the same medley of tracts, sewing-silk, darning-cotton, and
unimaginable old bonnets, which existed there of yore.
She has been heard to complain that she can't find things
as easily as once. Day before yesterday papa, Charley,
and I went down to Harpswell about seven o'clock in the
morning. The old spruces and firs look lovely as ever,
and I was delighted, as I always used to be, with every
step of the way. Old Getchell's mill stands as forlorn as
ever in its sandy wastes, and Mere Brook creeps on glassy
and clear beyond. Arriving at Harpswell a glorious hot
day, with scarce a breeze to ruffle the water, papa and
Charley went to fish for cunners, who soon proved too

cunning for them, for they ate every morsel of bait off the
hooks, so that out of twenty bites they only secured two
or three.   What they did get were fried for our dinner,
reinforced by a fine clam-chowder.   The evening was one
of the most glorious I ever saw, — a calm sea and round,
full moon; Mrs. Upham and I sat out on the rocks between
the mainland and the island until ten o'clock.   I never did
see a more perfect and glorious scene, and to add to it there
was a splendid northern light dancing like spirits in the
sky.   Had it not been for a terrible attack of mosquitoes in
our sleeping-rooms, that kept us up and fighting all night,
we should have called it a perfect success.

We went into the sea to bathe twice, once the day we
came, and about eight o'clock in the morning before we
went back.   Besides this we have been to Middle Bay,
where Charley, standing where you all stood before him,
actually caught a flounder with his own hand, whereat he
screamed loud enough to scare all the folks on Eagle Island.
We have also been to Maquoit.   We have visited the old
pond, and, if I mistake not, the relics of your old raft yet
float there; at all events, one or two fragments of a raft
are there, caught among rushes.

I do not realize that one of the busiest and happiest of
the train who once played there shall play there no more.
"He shall return to his house no more, neither shall his
place know him any more."   I think I have felt the healing touch of Jesus of Nazareth on the deep wound in my
heart, for I have golden hours of calm when I say: "Even
so, Father, for so it seemed good in thy sight."   So sure
am I that the most generous love has ordered all, that I
can now take pleasure to give this little proof of my un-
questioning confidence in resigning one of my dearest comforts to Him.   I feel very near the spirit land, and the
words, "I shall go to him, but he shall not return to me,"
are very sweet.

Oh, if God would give to you, my dear children, a view of the infinite beauty of Eternal Love, — if He would unite us in Himself, then even on earth all tears might be wiped away.   H. B. S.

She wrote to Lady Byron out of her open heart: —

ANDOVER, June 30.

MY DEAR FRIEND, — I did long to hear from you at a time when few knew how to speak, because I knew that you did know everything that sorrow can teach: you whose whole life has been a crucifixion, a long ordeal.   But I believe that the "Lamb," who stands forever in the midst of the throne "as it had been slain," has everywhere his followers, those who are sent into the world, as He was, to suffer for the redemption of others, and like Him they must look to the joy set before them of redeeming others.

I often think that God called you to this beautiful and terrible ministry when He suffered you to link your destiny with one so strangely gifted, so fearfully tempted, and that the reward which is to meet you, when you enter within the veil, where you must soon pass, will be to see the angel, once chained and defiled within him, set free from sin and glorified, and so know that to you it has been given, by your life of love and faith, to accomplish this glorious change.

And again from her chamber of sorrows she writes to her youngest daughter, Georgiana: —

February 12.

MY DEAR GEORGIE, — Why have n't I written? Because, dear Georgie, I am like the dry, dead, leafless tree, and have only cold, dead, slumbering buds of hope on the end of stiff, hard, frozen twigs of thought, but no leaves, no blossoms; nothing to send to a little girl who does n't know what to do with herself any more than a kitten. I am cold, weary, dead; everything is a burden to me.

I let my plants die by inches before my eyes, and do not water them, and I dread everything I do, and wish it was not to be done, and so when I get a letter from my little girl I smile and say, "Dear little puss, I will answer it;" and I sit hour after hour with folded hands, looking at the inkstand and dreading to begin. The fact is, pussy, mamma is tired. Life to you is gay and joyous, but to mamma it has been a battle in which the spirit is willing but the flesh weak; and she would be glad, like the woman in the St. Bernard, to lie down with her arms around the wayside cross, and sleep away into a brighter scene. Henry's fair, sweet face looks down upon me now and then from out a cloud, and I feel again all the bitterness of the eternal "No" which says I must never, never, in this life, see that face, lean on that arm, hear that voice. Not that my faith in God in the least fails, and that I do not believe that all this is for good. I do, and though not happy, I am blessed. Weak, weary as I am, I rest on Jesus in the innermost depth of my soul, and am quite sure that there is coming an inconceivable hour of beauty and glory when I shall regain Jesus, and He will give me back my beloved one, whom He is educating in a far higher sphere than I proposed. So do not mistake me, — only know that mamma is sitting weary by the wayside, feeling weak and worn, but in no sense discouraged.

Your affectionate mother,   H. B. S.

Mrs. Stowe's literary labors did not cease. In November she published in the "Atlantic Monthly" a brief allegory called "The Mourning Veil," and in the following year, in December, the first chapters of "The Minister's Wooing."

She was kept in good heart and spirit by the very strong

commendation of this story, from the moment of its appearance.   James Russell Lowell wrote of it: —

"It has always seemed to us that the anti-slavery element in the two former novels by Mrs. Stowe stood in the
way of a full appreciation of her remarkable genius, at least
in her own country.   It was so easy to account for the
unexampled popularity of 'Uncle Tom' by attributing it
to a cheap sympathy with sentimental philanthropy!   As
people began to recover from the first enchantment, they
began also to resent it and to complain that a dose of that
insane Garrison-root which takes the reason prisoner had
been palmed upon them without their knowing it, and that
their ordinary water-gruel of fiction, thinned with sentiment
and thickened with moral, had been hocused with the
bewildering hasheesh of Abolition.   We had the advantage
of reading that truly extraordinary book for the first time
in Paris, long after the whirl of excitement produced by
its publication had subsided, in the seclusion of distance,
and with a judgment unbiased by those political sympathies which it is impossible, perhaps unwise, to avoid at
home.   We felt then, and we believe now, that the secret
of Mrs. Stowe's power lay in that same genius by which
the great successes in creative literature have always been
achieved, — the genius that instinctively goes right to the
organic elements of human nature, whether under a white
skin or a black, and which disregards as trivial the conventional and factitious notions which make so large a part
both of our thinking and feeling.   Works of imagination
written with an aim to immediate impression are commonly
ephemeral, like Miss Martineau's 'Tales,' and Elliott's
'Corn-law Rhymes;' but the creative faculty of Mrs.
Stowe, like that of Cervantes in 'Don Quixote' and of
Fielding in 'Joseph Andrews,' overpowered the narrow
specialty of her design, and expanded a local and temporary
theme with the cosmopolitanism of genius."

In a private letter to Mrs. Stowe full of wit and wisdom on the same topic, Lowell says: —

Let your moral take care of itself, and remember that an author's writing-desk is something infinitely higher than a pulpit. What I call "care of itself" is shown in that noble passage in the February number about the ladder up to heaven. That is grand preaching and in the right way. I am sure that "The Minister's Wooing" is going to be the best of your products hitherto, and I am sure of it because you show so thorough a mastery of your material, so true a perception of realities, without which the ideality is impossible.

.   .   .   .

Woman charms a higher faculty in us than reason, God be praised, and nothing has delighted me more in your new story than the happy instinct with which you develop this incapacity of the lovers' logic in your female characters. Go on just as you have begun, and make it appear in as many ways as you like that, whatever creed may be true, it is *not* true and never will be that man can be saved by machinery. I can speak with some chance of being right, for I confess a strong sympathy with many parts of Calvinistic theology, and, . . . for one thing, believe in hell with all my might, and in the goodness of God for all that.

I have not said anything. What could I say? One might almost as well advise a mother about the child she still bears under her heart, and say, Give it these and those qualities, as an author about a work yet in the brain.

Only this I will say, that I am honestly delighted with "The Minister's Wooing;" that reading it has been one of my few editorial pleasures; that no one appreciates your genius more highly than I, or hopes more fervently that you will let yourself go without regard to this, that, or

t'other.   Don't read any criticisms on your story; believe
that you know better than any of us, and be sure that
everybody likes it.   That I know.   ¡There is not, and
never was, anybody so competent to write a true New
England poem as yourself, and have no doubt that you are
doing it.   The native sod sends up the best inspiration to
the brain, and you are as sure of immortality as we all are
of dying, — if you only go on with entire faith in yourself.

Faithfully and admiringly yours,   J. R. LOWELL.

Mrs. Stowe's genius was essentially dramatic.   She was
her own theatre; herself among the actors; the scenery
woven of her own brain.   In her early days and in the
places where she lived the theatre was unknown, and music,
save the homely singing of church and fireside, absolutely
non-existent.

Not only "Uncle Tom" but the slighter sketches of her
earlier years, and "Dred," have the power which only genius
possesses of sweeping you out of your own world into the
world of her imagination; a world too, so lighted by the
flame of truth that you feel your heart burn within you,
as the hearts of all true men burned when she first laid
the spell of her strong spirit upon them to breathe a new
life into her fellow-men.

We who knew Mrs. Stowe later saw her wrapped about
as it were with a kind of sacred awe; but her work then
bore the stamp of fatigue; the long agony of spirit for those
who were in bondage, the sympathy with the sorrows of humanity everywhere about her, the inexpressible woe which
she endured in the trials and losses of her children, made
writing a task for her.   She was more than ever wonderful
then in her conversation and personal communion with
others.   She literally poured her spirit out.   She became
one with the joy and the grief of others; she drew near to
the heart of every one with whom she really came in close

contact.   Every human being was to her a spirit walking
the brief road to the eternal life, and the shows of things
were the divine setting in which the Lord's jewels shone.
She loved beautiful things and the luxuries of the world
when she chanced to come across them, but they bound her
no more than if they were the cobweb lines of the Lillipu-
tians.

In the summer of 1859, Mrs. Stowe again went to
Europe for the last time, accompanied by her husband and
her youngest daughter.   They traveled two months in
England, visiting their friends and reviewing the scenes
which had become dear to her.   In the autumn her two
companions returned to America, to rejoin the youngest
son, the only member of the family who had been left behind.   Mrs. Stowe went on her way to Italy, and wrote to
Professor Stowe from Lausanne, whither she had gone to
meet her two eldest daughters, who had been left at school
in Paris: —

"Coming upstairs and opening the door, I found the
whole party seated with their books and embroidery about
a centre-table and looking as homelike and cosy as possible.
You may imagine the greetings, the kissing, laughing, and
good times generally."

From Lausanne the party voyaged comfortably towards
Italy.   They were joined on the way by her Brooklyn
friends, Mr. and Mrs. Howard and their children, her son
Frederick and a friend of his.   Before Christmas they
were established in Florence, whence Mrs. Stowe wrote to
Andover on Christmas Day: "We shall have quite a New
England party to-night, and shall sing Milton's Christmas
hymn in great force.   Hope you will all do the same in
the old stone cabin.

"Our parlor is all trimmed with laurel and myrtle, looking like a great bower, and our mantel and table are redo-
lent with bouquets of orange blossoms and pinks."

January 16.

MY DEAR HUSBAND, — Your letter received to-day
has raised quite a weight from my mind, for it shows that
at last you have received all mine, and that thus the chain
of communication between us is unbroken. What you said
about your spiritual experiences in feeling the presence of
dear Henry with you, and, above all, the vibration of that
mysterious guitar, was very pleasant to me. Since I have
been in Florence, I have been distressed by inexpressible
yearnings after him, — such sighings and outreachings, with
a sense of utter darkness and separation, not only from
him but from all spiritual communion with my God. But I
have become acquainted with a friend through whom I receive consoling impressions of these things, — a Mrs. E.,
of Boston, a very pious, accomplished, and interesting
woman, who has had a history much like yours in relation
to spiritual manifestations.

Without doubt she is what the spiritualists would regard
as a very powerful medium, but being a very earnest Christian, and afraid of getting led astray, she has kept carefully
aloof from all circles and things of that nature. She came
and opened her mind to me in the first place, to ask my
advice as to what she had better do, relating experiences
very similar to many of yours.

My advice was substantially to try the spirits whether
they were of God, — to keep close to the Bible and prayer,
and then accept whatever came. But I have found that
when I am with her I receive very strong impressions from
the spiritual world, so that I feel often sustained and comforted, as if I had been near to my Henry and other departed friends. This has been at times so strong as greatly
to soothe and support me. I told her your experiences, in
which she was greatly interested. She said it was so rare
to hear of Christian and reliable people with such peculiarities. . . .

One thing I am convinced of, — that spiritualism is a reaction from the intense materialism of the present age. Luther, when he recognized a personal devil, was much nearer right. We ought to enter fully, at least, into the spiritualism of the Bible. Circles and spiritual jugglery I regard as the lying signs and wonders, with all deceivableness of unrighteousness; but there is a real scriptural spiritualism which has fallen into disuse, and must be revived, and there are, doubtless, people who, from some constitutional formation, can more readily receive the impressions of the surrounding spiritual world. Such were apostles, prophets, and workers of miracles.

It was at this period that the editor of the present book first met Mrs. Stowe. We had both been invited to a large reception, one evening, in an old palace on the Arno. There were music and dancing, and there were lively groups of ladies and gentlemen strolling from room to room, contrasting somewhat strangely in their gayety with the solemn pictures hanging on the walls, and a sense of shadowy presence which seems to haunt those dusky interiors. A certain discrepancy between the modern company and the surroundings, a weird mingling of the past and the present, made any apparition appear possible, and left room only for a faint thrill of surprise when a voice by my side said, "There is Mrs. Stowe." In a moment she approached and I was presented to her, and after a brief pause she passed on. All this was natural enough, but a wave of intense disappointment swept over me. Why had I found no words to express or even indicate the feeling that had choked me? Was the fault mine? Oh, yes, I said to myself, for I could not conceive it to be otherwise, and I looked upon my opportunity, the gift of the gods, as utterly and forever wasted. I was depressed and sorrowing over the vanishing of a presence I might perhaps never

meet again, and no glamour of light or music or pictures
or friendly voices could recall any pleasure to my heart.
Meanwhile, the unconscious object of all this disturbance
was strolling quietly along, leaning on the arm of a friend,
hardly ever speaking, followed by a group of traveling companions, and entirely absorbed in the gay scene around her.
She was a small woman; and her pretty curling hair and
far-away dreaming eyes, and her way of becoming occupied
in what interested her until she forgot everything else for
the time, all this I first began to see and understand as I
gazed after her retreating figure.

In those days of our early acquaintance in Italy we had
ample opportunity to discover the affectionate qualities of
her character. If my first interview was a disappointment,
her second greeting a few days later had the warmth of old
acquaintance. From that moment we (my husband and I)
were continually meeting her, in galleries and out of them,
at Bellosguardo, which Hawthorne had just quitted, but
where Isa Blagden and Frances Power Cobbe still lingered,
or in Florence itself with Francesca Alexander and her
family, the Trollopes, or elsewhere. Our evenings were
commonly spent in each other's apartments.

Towards the end of February, the pleasant Florentine
residence was given up for a long visit in Rome. There,
one day, we went together to the rooms of the brothers
Castellani, the world-famous workers in gold. The collection of antique gems and the beautiful reproductions of
them were new to us. Mrs. Stowe was full of enthusiasm,
and we lingered long over the wonderful things which the
brothers brought forward to show. Among them was the
head of an Egyptian slave carved in black onyx. It was
an admirable work of art, and while we were enjoying it
one of them said to Mrs. Stowe, "Madam, we know what
you have been to the poor slave. We are ourselves but
poor slaves still in Italy; you feel for us; will you keep

this gem as a slight recognition of what you have done?"
She took the jewel in silence; but when we looked for
some response, her eyes were filled with tears, and it was
impossible for her to speak.

Great human tenderness was one of her chief characteristics. Although she was a reformer by nature there was
no sternness in her composition. Forgetfulness of others
there was certainly sometimes, arising from her hopeless
absent-mindedness and the preoccupation consequent upon
her work; but her whole life was swayed and ruled by her
affections.

Her love was a sheet anchor which held in the stormiest
seas. Of her household devotion it is impossible to speak
fitly; but there are few natures that can be said to have
been more dependent upon human love. Her tender ways
were inexpressibly touching.

In spite of Mrs. Stowe's love of society, she did not become a woman of society, properly so called. She was
greatly sought after and appreciated, but the habit of her
mind and, I am tempted to say, the sincerity of her heart
forbade it. A worldly-minded woman of great taste, ele-
gance, and appreciation, a friend of Mrs. Stowe, once said
to me, "Why is it that for some reason Mrs. Stowe does not
seem to go into the best society?" I could not help remembering how all society was at her command if she
had chosen to give herself to it, nor how her absorption
of mind and her devotion to a small circle made any large
currency impossible. The lady's question was one not to
be answered. Eyes cannot always be given to the blind;
but we recall what Goethe says of this class of person in
his wonderful correspondence with Schiller,— wonderful
because in those letters we see two men really speaking to
each other without reserve:—

"It is amusing to see what it is has offended this kind
of person; what they believe offends others; how hollow,

empty, and common they esteem an existence different from their own, how they direct their shafts against the outworks of appearances, how little they even dream in what an inaccessible castle that man lives who is always in earnest in regard to himself and everything around him."

Such a nature as Mrs. Stowe's was quite unlikely to help her in playing the part of a famous woman of the world with any success, and she did not attempt it. She was always reaching out to the friends of her adoption and drawing them closer to her side.

When the hours of our European play-days drew near the end, she began to lay plans for returning home in the steamer with those who had grown dear to her, and in one of her notes of that period she wrote to me : —

" On the strength of having heard that you were going home in the Europa June 16th, we also have engaged passage therein for that time, and hope that we shall not be disappointed. . . . It must be true, we can't have it otherwise. . . . Our Southern Italy trip was a glory ; it was a rose — a nightingale — all, in short, that one ever dreams, but alas ! it is over."

She wrote to Professor Stowe : —

Since my last letter a great change has taken place in our plans, in consequence of which our passage for America is engaged by the Europa, which sails the 16th of June ; so, if all goes well, we are due in Boston four weeks from this date. I long for home, for my husband and children, for my room, my yard and garden, for the beautiful trees of Andover. We will make a very happy home, and our children will help us.

Affectionately yours, HATTY.

CHAPTER IX

WE have now reached the period, both in the life of our country and of Mrs. Stowe, which, looked at with the eye of history, may be called the moment of culmination.

The red hand of war, dreaded in itself, inexorable in its touch, yet inevitable, as Daniel Webster and others had seen a quarter of a century earlier, was looked upon at last by the regenerators of our people as the red-hot iron which was to burn away our disease. This belief was the only consolation in the miserable deep of suffering into which the nation was plunged, and it held the hearts of men high with courage and good cheer.

All the private interests and emotions which necessarily occupied Mrs. Stowe were subservient in her heart to the interests of her country. To use her own words: —

"It was God's will that this nation — the North as well as the South — should deeply and terribly suffer for the sin of consenting to and encouraging the great oppressions of the South; that the ill-gotten wealth, which had arisen from striking hands with oppression and robbery, should be paid back in the taxes of war; that the blood of the poor slave, that had cried so many years from the ground in vain, should be answered by the blood of the sons from the best hearthstones through all the free States; that the slave mothers whose tears nobody regarded should have with them a great company of weepers, North and South, — Rachels weeping for their children and refusing to be comforted; that the free States, who refused to listen when they were told of lingering starvation, cold, privation, and barbarous cruelty, as perpetrated on the slave, should have lingering starvation, cold, hunger, and cruelty doing its work among their own sons, at the hands of these slave-masters, with whose sins our nation had connived."

"Mrs. Stowe spoke from personal experience," writes the Rev. C. E. Stowe, "having seen her own son go forth in the ranks of those who first responded to the President's call for volunteers. He was one of the first to place his name on the muster-roll of Company A of the First Massachusetts Volunteers." While his regiment was still at the camp in Cambridge, Mrs. Stowe was called to Brooklyn on important business, from which place she writes to her husband under the date June 11.

"Yesterday noon Henry" (Ward Beecher) "came in, saying that the Commonwealth, with the First (Massachusetts) Regiment on board, had just sailed by. Immediately I was of course eager to get to Jersey City to see Fred. Sister Eunice said she would go with me, and in a few minutes she and I were in a carriage, driving towards the Fulton Ferry. Upon reaching Jersey City we found that the boys were dining in the depot, an immense building with many tracks and platforms. It has a great cast-iron gallery just under the roof, apparently placed there with prophetic instinct of these times. There was a crowd of people pressing against the grated doors, which were locked, but through which we could see the soldiers. It was with great difficulty that we were at last permitted to go inside, and that object seemed to be greatly aided by a bit of printed satin that some man gave Mr. Scoville.

"When we were in, a vast area of gray caps and blue overcoats was presented. The boys were eating, drinking, smoking, talking, singing, and laughing. Company A was reported to be here, there, and everywhere. At last S. spied Fred in the distance, and went leaping across the

tracks towards him. Immediately afterwards a blue-over-
coated figure bristling with knapsack and haversack, and
looking like an assortment of packages, came rushing
towards us.

"Fred was overjoyed, you may be sure, and my first
impulse was to wipe his face with my handkerchief before
I kissed him. He was in high spirits, in spite of the
weight of blue overcoat, knapsack, etc., etc., that he
would formerly have declared intolerable for half an hour.
I gave him my handkerchief and Eunice gave him hers, with
a sheer motherly instinct that is so strong within her, and
then we filled his haversack with oranges.

"We stayed with Fred about two hours, during which
time the gallery was filled with people, cheering and waving their handkerchiefs. Every now and then the band
played inspiriting airs, in which the soldiers joined with
hearty voices. While some of the companies sang, others
were drilled, and all seemed to be having a general jollifi-
cation. The meal that had been provided was plentiful,
and consisted of coffee, lemonade, sandwiches, etc.

"On our way out, we were introduced to the Rev. Mr.
Cudworth, chaplain of the regiment. He is a fine-looking
man, with black eyes and hair, set off by a white havelock.
He wore a sword, and Fred, touching it, asked, 'Is this
for use or ornament, sir?'

"'Let me see you in danger,' answered the chaplain,
'and you 'll find out.'

"I said to him I supposed he had had many a one confided to his kind offices, but I could not forbear adding one
more to the number. He answered, 'You may rest assured, Mrs. Stowe, I will do all in my power.'

"We parted from Fred at the door. He said he felt lonesome enough Saturday evening on the Common in Boston,
where everybody was taking leave of somebody, and he
seemed to be the only one without a friend, but that this
interview made up for it all.

"I also saw young Henry. Like Fred he is mysteriously changed, and wears an expression of gravity and care. So our boys come to manhood in a day. Now I am watching anxiously for the evening paper to tell me that the regiment has reached Washington in safety."

"In November, 1862," says her son Charles, "Mrs. Stowe was invited to visit Washington, to be present at a great thanksgiving dinner provided for the thousands of fugitive slaves who had flocked to the city. She accepted the invitation the more gladly because her son's regiment was encamped near the city, and she should once more see him. He was now Lieutenant Stowe, having honestly won his promotion by bravery on more than one hard-fought field." She writes of this visit: —

Imagine a quiet little parlor with a bright coal fire, and the gaslight burning above a centre-table, about which Hatty, Fred, and I are seated. Fred is as happy as happy can be to be with mother and sister once more. All day yesterday we spent in getting him. First we had to procure a permit to go to camp, then we went to the fort where the colonel is, and then to another where the brigadier-general is stationed. I was so afraid they would not let him come with us, and was never happier than when at last he sprang into the carriage, free to go with us for forty-eight hours. "Oh!" he exclaimed in a sort of rapture, "this pays for a year and a half of fighting and hard work!"

We tried hard to get the five o'clock train out to Laurel, where J.'s regiment is stationed, as we wanted to spend Sunday all together; but could not catch it, and so had to content ourselves with what we could have. I have managed to secure a room for Fred next ours, and feel as though I had my boy at home once more. He is looking very well, has grown in thickness, and is as loving and affectionate as a boy can be.

I have just been writing a pathetic appeal to the brigadier-general to let him stay with us a week. I have also
written to General Buckingham in regard to changing him
from the infantry, in which there seems to be no prospect
of anything but garrison duty, to the cavalry, which is full
of constant activity.

General B. called on us last evening. He seemed to
think the prospect before us was, at best, of a long war.
He was the officer deputed to carry the order to General
McClellan, relieving him of command of the army. He
carried it to him in his tent about twelve o'clock at night.
Burnside was there. McClellan said it was very unexpected,
but immediately turned over the command. I said I
thought he ought to have expected it, after having so disregarded the President's order. General B. smiled and said
he supposed McClellan had done that so often before that
he had no idea any notice would be taken of it this time.

Now, as I am very tired, I must close, and remain as
always, lovingly yours,   HATTY.

Just before she left Hartford for Washington I received
the following hurried note from her: —

"I am going to Washington to see the heads of departments myself, and to satisfy myself that I may refer to the
Emancipation Proclamation as a reality and a substance,
not a fizzle out at the little end of the horn, as I should be
sorry to call the attention of my sisters in Europe to any
such impotent conclusion. . . . I mean to have a talk with
'Father Abraham' himself, among others."

Mrs. Stowe lost no time, but proceeded to carry out her
plan as soon as practicable. Of this visit to Washington
she says little in her letters beyond the following meagre
words: "It seems to be the opinion here, not only that the
President will stand up to his proclamation, but that the
Border States will accede to his proposition for emancipa-

tion.   I have noted the thing as a glorious expectancy!
. . . To-day to the home of the contrabands, seeing about
five hundred poor fugitives eating a comfortable Thanksgiving dinner, and singing, 'Oh, let my people go!' It
was a strange and moving sight."

During this visit Mrs. Stowe wrote and dispatched to
the "Atlantic Monthly" her most eloquent and noble appeal to the women of England.

Eight years earlier an address had been received from
England by Mrs. Stowe with the names of some of the
most distinguished women of Great Britain at the head,
urging the abolition of slavery.   This appeal was beautifully illuminated, and the twenty-six folio volumes which
accompanied it contain the signatures of more than half a
million of British women.

No published reply had as yet been made to this address.   Now, however, the conditions had changed.   The
North was giving her children, her possessions, her life, in a
vast struggle against slavery, and a strong party had arisen
in England in favor of the South.

Mrs. Stowe's reply was calm and strong, but written
with her heart's blood.   She begins: "Sisters," — and
after quoting their own words and describing the wonderful memorial in its oaken case as it stood before her, she
continues, — "The signatures to this appeal are not the
least remarkable part of it; for, beginning at the very steps
of the throne, they go down to the names of women in the
very humblest conditions in life, and represent all that
Great Britain possesses, not only of highest and wisest, but
of plain, homely common sense and good feeling.   Names
of wives of cabinet ministers appear on the same page with
the names of wives of humble laborers, — names of duch-
esses and countesses, of wives of generals, ambassadors,
savants, and men of letters, mingled with names traced in
trembling characters by hands evidently unused to hold the

pen, and stiffened by lowly toil. Nay, so deep and expansive was the feeling, that British subjects in foreign lands had their representation. Among the signatures are those of foreign residents, from Paris to Jerusalem. Autographs so diverse, and collected from sources so various, have seldom been found in juxtaposition. They remain at this day a silent witness of a most singular tide of feeling which at that time swept over the British community and *made* for itself an expression, even at the risk of offending the sensibilities of an equal and powerful nation.

"No reply to that address, in any such tangible and monumental form, has ever been possible. It was impossible to canvass our vast territories with the zealous and indefatigable industry with which England was canvassed for signatures. In America, those possessed of the spirit which led to this efficient action had no leisure for it. All their time and energies were already absorbed in direct efforts to remove the great evil, concerning which the minds of their English sisters had been newly aroused, and their only answer was the silent continuance of these efforts.

"From the slaveholding States, however, as was to be expected, came a flood of indignant recrimination and rebuke. No one act, perhaps, ever produced more frantic irritation, or called out more unsparing abuse. It came with the whole united weight of the British aristocracy and commonalty on the most diseased and sensitive part of our national life; and it stimulated that fierce excitement which was working before, and has worked since, till it has broken out into open war.

"The time has come, however, when such an astonishing page has been turned, in the anti-slavery history of America, that the women of our country, feeling that the great anti-slavery work to which their English sisters exhorted them is almost done, may properly and naturally feel moved to reply to their appeal, and lay before them the history of what has occurred since the receipt of their affectionate and Christian address.

"Your address reached us just as a great moral conflict was coming to its intensest point. The agitation kept up by the anti-slavery portion of America, by England, and by the general sentiment of humanity in Europe, had made the situation of the slaveholding aristocracy intolerable. As one of them at the time expressed it, they felt themselves under the ban of the civilized world. Two courses only were open to them: to abandon slave institutions, the sources of their wealth and political power, or to assert them with such an overwhelming national force as to compel the respect and assent of mankind. They chose the latter."

She then most eloquently and succinctly rehearses the steps of the struggle.

The whole paper is eminently worth reproduction, but it is already in print and we must therefore deny ourselves. Towards the end she says: —

Now, sisters of England, in this solemn, expectant hour, let us speak to you of one thing which fills our hearts with pain and solicitude. It is an unaccountable fact, and one which we entreat you seriously to ponder, that the party which has brought the cause of freedom thus far on its way during the past eventful year has found little or no support in England. Sadder than this, the party which makes slavery the chief corner-stone of its edifice finds in England its strongest defenders.

The voices that have spoken for us who contend for liberty have been few and scattering. God forbid that we should forget those few noble voices, so sadly exceptional in the general outcry against us! They are, alas! too few to be easily forgotten. False statements have blinded the minds of your community, and turned the most generous sentiments of the British heart against us. The North is fighting for supremacy and the South for independence, has been the voice. Independence? for what? to do what? To prove the doctrine that all men are *not* equal; to establish the doctrine that the white man may enslave the negro!

.   .   .   .

This very day the writer of this has been present at a solemn religious festival in the national capital, given at the home of a portion of those fugitive slaves who have fled to our lines for protection, — who, under the shadow of our flag, find sympathy and succor. The national day of thanksgiving was there kept by over a thousand redeemed slaves, and for whom Christian charity had spread an ample repast. Our sisters, we wish *you* could have witnessed the scene. We wish you could have heard the prayer of a blind old negro, called among his fellows John the Baptist, when in touching broken English he poured forth his thanksgivings. We wish you could have heard the sound of that strange rhythmical chant which is now forbidden to be sung on Southern plantations, — the psalm of this modern exodus, — which combines the barbaric fire of the Marseillaise with the religious fervor of the old Hebrew prophet: —

> "Oh, go down, Moses,
> Way down into Egypt's land!
> Tell King Pharaoh
> To let my people go!
> Stand away dere,
> Stand away dere,
> And let my people go!"

As we were leaving, an aged woman came and lifted up her hands in blessing. "Bressed be de Lord dat brought me to see dis first happy day of my life! Bressed be de Lord!" In all England is there no Amen?

We have been shocked and saddened by the question asked in an association of Congregational ministers in England, the very blood relations of the liberty-loving Puritans — "Why does not the North let the South go?"

What! give up the point of emancipation for these four
million slaves? Turn our backs on them, and leave them
to their fate? What! leave our white brothers to run a
career of oppression and robbery, that, as sure as there is a
God that ruleth in the armies of heaven, will bring down
a day of wrath and doom? Remember that wishing success to this slavery-establishing effort is only wishing to
the sons and daughters of the South all the curses that God
has written against oppression. *Mark our words!* If we
succeed, the children of these very men who are now fighting us will rise up to call us blessed. Just as surely as
there is a God who governs in the world, so surely all the
laws of national prosperity follow in the train of equity;
and if we succeed, we shall have delivered the children's
children of our misguided brethren from the wages of sin,
which is always and everywhere death.

And now, sisters of England, think it not strange if
we bring back the words of your letter, not in bitterness,
but in deepest sadness, and lay them down at your door.
We say to you, Sisters, you have spoken well: we have
heard you; we have heeded; we have striven in the cause,
even unto death. We have sealed our devotion by desolate hearth and darkened homestead, — by the blood of
sons, husbands, and brothers. In many of our dwellings
the very light of our lives has gone out; and yet we accept
the life-long darkness as our own part in this great and
awful expiation, by which the bonds of wickedness shall
be loosed, and abiding peace established on the foundation
of righteousness. Sisters, what have *you* done, and what
do you mean to do?

We appeal to you as sisters, as wives, and as mothers,
to raise your voices to your fellow-citizens, and your prayers
to God for the removal of this affliction and disgrace from
the Christian world.

In behalf of many thousands of American women,

HARRIET BEECHER STOWE.

John Bright and Archbishop Whately sent personal replies to this letter.   John Bright said: "Before this reaches you, you will have seen what large and earnest meetings have been held in all our towns in favor of abolition and the North.   No town has a building large enough to contain those who come to listen, to applaud, and to vote in favor of freedom and the Union.   The effect of this is evident on our newspapers and on the tone of Parliament, where now nobody says a word in favor of recognition, or mediation, or any such thing."

Mrs. Browning says: —

"I had much anxiety for you after the Seward and Adams speeches, but the danger seems averted by that fine madness of the South which seems judicial.   The tariff movement we should regret deeply (and do, some of us), only I am told it was wanted in order to persuade those who were less accessible to moral argument.   It's eking out the holy water with ditch water.   If the Devil flees before it, even so, let us be content.   How you must feel, *you* who have done so much to set this accursed slavery in the glare of the world, convicting it of hideousness.

"Meanwhile I am reading you in the ' Independent,' sent to me by Mr. Tilton, with the greatest interest.   Your new novel opens beautifully." [1]

Mrs. Stowe wrote to Mrs. Howard: —

"Can it be that New York is going into revolution?   I am writing on the decisive day (the 4th), yet ignorant what its vote.   Why did not Henry stump the state for Wadsworth rather than this thing should be?   We are all on tip-toe with anxiety.   I don't know that there will long be any use in investing in anything, if New York is going to rebel and join the South as the ' Tribune ' announces to-night.   I think I see her ' a doin' of it ' ! "

It was left for others to speak of Mrs. Stowe's interview

[1] The Pearl of Orr's Island.

with President Lincoln.   Her daughter was told that when
the President heard her name he seized her hand, saying,
"Is this the little woman who made this great war?"   He
then led her to a seat in the window, where they were
withdrawn, and undisturbed by other guests.   No one but
those two souls will ever know what waves of thought and
feeling swept over them in that brief hour.

Afterwards she heard these words pronounced in the
Senate Chamber in the Message of President Lincoln; it
was in the darkest hour of the war, Mrs. Stowe wrote,
when defeat and discouragement had followed the Union
armies and all hearts were trembling with fear: "If this
struggle is to be prolonged till there be not a home in
the land where there is not one dead, till all the treasure
amassed by the unpaid labor of the slave shall be wasted,
till every drop of blood drawn by the lash shall be
atoned by blood drawn by the sword, we can only bow
and say, 'Just and true are thy ways, thou King of
saints!'"

To the Duchess of Argyll Mrs. Stowe wrote from

ANDOVER, July 31.

MY DEAR FRIEND, — Your lovely, generous letter was
a real comfort to me, and reminded me that a year — and
alas! a whole year — had passed since I wrote to your dear
mother, of whom I think so often as one of God's noblest
creatures, and one whom it comforts me to think is still in
our world.

So many, good and noble, have passed away whose friendship was such a pride, such a comfort to me!   Your noble
father, Lady Byron, Mrs. Browning, — their spirits are as
perfect as ever passed to the world of light.   I grieve about
your dear mother's eyes.   I have thought about you all,
many a sad, long, quiet hour, as I have lain on my bed and
looked at the pictures on my wall; one, in particular, of

the moment before the Crucifixion, which is the first thing I look at when I wake in the morning. I think how suffering is, and must be, the portion of noble spirits, and no lot so brilliant that must not first or last dip into the shadow of that eclipse. Prince Albert, too, the ideal knight, the *King Arthur* of our times, the good, wise, steady head and heart we — that is, our world, we Anglo-Saxons — need so much. And the Queen! yes, I have thought of and prayed for her, too. But could a woman hope to have *always* such a heart, and yet ever be weaned from earth, "all this and heaven, too"?

Under my picture I have inscribed, "Forasmuch as Christ also hath suffered for us in the flesh, arm yourselves with the same mind."

This year has been one long sigh, one smothering sob, to me. And I thank God that we have as yet one or two generous friends in England who understand and feel for our cause.

The utter failure of Christian, anti-slavery England, in those *instincts* of a right heart which always can see where the cause of liberty lies, has been as bitter a grief to me as was the similar prostration of all our American religious people in the day of the Fugitive Slave Law. Exeter Hall is a humbug, a pious humbug, like the rest. But I saw *your* duke's speech to his tenants! That was grand! If *he* can see these things, they are to be seen, and why cannot Exeter Hall see them? It is simply the want of the honest heart.

Why do the horrible barbarities of *Southern* soldiers cause no comment? Why is the sympathy of the British Parliament reserved for the poor women of New Orleans? Why is *all* expression of sympathy on the *Southern* side? You wonder at my brother. He is a man, and feels a thousand times more than I can, and deeper than all he ever has expressed, the spirit of these things. You must

not wonder, therefore. Remember it is the moment when
every nerve is vital; it is our agony; we tread the wine-
press alone, and they whose cheap rhetoric has been for
years pushing us into it now desert *en masse*. I thank my
God I always loved and trusted those who now *do* stand
true, — your family, your duke, yourself, your noble mother. I have lost Lady Byron. Her great heart, her eloquent letters, would have been such a joy to me! And
Mrs. Browning, oh, such a heroic woman! None of her
poems can express what *she* was, — so grand, so compre-
hending, so strong, with such inspired insight! She stood
by Italy through its crisis. Her heart was with all good
through the world. Your prophecy that we shall come out
better, truer, stronger, will, I am confident, be true, and it
was worthy of yourself and your good lineage.

Slavery will be sent out by this agony. We are only in
the throes and ravings of the exorcism. The roots of the
cancer have gone everywhere, but they must die — will.
Already the Confiscation Bill is its natural destruction.
Lincoln has been too slow. He should have done it sooner,
and with an impulse, but come it must, come it will. Your
mother will live to see slavery abolished, *unless* England
forms an alliance to hold it up. England is the great
reliance of the slave-power to-day, and next to England
the faltering weakness of the North, which palters and
dare not fire the great broadside for fear of hitting friends.
These things *must* be done, and sudden, sharp remedies
are *mercy*. Just now we are in a dark hour; but whether
God be with us or not, I know He is with the slave, and
with his redemption will come the solution of our question.
I have long known *what* and who we had to deal with in
this, for when I wrote "Uncle Tom's Cabin" I had letters
addressed to me showing a state of society perfectly *inconceivable*. If I had written what I knew of the obscenity,
brutality, and cruelty of that society down there, society

would have cast out the books; and it is for their interest, the interest of the whole race in the South, that we should succeed. I wish *them* no ill, feel no bitterness, — they have had a Dahomian education which makes them savage. We don't expect any more of *them*, but if slavery is destroyed, one generation of education and liberty will efface these stains. They will come to themselves, these States, and be glad it is over.

I am using up my paper to little purpose. Please give my best love to your dear mother. I am going to write to her. If I only could have written the things I have often thought! I am going to put on her bracelet, with the other dates, that of the abolition of slavery in the District of Columbia. Remember me to the duke and to your dear children. My husband desires his best regards, my daughters also.

I am lovingly ever yours,

H. B. STOWE.

Mrs. Stowe heard from her son directly after the battle of Gettysburg. But it was the chaplain who wrote: —

GETTYSBURG, PA., Saturday, July 11, 9.30 P. M.

MRS. STOWE:

Dear Madam, — Among the thousands of wounded and dying men on this war-scarred field, I have just met with your son, Captain Stowe. If you have not already heard from him, it may cheer your heart to know that he is in the hands of good, kind friends. He was struck by a fragment of a shell, which entered his right ear. He is quiet and cheerful, longs to see some member of his family, and is, above all, anxious that they should hear from him as soon as possible. I assured him I would write at once, and though I am wearied by a week's labor here among scenes of terrible suffering, I know that, to a mother's anxious heart, even a hasty scrawl about her boy will be more than welcome.

May God bless and sustain you in this troubled time! Yours with sincere sympathy,

J. M. CROWELL.

In the autumn of 1864 she wrote to me:- "I feel I need to write in these days, to keep from thinking of things that make me dizzy and blind, and fill my eyes with tears so that I cannot see the paper. I mean such things as are being done where our heroes are dying as Shaw died. It is not wise that all our literature should run in a rut cut through our hearts and red with our blood. I feel the need of a little gentle household merriment and talk of common things, to indulge which I have devised the following."

Notwithstanding her view of the need and her skillfully devised plans to meet it, she soon sent another epistle, showing how impossible it was to stem the current of her thought.

She wrote to the Editor of the Atlantic: —

November 29, 1864.

MY DEAR FRIEND, — I have sent my New Year's article, the result of one of those peculiar experiences which sometimes occur to us writers. I had planned an article, gay, sprightly, wholly domestic; but as I began and sketched the pleasant home and quiet fireside, an irresistible impulse *wrote for me* what followed, — an offering of sympathy to the suffering and agonized whose homes have forever been darkened. Many causes united at once to force on me this vision, from which generally I shrink, but which sometimes will not be denied, — will make itself felt.

Just before I went to New York two of my earliest and most intimate friends lost their oldest sons, captains and

majors, — splendid fellows physically and morally, beautiful, brave, religious, uniting the courage of soldiers to the
faith of martyrs, — and when I went to Brooklyn it seemed
as if I were hearing some such thing almost every day; and
Henry, in his profession as minister, has so many letters
full of imploring anguish, the cry of hearts breaking that
ask help of him. . . .

In writing to Mrs. Howard at this time she says: "I left
my poor Fred at home. I do hope he will get a good ship.
The sea air works marvels in our family. That wound in
his head will never heal unless by a general tonic to the
whole system. . . . I feel a weight of solicitude for the
poor fellow which I can only lay where you lay yours."

At last the war was ended, and she wrote to the Duchess
of Argyll: —

HARTFORD, February 19.

MY DEAR FRIEND, — Your letter was a real spring of
comfort to me, bringing refreshingly the pleasant library at
Inveraray and the lovely day I spent there.

.   .   .   .

Oh, my friend, when I think of what has been done
these last few years, and of what is now doing, I am lost
in amazement. I have just, by way of realizing it to myself, been reading "Uncle Tom's Cabin" again, and when I
read that book, scarred and seared and burned into with
the memories of an anguish and horror that can never be
forgotten, and think it is all over now, all past, and that
now the questions debated are simply of more or less time
before granting legal suffrage to those who so lately were
held only as articles of merchandise, — when this comes
over me I think no private or individual sorrow can ever
make me wholly without comfort. If my faith in God's
presence and real, living power in the affairs of men ever
grows dim, this makes it impossible to doubt.

I have just had a sweet and lovely Christian letter from Garrison, whose beautiful composure and thankfulness in his hour of victory are as remarkable as his wonderful courage in the day of moral battle. His note ends with the words, "And who but God is to be glorified?" Garrison's attitude is far more exalted than that of Wendell Phillips. He acknowledges the great deed done. He suspends his "Liberator" with words of devout thanksgiving, and devotes himself unobtrusively to the work yet to be accomplished for the freedmen; while Phillips seems resolved to ignore the mighty work that has been done, because of the inevitable shortcomings and imperfections that beset it still. We have a Congress of splendid men, — men of stalwart principle and determination. We have a President[1] honestly seeking to do right; and if he fails in knowing just what right is, it is because he is a man born and reared in a slave State, and acted on by many influences which we cannot rightly estimate unless we were in his place. My brother Henry has talked with him earnestly and confidentially, and has faith in him as an earnest, good man seeking to do right. Henry takes the ground that it is unwise and impolitic to endeavor to force negro suffrage on the South at the point of the bayonet. His policy would be, to hold over the negro the protection of our Freedman's Bureau until the great laws of free labor shall begin to draw the master and servant together; to endeavor to soothe and conciliate, and win to act with us, a party composed of the really good men at the South.

For this reason he has always advocated lenity of measures towards them. He wants to get them into a state in which the moral influence of the North can act upon them beneficially, and to get such a state of things that there will be a party *at the South* to protect the negro.

Charles Sumner is looking simply at the abstract *right*

[1] Andrew Johnson

of the thing. Henry looks at actual probabilities. We all know that the state of society at the South is such that laws are a very inadequate protection even to white men. Southern elections always have been scenes of mob violence *when only white men voted.*

Multitudes of lives have been lost at the polls in this way, and if against their will negro suffrage were forced upon them, I do not see how any one in their senses can expect anything less than an immediate war of races.

If negro suffrage were required as a condition of acquiring political position, there is no doubt the slave States would grant it; grant it nominally, because they would know that the grant never could or would become an actual realization. And what would then be gained for the negro?

I am sorry that people cannot differ on such great and perplexing public questions without impugning each other's motives. Henry has been called a backslider because of the lenity of his counsels, but I cannot but think it is the Spirit of Christ that influences him. Garrison has been in the same way spoken of as a deserter, because he says that a work that *is* done shall be called done, and because he would not keep up an anti-slavery society when slavery is abolished; and I think our President is much injured by the abuse that is heaped on him, and the selfish and unworthy motives that are ascribed to him by those who seem determined to allow to nobody an honest, unselfish difference in judgment from their own.

Henry has often spoken of you and your duke as pleasant memories in a scene of almost superhuman labor and excitement. He often said to me: "When this is all over, — when we have won the victory, — *then* I will write to the duchess." But when it was over and the flag raised again at Sumter his arm was smitten down with the news of our President's death! We all appreciate your noble and true sympathy through the dark hour of our national trial. You and yours are almost the only friends we now have left in England. You cannot know what it was, unless you could imagine your own country to be in danger of death, extinction of nationality. *That*, dear friend, is an experience which shows us what we are and what we can feel. . . . It seems almost like a dream to look back to those pleasant days with you all. I am glad to see you still keep some memories of our goings on. Georgie's marriage is a very happy one to us. They live in Stockbridge, the loveliest part of Massachusetts, and her husband is a most devoted pastor, and gives all his time and property to the great work which he has embraced, purely for the love of it. My other daughters are with me, and my son, Captain Stowe, who has come with weakened health through our struggle, suffering constantly from the effects of a wound in his head received at Gettysburg, which makes his returning to his studies a hard struggle. My husband is in better health since he resigned his professorship, and desires his most sincere regards to yourself and the duke, and his profound veneration to your mother. Sister Mary also desires to be remembered to you, as do also my daughters. Please tell me a little in your next of Lady Edith; she must be very lovely now.

I am, with sincerest affection, ever yours,

H. B. STOWE.

The labor, the shock, were past, but the fatigue and the strain of the long struggle for freedom which she carried always on her own heart could never be over-lived. She was already, as Mrs. Hawthorne used to say, "tired far into the future." The woman who had written "Uncle Tom" was not to continue a series of equally exciting stories, but she was to bear the burden and heat of much every-day labor with the patience and the rejoicing of all faithful souls.

We are reminded, as we study Mrs. Stowe's life, of Swinburne's noble tribute to Sir Walter Scott after reading his Journals, which appeared in full only five or six years ago. He says: "Now that we have before us in full — in all reasonable or desired completeness — the great man's own record of his troubles, his emotions, and his toils, we find it, from the opening to the close, a record, not only of dauntless endurance, but of elastic and joyous heroism. . . . It is no longer pity that any one may presume to feel for him at the lowest ebb of his fortunes or his life; it is rapture of sympathy, admiration, and applause."

The wound received by her son in his head was one from which he was never entirely to recover. "After weary months of intense suffering," his brother says, "it only imperfectly healed; the cruel iron had too nearly touched the brain of the young officer. He was never to be himself again. Soon after the war his mother bought a plantation in Florida, largely in the hope that the out-of-door life connected with its management might be beneficial to her afflicted son."

No more harrowing experience than this was endured during our war; it is impossible to imagine anything more painful, in its slow continuance; the doubt respecting her boy's ultimate return to health; the methods to be employed for his best welfare; the constantly increasing incompetence, and the final silence. She who was always a comforter for the sorrowful still wrote from the centre of divine peace: —

"When winds are raging o'er the upper ocean
    And billows wild contend with angry roar,
 'T is said, far down beneath the wild commotion,
    That peaceful stillness reigneth evermore.

  .   .   .   .

"Far, far away, the roar of passion dieth,
    And loving thoughts rise calm and peacefully;
 And no rude storm, how fierce soe'er it flieth,
    Disturbs the soul that dwells, O Lord, in thee."

CHAPTER X

IN a period of great public excitement a contrast is always to be observed. Private life still goes on, and it depends upon the temperament, the religion, the imagination of individuals whether the surface of their existence is greatly deflected from ordinary channels by the public necessity. With Mrs. Stowe, as we have seen, thought, feeling, and her spiritual life on earth, if we may say so, were swallowed up in the struggle; but as men lived on from day to day and the war stretched its dreadful length over years of time, life often appeared hardly more exciting to some persons than in certain periods before the strife began. We shall see how during this time Mrs. Stowe kept steadily at her desk, providing stories which were eagerly read by a large public.

In order to make the picture of her life during the war a true one, we must return to the month of June, 1860, in which she left England for the last time. She was about leaving Paris for Liverpool when the news reached her of the sudden death of Annie Howard, the beautiful young daughter of her friend, and the companion of her children. Mrs. Stowe at once wrote Mrs. Howard: "Oh, my dear sister! Why am I not with you . . . the blow has almost crushed us all. . . . We have thought of all things that we could do, — we thought of waiting here for you, but we have no hope that you *could* be here. . . . Our fears are for you, dear child, but we can only commend you to God. . . . How many stings and agonies and living thorns there are for every hour and moment in a wrench like this, God only knows — but God will reveal himself to you in the deep waters. 'When thou passest through the waters they shall not overflow thee, for I am with thee.' . . . Sorrow not, even as others, who have no hope. For, if we believe that Jesus died and rose again, even so also them that sleep in Jesus shall God bring with Him."

SWAYLANDS, PENSHURST, June 10.

MY DEAR SUSIE, — We are resting a day or two in this peaceful retreat under the shaded skies of England, — literally amid green pastures, and my thoughts return to you, as this letter will find you weary and desolate on your way to Paris. . . .

Ah! Susie, I who have walked in this dark valley for now three years, what can I say to you who are entering it? One thing I can say — be not afraid and confounded if you find no apparent religious support at first. When the heartstrings are all suddenly cut, it is, I believe, a physical impossibility to feel faith or resignation; there is a revolt of the instinctive and animal system, and though we may submit to God it is rather by a constant painful effort than by a sweet attraction. There are cases when a superhuman grace is given and the soul is buoyed above itself, but more often we can only bleed in silent pain. . . .

For such deep places there is nothing but the remembrance of Him who *though He were a son*, yet learned obedience by the things which He suffered. We see that it cost Him a conflict with agony and bloody sweat to say, Not my will but thy will. It did not come *easily* even to Him, and He said it over and over in his anguish as we must. Since that fearful night at your home" [the night when Mrs. Stowe heard of the death of her son] "every hour of life has been to me with an upper and an under

current, and every day I have been making again and again
that hard sacrifice, and it is a submission now as painful
as at first.

> " Time but the impression stronger makes
> As streams their channels deeper wear."

and I know all the strange ways in which this anguish will
reveal itself, — the prick, the thrust, the stab, the wearing
pain, the poison that is mingled with every bright remembrance of the past, — I have felt them all, — and all I can
say is that, though "faint," I am "pursuing," although
the crown of thorns secretly pressed to one's heart never
ceases to pain.   Yet as the day is the strength will be.
So often this summer I have looked on you with your
children all round you prosperous and happy, and thought
in what peace and prosperity your life was passing, and
how little you could know of the inner cell in my heart
where I spend so many sad hours.   But I *know* whose
hand holds ours . . . and *that He makes no mistakes.* . . .

These are our weanings from earth, and we fill the long
night with tossings and moanings. . . . Our Father, loving
us better than we love ourselves, will educate us for our
inheritance.   It is no small thing, — this eternal glory,
and we must suffer something for it. . . . I am very
poorly, but I am going to finish by copying one of the
Plymouth hymns, which I have said over almost every
day this winter and which I hope one day will be the expression of my feelings.

> "I worship thee, sweet will of God,
> And all thy ways adore;
> And every day I live, I long
> To love thee more and more."

.   .   .   .

To this I add some lines that I thought of much after
Henry's death: —

> "God never does, nor suffers to be done,
> But that *which we would do*, if we could see
> The end of all events as well as He."

On board the Europa, June.

My dear Susie, — We had a great fright yesterday coming on in the express train. H—— was faint and we thought she was restored, but just as we were stopping at the next station she called out that she was dying, and must be taken into the air. . . . We hurried out, all of us, on to the platform with her, — we had been sitting with our hats off and had no time to put them on, — got her in all haste into a chamber of the railroad hotel, for she seemed to be in a death agony. . . . At last she began to be more comfortable and we telegraphed to know when the ship would sail; put her on a mattress, caught the next express, found a physician, who gave her a tonic, and she had a tolerable night. I think all this the culmination of the excitement and fatigue of the last few weeks. . . . I thought I had lost her, and felt all calm, for I know she is Christ's, whether it is yet made clear to her sad heart or not. . . . She has not been well since the shock of the sad news. . . . We are now lying by in Cork Harbor, with the prospect of spending the rest of the day here. . . . H. seems much better this morning, is dressed and on deck like anybody else. Each of you had a letter in Paris from one or another of us.

Ever affectionately yours,   H. B. Stowe.

It was a beautiful voyage in every sense; and at that period a voyage was no little matter of six days, but a good fourteen days of sitting together on deck in pleasant summer weather, and having time enough and to spare. Hawthorne and his family also concluded to join the party. Mrs. Hawthorne, who was always the romancer in conversation, filled the evening hours by weaving magic webs of her fancies, until we looked upon her as a second Scheherezade, and the day the head was to be cut off was the day we should come to shore. "Oh," said Hawthorne, "I

wish we might never get there." But the good ship
moved steadily as fate. Meanwhile, Mrs. Stowe often
took her turn at entertaining the little group. She was
seldom tired of relating stories of New England life and
her early experiences.

When the ship came to shore, Mrs. Stowe and her
daughters went at once to Andover, where Professor Stowe
had remained at his post during the long winter. She
went also with equal directness to her writing-desk; and
though there are seldom any dates upon her letters, the
following note must have been written shortly after her
return: —

MY DEAR MR. FIELDS, — "Agnes of Sorrento" was
conceived on the spot, — a spontaneous tribute to the exceeding loveliness and beauty of all things there.

One bright evening, as I was entering the old gateway,
I saw a beautiful young girl sitting in its shadow selling
oranges. She was my Agnes. Walking that same evening through the sombre depths of the gorge, I met "Old
Elsie," walking erect and tall, with her piercing black eyes,
Roman nose, and silver hair, — walking with determination in every step, and spinning like one of the Fates glitter-
ing silver flax from a distaff she carried in her hands.

A few days after, our party, being weatherbound at Sa-
lerno, had to resort to all our talents to pass the time, and
songs and stories were the fashion of the day. The first
chapter was my contribution to that entertainment. The
story was voted into existence by the voices of all that
party, and by none more enthusiastically than by one
young voice which will never be heard on earth more.
It was kept in mind and expanded and narrated as we
went on to Rome over a track that the pilgrim Agnes is to
travel. To me, therefore, it is fragrant with love of Italy
and memory of some of the brightest hours of life.

I wanted to write something of this kind as an author's introduction to the public. Could you contrive to print it on a fly-leaf, if I get it ready, and put a little sort of dedicatory poem at the end of it? I shall do this at least in the book, if not now.

She wrote to Mrs. Howard, Sunday, August 3,

We have watched your course across the ocean from the first day of your sailing until now, every day, noting the wind and weather. . . . I feel as if I had a sort of right in you which I never had before, as if you and I were united by a bond that could unite no others. . . . It was you who broke to me the sudden news of my life, and I no less seem to be associated in your kindred sorrow. Will you not therefore come to us as soon as you can? . . . The old stone cabin will open wide its arms . . . when the ship arrives that brings the dear form — no longer Annie, but associated with her parted spirit; then we shall come to Brooklyn and mingle our tears with yours. To-day we have been reading Henry's sermon, "The Sepulchre in the Garden." "Italy," H. said, "was the lovely garden where we found the unexpected tomb." . . . Do come to us as soon as you can. It is calm, quiet, still, and shady, and we all long for you. . . . My health has been very poor since I came home. A most oppressive languor has weighed upon me. I have felt entirely prostrate and longed for friends to lean on. . . .

Your sister,   H. B. S.

A network of difficulties seems to have closed about her at this time, because in spite of her interest in the new story and the hopeful view which she took of its speedy completion, several months passed by before anything definite came respecting her literary plans.

Meanwhile she had been tempted into beginning "The Pearl of Orr's Island," a story good enough, if she had been left to herself and not overridden by greedy editors and publishers, to have added a lustre even to *her* name. It is to this she refers in the following letter when she speaks of her "Maine story." Unhappily the first number, which is one of her finest pieces of writing, drew off power which belonged to "Agnes of Sorrento," and Agnes served to prevent her from ending "The Pearl of Orr's Island" in a manner worthy of its first promise.

She says, writing in January, "Authors are apt, I suppose, like parents, to have their unreasonable partialities. Everybody has, — and I have a pleasure in writing ' Agnes of Sorrento ' that gilds this icy winter weather. I write my Maine story with a shiver, and come back to this as to a flowery home where I love to rest.

"My manuscripts are always left to the printers for punctuation, — as you will observe; I have no time for copying."

These incessant drafts upon Mrs. Stowe's energy had greatly enfeebled her; but her spirit was indomitable, and when she was weary a brief visit to Boston was, she considered, sufficient to restore her nervous force. During these visits she sometimes rehearsed the story of the early days of her married life when, as we have seen, she fought her way through difficulties and under the burden of sorrows which would have crushed many another woman.

In an unpublished prefatory note for "The Pearl of Orr's Island," the first seventeen chapters of which appeared in April of this year, Mrs. Stowe wrote in November: "The writer was applied to a year ago to furnish a serial story for ' The Independent.' This offer she promptly and decidedly declined, on the ground that she had not time nor strength, having just come under engagements to furnish one to the ' Cornhill Magazine,' simultaneously with the 'Atlantic Monthly,' in America. [This was "Agnes of Sorrento."] The engagement for this story lasted from May, 1861, to May, 1862, and Mrs. Stowe thought it would absorb all her time and strength.

"The editor of 'The Independent' subsequently wrote to know whether she could not furnish a short story to run through four or five numbers. . . . She responded that it had always been her experience that a short story once begun was taken possession of by certain spirits." . . .

In spite of her better reason she was induced to begin, and found, as she says in continuing: "a Captain Kittridge with his garrulous yarns, Misses Roxy and Ruey given to talk," and herself on the verge of her engagement for the "Atlantic Monthly" quite unprepared.

Mrs. Stowe then wrote to "The Independent," proposing to stop her story then and there in two numbers, or to promise a continuation after six months, beginning again in December. The latter scheme was accepted. "But," she says, "the agitations and mental excitements of the war have, in the case of the writer, as in the case of many others, used up the time and strength which would have been devoted to authorship.

"Who could write on stories that had a son to send to battle, with Washington beleaguered and the whole country shaken as with an earthquake? Who could write fiction when fact was so imperious and terrible, in the days of Bull Run and Big Bethel? But the author has labored assiduously on her literary engagements, and if she must commence a month or two later in the autumn than she expected, it is no greater delay than the war has caused everywhere and in every department of business.

"The readers will see by this frank statement that there has been no intention of dealing unfairly with them, but only the result of unforeseen circumstances. The story will be resumed the first of December."

Accordingly the second part, beginning with what is now chapter eighteenth, was begun in the number for December, and completed in April. Upon taking up the story again, Mrs. Stowe issued in "The Independent" the following card: —

TO OUR READERS

In commencing again "The Pearl of Orr's Island," the author meets the serious embarrassment of trying to revive for the second time an unexpected pleasure.

That a story so rustic, so woodland, so pale and colorless, so destitute of all that is ordinarily expected in a work of fiction, should be advertised in the columns of "The Independent" as this was last week, as "Mrs. So-and-So's *great* romance," or with words to that effect, produces an impression both appalling and ludicrous.

It is as if some golden-haired baby, who had touched her mother's heart by singing: —

"Jesus, tender shepherd, hear us!"

should forthwith be announced with flaming playbills, to sing in the Boston Theatre as the celebrated Prima Donna, Madame Trottietoes!

We beg our readers to know that no great romance is coming, — only a story pale and colorless as real life, and sad as truth.

You will not be interested as you have been, kind friends, — we cannot hope it; your expectations are raised only to be dashed; for our characters have no strange and wonderful adventures of outward life, and the changes that occur to them and the history they make is that of the inner life, that "cometh not with observation."

We are most sorry for our dear little child-audience, who, now that Mara and Moses have grown up, will, we fear, lose their interest in them. What a pity, boys and girls, that you are not grown up too in these six months,

—and then Mara and Moses would not seem to you to be getting dull, and talking all sorts of unintelligible talk.

But no, dear little folks, we don't wish it, either. We pray you may stay long little and believing, and able to be pleased with child's stories; for Christ says of such as you is the kingdom of heaven. We must try and see what can be done for you, and whether Captain Kittridge has not a story or two left in his pocket, with which to beguile your time.

She speaks of the severe winter in her letters to Mrs. Howard: "Snow over the fences—up to the frames of the kitchen window. No cyclamen to be looked for yet, — no violets or anemones, nothing but wintry white, — and after this is gone will come unlimited water and slush. We have seemed to be on an island in the frozen ocean, — going nowhere and seeing nobody." . . .

"Thursday evening of this week we inaugurated a society to be called the Pic-nic, to meet every week for mutual amusement, — pieces are to be written, songs sung, plays played. The first one was a brilliant success and we are in hopes to make the snows tolerable. I appoint you all corresponding members. Send us something."

Thus we see the days wore on during this winter, while she was struggling against failing strength, much labor, and the hard weather, but cheerful still, as we who saw her in Boston know. It was during these war years that Mrs. Stowe exchanged many letters with three distinguished persons whose correspondence was always a joy to her: Mrs. Browning, Mr. Ruskin, and Dr. Holmes. She writes to the latter: —

ANDOVER.

DEAR DR. HOLMES, — I have had an impulse upon me for a long time to write you a line of recognition and sympathy, in response to those that reached me monthly in your late story in the "Atlantic" ("Elsie Venner").

I know not what others may think of it, since I have seen nobody since my return; but to me it is of deeper and broader interest than anything you have done yet, and I feel an intense curiosity concerning that under-world of thought from which like bubbles your incidents and remarks often seem to burst up. The foundations of moral responsibility, the interlacing laws of nature and spirit, and their relations to us here and hereafter, are topics which I ponder more and more, and on which only one medically educated can write *well*. I think a course of medical study ought to be required of all ministers. How I should like to talk with you upon the strange list of topics suggested in the schoolmaster's letter! They are bound to agitate the public mind more and more, and it is of the chiefest importance to learn, if we can, to think soundly and wisely of them. Nobody can be a sound theologian who has not had his mind drawn to think with reverential fear on these topics.

Allow me to hint that the monthly numbers are not long enough. Get us along a little faster. You must work this well out. Elaborate and give us all the particulars. Old Sophie is a jewel; give us more of her. I have seen her. Could you ever come out and spend a day with us? The professor and I would so like to have a talk on some of these matters with you!

Very truly yours,   H. B. STOWE.

ANDOVER, February 18.

DEAR DOCTOR, — I was quite indignant to hear yesterday of the very unjust and stupid attack upon you in the ——. Mr. Stowe has written to them a remonstrance which I hope they will allow to appear as he wrote it, and over his name. He was well acquainted with your father and feels the impropriety of the thing.

But, my dear friend, in being shocked, surprised, or displeased personally with such things, we must consider other people's natures. A man or woman may wound us to the quick without knowing it, or meaning to do so, simply through difference of fibre. As Cowper hath somewhere happily said: —

> " Oh, why are farmers made so coarse,
> Or clergy made so fine?
> A kick that scarce might move a horse
> Might kill a sound divine."

When once people get ticketed, and it is known that one is a hammer, another a saw, and so on, if we happen to get a taste of their quality we cannot help being hurt, to be sure, but we shall not take it ill of them. There be pious, well-intending beetles, wedges, hammers, saws, and all other kinds of implements, good, — except where they come in the way of our fingers, — and from a beetle you can have only a beetle's gospel.

I have suffered in my day from this sort of handling, which is worse for us women, who must never answer, and once when I wrote to Lady Byron, feeling just as you do about some very stupid and unkind things that had invaded my personality, she answered me, "Words do not kill, my dear, or I should have been dead long ago."

There is much true religion and kindness in the world, after all, and as a general thing he who has struck a nerve would be very sorry for it if he only knew what he had done.

I would say nothing, if I were you. There is eternal virtue in silence.

I must express my pleasure with the closing chapters of "Elsie." They are nobly and beautifully done, and quite come up to what I wanted to complete my idea of her character. I am quite satisfied with it now. It is an artistic creation, original and beautiful.

Believe me to be your true friend,   H. B. STOWE.

Mrs. Stowe's correspondence with George Eliot did not begin until a few years later, although the letter written by Mrs. Stowe to Mrs. Follen, printed in the earlier pages of this volume, had already awakened a strong feeling for the writer in Mrs. Lewes. She said of it, "The whole letter is most fascinating and makes me love her."

Mrs. Stowe's replies to the interesting letters of Mr. Ruskin have not been found, nor those written to Mrs. Browning. We can only judge of their contents by the intimate and affectionate answers, portions of which are reproduced here, where they bear upon the subjects of the time.

The ceaseless mill, whose engine was her own pen, still went on whatever interruptions or preoccupations came to her.

The varied currents of thought and feeling excited by the war, and her trouble with two serial stories, made Mrs. Stowe's work much more difficult, although she would not recognize it even in her own mind. She explained herself sometimes to Mrs. Howard by saying: "I never was so hard run in writing as I have been lately, so you must appreciate this so large letter writ with my own hand."

In April, she writes the same friend: "At last I am free. Both stories are finished, and the last copy sent to England, thanks to the girls' busy copying fingers. I have been pressed and overdriven. . . . Next I have to go to Canada and spend ten days or a fortnight securing copyright. Not a pleasant journey, but we shall try to make the best of it."

From the moment of our return from Europe together Mrs. Stowe began to form the habit of getting a little much-needed rest and change by coming to us for brief visits in Boston.

During these vacations she was always interested to observe the benevolent work going on about her and to lend a hand if it were possible.   One incident flavored with a strong touch of the ludicrous still lingers in my memory. We had fallen in somewhere with a poor little waif of a boy, one easily to be recognized by the practiced eye of to-day as a good specimen of the street Arab.   This little being was taken up by us and brought home.   His arrival was looked upon with horror by the servants, who recognized existing facts and foresaw future miseries veiled from our less educated vision.   A visit to the bathroom was at once suggested; but as none of the house maidens offered to take charge of the business, Mrs. Stowe announced herself as more than equal to the occasion and proceeded to administer the first bath probably ever known to that specimen of the human family.   Hawthorne's clasping the leprous child was but a shadow compared to that hour, but happily Mrs. Stowe was not Hawthorne and she combed and scrubbed faithfully.

I cannot recall the precise ending of the tale.   I can only remember the whole house being aroused at some unearthly hour of that night by the child's outcries, from his unusual indulgence in a good supper, and Mrs. Stowe's amusement at the situation.   She declared the household was far better constituted to look after young cherubim than young male humans.   Something of the canary-bird order would be much more in its line, she said.   I believe he ran away the next day, probably understanding the fitness of things better than ourselves.   At any rate I find a comforting note on the subject from Andover saying: "If we can do no more we must let him go.   He certainly stands a better chance in his life's journey for the little good we have been able to put into him.   When we try a little to resist the evil current and to pull one out here and there, we learn how dreadful is the downward gravitation, the sweep and whirl of the maelstrom.   Let us hope all these have a Father, who charges Himself with

them somewhere further on in their eternal pilgrimage
when our weak hold fails."

In the autumn a plan for leaving Andover altogether
was finally matured. She wrote, "You have heard that
we are going to Hartford to live, and I am now in all
the bustle of house planning, to say nothing of grading,
under-draining, and setting out trees around our future
home. It is four acres and a half of lovely woodland on
the banks of a river and yet within an easy walk of Hartford; in fact, in the city limits; and when our house is
done you and yours must come and see us. I would
rather have made the change in less troublous times, but
the duties here draw so hardly on Mr. Stowe's strength
that I thought it better to live on less and be in a place of
our own, and with no responsibilities except those of common gentlefolk."

Mrs. Stowe's love of home, of the fireside, and her faith
in family ties were marked characteristics of her nature.
For the first time in her life she was now to make the
material house, at least, after her own idea, and for many
months she was absorbed in the enjoyment of forming
plans for her Hartford home.

In November she was in Hartford superintending the
growing establishment. She wrote, — "My house with
eight gables is growing wonderfully. I go over every
day to see it. I am busy with drains, sewers, sinks,
digging, trenching, and above all with manure! You
should see the joy with which I gaze on manure heaps in
which the eye of faith sees Delaware grapes and D'Angou-
lême pears, and all sorts of roses and posies, which at some
future day I hope you will be able to enjoy.

"Do tell me if our friend Hawthorne praises that arch
traitor Pierce in his preface, and your loyal firm publishes
it. I never read the preface, and have not yet seen the
book, but they say so here, and I can scarcely believe it

of you, if I can of him.   I regret that I went to see him
last summer.   What! patronize such a traitor to our faces!
I can scarce believe it.

"Meanwhile old Hartford seems fat, rich, and cosy, —
stocks higher than ever, business plenty, — everything as
tranquil as possible.   The drawings of our house, that is to
be, are now finished, the spot where it is to stand is staked
out, and if you will come here I will show you both.   To-
night I was there, and the great full moon shining down
on the river and the red trees growing redder in the twilight made a beautiful picture."

The year proved an eventful one to Mrs. Stowe.   "In
the first place," says her son Charles, "the long and pleasant Andover connection of Professor Stowe was about to
be severed, and the family were to remove to Hartford.
They were to occupy a house that Mrs. Stowe was building on the bank of Park River.   It was erected in a
grove of oaks that had in her girlhood been one of Mrs.
Stowe's favorite resorts.   Here, with her friend Georgiana
May, she had passed many happy hours, and had often
declared that if she were ever able to build a house, it
should stand in that very place.   Here, then, it was built;
and as the location was at that time beyond the city
limits, it formed, with its extensive, beautiful groves, a
particularly charming place of residence.   Beautiful as it
was, however, it was occupied by the family for only a
few years.   The needs of the growing city caused factories
to spring up in the neighborhood, and to escape their en-
croachments ten years later, Mrs. Stowe bought and moved
into the house on Forest Street that was ever afterward her
Northern home.   Thus the only house Mrs. Stowe ever
planned and built for herself has been appropriated to the
use of factory hands, and is now a tenement occupied by
several families."

In this year, also, was finally published "Agnes of
Sorrento."

In the month of May came the first letter to her publisher from the new place.   Already we find that the ever-
present need has driven Mrs. Stowe to print her thoughts
about "House and Home."

                              HARTFORD, OAKWOLD, May 1.
MY DEAR FRIEND, — I came here a month ago to hurry
on the preparations for our house, in which I am now
writing, in the high bow window of Mr. Stowe's study,
overlooking the wood and river.   We are not moved in
yet, only our things, and the house presents a scene of the
wildest chaos, the furniture having been tumbled in and
lying boxed and promiscuous.
     I sent the sixth number of "House and Home Papers"
a week ago, and, not having heard from it, am a little
anxious.   I always want faith that a bulky manuscript
will go safe, — for all I never lost one. . . . I should
like to show you the result here when we are fairly in,
and the spring leaves are out.   It is the brightest, cheer-
fulest, homeliest home that you could see, — not even
excepting yours.

     The pursuit of literature under such circumstances is
neither natural nor profitable.   In Mrs. Stowe's case it
proved that she was pursuing, not literature, but the ne-
cessities of life.   Everything in the household economy
now depended upon her; and however strong her tenden-
cies were naturally, she no longer possessed the reserved
strength to forge the work from her brain.   In the writing
of "Uncle Tom," great as were the odds against her, she
had been preparing to that end from the moment of her
birth.   Her father's fiery powers of expression; her mother's nature, absorbed in the still dream of love and duty;
her own solitary childhood in spite of the enormous household in which she was brought up; above all her brooding

nature quietly absorbing and assimilating the knowledge and thought which were finding expression around her; the first years of married life in Cincinnati, where the slaves were continually harbored and assisted, notwithstanding the risks to life and property, — everything, in short, within and around her was nourishing the child of her genius which was to leap into being and gather the armies of America.

On the whole we may rather wonder at the high average value of the literary work by which she lived, especially when we follow the hints given in her letters of her interrupted and crowded existence.

In June she says, — "I wrote my piece in a sea of troubles. I had, as you see, to write by amanuensis, and yet my little senate of girls say they like it better than anything I have written yet." It was a touching characteristic to see how the "senate of girls," or of such household friends as she could muster wherever she might be, were always called in to keep up her courage and to give her a sympathetic stimulus. During the days when she was writing, it was never safe to be far away, for she was rapid as light itself, and before a brief hour was ended we were pretty sure to hear her voice calling "Do come, come and hear and tell me how you like it."

Her June letter continues: "Can I begin to tell you what it is to begin to keep house in an unfinished home and place, dependent on a carpenter, a plumber, a mason, a bell-hanger, who come and go at their own sweet will, breaking in, making all sorts of chips, dust, dirt, going off in the midst leaving all standing, — reappearing at uncertain intervals and making more dust, chips, and dirt. One parlor and my library have thus risen piecemeal by disturbance and convulsions. They are now almost done, and the last box of books is almost unpacked, but my head aches so with the past confusion that I cannot get up any feeling of rest.   I can't enjoy — can't feel a minute to sit down and say ' It is done.'

"The fountain plays, the plants flourish, and our front hall minus the stair railing looks beautifully; my pictures are all hung in parlor and library, and yet I feel so unsettled.   Well, in a month more perhaps I shall get my brains right side up."

The following year was made memorable in Mrs. Stowe's life by the marriage of her youngest daughter. Again I find that no description can begin to give as clearly as the glimpses in her own letters the multifarious responsibilities which beset her.   She says: "I am in trouble, — have been in trouble ever since my turtle-doves announced their intention of pairing in June instead of August, because it entailed on me an immediate necessity of bringing everything out of doors and in to a state of completeness for the wedding exhibition in June.   The garden must be planted, the lawn graded, harrowed, rolled, seeded, and the grass up and growing, stumps got out and shrubs and trees got in, conservatory made over, belts planted, holes filled, — and all by three very slippery sort of Irishmen who had rather any time be minding their own business than mine.   I have back doorsteps to be made, and troughs, screens, and what not; papering, painting, and varnishing, hitherto neglected, to be completed; also spring house-cleaning; also dressmaking for one bride and three ordinary females; also —— and —— and ——'s wardrobes to be overlooked; also carpets to be made and put down; also a revolution in the kitchen cabinet, threatening for a time to blow up the whole establishment altogether."   And so the letter proceeds with two more sheets, adding near the end: "I send you to-day a ' Chimney Corner ' on ' Our Martyrs,' which I have written out of the fullness of my heart. . . . It is an account of the martyrdom of a Christian boy of our own town of Andover, who died of starvation and want in a Southern prison on last Christmas Day."

Just one month before the marriage she writes again: "The wedding is indeed an absorbing whirlpool, but amid it all I have the next 'Chimney Corner' in good train and shall send it on to-morrow or next day."

How small a portion of the world outside can understand the lives of writers, actors, and those whose professions compel them to depend directly upon the public! No private joy, no private sorrow, no rest, no change, is recognized by this taskmaster. It is well: on the whole we would not have it otherwise; because those who can minister to the great Public embrace their profession in a spirit of conscious or unconscious self-denial. In either case the result is the same: development, advancement, and sometimes attainment.

The wedding is not two days over when another letter arrives full of her literary work, yet adding that she longs for rest and if we will only tell her where Campton is, whither we had gone, she would gladly join us. "I was a weary idiot," she continues, "by the time the wedding was over, and said 'Yes ma'am' to the men and 'No sir' to the women in sheer imbecility."

Nevertheless she did not get to Campton, but kept on, with the exception of a few brief visits at Peekskill and elsewhere until the autumn. In one of her notes she says: "I have returned to my treadmill. A——— is to leave as soon as she can get ready, and I am trying to see her off, — helping her to get her things together, and trying to induce her to take a new stand in a new place and make herself a respectable woman. When she is gone a load will be off my back. If it were not for the good that is still left in our fellows our task would be easier than it is — we could cut them adrift and let them swim; but while we see much that may be turned to good account in

them we hang on, or let them hang on, and our boat
moves slow. So behold me fighting my good fight of
womanhood against dust and disorganization and the universal downward tendency of everybody, hoping for easier
times by and by."

With her heroic nature she was always ready to lead
the forlorn hope. The child no one else was willing to
provide for, the woman the world despised, were brought
into her home and cared for as her own. Unhappily, her
delicate health at this time (though she was naturally
strong), her constant literary labors, her uncertain income,
her private griefs, all united, caused her to fall short in
ability to accomplish what she undertook; hence there
were often crises from sudden illness and non-fulfillment
of engagements which were very serious in their effects,
but the elasticity of her spirits was something marvelous
and carried her over many a hard place.

The truth was, and it may seem a singular antithesis to
say of the writer of one of the greatest stories the world
has yet produced, that she was not a student of literature.
Books as a medium of the ideas of the age, and as the
promulgators of morals and religion, were of course like
the breath of her life; but a study of the literature of the
past as the only true foundation for a literature of the
present was outside the pale of her occupations, and for
the larger portion of her life outside of her interest.
During the riper season of her activity with the pen, the
necessity of studying style and the thoughts of others
gained a larger hold upon her mind; but she always said,
with a twinkle of amusement and pride, that she never
could have done anything without Mr. Stowe. He knew
everything, and all she had to do was to go to him. All
this double service, the impossibility of devoting herself
to a career which was after all her appointed work, made
her work exceptionally difficult.

All her life she stimulated the activity of her pen rather by her sympathy with humanity than by studies of literature. In one of her letters she says: "You see whoever can write on home and family matters, on what people think of and are anxious about and want to hear from, has an immense advantage. The success of the 'House and Home Papers' shows me how much people want this sort of thing, and, now I am bringing the series to a close, I find I have ever so much more to say; in fact, the idea has come in this shape. . . . A set of papers for the next year to be called 'Christopher's Evenings,' which will allow great freedom and latitude; a capacity of striking anywhere when a topic seems to be in the public mind and that will comprise a little series of sketches or rather little groups of sketches out of which books may be made. You understand Christopher writes these for the winter-evening amusement of his family. One set will be entitled 'An Account of the Seven Little Foxes that spoil the Vines.' This will cover seven sketches of certain domestic troubles. Another set is the 'Cathedral; or, the Shrines of Home Saints,' under which I shall give certain sketches of home characters contrasting with that of the legends of the saints: the shirt-making, knitting, whooping-cough-tending saints, the Aunt Esthers and Aunt Marias. . . . Hum" [her-humming bird] "is well — notwithstanding the dull weather; we keep him in a sunny upper chamber and feed him daily on sugar and water, and he catches his own mutton."

Thus in swift succession we find, not only charming little idyls here and there like her story of "Hum the Son of Buzz" in "Our Young Folks," being the tale of her captured and tamed humming-bird, but also "Little Foxes," "The Chimney Corner," a volume of collected Poems, "Oldtown Folks," "Sam Lawson's Fireside Tales," and others, following with tireless rapidity, bear-

ing the same stamp of living sympathy with difficulties of
the time and breathing a spirit of helpfulness and faith.

The world is yet to recognize the value of her writings
in their influence upon the suffering of our common humanity. When this power was concentrated upon the evil of
slavery the response was national, universal, and unprecedented; but such papers as "The Ministries of Departed
Friends; A New Year Reverie," and others of like character, will long keep her pages sacred to the dwellers in
silent places.

CHAPTER XI

AFTER the close of the war, the infirm condition of her son being ever in her mind, Mrs. Stowe began to discuss projects for making a winter home in Florida. "She was also," writes her son Charles, "most anxious to do her share towards educating and leading to a higher life those colored people whom she had helped so largely to set free, and who were still in the state of profound ignorance imposed by slavery." In writing of her hopes and plans to her brother Charles Beecher, in 1866, she says: —

"My plan of going to Florida, as it lies in my mind, is not in any sense a mere worldly enterprise. I have for many years had a longing to be more immediately doing Christ's work on earth. My heart is with that poor people whose cause in words I have tried to plead, and who now, ignorant and docile, are just in that formative stage in which whoever seizes has them.

"Corrupt politicians are already beginning to speculate on them as possible capital for their schemes, and to fill their poor heads with all sorts of vagaries. Florida is the State into which they have, more than anywhere else, been pouring. Emigration is positively and decidedly setting that way; but as yet it is mere worldly emigration, with the hope of making money, nothing more.

"The Episcopal Church is, however, undertaking, under direction of the future Bishop of Florida, a wide-embracing scheme of Christian activity for the whole State. In this work I desire to be associated, and my plan is to

locate at some salient point on the St. John's River, where
I can form the nucleus of a Christian neighborhood, whose
influence shall be felt far beyond its own limits."

During this year Mrs. Stowe partially carried her plan
into execution by hiring an old plantation called "Laurel
Grove," on the west side of the St. John's River, near
the present village of Orange Park. Here she established
her son Frederick as a cotton planter, and here he remained for two years. The situation did not, however,
prove entirely satisfactory, nor did the raising of cotton
prove to be, under the circumstances, a profitable business.
After visiting Florida towards the spring, at which time her
attention was drawn to the beauties and superior advantages of Mandarin on the east side of the river, Mrs. Stowe
wrote from Hartford to Rev. Charles Beecher: —

MY DEAR BROTHER, — We are now thinking seriously
of a place in Mandarin much more beautiful than any
other in the vicinity. It has on it five large date palms,
an olive-tree in full bearing, besides a fine orange grove
which this year will yield about seventy-five thousand
oranges. If we get that, then I want you to consider the
expediency of buying the one next to it. It contains
about two hundred acres of land, on which is a fine orange
grove, the fruit from which last year brought in two thousand dollars as sold at the wharf. It is right on the river,
and four steamboats pass it each week, on their way to
Savannah and Charleston. There is on the place a very
comfortable cottage, as houses go out there, where they do
not need to be built as substantially as with us.

I am now in correspondence with the Bishop of Florida,
with a view to establishing a line of churches along the
St. John's River, and if I settle, at Mandarin, it will be
one of my stations. Will you consent to enter the Episcopal Church and be our clergyman? You are just the

man we want.   If my tastes and feelings did not incline
me toward the Church, I should still choose it as the best
system for training immature minds such as those of our
negroes.   The system was composed with reference to the
wants of the laboring class of England, at a time when
they were as ignorant as our negroes now are.

I long to be at this work, and cannot think of it without my heart burning within me.   Still I leave all with
my God, and only hope He will open the way for me to
do all that I want to for this poor people.

Affectionately yours,   H. B. STOWE.

"Mrs. Stowe," writes her son, "had some years before
this joined the Episcopal Church, for the sake of attending the same communion as her daughters, who were Epis-
copalians."   This change was not remarkable when we
remember that Mrs. Stowe's mother was an Episcopalian.
Henry Ward Beecher said of their mother: "She was born
in the Episcopal church, and while a devout adherent to
that faith and government married my father.   She was
a sensible woman, evinced not only by that but by the
fact that she united herself to the Congregational church
in Litchfield.   She was a woman of extraordinary graces
and gifts; a woman not demonstrative, with a profound
philosophical nature and of wonderful depth of affection,
but with a serenity that was simply charming.   While my
father was in the early religious experience under Calvinistic teaching, debating and swelling and floating here and
there and tormenting himself, she threw the oil of faith
and trust on the waters, and they were quieted, for she
trusted in God."   Their brother Charles did not, however,
see fit to change his creed, and though he went to Florida, he settled a hundred and sixty miles west from the
St. John's River, at Newport, near St. Marks, on the Gulf
coast, and about twenty miles from Tallahassee.   Here

he lived every winter and several summers for fifteen years, and here he left the impress of his own remarkably sweet and lovely character upon the scattered population of the entire region.

"Mrs. Stowe in the mean time purchased the property, with its orange grove and comfortable cottage, that she had recommended to him, and thus Mandarin became her winter home. No one who has ever seen it can forget the peaceful beauty of this Florida home and its surroundings. The house, a story and a half cottage of many gables, stands on a bluff overlooking the broad St. John's, which is five miles wide at this point. It nestles in the shade of a grove of superb, moss-hung live-oaks, around one of which the front piazza is built. Several fine old orange-trees also stand near the cottage, scenting the air with the sweet perfume of their blossoms in the early spring, and offering their golden fruit to whoever may choose to pluck it during the winter months. Back of the house stretches the well-tended orange grove in which Mrs. Stowe took such genuine pride and pleasure. Everywhere about the dwelling and within it were flowers and singing birds, while the rose garden in front, at the foot of the bluff, was the admiration of all who saw it."

Her own times for going and coming were somewhat uncertain, depending upon her work, upon printers, binders, and publishers; also, perchance, upon the weather and the state of her own health. She wrote to Mrs. Howard: "I have been very hard driven of late, owing to a promise inadvertently given to a publishing firm here in Hartford that I would get a book called 'Men of our Times' ready for them this fall. I have been obliged to stop printing my story, and work incessantly to get that off my hands, and have written so much every day that to write even a note in addition seemed more than I could do."

Nevertheless in one of her pleasant familiar letters to me she gives the following cheerful picture: —

"My conservatory is doing splendidly. I wish you could see two crimson camellias on one stem that are opening now in front of my door as I sit writing. My ferns and ivies that I brought from Brooklyn are all doing well, — my bulbs all asleep in pots under a blanket of earth four inches deep in the cellar. I shall expect them up about January, and in February shall have a gay time with them."

At last, having an accessible home in the pleasant city of Hartford, strangers and travelers often sought and found her. In one of her familiar notes she says: "The Amberleys have written that they are coming to us to-morrow, and of all times, accordingly, our furnace must spring a leak. We are hoping to make all right before they get here, but I am really ashamed to show such weather at this time of year. Poor America! It's like having your mother expose herself by a fit of ill temper before strangers. . . . Do, I beg, write to a poor sinner laboring under a book." And again, a little later: "*The book* is almost done — hang it! but done *well*, and will be a good thing for young men to read, and young women too, and so I'll send you one. You'll find some things in it, I fancy, that I know and you don't, about the times before you were born, when I was 'Hush, hush, my dearing' in Cincinnati. . . . I smell spring afar off — sniff — do you? Any smell of violets in the distance? I think it comes over the water from the Pamfili Doria."

It was during one of Mrs. Stowe's visits to Boston about this time that she chanced to talk with greater fullness and openness than she had done before on the subject of Spiritualism. In the simplest way she affirmed her entire belief in possible manifestations of the nearness and individual life of those who had passed to the unseen world and gave vivid illustrations of the reasons why her faith was thus assured. She never sought after such testimony unless she found herself sitting with others who were interested and who wished to try experiments, but her conclusions were definite and unvarying. At that period such a declaration of faith required a good deal of bravery; now the subject has assumed a different phase and there are few thinking persons who do not recognize a certain truth hidden within the shadows. She spoke with tender seriousness of such manifestations as are recorded in the Old and New Testament. Her husband had possessed the peculiar power from his early youth of seeing persons moving about him who could not be perceived by others. These visions were so distinct that it was impossible for him to distinguish at times between the real and the unreal. I recall one illustration which had occurred only a few years previous to their departure from Andover. She had been called to Boston one day on business. Making her preparations hurriedly, she bade the household farewell, and rushed to the station, only to see the train go out as she arrived. There was nothing to do but to return home and wait patiently for the next train; but wishing not to be disturbed, she quietly opened a side door and crept noiselessly up the staircase leading to her own room, sitting down by her writing-table in the window. She had been seated about half an hour when Professor Stowe came in, looked about him with a preoccupied air, but did not speak to her. She thought his behavior strange, and amused herself by watching him; at last the situation became so extraordinary that she began to laugh. "Why," he exclaimed, with a most astonished air, "is that you? I thought it was one of my visions!"

Mrs. Stowe wrote out one day for her children her own mature views upon the subject of Spiritualism. She says: —

"Each friend takes away a portion of ourselves. There was some part of our being related to him as to no other, and we had things to say to him which no other would understand or appreciate. A portion of our thoughts has become useless and burdensome, and again and again, with involuntary yearning, we turn to the stone at the door of the sepulchre. We lean against the cold, silent marble, but there is no answer; no voice, neither any that regardeth.

"There are those who would have us think that in *our* day this doom is reversed; that there are those who have the power to restore to us the communion of our lost ones. How many a heart, wrung and tortured with the anguish of this fearful silence, has throbbed with strange, vague hopes at the suggestion! When we hear sometimes of persons of the strongest and clearest minds becoming credulous votaries of certain spiritualist circles, let us not wonder: if we inquire, we shall almost always find that the belief has followed some stroke of death; it is only an indication of the desperation of that heart-hunger which in part it appeases.

"Ah, *were* it true! Were it indeed so that the wall between the spiritual and material is growing thin, and a new dispensation germinating in which communion with the departed blest shall be among the privileges and possibilities of this our mortal state! Ah, were it so that when we go forth weeping in the gray dawn, bearing spices and odors which we long to pour forth for the beloved dead, we should indeed find the stone rolled away and an angel sitting on it!

"But for us the stone must be rolled away by an *unquestionable* angel, whose countenance is as the lightning, who executes no doubtful juggle by pale moonlight or starlight, but rolls back the stone in fair, open morning, and sits on it. Then we could bless God for his mighty gift, and with love, and awe, and reverence take up that blessed fellowship with another life, and weave it reverently and trustingly into the web of our daily course.

"But no such angel have we seen, — no such sublime, unquestionable, glorious manifestation. And when we look at what is offered to us, ah! who that has friends in heaven could wish them to return in such wise as this? The very instinct of a sacred sorrow seems to forbid that our beautiful, our glorified ones should stoop lower than even to the medium of their cast-off bodies, to juggle, and rap, and squeak, and perform mountebank tricks with tables and chairs; to recite over in weary sameness harmless truisms, which we were wise enough to say for ourselves; to trifle, and banter, and jest, or to lead us through endless moonshiny mazes. Sadly and soberly we say that, if this be communion with the dead, we had rather be without it. We want something a little in advance of our present life, and not below it. We have read with some attention weary pages of spiritual communication purporting to come from Bacon, Swedenborg, and others, and long accounts from divers spirits of things seen in the spirit land, and we can conceive of no more appalling prospect than to have them true.

"If the future life is so weary, stale, flat, and unprofitable as we might infer from these readings, one would have reason to deplore an immortality from which no suicide could give an outlet. To be condemned to such eternal prosing would be worse than annihilation.

"Is there, then, no satisfaction for this craving of the soul? There is One who says: 'I am he that liveth and was dead, and behold I am alive for evermore, and I have the keys of hell and of death;' and this same being said once before: 'He that loveth me shall be loved of my Father, and I will love him and will manifest myself unto him.' This is a promise direct and personal; not confined to the first apostles, but stated in the most general way as

attainable by any one who loves and does the will of
Jesus. It seems given to us as some comfort for the unavoidable heart-breaking separations of death that there
should be, in that dread unknown, one all-powerful Friend
with whom it is possible to commune, and from whose
spirit there may come a response to us. Our Elder Brother, the partaker of our nature, is not only in the spirit
land, but is all-powerful there. It is He that shutteth
and no man openeth, and openeth and no man shutteth.
He whom we have seen in the flesh, weeping over the
grave of Lazarus, is He who hath the keys of hell and of
death. If we cannot commune with our friends, we can
at least commune with Him to whom they are present,
who is intimately with them as with us. He is the true
bond of union between the spirit world and our souls; and
one blest hour of prayer, when we draw near to Him and
feel the breadth, and length, and depth, and height of
that love of his that passeth knowledge, is better than all
those incoherent, vain, dreamy glimpses with which longing hearts are cheated.

"They who have disbelieved all spiritual truth, who
have been Sadduceeic doubters of either angel or spirit,
may find in modern spiritualism a great advance. But
can one who has ever really had communion with Christ,
who has said with John, 'Truly our fellowship is with
the Father and the Son,' — can such an one be satisfied
with what is found in the modern circle?

"Let us, then, who long for communion with spirits,
seek nearness to Him who has promised to speak and commune, leaving forever this word to his church: —

"'I will not leave you comfortless. I will come to
you.'"

In these busy years she went away upon her Boston
trips more and more rarely, but she writes after her return

from one of them: "I don't think I *ever* enjoyed Boston
so much as in this visit. Why was it? Every cloud seemed
to turn out its silver lining, everybody was delightful, and
the music has really done me good. I feel it all over
me now. I think of it with a sober certainty of waking
bliss! Our little 'hub' is a grand 'hub.' Three cheers
for it! . . . I have had sent me through the War Department a French poem which I think is full of real nerve
and strength of feeling. I undertook the reading only as
a duty, but found myself quite waked up. The indignation and the feeling with which the author denounces
modern skepticism, that worst of all unbelief, the denial
of all good, all beauty, all generosity, all heroism, is splendid. He is a live man this, and I wish you would read
his poem and send it to Longfellow, for it does one's heart
good to see the French made the vehicle of so much real
heroic sentiment. The description of a slave hunt is
splendidly and bitterly satirical and indignant and full of
fine turns of language. Thank God *that* is over. No
matter what happens to you and me, *that* great burden of
sin and misery has tumbled off from our backs and rolled
into the sepulchre, where it shall never arise more. . . .
I have been the most industrious of beings since my return, and am steaming away on the obstacle that stands
between me and my story, which I long to be at. . . . I
want to get one or two special bits of information out of
Garrison, and so instead of sending my letter at random
to Boston I will trouble you (who have little or nothing
to do!) to get this letter to him. *My own book,* instead
of cooling, boils and bubbles daily and nightly, and I am
pushing and spurring like fury to get to it. I work like
a dray-horse, and I'll *never* get in such a scrape again.
It isn't my business to make up books, but to make them.
I have lots to say."

The story which had so taken possession of her mind

and heart was "Oldtown Folks," the one which she at the time fancied the best calculated of all her works to sustain the reputation of the author of "Uncle Tom's Cabin." The many proofs of her own interest in it seem to show that she had been moved to a livelier and deeper satisfaction in this creation than in any of her later productions. She writes respecting it: "It is more to me than a story; it is my résumé of the whole spirit and body of New England, a country that is now exerting such an influence on the civilized world that to know it truly becomes an object." But there were weary lengths of roads to be traveled, by a woman already overladen with responsibilities and in delicate health, before such a book could reach its consummation.

"I must cry you mercy," she begins one of the notes to her publisher, and explain my condition to you as well as possible." The "condition" was frequently to be explained! Proofs were not ready when they were promised, the press was stopped, and both author and publisher required all the tender regard they really had for each other and all the patience they possessed to keep in tune. She says, "I am sorry to trouble you or derange your affairs, but one can't always tell in driving such horses as we drive where they are going to bring up."

She started off in this long journey very hopefully, writing that she would like to begin printing at once, because "to have the first part of my book in type will greatly assist me in the last." A month later she writes: "Here goes the first of my nameless story, of which I can only say it is as unlike everything else as it is like the strange world of folks I took it from. There is no fear that there will not be as much matter as 'Uncle Tom's Cabin;' there will. There could be an endless quantity if I only said all I can see and think that is strange and curious. I partake in ——'s disappointment that it is not done, but it is of that class of things that cannot be commanded; as my friend Sam Lawson (*vide* MSS.) says, 'There 's things that can be druv and then agin there 's things that can't,' and this is that kind; as had to be humored. Instead of rushing on, I have often turned back and written over with care, that nothing that I wanted to say might be omitted; it has cost me a good deal of labor to elaborate this first part, namely, to build my theatre and to introduce my actors. My labor has all, however, been given to the literary part. My printers always inform me that I know nothing of punctuation, and I give thanks that I have no responsibility for any of its absurdities! Further than beginning my sentence with a capital, I go not, — so I hope my friend Mr. Bigelow, who is a direct and lineal descendant of 'my Grandmother,' will put those things all right."

Who so well as authors can fully understand and sympathize with the burden of a long story in the head, long bills on the table, tempting offers to write for this and that in order to bring in two hundred dollars from a variety of pleasant editors who desire the name on their list, house and grounds to be looked after, cooks to be pacified, visits to be made — it is no wonder that Mrs. Stowe wrote: "The thing has been an awful tax and labor, for I have tried to do it well. I say also to you confidentially, that it has seemed as if every private care that could hinder me as woman and mother has been crowded into just this year that I have had this to do."

Happily more peaceful days were in store for her. Her daughters, now grown to womanhood, were beginning to take the reins of home work and government into their own hands; and as the darkest hour foreruns the dawn, so almost imperceptibly to herself her cares began to fade away from her.

A new era opened in Mrs. Stowe's life when she made

her first visit to Florida. She was tired and benumbed
with care and cold. Suddenly the thought came to her
that she would go to the South, herself, and see what the
stories were worth which she was constantly hearing about
its condition. In the mean time, if she could, she would
enjoy the soft air, and find retirement in which she might
continue her book. She says in one of her letters: —

"Winter weather and cold seem always a kind of nightmare to me. I am going to take my writing-desk and go
down to Florida to F——'s plantation, where we have
now a home, and abide there until the heroic agony of be-
tweenity, the freeze and thaw of winter, is over, and then
I doubt not I can write my three hours a day. Meanwhile, I have a pretty good pile of manuscript. . . . The
letters I have got about blossoming roses and loungers in
linen coats, while we have been frozen and snowed up,
have made my very soul long to be away. Cold weather
really seems to torpify my brain. I write with a heavy
numbness. I have not yet had a *good* spell of writing,
though I have had all through the story abundant clairvoy-
ance, and see just how it must be written; but for writing
some parts I want *warm* weather, and not to be in the
state of a 'froze and thawed apple.' . . . The cold affects
me precisely as extreme hot weather used to in Cincinnati,
—gives me a sort of bilious neuralgia. I hope to get a
clear, bright month in Florida, when I can say something
to purpose.

"I did want to read some of my story to you before I
went. I have read it to my husband; and though one
may think a husband a partial judge, yet mine is so nervous and so afraid of being bored that I feel as if it were
something to hold him; and he likes it — is quite wake-
ful, so to speak, about it. All I want now, to go on, is
a good *frame*, as father used to say about his preaching.
I want calm, soft, even dreamy, enjoyable weather, sun-

shine and flowers.   Love to dear A——, whom I so much
want to see once more."

Unhappily, she could not get away so soon as she desired.   There were contracts to be signed and other busi-
nesses to arrange.   These delays made her visit southward
much shorter than she intended, but it proved to be only
the introduction, the first brief chapter, as it were, of her
future winter life in Florida.   Before leaving she wrote
to Mr. Fields: —

"I am so constituted that it is absolutely fatal to me
to agree to have *any* literary work done at certain dates.
I *mean* to have this story done by the 1st of September.
It would be greatly for my pecuniary interest to get it
done before that, because I have the offer of eight thousand dollars for the newspaper use of the story I am planning to write after it.   But I am bound by the laws of
art.   Sermons, essays, lives of distinguished people, I can
write to order at times and seasons.   A story comes, grows
like a flower, sometimes will and sometimes won't, like
a pretty woman.   When the spirits will help, I can write.
When they jeer, flout, make faces, and otherwise maltreat
me, I can only wait humbly at their gates, watch at the
posts of their doors.

"This story grows even when I do not write.   I spent
a month in the mountains in Stockbridge *composing* before
I wrote a word.

"I only ask now a good physical condition, and I go to
warmer climes hoping to save time there.   I put everything and everybody off that interferes with this, except
Pussy Willow, which will be a pretty story for a child
series."

At last she sailed away, about the first of March, and
with that delightful power of knowing what she wanted,
and being content when she attained her end, which is
too rare, alas! her letters glowed and blossomed and shone

with the fruit and flowers and sunshine of the South. It was hardly to be expected that her literary work could actually reach the printers' hands under these circumstances as rapidly as if she had been able to write at home; therefore it was with no sense of surprise that we received from her, during the summer, what proved to be a chapter of excuses instead of a chapter of her book: "I have a long story to tell you of *what* has prevented my going on with my story, which you must see would so occupy all the nerve and brain force I have that I have not been able to write a word except to my own children. To them in their needs I *must* write *chapters* which would otherwise go into my novel."

In the autumn she found herself able to come again to Boston for a few days' visit. There were often long croonings over the fire far into the night; her other-worldliness and abstractions brought with them a dreamy quietude, especially to those whose harried lives kept them only too much awake. Her coming was always a pleasure, for she made holidays by her own delightful presence, and asked nothing more than what she found in the companionship of her friends.

After her return to Hartford and in December of the same year, I find some curious notes showing how easily she was attracted by new subjects of interest away from the work she had in hand; not that she saw it in that light, or was aware that her story was in the least retarded by such digressions, but her keen sympathy with everything and everybody made it more and more difficult to concentrate herself upon the long story she held after all to be of the first importance. She writes to the editor of the "Atlantic Monthly:" "I see that all the leading magazines have articles on 'Planchette.'

"There is a lady of my acquaintance who has developed more remarkable facts in this way than any I have ever seen; I have kept a record of these communications for some time past, and everybody is very much struck with them.

"I have material to prepare a very curious article. Shall you want it? And when?"

We can imagine the feeling of a publisher waiting for copy of her promised story on reading this note! Also the following of a few days later: —

"I am beginning a series of articles called 'Learning to Write,' designed to be helpful to a great many beginners. . . . I shall instance Hawthorne as a model and speak of his 'Note-Book' as something which every young author aspiring to write should study. . . . My materials for the 'Planchette' article , are really very extraordinary, . . . but I don't want to write it now when I am driving so hard upon my book. . . . It costs some patience to you and certainly to me to have it take so long, yet I have conscientiously done all I could, since I began. Now the end of it is in plain sight, but there is a good deal to be done to bring it out worthily, and I work upon it steadily and daily. I never put so much work into anything before."

A week later she says again: —

"I thank you very much for your encouraging words, for I really need them. I have worked so hard that I am almost tired. I hope that you will still continue to read, and that you will not find it dull. . . . I have received the books. What a wonderful fellow Hawthorne was!"

Happily the time was near for a second flight to Florida, and she wrote with her own rested hand *en route* from Charleston: —

"Room fragrant with violets, banked up in hyacinths, flowers everywhere, windows open, birds singing."

She inclosed some fans, upon which she had been painting flowers busily during the journey in order to send them back to Boston to be sold at a fair in behalf of the Cretans: "Make them do the Cretes all the good you can," she said.

"At last," she writes a few days later, "after waiting a day and a half in Charleston, we arrived at Mandarin about ten o'clock Saturday morning, just a week from the day we sailed. The house looked so pretty, and quiet, and restful, the day was so calm and lovely, it seemed as though I had passed away from all trouble, and was looking back upon you all from a secure resting-place. Mr. Stowe is very happy here, and is constantly saying how pleasant it is, and how glad he is that he is here. He is so much improved in health that already he is able to take a considerable walk every day.

"We are all well, contented, and happy, and we have six birds, two dogs, and a pony. Do write more and oftener. Tell me all the little nothings and nowheres. You can't imagine how they are magnified by the time they have reached into this remote corner."

In the summer a new experience came to her. The death of Lady Byron a few years before had closed an episode in Mrs. Stowe's earthly affections. Lady Byron possessed for her a strong personal fascination. She said once: "When I was first introduced to her I felt in a moment the words of her husband: —

> "There was awe in the homage that she drew;
> Her spirit seemed as seated on a throne."

It was altogether natural that with Mrs. Stowe's temperament and the sincere affection which ripened between her and Lady Byron, she should have attempted after her death to try to prove to the world the exceptional purity of her character and her devotion to her marriage oath. Mrs. Stowe wrote to Dr. Holmes upon this subject: —

DEAR DOCTOR, — I am going to ask help of you, and I feel that confidence in your friendship that leads me to be glad that I have a friend like you to ask advice of. In order that you may understand fully what it is, I must go back some years and tell you about it.

When I went to England the first time, I formed a friendship with Lady Byron which led to a somewhat interesting correspondence. When there the second time, after the publication of "Dred" in 1856, Lady Byron wrote to me that she wished to have some private confidential conversation with me, and invited me to come spend a day with her at her country seat near London. I went, met her alone, and spent an afternoon with her. The object of the visit she then explained to me. She was in such a state of health that she considered she had very little time to live, and was engaged in those duties and reviews which every thoughtful person finds who is coming deliberately, and with their eyes open, to the boundaries of this mortal life.

Lady Byron, as you must perceive, has all her life lived under a weight of slanders and false imputations laid upon her by her husband. Her own side of the story has been told only to that small circle of confidential friends who needed to know it in order to assist her in meeting the exigencies which it imposed on her. Of course it has thrown the sympathy mostly on his side, since the world generally has more sympathy with impulsive incorrectness than with strict justice.

At that time there was a cheap edition of Byron's works in contemplation, meant to bring them into circulation among the masses, and the pathos arising from the story of his domestic misfortunes was one great means relied on for giving it currency.

Under these circumstances some of Lady Byron's friends

had proposed the question to her whether she had not a responsibility to society for the truth; whether she did right to allow these persons to gain influence over the popular mind by a silent consent to an utter falsehood. As her whole life had been passed in the most heroic self-abnegation and self-sacrifice, the question was now proposed to her whether one more act of self-denial was not required of her, namely, to declare *the truth*, no matter at what expense to her own feelings.

For this purpose she told me she wished to recount the whole story to a person in whom she had confidence, — a person of another country, and out of the whole sphere of personal and local feelings which might be supposed to influence those in the country and station in life where the events really happened, — in order that I might judge whether anything more was required of her in relation to this history.

The interview had almost the solemnity of a death-bed confession, and Lady Byron told me the history which I have embodied in an article to appear in the "Atlantic Monthly." I have been induced to prepare it by the run which the Guiccioli book is having, which is from first to last an unsparing attack on Lady Byron's memory by Lord Byron's mistress.

When you have read my article, I want, *not* your advice as to whether the main facts shall be told, for on this point I am so resolved that I frankly say advice would do me no good. But you might help me, with your delicacy and insight, to make the *manner of telling* more perfect, and I want to do it as wisely and well as such story can be told."

Dr. Holmes mentions the subject several times in writing to his friend Lothrop Motley. "Mr. Fields was absent in Europe," he says, "and his sub-editor, fearing to lose Mrs. Stowe as a contributor altogether, assented to her request to print the Byron paper." In another letter he writes: "We have had three storms this autumn: first, the great gale of September 8, which I recognized while it was blowing as the greatest for fifty-four years, for you remember that I remember the September gale; second, the Byron whirlwind, which began here and swiftly traveled across the Atlantic; and third, the gold-storm, as I christened the terrible financial conflict of the last week."

That Lady Byron should herself have contemplated the publication of the statements made to Mrs. Stowe just before her death and should have sought her advice on the subject, proves how deeply she had suffered. Mrs. Stowe and her sister advised against this step, but all the more we can conceive of the responsibility accepted by Mrs. Stowe in saving her friend from public obloquy at the moment of her failing health. In finally answering Lady Byron's question Mrs. Stowe wrote: —

On that subject on which you spoke to me the last time we were together, I have thought often and deeply. I have changed my mind somewhat. Considering the peculiar circumstances of the case, I could wish that the sacred veil of silence, so bravely thrown over the past, should never be withdrawn during the time that you remain with us. I would say then, leave all with some discreet friends, who, after both have passed from earth, shall say what was due to justice. I am led to think this by seeing how low, how unworthy, the judgments of this world are; and I would not that what I so much respect, love, and revere should be placed within reach of its harpy claw, which pollutes what it touches. The day will yet come which will bring to light every hidden thing. "There is nothing covered that shall not be revealed, neither hid that shall not be known;" and so justice will not fail.

Such, my dear friend, are my thoughts; different from what they were since first I heard that strange, sad history. Meanwhile I love you forever, whether we meet again on earth or not.

Affectionately yours,   H. B. S.

The subject lay in abeyance in Mrs. Stowe's mind for several years after Lady Byron's death until the publication of the Guiccioli memoirs, succeeded by an article in "Blackwood's Magazine," where Lady Byron was spoken of in a way to sting Mrs. Stowe to the quick.

Nothing more was needed. She arranged the statements given her by Lady Byron and published them in the "Atlantic Monthly," showing them, as we have seen, to Dr. Holmes.

To a more worldly minded person such a step would have been impossible, but to Mrs. Stowe's love and to her sense of right nothing was impossible, and she braved the world for her friend's sake, hardly knowing that she was brave. She always spoke and behaved as if she recognized herself to be an instrument breathed upon by the Divine Spirit. When we consider how this idea absorbed her to the prejudice of what appeared to others a wholesome exercise of human will and judgment, it is not wonderful that the world was offended when she made conclusions contrary to the opinion of the public, and thought best to publish them. But the world could not understand the motives which moved her.

She wrote to Mrs. Howard: "It is worth while to have a *storm* of abuse once in a while, for *one* reason to read the Psalms, — they are a radiant field of glory that never shines unless the night shuts in. Sometimes in my sleep I have such nearness to the blessed, it is almost as if one voice after another whispers to me, 'Thou shalt tread upon the lion and the adder.' 'The eternal God is thy refuge, and underneath thee are the everlasting arms.' . . . It's worth while to have trouble to have friends stand by one as mine do by me. . . . Depend upon it, the spirit of the Lord did n't pitch me into this seething caldron for nothing, and the Son of Man walketh with me in the fire. Eternal right and justice are with me and I shall triumph by and by on the other side of the river and here too. . . . Your letter and one from Sister Mary gave me more support than any other. At first I thought the world's people must have all lost their senses, — or I — *Could* that account be called uncalled-for!"

One is reminded in all this of Tennyson's lines written at about the same epoch, where Arthur says: —

> "And some among you held, that if the King
> Had seen the sight he would have sworn the vow;
> Not easily, seeing that the King must guard
> That which he rules, and is but as the hind
> To whom a space of land is given to plough,
> Who may not wander from the allotted field
> Before his work be done; but being done
> Let visions of the night or of the day
> Come as they will . . .
> In moments when he feels he cannot die."

Perhaps a deeper sense of reverence for poetic genius with which alone the world has learned to concern itself in regard to Byron, would have suggested continued silence and the Scripture warning, "Vengeance is mine, saith the Lord;" but Mrs. Stowe felt her message as from the Most High, and who are we to condemn her?

Meanwhile her legitimate work, "Oldtown Folks," for which the publishers had impatiently waited long after the promised time, was at length fairly off her hands. The book was published in the spring or early summer, and she was free once more.

During the following winter she appeared to enjoy Mandarin with peculiar zest, and wrote contentedly therefrom save for a vision of having to go to Canada in the early spring to obtain the copyright of her story.

The visits to Florida had now become necessary to her
health, and before long she perceived that to pass the
entire season there, and to surrender her large house in
Hartford, was the next step for her to take. She wrote:
"I am leaving the land of flowers on the 1st of June with
tears in my eyes; but having a house in Hartford, it must
be lived in. I wish you and —— would just come to see
it. You have no idea what a lovely place it has grown to
be, and I am trying to sell it as hard as a snake to crawl
out of his skin. Thus on, till reason is pushed out of life.
There's no earthly sense in having anything, — lordy
massy, no! By the bye, I must delay sending you "The
Ghost in the Captain Brown House" till I can go to Natick,
and make a personal inspection of the premises and give it
to you hot."

Her busy brain was again at work with new plans for
future books and articles for magazines. "Gladly would
I fly to you on the wings of the wind," she says, "but I
am a slave, a bound thrall to *work*, and I cannot work
and play at the same time. After this year I hope to
have a little rest, and above all things I won't be hampered with a serial to write. . . . We have sold out in
Hartford."

All this routine of labor was to have a new form of in-
terruption, which gave her intense joy. "I am doing just
what you say," she wrote, "being first lady-in-waiting on
his new majesty. He is very pretty, very gracious and
good, and his little mamma and he are a pair. . . . I am
getting to be an old fool of a grandma, and to think there
is no bliss under heaven to compare with a baby." Later
she wrote on the same subject: "You ought to see my
baby. I have discovered a way to end the woman contro-
versy. Let the women all say that they won't take care
of the babies till the laws are altered. One week of this
discipline would bring all the men on their marrow-bones.

Only tell us what you want, they would say, and we will
do it. Of course you may imagine me trailing after our
little king, — first granny-in-waiting."

Only those who have followed Mrs. Stowe through
the exciting episodes of her life can know what the repose
of those winters in Florida became to her. Her human
interests were still fed and nourished by her wish to help
the freed people and to build a church for them, and poor
as she was herself at this time, she was able through her
busy pen and by writing letters to her friends to get
money enough together to carry out her projects for them.
But she was removed from much of the stress and strain of
life in New England. In spite of all her previous labors
the year 1870 was one of the hardest of her life. She
writes fully on the question to young Mr. Howard, who
was not only her friend, but also a member of a publishing
firm and one of the editors of the "Christian Union:" —

MANDARIN, February, 1870.

George Eliot writes me that she and Mr. Lewes have
both read Henry's sermon, and, lying on their parlor table,
it has often been borrowed and read. . . . I was encouraged, and have sent her another lately on "The Comforting
God." They have just lost a son, — *his* son, not hers,
— but she is a warm-hearted, devoted woman, and was
attached to him as a mother. It is the real religious element, the deep *reality* of a life in God that gives these
things their power, that must give your paper its *distinctive* power, if it is to have any. Every denomination has
its paper, — but there is a yearning after a centralizing
point, a point where all shall feel themselves *one*. That
feeling is the one to which a new religious paper may
address itself with mighty power.

I wish I could settle on a story. I am like a spider
that is puzzled where to attach its threads for a web.

She had invested, she tells him, thirty-four thousand dollars in various ways, none of which could give her any immediate income. She had persuaded Professor Stowe to give up his position in Andover, which she thought too laborious for him, and of course, in consequence, any mention of her difficulties to him was out of the question. There was probably no human being except Mr. Howard to whom she could confide her anxieties and troubles, and she pours herself out to him. During the three previous years Mr. Fields had given her ten thousand dollars for "Oldtown Folks," — much of it in prepayments, that she might write with a mind at leisure. This sum was not sufficient, it appeared, in spite of her calculations, and much to her publisher's dismay she had undertaken, as we have seen, the editorship of "Men of our Times," the completion of "The Pearl of Orr's Island," and had contemplated other projects, while her story sometimes halted altogether, and sometimes progressed under conditions of extreme exhaustion.

All these conditions were renewed with Mr. Howard. She was deeply solicitous for the success of the "Christian Union," of which her brother, Henry Ward Beecher, was called the editor, and where his sermons were published. She believed that a good religious paper was necessary, and she was willing to write for it, as she said, for nothing. On the other hand she had no income for the year. If she would promise a serial story, she asked him, would he guarantee her a certain sum of money every month? Would he accept some very interesting papers from her husband on the Old Testament, to be counted at the same value as her own work? Would he remember how deeply she believed in the necessity of the strictly religious character of the paper and allow her to write a series of unsigned articles on religious topics only? · Indeed, with her poor, tired little hand she wrote a volume

of letters to Mr. Howard during the year, showing the
anxieties which beset her.

"My investment in this Southern place," she wrote, "is
still one whose returns are in the future, and so, as I say,
I need to use my talents to bring an immediate return for
a year or two;" and again she says, "My mind is bubbling
and boiling, and I think of so many stories I could write
that I don't settle upon any." "I see," she writes again,
"you have advertised a serial story from me as one of the
attractions of the year to come, and I ought therefore to
be thinking what to write. On looking back to the time
when 'Uncle Tom's Cabin' came forth, I see myself then
a woman with no particular capital of reputation, driven
to write then as now by the necessity of making some
income for family expenses. In this mood, with a mind
burning with the wrongs of slavery, I undertook to write
some loose sketches of slave life in the 'National Era,' and
out of that attempt grew 'Uncle Tom's Cabin.' If there
had been a grand preparatory blast of trumpets or had it
been announced that Mrs. Stowe would do this or that, I
think it likely I could not have written; but nobody expected anything, nobody said anything, and so I wrote
freely. Now what embarrasses me is to be announced as
an attraction, — to have eyes fixed on me, and people all
waiting. . . . I have a desire, a longing to express myself
once more on a certain subject, but a story ought to *grow*
out of one's heart like a flower and not be measured off by
the yard. . . . There is a misery — a desolation — an
anguish deeper than that of the slave; there is a cause
where every soul ought to be roused, but how to do it?
Temperance stories have been thick as pigweed in rich
land. I think I see how a better one could be written,
but am not sure yet," — and thus the painful effort
went on in her mind. Sometimes she wished to write
about the church, sometimes about society, but something

which publishers and editors needed enough to give her a salary, that was what she must find. Mr. Howard did everything in his power, but the result was she wrote continually upon whatever subject moved her. There was one story called "My Wife and I," which fulfilled the promise of the much hated advertisement, but she threw the weight of her influence upon the religious character of the paper and also secured some valuable contributors. "To have a paper," she wrote, "that, passing with the power of a strong magnet over the confused heap of modern thought, shall make every fragment of pure Christian faith start up and show itself, and come into such nearness that the furnace of love may smelt them all together, that would be something worth praying for." She adds, "Perhaps it must be ready to lose subscribers or get them slowly and not to be a brilliant financial success."

"I feel, the more I think of it, sure that the *world* that hates Christ is just as real in our times as it was in his. Under the various forms of sentimental religion, spiritualism, free inquiry, and philanthropic reform, there is a spirit working that is not subject to the law of God, neither, indeed, can be. How in such a world is a paper, the animus of which is that of Christ and the apostles, to succeed? I have pondered that question in relation to Henry's popularity; but I feel that the world really does *hate* him to a degree that makes it safe to hope that he is about right. Such demonstrations as now and then occur show that they are only waiting for him to be down to spring on him, . . . in proportion as he makes Christianity aggressive on sin they are malignant and spring joyfully on him when their time comes."

She wrote to Mrs. Howard from Florida in January: "I cannot realize what time of year it is. Here the spring is coming on with such a rush that there is no time for anything. I have been down seeing about my own little

flower garden and setting out the plants I brought down
from my greenhouse, and have just finished tying up the
wax plant to the sides of the veranda, where it looks quite
green and handsome. Yesterday we had service in our
mission church for the first time. There has been no
preaching and no religious exercises of any sort except
those held by the negroes, since last May, except one
Sunday. Now we have a neat little building that will
hold three hundred, and yesterday on short notice we got
quite an audience. Mr. Stowe preached. He is going to
hold service for the colored folks in the morning. We
need a bell, as we live so scattered through the woods. I
wish you would inquire what the cost of a small bell
would be. It would be a new sound in these woods, and
if we get it, I shall see that everybody within three miles
shall awake to the consciousness of a ' first bell ' on Sunday morning and a Sunday - school bell and a ' meeting
bell.' I bought a little Mason and Hamlin's organ in
New York and brought it down. H—— plays, and the
others make quite a choir in which I humbly join. . . .
The white school moved into the new building to-day; the
colored school is not yet organized, but you see we are
like to have our hands full. . . . We have had an unusual spell of damp, chilly, sultry weather, which is very
provoking, as our climate is our only strong point. Florida is like a woman whose good temper is her beauty, —
our sunny days are what must cover a multitude of sins,
and when we don't have them, of course the sins have no
cloak. . . . What will the World, the Flesh, and the
Devil do to Henry now that he won't take twenty thousand dollars, and yet has had it *offered!*

"I have had a very handsome letter from Professor
Phelps of Andover, written purposely to express his strong
unqualified sympathy with my course in the Byron matter.
The ' Congregationalist' has also a strong article. But I

don't dwell on that. It is a duty done and left with God who takes care of duties done. I have no more concern with it."

The work of writing her story and other papers promised to the "Christian Union" was not accomplished without painful delays. In the summer she found herself in a weak physical condition. "I must have a little time to recuperate before I begin," she wrote Mr. Howard. "I should do you no good writing feebly. I am not one of those who, if they have three months before them, do not write till almost the end. I have all the plod and regularity about me of a plough horse, and I have worked mostly up towards my engagements, but every hot spell has thrown me upon my back and lasts me sometimes a week or ten days. It is dangerous to try to write when you feel that the brain and spinal system are prostrate or inflamed. There is nothing for it but to *wait* then, and thus I am behindhand. . . . I know all your burdens and worries, and be assured I shall do all I can daily."

At this time her youngest daughter fell under a nervous disease which finally, after many years of intense suffering, ended her life. At first it was "sudden and utter prostration with nervous sleeplessness and such depression of spirits as made her, so gay and buoyant, a distress to look at." The suffering of this illness reacted upon Mrs. Stowe, occupied all her thought, and prevented her from sleep. Happily, as time went on, and she saw her daughter less seldom, she was able to return to her work. "I cannot positively come under binding engagements," she says in October, "to begin my story next month, yet *I think* I shall be ready, unless such heavy blows of family afflictions fall as paralyze me. I wanted to begin with a month's supply ahead. . . . I have not been *writing*, but I have been *composing* the story all this time in the intervals of nursing and tending baby, and now I feel a

degree of assurance respecting it; though I am never sanguine in anything, but am a waiter on Providence.
    "The blow has fallen! My dear brother" (the husband
of her sister Mary, Thomas C. Perkins) "has left us. Nowhere in the world had I a truer friend. It is a blow
that strikes deep on my life and makes me feel that it is
like ice breaking under my feet. Those who truly love us,
and on whom we can at all times depend, are not many,
and all my life he has been one of these."
    From this period, although she continued to write, she
lived chiefly in the retirement of the Florida orange grove,
which she always enjoyed. Her sympathy was strong
with the new impetus benevolent work in cities had received, and she helped it from her "grotto" in more ways
than one. Sometimes she would write soothing or inspiriting letters, as the case might demand, to individuals.
    The following note, written at the time of the Boston
fire in 1872, will show how alive she was to the need of
that period.
    "I send inclosed one hundred dollars to the fund for
the firemen. I could wish it a hundred times as much,
and then it would be inadequate to express how much I
honor those brave, devoted men who put their own lives
between Boston and mine. No soldiers that fell in battle
for our common country ever deserved of us all greater
honor than the noble men whose charred and blackened
remains have been borne from the ruins of Boston; they
are worthy to be inscribed on imperishable monuments.
    "I would that some such honorary memorial might com-
memorate their heroism."
    In the autumn we find her writing to her daughters as
follows regarding her work: —
    "I have at last finished all my part in the third book of
mine that is to come out this year, to wit, 'Oldtown Fireside Stories,' and you can have no idea what a perfect

luxury of rest it is to be free from all literary engagements, of all kinds, sorts, or descriptions.   I feel like a
poor woman I once read about, —

> " ' Who always was tired,
> 'Cause she lived in a house
> Where help was n't hired,'

and of whom it is related that in her dying moments,

> " ' She folded her hands
> With her latest endeavor,
> Saying nothing, dear nothing,
> Sweet nothing forever.'

"I am in about her state of mind.   I luxuriate in laziness.   I do not want to do anything or go anywhere.   I
only want to sink down into lazy enjoyment of living."

"I am very much gratified," she writes Mr. Howard,
"with the success of ' My Wife and I.'   I get a great many
more letters about it than I received about anything except ' Uncle Tom.'   An English novelist has purloined my
title and published ' My Wife and I ' in Queensland.   The
title was a good hit, more shame to him for stealing it.
When you advertise again there is no harm in saying how
many you have sold.   I like people to know it for very
many reasons.   A letter from the Duchess of Argyll to-
day, by which it appears she has been reading it."

She writes, also, to her friend's husband, from Mandarin, after the death of their son Frank: "I hoped fully to
see him down here, but he has gone where the flowers
never fade, —

> " Each new morning ray
> Brings no sigh for yesterday."

This is my idea of heaven, — a land where we can recall
nothing to sigh for; the present overpays the past.

"Of late I have seen the glory so wonderful, — so over-
powering — that it seems too much to be ours, as if one
longed to suffer or endure a little something before one is
weighed down with such an overplus of joy.

"Your Frank, like my Henry, was your heart's flower, and Christ honored each by taking them for his bosom. When you look over a bush for a flower to wear in your bosom, it is not the mildewed or imperfect ones you choose, but the very ones whose loss makes the bush empty. . . . Oh, my dear brother, think of your blessedness by my sorrow. Where is my poor Fred? You know where Frank is, and that he is safe and blessed. I never forget my boy. *Can* a woman forget her child?"

Her son Frederick had remained on the Florida plantation which Mrs. Stowe bought for his sake for several years. At last he was possessed by the idea that a long sea-voyage would do him more good than anything else. He sailed away from New York to San Francisco around the Horn. His brother says: "That he reached the latter city in safety is known; but that is all. No word from him or concerning him has ever reached the loving hearts that have waited so anxiously for it, and of his ultimate fate nothing is known."

In August Mrs. Stowe writes: "I find it is a good thing for me sometimes to fly from place to place, so that I cannot think continuously. It shakes out morbid thoughts and brooding ones, and my nature is such that I need just that to keep the whole stream of thought from running inward. I hope I have learned something on the way to the ' other and better ' to which we are all hastening."

There was at this time a pleasant home at St. John's Wood, in London, which possessed peculiar attractions to the lovers of best society. Other houses were as comfortable to look at, other hedges were as green, other drawing-rooms were gayer, but this was the home of George Eliot, and on Sunday afternoons the resort of those who desired the best that London had to give. Here it was that she told me of her admiration and deep regard, her affec-

tion, for Mrs. Stowe.   Her reverence and love were expressed with such tremulous sincerity that the speaker won
our hearts by her love for our friend.   Many letters had
already passed between Mrs. Stowe and herself, and she
confided to us her amusement at a fancy Mrs. Stowe had
taken that Casaubon, in "Middlemarch," was drawn from
the character of Mr. Lewes.   Mrs. Stowe took it so entirely
for granted in her letters that it was impossible to dis-
possess her mind of the illusion.   Evidently it was the
source of much harmless household amusement at St. John's
Wood.   I find in Mrs. Stowe's letters some pleasant allusions to this correspondence.   She writes: "We were all
full of George Eliot when your note came, as I had received a beautiful letter from her in answer to one I wrote
from Florida.   She is a noble, true woman; and if anybody does n't see it, so much the worse for *them*, and not
her."   Again Mrs. Stowe says she is coming to Boston,
and will bring George Eliot's letters with her that we may
read them together; but that pleasant plan was only one
of the imagination, and was never carried out.

Later George Eliot wrote Mrs. Stowe to comfort her anxieties about the success of "Oldtown Folks" in England:

"I have good hopes that your fears are groundless as to
the obstacles your new book ('Oldtown Folks') may find
here from its thorough American character.   Most readers
who are likely to be really influenced by writing above the
common order will find that special aspect an added reason
for interest and study; and I dare say you have long seen,
as I am beginning to see with new clearness, that if a book
which has any sort of exquisiteness happens also to be a
popular, widely circulated book, the power over the social
mind for any good is, after all, due to its reception by a
few appreciative natures, and is the slow result of radiation
from that narrow circle.   I mean that you can affect a
few souls, and that each of these in turn may affect a few

more, but that no exquisite book tells properly and directly
on a multitude, however largely it may be spread by type
and paper. Witness the things the multitude will say
about it, if one is so unhappy as to be obliged to hear their
sayings. I do not write this cynically, but in pure sadness and pity. Both traveling abroad and staying at home
among our English sights and sports, one must continually
feel how slowly the centuries work toward the moral good
of men, and that thought lies very close to what you say
as to your wonder or conjecture concerning my religious
point of view. I believe that religion, too, has to be
modified according to the dominant phases; that a religion
more perfect than any yet prevalent must express less care
of personal consolation, and the more deeply awing sense
of responsibility to man springing from sympathy with
that which of all things is most certainly known to us, —
the difficulty of the human lot. Letters are necessarily
narrow and fragmentary, and, when one writes on wide
subjects, are likely to create more misunderstanding than
illumination. But I have little anxiety in writing to you,
dear friend and fellow-laborer; for you have had longer
experience than I as a writer, and fuller experience as
a woman, since you have borne children and known a
mother's history from the beginning. I trust your quick
and long-taught mind as an interpreter little liable to
mistake me."

Mrs. Stowe replies: —

MANDARIN, February 8, 1872.

DEAR FRIEND, — It is two years nearly since I had
your last very kind letter, and I have never answered because two years of constant and severe work have made it
impossible to give a drop to anything beyond the needs of
the hour. Yet I have always thought of you, loved you,
trusted you all the same, and read every little scrap from
your writing that came to hand.

One thing brings you back to me. I am now in Florida in my little hut in the orange orchard, with the broad expanse of the blue St. John's in front, and the waving of the live-oaks with their long, gray mosses overhead, and the bright gold of oranges looking through dusky leaves around. It is like Sorrento, — so like that I can quite dream of being there. And when I get here I enter another life. The world recedes — I am out of it; it ceases to influence; its bustle and noise die away in the far distance; and here is no winter, an open-air life, — a quaint, rude, wild wilderness sort of life, both rude and rich: but when I am here I write more letters to friends than ever I do elsewhere. The mail comes only twice a week, and then is the event of the day. My old rabbi and I here set up our tent, he with German, and Greek, and Hebrew, devouring all sorts of black-letter books, and I spinning ideal webs out of bits that he lets fall here and there.

I have long thought that I would write you again when I got here, and so I do. I have sent North to have them send me the "Harper's Monthly," in which your new story is appearing, and have promised myself leisurely to devour and absorb every word of it.

.   .   .   .

In regard to the subject of Spiritualism I am of the opinion of Goethe that "it is just as absurd to deny the facts of Spiritualism now as it was in the middle ages to ascribe them to the devil."

I think Mr. Owen attributes too much value to his facts. I do not think the things contributed from the ultra-mundane sphere are particularly valuable, apart from the evidence they give of continued existence after death.

I do not think there is yet any evidence to warrant the idea that they are a supplement or continuation of the revelations of Christianity, but I do regard them as an interesting and curious study in psychology. . . . I am

perfectly aware of the frivolity and worthlessness of much
of the revealings purporting to come from spirits. In my
view, the worth or worthlessness of them has nothing to
do with the question of fact.

Do invisible spirits speak in any wise, — wise or foolish ? — is the question *a priori.* I do not know of any
reason why there should not be as many foolish virgins in
the future state as in this. As I am a believer in the
Bible and Christianity, I don't need these things as confir-
mations, and they are not likely to be a religion to me.
I regard them simply as I do the phenomena of the Aurora
Borealis, or Darwin's studies on natural selection, as curious studies into nature. Besides, I think some day we
shall find a law by which all these facts will fall into their
places.

I hope now this subject does not bore you; it certainly
is one that seems increasingly to insist on getting itself
heard. It is going on and on, making converts, who are
many more than dare avow themselves, and for my part
I wish it were all brought into the daylight of inquiry.

Let me hear from you if ever you feel like it. I know
too well the possibilities and impossibilities of a nature
like yours to ask more, but it can do you no harm to know
that I still think of you and love you as ever.

Faithfully yours,   H. B. Stowe.

Mrs. Stowe paid a visit to her brother Charles in Florida
during the winter, and, continuing her journey to New
Orleans, was made to feel how little of bitterness towards
her was felt by the best class of Southerners. In both
New Orleans and Tallahassee she was warmly welcomed,
and tendered public receptions that gave equal pleasure to
her and to the throngs of cultivated people who attended
them. She was also greeted everywhere with intense enthusiasm by the colored people, who, whenever they knew of

her coming, thronged the railway stations in order to obtain
a glimpse of her whom they venerated above all women.

Finding by George Eliot's former letter that she was
not quite well, Mrs. Stowe wrote again: —

(Begun April 4.)   MANDARIN, FLORIDA, May 11.

MY DEAR FRIEND, — I was very glad to get your dear
little note, — sorry to see by it that you are not in your
full physical force.   Owing to the awkwardness and misunderstanding of publishers, I am not reading "Middlemarch," as I expected to be, here in these orange shades;
they don't send it, and I am too far out of the world
to get it.   I felt, when I read your letters, how glad I
should be to have you here in our Florida cottage, in the
wholly new, wild, woodland life.   Though resembling
Italy in climate, it is wholly different in the appearance
of nature, — the plants, the birds, the animals, all different.   The green tidiness and culture of England here
gives way to a wild and rugged savageness of beauty.
Every tree bursts forth with flowers; wild vines and
creepers execute delicious gambols, and weave and inter-
weave in interminable labyrinths.   Yet here, in the great
sandy plains back of our house, there is a constant sense
of beauty in the wild, wonderful growths of nature.   First
of all, the pines — high as the stone pines of Italy — with
long leaves, eighteen inches long, through which there is
a constant dreamy sound, as if of dashing waters.   Then
the live-oaks and the water-oaks, narrow-leaved evergreens,
which grow to enormous size, and whose branches are
draped with long festoons of the gray moss.   There is a
great, wild park of these trees back of us, which, with the
dazzling, varnished green of the new spring leaves and the
swaying drapery of moss, looks like a sort of enchanted
grotto.   Underneath grow up hollies and ornamental flowering shrubs, and the yellow jessamine climbs into and

over everything with fragrant golden bells and buds, so that sometimes the foliage of a tree is wholly hidden in its embrace.

This wild, wonderful, bright and vivid growth, that is all new, strange, and unknown by name to me, has a charm for me. It is the place to forget the outside world, and live in one's self. And if you were here, we would go together and gather azaleas, and white lilies, and silver bells, and blue iris. These flowers keep me painting in a sort of madness. I have just finished a picture of white lilies that grow in the moist land by the watercourses. I am longing to begin on blue iris. Artist, poet as you are by nature, you ought to see all these things, and if you would come here I would take you in, heart and house, and you should have a little room in our cottage. The history of the cottage is this: I found a hut built close to a great live-oak twenty-five feet in girth, and with overarching boughs eighty feet up in the air, spreading like a firmament, and all swaying with mossy festoons. We began to live here, and gradually we improved the hut by lath, plaster, and paper. Then we threw out a wide veranda all round, for in these regions the veranda is the living-room of the house. Ours had to be built around the trunk of the tree, so that our cottage has a peculiar and original air, and seems as if it were half tree, or a something that had grown out of the tree. We added on parts, and have thrown out gables and chambers, as a tree throws out new branches, till our cottage is like nobody else's, and yet we settle into it with real enjoyment. There are all sorts of queer little rooms in it, and we are accommodating at this present a family of seventeen souls. In front, the beautiful, grand St. John's stretches five miles from shore to shore, and we watch the steamboats plying back and forth to the great world we are out of. On all sides, large orange-trees, with their dense shade and ever-vivid green,

shut out the sun so that we can sit, and walk, and live in
the open air. Our winter here is only cool, bracing out-
door weather, without snow. No month without flowers
blooming in the open air, and lettuce and peas in the garden. The summer range is about 90°, but the sea-breezes
keep the air delightfully fresh. Generally we go North,
however, for three months of summer. Well, I did not
mean to run on about Florida, but the subject runs away
with me, and I want you to visit us in spirit if not personally.

My poor rabbi! — he sends you some Arabic, which I
fear you cannot read: on diablerie he is up to his ears in
knowledge, having read all things in all tongues, from the
Talmud down. . . .

Ever lovingly yours,   H. B. STOWE.

BOSTON, September 26, 1872.

MY DEAR FRIEND, — I think when you see my name
again so soon, you will think it rains, hails, and snows
notes from this quarter. Just now, however, I am in this
lovely little nest in Boston, where dear ——, like a dove,
"sits brooding on the charmèd wave." We are both wishing we had you here with us, and she has not received any
answer from you as yet in reply to the invitation you
spoke of in your last letter to me. It seems as if you
must have written, and the letter somehow gone astray,
because I know, of course, you would write. Yesterday
we were both out of our senses with mingled pity and
indignation at that dreadful stick of a Casaubon, — and
think of poor Dorothea dashing like a warm, sunny wave
against so cold and repulsive a rock! He is a little too
dreadful for anything; there does not seem to be a drop
of warm blood in him, and so, as it is his misfortune and
not his fault to be cold-blooded, one must not get angry
with him. It is the scene in the garden, after the inter-

view with the doctor, that rests on our mind at this present. There was such a man as he over in Boston, high in literary circles, but I fancy his wife was n't like Dorothea, and a vastly proper time they had of it, treating each other with mutual reverence, like two Chinese mandarins.

My love, what I miss in this story is just what we would have if you would come to our tumble-down, jolly, improper, but joyous country, — namely, "jollitude." You write and live on so high a plane! It is all self-abnegation. We want to get you over here, and into this house, where, with closed doors, we sometimes make the rafters ring with fun, and say anything and everything, no matter what, and won't be any properer than we 's a mind to be. I am wishing every day you could see our America, — travel, as I have been doing, from one bright, thriving, pretty, flowery town to another, and see so much wealth, ease, progress, culture, and all sorts of nice things. This dovecot where I now am is the sweetest little nest imaginable; fronting on a city street, with back windows opening on a sea view, with still, quiet rooms filled with books, pictures, and all sorts of things, such as you and Mr. Lewes would enjoy. Don't be afraid of the ocean, now! I 've crossed it six times, and assure you it is an overrated item. Froude is coming here — why not you? Besides, we have the fountain of eternal youth here, that is, in Florida, where I live, and if you should come you would both of you take a new lease of life, and what glorious poems, and philosophies, and whatnot, we should have! My rabbi writes, in the seventh heaven, an account of your note to him. To think of his setting-off on his own account when I was away!

Come now, since your answer to dear Mrs. Fields is yet to come, let it be a glad yes, and we will clasp you to our heart of hearts.

Your ever loving,   H. B. S.

The following season she wrote with her usual sense of calm from Florida: —

"I am writing as a pure recreative movement of mind, to divert myself from the stormy, unrestful present. . . . I am being *chatelaine* of a Florida farm. I have on my mind the creation of a town on the banks of the St. John. The three years since we came this side of the river have called into life and growth a thousand peach-trees, a thousand orange-trees, about five hundred lemons, and seven or eight hundred grapevines. A peach orchard, a vineyard, a lemon grove, will carry my name to posterity. I am founding a place which, thirty or forty years hence, will be called the old Stowe place. . . . You can have no idea of this queer country, this sort of strange, sandy, half-tropical dreamland, unless you come to it. Here I sit with open windows, the orange buds just opening and filling the air with sweetness, the hens drowsily cackling, the men planting in the field, and callas and wild roses blossoming out of doors. We keep a little fire morning and night. We are flooded with birds; and by the bye, it is St. Valentine's Day. . . . I think a uniform edition of Dr. Holmes's works would be a good thing. Next to Hawthorne he is our most exquisite writer, and in many passages he goes far beyond him. What is the dear Doctor doing? If you know any book good to inspire dreams and visions, put it into my box. My husband chews endlessly a German cud. I must have English. Has the French book on Spiritualism come yet? If it has, put it in. . . . I wish I could give you a plateful of our oranges. . . . We had seventy-five thousand of these same on our trees this year, and if you will start off quick, they are not all picked yet. Florida wants one thing, — grass. If it had grass, it would be paradise. But nobody knows what grass is till they try to do without it."

Three months later she wrote: "I hate to leave my

calm isle of Patmos, where the world is not, and I have such quiet long hours for writing. Emerson could *insulate* himself here and keep his electricity. Hawthorne ought to have lived in an orange grove in Florida. . . . You have no idea how small you all look, you folks in the world, from this distance. All your fusses and your fumings, your red hot hurrying newspapers, your clamor of rival magazines, — why, we see it as we see steamboats fifteen miles off, a mere speck and smoke."

Again she writes: "You ought to see us riding out in our mule-cart. Poor 'Fly!' the last of pea-time, who looks like an animated hair-trunk, and the wagon and harness to match! It is too funny, but we enjoy it hugely. There are now in our solitude five Northern families, and we manage to have quite pleasant society.

"But think of our church and school house being burned down just as we were ready to do something with it. I feel it most for the colored people, who were so anxious to have their school and now have no place to have it in. We have all been trying to raise what we can for a new building and intend to get one up by March.

"If I were North now I would try giving some readings for this and perhaps raise something."

CHAPTER XII

IT was a strange contrast to Mrs. Stowe's usual life, and one at variance with her natural taste, when she appeared before the public as a reader of her own stories in the autumn and winter of 1872–73. She was no longer able to venture on the effort of a long story, therefore it was manifestly unwise for her to forego the income which was offered through this proposed channel. She wrote to her friends in Boston: "I have had a very urgent business letter, saying that the lyceums of different towns were making up their engagements, and that if I were going into it I must make my engagements now. It seems to me that I cannot do this. The thing will depend so much on my health and ability to do. You know I could not go round in cold weather. . . . I feel entirely uncertain, and, as the Yankees say, 'did n't know what to do nor to don't.' My state in regard to it may be described by the phrase 'Kind o' love to — hate to — wish I did n't — want ter.' I suppose the result will be I shall not work into their lecture system."

In April she wrote from Mandarin: "I am painting a *Magnolia grandiflora*, which I will show you. . . . I am appalled by finding myself booked to read. But I am getting well and strong, and trust to be equal to the emergency. But I shrink from Tremont Temple, and —— does not think I can fill it. On the whole I should like to begin in Boston." And in August she said: "I am to begin in Boston in September. . . . It seems to me that

is a little too early for Boston, isn't it? Will there be
anybody in town then? I don't know as it's my business, which is simply to speak my piece and take my
money."

Her first reading actually took place in Springfield, not
Boston, and the next day she unexpectedly arrived at our
cottage at Manchester-by-the-Sea. She had read the previous evening in a large public hall, had risen at five
o'clock that morning, and found her way to us. Her next
readings were given in Boston, the first in the afternoon,
at the Tremont Temple. She was conscious that her
effort at Springfield had not been altogether successful, —
she had not held her large audience; and she was determined to put the whole force of her nature into this afternoon reading at the Tremont Temple. She called me into
her bedroom, where she stood before the mirror, with her
short gray hair, which usually lay in soft curls around her
brow, brushed erect and standing stiffly. "Look here,
my dear," she said; "now I am exactly like my father,
Dr. Lyman Beecher, when he was going to preach," and
she held up her forefinger warningly. It was easy to see
that the spirit of the old preacher was revived in her
veins, and the afternoon would show something of his
power. An hour later, when I sat with her in the ante-
room waiting for the moment of her appearance to arrive,
I could feel the power surging up within her. I knew
she was armed for a good fight.

That reading was a great success. She was alive in
every fibre of her being; she was to give portions of
"Uncle Tom's Cabin" to men, women, and children who
could hardly understand the crisis which inspired it, and
she determined to effect the difficult task of making them
feel as well as hear. With her presence and inspiration
they could not fail to understand what her words had sig-
nified to the generation that had passed through the strug-

gle of our war.   When her voice was not sufficient to
make the audience hear, men and women rose from their
seats and crowded round her, standing gladly, that no
word might be lost.   It was the last leap of the flame
which had burned out a great wrong.

One of her lively and observant hearers in another city
described Mrs. Stowe as "small in stature, with a complexion bordering on the blonde, and with the merriest twinkle
in her eye, betokening a reservoir of fun and mirth sufficient to explode a funeral assembly with laughter. . . .
In some parts of the scene between Eva and Topsy, she
reached the hearts of her audience, and many a tear was
pushed out of sight by finger tips and umbrella handles.

"In ' part third,' " continues this writer, " ' Laughing in
Meeting,' a constant ripple of laughter followed her reading till she reached the point where the deacon was sent
sprawling in the centre aisle of the church, when the entire
audience ' broke out ' and shook the hall with laughter and
applause."

These readings were conducted for her by a Lecture
Bureau, who made her a very liberal offer if she would
give forty readings in the New England States.   She
agreed to this plan with the understanding that the readings should be over before December in order to allow her
to go at once to Florida.

She wrote to her husband during this tour at a time
when he was peculiarly depressed, from Westfield, Massachusetts: —

"I have never had a greater trial than being forced to
stay away from you now.   I would not, but that my
engagements have involved others in heavy expense, and
should I fail to fulfill them, it would be doing a wrong.

"God has given me strength as I needed it, and I never
read more to my own satisfaction than last night.

"Now, my dear husband, please do *want*, and try, to

remain with us yet a while longer, and let us have a little quiet evening together before either of us crosses the river. My heart cries out for a home with you; our home to-gether in Florida. Oh, may we see it again! Your ever loving wife."

Again she told him that she had driven to Chelsea and found no hotel there. "So," she continues, "I turned at once toward 148 Charles Street, where I tumbled in on the Fieldses before they had got their things off. We had a good laugh, and I received a hearty welcome. I was quickly installed in my room, where, after a nice dinner, I curled up for my afternoon nap. At half past seven the carriage came for me, and I was informed that I should not have a hard reading, as they had engaged singers to take part. So, when I got into the carriage, who should I find, beshawled, and beflowered, and betoggled in blue satin and white lace, but ——, now become Madame Thingumbob, of European celebrity. She had studied in Italy, come out in Milan, sung there in opera for a whole winter, and also in Paris and London.

"Well, she sings very sweetly and looks very nice and pretty. Then we had a little rosebud of a Chelsea girl who sang, and a pianist. I read 'Minister's House-keeper' and Topsy, and the audience was very jolly and appreciative. Then we all jogged home."

"One woman in Portland the other night," she wrote again, "totally deaf, came to me afterwards and said: 'Bless you. I come jist to see you. I'd rather see you than the Queen.' Another introduced her little girl named Harriet Beecher Stowe, and another, older, named Eva. She said they had traveled fifty miles to hear me read. An incident like that appeals to one's heart, does it not?

"The people of Bangor were greatly embarrassed by the horse disease; but the mayor and his wife walked over from their house, a long distance off, to bring me flowers, and at the reading he introduced me. I had an excellent audience, notwithstanding that it rained tremendously, and everybody had to walk because there were no horses. The professors called on me, also Newman Smyth, now a settled minister here.

"It stormed all the time I was in Portland and Bangor, so I saw nothing of them. Now I am in a palace car riding alongside the Kennebec, and recalling the incidents of my trip. I certainly had very satisfactory houses; and these pleasant little visits, and meetings with old acquaintance, would be well worth having, even though I had made nothing in a pecuniary sense. On the whole it is as easy a way of making money as I have ever tried, though no way of making money is perfectly easy, — there must be some disagreeables. The lonesomeness of being at a hotel in dull weather is one, and in Portland it seems there is nobody now to invite us to their homes. Our old friends there are among the past. They have gone on over the river. I send you a bit of poetry that pleases me. The love of the old for each other has its poetry. It is something sacred and full of riches. I long to be with you and to have some more of our good long talks.

"The Lord bless and keep you. It grieves me to think you are dull and I not with you. By and by we will be together and stay together. Good-by, dear. Your ever loving wife,   H. B. S."

She continues in another letter to her husband: —

"Well, my course is almost done, and if I get through without any sickness, cold, or accident, how wonderful it will seem. I have never felt the near, kind presence of our Heavenly Father so much as in this. 'He giveth strength to the faint, and to them of no might He increaseth strength.' I have found this true all my life."

From Newport she writes, November 26: —

"It was a hard, tiring, disagreeable piece of business to read in New London. Had to wait three mortal hours in Palmer. Then a slow, weary train, that did not reach New London until after dark. There was then no time to rest, and I was so tired that it did seem as though I could not dress. I really trembled with fatigue. The hall was long and dimly lighted, and the people were not seated compactly, but around in patches. The light was dim, except for a great flaring gas jet arranged right under my eyes on the reading desk, and I did not see a creature whom I knew. I was only too glad when it was over and I was back again at my hotel. There I found that I must be up at five o'clock to catch the Newport train.

"I started for this place in the dusk of a dreary, foggy morning. Traveled first on a ferry, then in cars, and then in a little cold steamboat. Found no one to meet me, in spite of all my writing, and so took a carriage and came to the hotel. The landlord was very polite to me, said he knew me by my trunk, had been to our place in Mandarin, etc. All I wanted was a warm room, a good bed, and unlimited time to sleep. Now I have had a three hours' nap, and here I am, sitting by myself in the great, lonely hotel parlor.

"Well, dear old man, I think lots of you, and only want to end all this in a quiet home where we can sing 'John Anderson, my Jo' together. I check off place after place as the captive the days of his imprisonment. Only two more after to-night. Ever your loving wife."

These difficult experiences of which she made so light were continued one more year. She wrote to her son Charles, then in Harvard, in October, 1873: —

"I read two successive evenings in Chicago, and traveled the following day for thirteen hours, a distance of about three hundred miles, to Cincinnati. We were compelled

to go in the most uncomfortable cars I ever saw, crowded
to overflowing, a fiend of a stove at each end burning up
all the air, and without a chance to even lay my head
down.   This is the grand route between Chicago and Cincinnati, and we were on it from eight in the morning until
nearly ten at night.

.   .   .   .

"Those who planned my engagements failed to take into
account the fearful distances and wretched trains out here.
On none of these great Western routes is there a drawing-
room car.   Mr. Saunders tried in every way to get them
to put one on for us, but in vain.   They are all reserved
for the night trains; so that there is no choice except to
travel by night in sleeping cars, or take such trains as I
have described in the daytime.

"I had a most sympathetic audience in Cincinnati; they
all seemed delighted and begged me to come again.   The
next day George took us for a drive out to Walnut Hills,
where we saw the seminary buildings, the house where
your sisters were born, and the house in which we afterwards lived.   In the afternoon we had to leave and hurry
away to a reading in Dayton.   The next evening another
in Columbus, where we spent Sunday with an old friend.

"By this time I am somewhat rested from the strain
of that awful journey; but I shall never again undertake
such another.   It was one of those things that have to be
done once, to learn not to do it again.   My only reading
between Columbus and Pittsburgh is to be here in Zanes-
ville, a town as black as Acheron, and where one might
expect to see the river Styx.

.   .   .   .

"I met the other day at Dayton a woman who now has
grandchildren; but who, when I first came West, was a
gay, rattling girl.   She was one of the first converts of
brother George's seemingly obscure ministry in the little

new town of Chillicothe. Now she has one son who is a judge of the supreme court, and another in business. Both she and they are not only Christians, but Christians of the primitive sort, whose religion is their all; who triumph and glory in tribulation, knowing that it worketh patience. She told me, with a bright sweet calm, of her husband killed in battle the first year of the war, of her only daughter and two grandchildren dying in the faith, and of her own happy waiting on God's will, with bright hopes of a joyful reunion. Her sons are leading members of the Presbyterian Church, and most active in stirring up others to make their profession a reality, not an empty name. When I thought that all this came from the conversion of one giddy girl, when George seemed to be doing so little, I said, 'Who can measure the work of a faithful minister?' It is such living witnesses that maintain Christianity on earth."

At last Mrs. Stowe was again installed in the calm of her Florida home, where she wrote a series of Florida sketches, called "Palmetto Leaves." She sends a note to her brother Charles at Newport, Florida: —

"I cannot leave Florida without saying good-by. I send you the 'Palmetto Leaves' and my parting love. If I could either have brought or left my husband, I should have come to see you this winter. The account of your roses fills me with envy.

"We leave on the San Jacinto next Saturday, and I am making the most of the few charming hours yet left; for never did we have so delicious a spring. I never knew such altogether perfect weather. It is enough to make a saint out of the toughest old Calvinist that ever set his face as a flint. How do you think New England theology would have fared if our fathers had been landed here instead of on Plymouth Rock?

"The next you hear of me will be at the North, where

our address is Forest Street, Hartford. We have bought
a pretty cottage there, near to Belle, and shall spend the
summer there."

Again this heart, which was never allowed to rest from
ceaseless anxieties, was to be put to another proof. Mrs.
Stowe wrote to her friend, Mrs. Howard: —

"We are on our way to Cambridge for Charley's Class
Day, and of course my heart and hands are full of his
feelings and joys and interests. . . . But amid all these
scenes there is a deep undercurrent of fellow-suffering
with you all in this great trial, and my heart is constantly
ascending in silent prayer. I prayed without ceasing for
Henry, that his strength, health, and courage might not
fail, and when I saw the report of the Friday night meeting I was comforted. I saw that God was manifestly
with you, and since then my heart has been at rest. But
I am all on fire to hear more, and cannot buy a 'Tribune.'"

The notorious scandal aroused against her brother,
Henry Ward Beecher, has been very clearly outlined by
the Rev. Lyman Abbott, D. D. It may be considered
that Mr. Abbott has made the final report. He has
studied the subject and sifted the evidence with the careful conscience of a man of truth, and his words may well
be reprinted here to make the reasons for Mrs. Stowe's
sufferings and consolations more distinct to future readers.

Dr. Abbott says: "It is certain no other man in America
could have lived and retained his position and influence
through such a scandal. . . . He had formerly been editor
of the 'Independent,' but had resigned in favor of Mr.
Tilton, who for some years was extremely successful and
popular, but at last fell under a cloud. Finding his own
morality impeached, he adopted the peculiar defense of
darkly insinuating that Mr. Beecher (who was now the
successful editor of the 'Christian Union') was open to

grave suspicion in the same direction. He determined
to drive him from his pulpit, and the city, accused Mr.
Beecher of improper advances to his wife, whispered to
his friends that Mrs. Tilton had become the victim of a
morbid passion, which had utterly wrecked her happiness
and health. This last coming to Mr. Beecher's ears, he
believed he had not been sufficiently discreet, and with
the instinct of a true gentleman overwhelmed himself with
reproaches both by word and by letter. . . . Finally a
direct charge appeared against him in the newspapers;
whereupon he appointed a committee to look into the
matter, consisting of some of the most eminent and re-
spected members of his church and society. They reported
unanimously, after giving Mr. Tilton a full hearing, that
the charge was entirely false. . . . Tilton, however,
brought an action at law; the trial lasted six months, when
Mr. Beecher was entirely acquitted. The suit was never
tried again.

.   .   .   .

"A council of Congregational churches and ministers was
then called in Plymouth Church, . . . including many
men of strong prejudices against Mr. Beecher on theological grounds, and some men full of suspicions engendered
by the trial and public reports. . . . After nearly a week
spent in a most thorough and scrutinizing inquiry, it extended to Mr. Beecher, without a dissenting voice, the confidence of the entire council in his integrity. The whole
affair was complicated in the public mind by Mr. Beecher's
unwisdom in the selection of some confidential friends at
this trying period of his life, prior to the first publication
of the scandal, and by his evident endeavor to keep it from
becoming public, an endeavor not only not strange, but
abundantly justified by the injurious effects of its publication.

.   .   .   .

"Dreadful as was the ordeal through which Mr. Beecher was dragged, and fearful as his sufferings must have been at times, the sufferings of his people were little less than agony. Strong men with faltering voice and falling tears attested the sympathy and intense love of his people for their pastor, and how completely they made his trouble their own. His support, serenity, and cheerfulness, his ability to preach as he did every Sabbath during those dark, dark months, showing almost no appearance of wear or suffering, was, and still is, an unsolved wonder to those who did not see the position occupied by his church. Its members suffered more than the pastor. Their prayers and sympathies buoyed him up, rendering him almost unconscious of the malignant billows that were dashing against him. During those dreadful days no one ever intruded upon Mr. Beecher; the love and sympathy of his people were not kept alive by personal intercourse with him, and not one in a hundred of his people had a moment's conversation with him then or since about these fearful troubles."

No one can understand the life of Mrs. Stowe without some knowledge of this trial. If his people suffered, if Plymouth Church prayed, what were her sufferings and prayers, whose existence was so bound up in affection for her brother! Her strength, continually tried to the full by the daily work at her desk, visibly failed. She sought refuge as much as possible in Florida, where, remote from newspapers and the battle of the world, her exhausted forces found space to recuperate. She wrote once: "Christ says, that amid the vaster ruins of man's desolation, ruins more dreadfully suggestive than those of sculptured frieze and architrave, we can yet live a bird's life of unconscious joy; or as Martin Luther beautifully paraphrases it, 'We can be like a bird that sits singing on his twig and lets God think for him.'"

Her confidence in her brother was never for a moment shaken, but she could neither write much nor speak with him.   Her friends, Mr. and Mrs. Howard, at this crisis gave her great comfort.   She wrote to Mrs. Howard: —

"Tell me how Henry is, — how you all are.   I am increasing in the hope and belief that the Lord will yet manifest himself and scatter this wicked host.   Prayer and hope are our trust.   Lately I have thought often of what the Lord said to Moses when the army of Pharaoh was behind, the mountains on one side, and the sea in front, and the rebellious people cried to God: 'Wherefore liest thou on thy face?   Speak unto the children of Israel, that they go forward.'   They went forward and the sea divided for them, but drowned their adversaries.   It is for us these things were done.   We are heirs of them that through faith and patience inherit the promises."

It was in this spirit that she endured the agony which had fallen upon her in behalf of her beloved brother. From the Twin Mountain House, where she had been with Mr. Beecher, she wrote: "We leave to-morrow, and you must not fail to be at home.   There is preparing a reception for Henry that shall show him, on his return, how his people feel.   I am coming down, and we Plymouthites must all be together and have one sing.   We have had serene and lovely times here sitting in heavenly places; prayers every morning with so many of the church around that it seemed quite natural; some also of the best and loveliest of our land.   Not a breath of the slander reaches here.   Sundays, there is great crowding to hear the word! Twenty-four or five cars! and so much tenderness and emotion and love!   Truly it has been good to be here!"

DEAR SUSIE, — Suffer a word!   This crisis must be met in the closet and with the Father that seeth in secret. All looking here and there, rushing to and fro, listening to *reports*, guesses, apprehensions, only exhaust the strength, and take away the power of endurance. Thank God, He not only can help, but is not displeased to be importuned. If God could be wearied and made impatient by importunity, it were hard with us when we have troubles that will not let us rest, and keep us saying the same thing again and again. But He, our Lord, prayed in an agony three times, saying the same words. . . . God bless you, and help us all.

I have been thinking much how Christ, when they were binding Him, asked a moment's delay that He might touch the ear of Malchus and *heal* him.

What unruffled sweetness of nature was in this! Malchus perhaps was forward and provoking, and thus drew on himself the attack of Peter; but Christ was, as He is always, not a destructive but a healing force. Across all this gulf of misery and scandal and sin that has swallowed so many who seemed to be Christ's, I look and pray for his healing power.

I cannot but look on T——'s history as most pitiable and no subject for scorn. . . .

> "Scorn! would the angels laugh to see
> A bright soul driven
> Fiend-dragged adown the awful track
> To Hell from Heaven!"

Some of his letters, written in better moments, reminding me that he had been at our prayer-meetings and our sacraments . . . fill me with a sense of the pitiableness of his mind. Then, too, he is the father of those poor, innocent children, the husband of that poor wife. . . . I have read a great deal in "Pilgrim's Progress" lately, and his case seems to me like that of the man in the iron cage.

The man said, "'I was once a fair and flourishing professor of religion both in my own eyes and those of others. I was once, as I thought, fair for the Celestial City and had

then even joy at the thought that I should get thither.'
'Well, but what art thou now?' 'I am now a man of
despair. I am shut up in this iron cage. I cannot get
out! Oh, now I cannot!' 'But how camest thou in this
condition?' 'I left off to watch and be sober; I laid the
reins on the neck of my lusts; I sinned against the light
of the word and the goodness of God. I grieved the
Spirit and He is gone. I tempted the devil and he is
come to me; I have provoked God to anger, and He has
left me; I have hardened my heart so that I cannot re-
pent.'"

This to all human view is his miserable state. . . .
I have been quite unwell for two days, and no letter
comes! . . . Meanwhile, faithful friend, cease not to
write, for your letters are as cold water to a thirsty soul.

Again she says: "I find since Henry's testimony that it
is impossible for me to pray for ——. Do you suppose Mary
and John joined in the 'Father, forgive them,' when they
saw the nails driven? No! I pray, 'Oh, God, to whom
vengeance belongeth, lift up Thyself!' . . . Pity me and
stick to me, to the end. I am perfectly heartsick and
homesick to be with you once more, but when I consider
that Mr. Stowe is pastor and preacher, and that the Sunday services, Sunday-school, and all, depend on us, I feel
it would be a mere yielding to my feelings to leave our
few poor sheep in the wilderness."

Later in the same year she writes from Hartford: "I
am more and more impressed with a sense of the dreadful,
irreparable wrong and injustice this wicked husband has
done to his wife, and which to her is deadly; for as he
forced her into sinful and weak compliances, he did the
greatest injury to her possible to a human being. God
only knows the limit of endurance, but I think she is to
be judged of as the poor witches who, under torture, sleep-

lessness, and exhaustion, criminated themselves and others at the will of barbarous persecutors. . . . The way the slanderer of St. Francis de Sales was brought to confess often occurs to me, and I beg and pray that something like that be done in this case."

To her sister Mary she says: "To think that Henry, who never would listen to an indelicate word, who has kept all this nauseous thing out of his mind, being obliged to sit in open court and have this foulness dribbled out before him! It seems as if it was not permitted to him to avoid drinking this most nauseous cup to the dregs. If he can pity and forgive *now* he does it with his eyes open and with full consciousness of what he forgives."

Happily there was always Florida, bright beautiful soothing Florida, to help her through the deep waves of trouble, and there were also the letters of her friends.

She writes: "We have had heavenly weather, and we needed it; for our house was a cave of spider-webs, cock-roaches, dirt, and all abominations, but less than a week has brought it into beautiful order. It now begins to put on that quaint, lively, pretty air that so fascinates me. Our weather is, as I said, heavenly, neither hot nor cold; cool, calm, bright, serene, and so tranquillizing. There is something indescribable about the best weather we have down here. It does not debilitate me like the soft October air in Hartford."

During the following February she writes in reply to an invitation to visit a Northern watering-place later in the season: "I shall be most happy to come, and know of nothing to prevent. I have, thank goodness, no serial story on hand for this summer, to hang like an Old Man of the Sea about my neck, and hope to enjoy a little season of being like other folks. It is a most lovely day to-day, most unfallen-Eden-like."

In a letter written later in the same season, March 28,

Mrs. Stowe gives us a pleasant glimpse at their preparations for the proper observance of Easter Sunday in the
little Mandarin schoolhouse. She says: "It was the week
before Easter, and we had on our minds the dressing of
the church. There my two Gothic fireboards were to be
turned into a pulpit for the occasion. I went to Jack-
sonville and got a five-inch moulding for a base, and then
had one fireboard sawed in two, so that there was an arched
panel for each end. Then came a rummage for something
for a top, and to make a desk of, until it suddenly occurred
to me that our old black walnut extension table had a set
of leaves. They were exactly the thing. The whole was
trimmed with a beading of yellow pine, and rubbed, and
pumice-stoned, and oiled, and I got out my tubes of paint
and painted the nail-holes with Vandyke brown. By
Saturday morning it was a lovely little Gothic pulpit, and
Anthony carried it over to the schoolhouse and took away
the old desk which I gave him for his meeting-house.
That afternoon we drove out into the woods and gathered
a quantity of superb Easter lilies, papaw, sparkleberry,
great fern-leaves, and cedar. In the evening the girls
went over to the Meads to practice Easter hymns; but I
sat at home and made a cross, eighteen inches long, of
cedar and white lilies. This Southern cedar is the most
exquisite thing; it is so feathery and delicate.

"Sunday morning was cool and bright, a most perfect
Easter. Our little church was full, and everybody seemed
delighted with the decorations. Mr. Stowe preached a
sermon to show that Christ is going to put everything
right at last, which is comforting. So the day was one
of real pleasure, and also, I trust, of real benefit, to the poor
souls who learned from it that Christ is indeed risen for
them."

During the season of her great trouble George Eliot
wrote to her: —

My dear Friend, — The other day I had a letter from Mrs. Fields, written to let me know something of you under that heavy trouble, of which such information as I have had has been quite untrustworthy, leaving me in entire incredulity in regard to it except on this point, that you and yours must be suffering deeply. Naturally I thought most of you in the matter (its public aspects being indeterminate), and many times before our friend's letter came I had said to Mr. Lewes: "What must Mrs. Stowe be feeling!" I remember Mrs. Fields once told me of the wonderful courage and cheerfulness which belonged to you, enabling you to bear up under exceptional trials, and I imagined you helping the sufferers with tenderness and counsel, but yet, nevertheless, I felt that there must be a bruising weight on your heart. Dear, honored friend, you who are so ready to give warm fellowship, is it any comfort to you to be told that those afar off are caring for you in spirit, and will be happier for all good issues that may bring you rest?

I cannot, dare not, write more in my ignorance, lest I should be using unreasonable words. But I trust in your not despising this scrap of paper which tells you, perhaps rather for my relief than yours, that I am always in grateful, sweet remembrance of your goodness to me and your energetic labors for all.

To this letter Mrs. Stowe replies after a delay of more than two years: —

Orange-blossom time,
MANDARIN, March 18, 1876.

My dear Friend, — I always think of you when the orange-trees are in blossom; just now they are fuller than ever, and so many bees are filling the branches that the air is full of a sort of still murmur. And now I am beginning to hear from you every month in "Harper's." It is as good

as a letter. "Daniel Deronda" has succeeded in awaking
in my somewhat worn-out mind an interest. So many
stories are tramping over one's mind in every modern
magazine nowadays that one is macadamized, so to speak.
It takes something unusual to make a sensation. This
does excite and interest me, as I wait for each number
with eagerness. I wish I could endow you with our long
winter weather, — not winter, except such as you find in
Sicily. We live here from November to June, and my
husband sits outdoors on the veranda and reads all day.
We emigrate in solid family: my two dear daughters,
husband, self, and servants come together to spend the
winter here, and so together to our Northern home in
summer. My twin daughters relieve me from all domestic
care; they are lively, vivacious, with a real genius for
practical life. We have around us a little settlement of
neighbors, who like ourselves have a winter home here,
and live an easy, undress, picnic kind of life, far from the
world and its cares. Mr. Stowe has been busy on eight
volumes of Görres on the mysticism of the Middle Ages.
This Görres was Professor of Philosophy at Munich, and
he reviews the whole ground of the shadow-land between
the natural and the supernatural, — ecstasy, trance, prophecy, miracles, spiritualism, the stigmata, etc. He was
a devout Roman Catholic, and the so-called facts that he
reasons on seem to me quite amazing; and yet the possibilities that lie between inert matter and man's living, all-
powerful, immortal soul may make almost anything credible.
The soul at times can do anything with matter. I have
been busying myself with Sainte-Beuve's seven volumes on
the Port Royal development. I like him (Sainte-Beuve).
His capacity of seeing, doing justice to all kinds of natures
and sentiments, is wonderful. I am sorry he is no longer
our side the veil.

There is a redbird (cardinal grosbeak) singing in the orange-trees fronting my window, so sweetly and insistently as to almost stop my writing. I hope, dear friend, you are well, — better than when you wrote last.

It was very sweet and kind of you to write what you did last. I suppose it is so long ago you may have forgotten, but it was a word of tenderness and sympathy about my brother's trial; it was womanly, tender, and sweet, such as at heart you are. After all, my love of you is greater than my admiration, for I think it more and better to be really a woman worth loving than to have read Greek and German, and written books. And in this last book I read, I feel more with you in some little, fine points, — they stare at me as making an amusing exhibition. For, my dear, I feel myself at last as one who has been playing and picnicking on the shores of life, and waked from a dream late in the afternoon to find that everybody almost has gone over to the beyond. And the rest are sorting their things and packing their trunks, and waiting for the boat to come and take them.

It seems now but a little time since my brother Henry and I were two young people together. He was my two years' junior, and nearest companion out of seven brothers and three sisters. I taught him drawing and heard his Latin lessons, for you know a girl becomes mature and womanly long before a boy. I saw him through college, and helped him through the difficult love affair that gave him his wife; and then he and my husband had a real German, enthusiastic love for each other, which ended in making me a wife. Ah! in those days we never dreamed that he, or I, or any of us, were to be known in the world. All he seemed then was a boy full of fun, full of love, full of enthusiasm for protecting abused and righting wronged people, which made him in those early days write editorials, and wear arms and swear himself a special policeman to protect the poor negroes in Cincinnati, where we then lived, when there were mobs instigated by the slaveholders of Kentucky.

Then he married, and lived a missionary life in the new West, all with a joyousness, an enthusiasm, a chivalry, which made life bright and vigorous to us both. Then in time he was called to Brooklyn, just as the crisis of the great anti-slavery battle came on, and the Fugitive Slave Law was passed. I was then in Maine, and I well remember one snowy night his riding till midnight to see me, and then our talking, till near morning, what we could do to make headway against the horrid cruelties that were being practiced against the defenseless blacks. My husband was then away lecturing, and my heart was burning itself out in indignation and anguish. Henry told me then that he meant to fight that battle in New York; that he would have a church that would stand by him to resist the tyrannic dictation of Southern slaveholders. I said: "I, too, have begun to do something; I have begun a story, trying to set forth the sufferings and wrongs of the slaves." "That's right, Hattie," he said; "finish it, and I will scatter it thick as the leaves of Vallombrosa," and so came "Uncle Tom," and Plymouth Church became a stronghold where the slave always found refuge and a strong helper. One morning my brother found sitting on his doorstep poor old Paul Edmondson, weeping; his two daughters, of sixteen and eighteen, had passed into the slave warehouse of Bruin & Hill, and were to be sold. My brother took the man by the hand to a public meeting, told his story for him, and in an hour raised the two thousand dollars to redeem his children. Over and over again, afterwards, slaves were redeemed at Plymouth Church, and Henry and Plymouth Church became words of hatred and fear through half the Union. From that time until we talked together about the Fugitive Slave Law, there

was not a pause or stop in the battle till we had been
through the war, and slavery had been wiped out in blood.
Through all he has been pouring himself out, wrestling,
burning, laboring, everywhere, making stump speeches
when elections turned on the slave question, and ever
maintaining that the cause of Christ was the cause of the
slave.   And when all was over, it was he and Lloyd Garrison who were sent by government once more to raise our
national flag on Fort Sumter.   You must see that a man
does not so energize without making many enemies.   Half
of our Union has been defeated, a property of millions
annihilated by emancipation, a proud and powerful slave
aristocracy reduced to beggary, and there are those who
never saw our faces that to this hour hate him and me.
Then he has been a progressive in theology.   He has been
a student of Huxley, and Spencer, and Darwin, — enough
to alarm the old school, — and yet remained so ardent a
supernaturalist as equally to repel the radical destruction-
ists in religion.   He and I are Christ-worshipers, adoring
Him as the Image of the Invisible God and all that comes
from believing this.   Then he has been a reformer, an
advocate of universal suffrage and woman's rights, yet not
radical enough to please that reform party who stand where
the Socialists of France do, and are for tearing up all
creation generally.   Lastly, he has had the misfortune of
a popularity which is perfectly phenomenal.   I cannot
give you any idea of the love, worship, idolatry, with
which he has been overwhelmed.   He has something
magnetic about him that makes everybody crave his society,
— that makes men follow and worship him.   I remember
being at his house one evening in the time of early flowers,
and in that one evening came a box of flowers from Maine,
another from New Jersey, another from Connecticut, — all
from people with whom he had no personal acquaintance,
who had read something of his and wanted to send him

some token. I said, "One would think you were a *prima donna*. What does make people go on so about you?"

My brother is hopelessly generous and confiding. His inability to believe evil is something incredible, and so has come all this suffering. You said you hoped I should be at rest when the first investigating committee and Plymouth Church cleared my brother almost by acclamation. Not so. The enemy have so committed themselves that either they or he must die, and there has followed two years of the most dreadful struggle. First, a legal trial of six months, the expenses of which on his side were one hundred and eighteen thousand dollars, and in which he and his brave wife sat side by side in the court-room, and heard all that these plotters, who had been weaving their webs for three years, could bring. The foreman of the jury was offered a bribe of ten thousand dollars to decide against my brother. He sent the letter containing the proposition to the judge. But with all their plotting, three fourths of the jury decided against them, and their case was lost. It was accepted as a triumph by my brother's friends; a large number of the most influential clergy of all denominations so expressed themselves in a public letter, and it was hoped the thing was so far over that it might be lived down and overgrown with better things.

But the enemy, intriguing secretly with all those parties in the community who wish to put down a public and too successful man, have been struggling to bring the thing up again for an ecclesiastical trial. The cry has been raised in various religious papers that Plymouth Church was in complicity with crime, — that they were so captivated with eloquence and genius that they refused to make competent investigation. The six months' legal investigation was insufficient; a new trial was needed. Plymouth Church immediately called a council of ministers and laymen, in

number representing thirty-seven thousand Congregational
Christians, to whom Plymouth Church surrendered her
records, — her conduct, — all the facts of the case, and
this great council unanimously supported the church and
ratified her decision; recognizing the fact that, in all the
investigations hitherto, nothing had been proved against
my brother.   They at his request, and that of Plymouth
Church, appointed a committee of five to whom within
sixty days any one should bring any facts that they could
prove, or else forever after hold their peace.   It is thought
now by my brother's friends that this thing must finally
reach a close.   But you see why I have not written.
This has drawn on my life, — my heart's blood.   He is
myself; I know you are the kind of woman to understand
me when I say that I felt a blow at him more than at
myself.   I, who know his purity, honor, delicacy, know
that he has been from childhood of an ideal purity, — who
reverenced his conscience as his king, whose glory was
redressing human wrong, who spake no slander, no, nor
listened to it.

Never have I known a nature of such strength, and
such almost childlike innocence.   He is of a nature so
sweet and perfect that, though I have seen him thunder-
ously indignant at moments, I never saw him fretful or
irritable, — a man who continuously, in every little act of
life, is thinking of others; a man that all the children on
the street run after, and that every sorrowful, weak, or
distressed person looks to as a natural helper.   In all this
long history there has been no circumstance of his relation
to any woman that has not been worthy of himself, —
pure, delicate, and proper; and I know all sides of it, and
certainly should not say this if there were even a misgiv-
ing.   Thank God, there is none, and I can read my New
Testament and feel that by all the beatitudes my brother
is blessed.

His calmness, serenity, and cheerfulness through all this time has uplifted us all. Where he was, there was no anxiety, no sorrow. My brother's power to console is something peculiar and wonderful. I have seen him at death-beds and funerals, where it would seem as if hope herself must be dumb, bring down the very peace of Heaven and change despair to trust. He has not had less power in his own adversity. You cannot conceive how he is beloved, by those even who never saw him, — old, paralytic, distressed, neglected people, poor seamstresses, black people, who have felt these arrows shot against their benefactor as against themselves, and most touching have been their letters of sympathy.

In your portrait of Deronda, you speak of him as one of those rare natures in whom a private wrong bred no bitterness. "The sense of injury breeds, not the will to inflict injuries, but a hatred of all injury;" and Henry's friends and lawyers have sometimes been aroused and sometimes indignant with his habitual caring for others, and his habit of vindicating and extending even to his enemies every scrap and shred of justice that might belong to them. From first to last of this trial he has never for a day intermitted his regular work. Preaching to crowded houses, preaching even in his short vacations at watering-places, carrying on his missions which have regenerated two once wretched districts of the city, editing a paper, and in short giving himself up to work. He cautioned his church not to become absorbed in him and his trials, to prove their devotion by more faithful church work and a wider charity; and never have the Plymouth missions among the poor been so energetic and effective. He said recently, "The worst that can befall a man is to stop thinking of God and begin to think of himself; if trials make us self-absorbed, they hurt us." Well, dear, pardon me for this outpour. I loved you — I love you — and therefore wanted you to know just what I felt. Now, dear, this is over, don't think you must reply to it or me. I know how much you have to do, — yes, I know all about an aching head and an overtaxed brain. This last work of yours is to be your best, I think, and I hope it will bring you enough to buy an orange grove in Sicily, or somewhere else, and so have lovely weather such as we have.

Your ancient admirer, who usually goes to bed at eight o'clock, was convicted by me of sitting up after eleven over the last installment of "Daniel Deronda," and he is full of it. We think well of Guendoline, and that she isn't much more than young ladies in general so far.

Next year, if I can possibly do it, I will send you some of our oranges. I perfectly long to have you enjoy them.

Your very loving   H. B. STOWE.

P. S.   I am afraid I shall write you again when I am reading your writings, they are so provokingly suggestive of things one wants to say.   H. B. S.

This friendship was one that greatly enlisted Mrs. Stowe's sympathies and enriched her life. Her interest in any woman who was supporting herself, and especially in any one who found a daily taskmaster in the pen, and above all when, as in this case, the woman was one possessed of great moral aspiration half paralyzed in its action by finding itself in an anomalous and (to the world in general) utterly incomprehensible position, made such a woman like a magnet to Mrs. Stowe. She inherited from her father a faith in the divine power of sympathy, which only waxed greater with years and experience. Wherever she found a fellow-mortal suffering trouble or dishonor, in spite of hindrance her feet were turned that way. The genius of George Eliot and the contrasting elements of her life and character drew Mrs. Stowe to her side in sisterly solicitude. Her attitude, her sweetness, her sincerity, could not fail to win the heart of George Eliot. They became loving friends.

It was the same inborn sense of fraternity which led her, when a child, on hearing of the death of Lord Byron, to go out into the fields and fling herself, weeping, on the mounded hay, where she might pray alone for his forgiveness and salvation. It is wonderful to observe the influence of Byron upon that generation. It is on record that when Tennyson, a boy of fifteen, heard some one say, "Byron is dead," he thought the whole world at an end. "I thought," he said one day, "everything was over and finished for every one; that nothing else mattered. I remember that I went out alone and carved 'Byron is dead' into the sandstone."

Mrs. Stowe belonged to the sympathetic order of genius; but it is to be observed how little of the "vatis irritabile" was to be found in her. She wrote to Dr. Holmes, putting aside all mention of the sorrows which had so weighed her down: —

MANDARIN, February 23.

DEAR DOCTOR, — How kind it was of you to write me that very beautiful note! and how I wish you were just where I am, to see the trees laden at the same time with golden oranges and white blossoms! I should so like to cut off a golden cluster, leaves and all, for you. Well, Boston seems very far away and dreamy, like some previous state of existence, as I sit on the veranda and gaze on the receding shores of the St. John's.

Dear doctor, how time slips by! I remember when Sumner seemed to me a young man, and now he has gone. And Wilson has gone, and Chase, whom I knew as a young man in society in Cincinnati, has gone, and Stanton has gone, and Seward has gone, and yet how lively the world races on! A few air-bubbles of praise or lamentation, and away sails the great ship of life, no matter over whose grave!

Well, one cannot but feel it! To me, also, a whole generation of friends has gone from the other side of the water since I was there and broke kindly bread with them. The Duchess of Sutherland, the good old duke, Lansdowne, Ellesmere, Lady Byron, Lord and Lady Amberley, Charles Kingsley, the good Quaker, Joseph Sturge, all are with the shadowy train that has moved on. Among them were as dear and true friends as I ever had, and as pure and noble specimens of human beings as God ever made. They are living somewhere in intense vitality, I must believe, and you, dear doctor, must not doubt.

I think about your writings a great deal, and one element in them always attracts me. It is their pitiful and sympathetic vein, the pity for poor, struggling human nature. In this I feel that you must be very near and dear to Him whose name is Love.

You wrote some verses once that have got into the hymn-books, and have often occurred to me in my most sacred hours as descriptive of the feelings with which I bear the sorrow and carry the cares of life. They begin:

"Love Divine, that stooped to share ;"

I have not all your books down here, and am haunted by gaps in the verses that memory cannot make good; but it is that "Love Divine" which is my stay and comfort and hope, as one friend after another passes beyond sight and hearing. Please let me have it in your handwriting.

I remember a remark you once made on spiritualism. I cannot recall the words, but you spoke of it as modifying the sharp angles of Calvinistic belief, as a fog does those of a landscape. I would like to talk with you some time on spiritualism, and show you a collection of very curious facts that I have acquired through mediums *not* professional.

I have long since come to the conclusion that the marvels of spiritualism are natural, and not supernatural phenomena, — an uncommon working of natural laws. I believe that the door between those *in* the body and those *out* has never in any age been entirely closed, and that occasional perceptions within the veil are a part of the course of nature, and therefore not miraculous. Of course such a phase of human experience is very substantial ground for every kind of imposture and superstition, and I have no faith whatever in mediums who practice for money. In their case I think the law of Moses, that forbade consulting those who dealt with "familiar spirits," a very wise one.

Do write some more, dear doctor. You are too well off in your palace down there on the new land. Your Centennial Ballad was a charming little peep; now give us a full-fledged story. Mr. Stowe sends his best regards, and wishes you would read "Görres."[1] It is in French also, and he thinks the French translation better than the German.

Yours ever truly,   H. B. STOWE.

Writing in the autumn to her son Charles, who was at that time abroad, studying at Bonn, Mrs. Stowe describes a most tempestuous passage between New York and Charleston, during which she and her husband and daughters suffered so much that they were ready to forswear the sea forever. The great waves, as they rushed boiling and seething past, would peer in at the little bull's-eye window of the stateroom, as if eager to swallow up ship and passengers. From Charleston, however, they

---

[1] *Die Christliche Mystik,* by Johann Joseph Görres, Regensburg, 1836–42.

had a most delightful run to their journey's end. She writes: "We had a triumphal entrance into the St. John's, and a glorious sail up the river. Arriving at Mandarin, at four o'clock, we found all the neighbors, black as well as white, on the wharf to receive us. There was a great waving of handkerchiefs and flags, clapping of hands and cheering, as we drew near. The house was open and all ready for us, and we are delighted to be once more in our beautiful Florida home."

In 1877 she writes her son: "I am again entangled in writing a serial, a thing I never mean to do again, but the story, begun for a mere Christmas brochure, grew so under my hands that I thought I might as well fill it out and make a book of it. It is the last thing of the kind I ever expect to do. In it I condense my recollections of a bygone era, that in which I was brought up, the ways and manners of which are now as nearly obsolete as the Old England of Dickens's stories is.

"I am so hampered by the necessity of writing this story that I am obliged to give up company and visiting of all kinds and keep my strength for it. I hope I may be able to finish it, as I greatly desire to do so, but I begin to feel that I am not so strong as I used to be. Your mother is an old woman, Charley mine, and it is best she should give up writing before people are tired of reading her.

"I would much rather have written another such a book as 'Footsteps of the Master,' but all, even the religious papers, are gone mad on serials. Serials they demand and will have, and I thought, since this generation will listen to nothing but stories, why not tell them?"

She was speaking in this letter of "Poganuc People," one of the most exquisite of her books of sketches. The flame of her genius seemed to awaken once more as she wrote, and the tenderness in its pages, the power to move both laughter and tears, is of her very own and of her very best. It was her last long book. The habit of her life was to write, and she did not lose it, but she was nearing her seventieth year, and the responsibility of a serial story was never assumed by her again.

In January she wrote from Mandarin to Dr. Holmes: —

DEAR DOCTOR, — I wish I could give to you and Mrs. Holmes the exquisite charm of this morning. My window is wide open; it is a lovely, fresh, sunny day, and a great orange-tree hung with golden balls closes the prospect from my window. The tree is about thirty feet high, and its leaves fairly glisten in the sunshine.

I sent "Poganuc People" to you and Mrs. Holmes as being among the few who know those old days. It is an extremely quiet story for these sensational days, when heaven and earth seem to be racked for a thrill; but as I get old I do love to think of those quiet, simple times when there was not a poor person in the parish, and the changing glories of the year were the only spectacle. We, that is the professor and myself, have been reading with much interest Motley's Memoir. That was a man to be proud of, a beauty, too (by your engraving). I never had the pleasure of a personal acquaintance.

I feel with you that we have come into the land of leave-taking. Hardly a paper but records the death of some of Mr. Stowe's associates. But the river is not so black as it seems, and there are clear days when the opposite shore is plainly visible, and now and then we catch a strain of music, perhaps even a gesture of recognition. They are thinking of us, without doubt, on the other side. My daughters and I have been reading "Elsie Venner" again. Elsie is one of my especial friends, — poor, dear child! — and all your theology in that book I subscribe to with both hands.

Does not the Bible plainly tell us of a time when there shall be no more pain? That is to be the end and crown of the Messiah's mission, when God shall wipe all tears away. My face is set that way, and yours, too, I trust and believe.

Mr. Stowe sends hearty and affectionate remembrance both to you and Mrs. Holmes, and I am, as ever, truly yours,   H. B. STOWE.

There is one more letter to her son Charles and his wife, which must close the record of her seventy years.

"Dear children," she says, writing from Florida to Saco, Maine, where her son was busy in his parish, — "Well, we have stepped from December to June, and this morning is sunny and dewy, with a fresh sea-breeze giving life to the air. I have just been out to cut a great bunch of roses and lilies, though the garden is grown into such a jungle that I could hardly get about in it. The cannas, and dwarf bananas, and roses are all tangled together so that I can hardly thread my way among them. I never in my life saw anything range and run rampant over the ground as cannas do. The ground is littered with fallen oranges, and the place looks shockingly untidy, but so beautiful that I am quite willing to forgive its disorder. . . .

"Your father is quite well. The sea had its usual exhilarating effect upon him. Before we left New York he was quite meek, and exhibited such signs of grace and submission that I had great hopes of him. He promised to do exactly as I told him, and stated that he had entire confidence in my guidance. What woman couldn't call such a spirit evidence of being prepared for speedy translation? I was almost afraid he could not be long for this world. But on the second day at sea his spirits rose, and his appetite reasserted itself. He declared in loud tones

how well he felt, and quite resented my efforts to take
care of him. I reminded him of his gracious vows and
promises in the days of his low spirits, but to no effect.
The fact is, his self-will has not left him yet, and I have
now no fear of his immediate translation. He is going to
preach for us this morning."

Still well, but not at all strong, we must leave her here
upon the entrance of the long valley of age.

This woman, who seems to have touched every note
in the gamut of human joy and suffering; she who had
known physical weakness, overwork, poverty on one hand,
and on the other great success, who had possessed devoted friends and household happiness; she who had lived
through the sorrows of war, had lost her two sons, who
had watched a large company pass into the unseen land
of those who made this world lovely to her; she who
had seen the great of the earth fall away and despise her
for works she felt herself called upon to perform; who
had seen one dearest to her cast down from the high places
and trampled on, was now to experience a slow descent
towards the dark gate of death. There was to be no sudden release from decadence, but every step of the journey
of life was to be painfully traversed.

A sense of fellowship in the joys and sorrows of humanity was as I have said, a characteristic of her nature; but
this sacred fellowship was not alone born of imagination and
tenderness of feeling; she was indeed in harmony with the
children of men in that she walked with them through the
low gates of failure and decay, yet the light of her faith so
irradiated her whole nature that she always had the secret
of unspeakable peace if not of joy to give to those who
were walking the same road.

CHAPTER XIII

AFTER the many instances of Mrs. Stowe's natural eloquence which have been quoted in these pages, it is scarcely necessary to say that she was a delightful talker. Nevertheless, the affectionateness of her character, her intense interest in all human experience, qualified her for personal communion to a most uncommon degree. She loved to gather a small circle of friends around a fireside, when she easily took the lead in fun and story telling. This was her own ground, and upon it she was not to be outdone. "Let me put my feet upon the fender," she would say, "and I can talk till all is blue."

It appeared to those who listened most frequently to her conversation that a large part of the charm of her tales was often lost in the writing down; yet with all her unusual powers she was an excellent listener herself. Her natural modesty was such that she took keen pleasure in gathering fresh thought and inspiration from the conversation of others. Nor did the universal homage she received from high and low leave any unworthy impression upon her self-esteem. She was grateful and pleased and humble, and the only visible effect produced upon her was the heightened pleasure she received from the opportunities of knowing men and women who excited her love and admiration. Her name was a kind of sacred talisman, especially in New and Old England. It was a banner which had led men to battle against slavery. Therefore it was often a cause of surprise and social embarrassment when the bearer of this name proved to be sometimes too modest, and sometimes too absent-minded, to remember that anything was expected of her on great occasions, or anything arranged for her special entertainment. I have already told how she was utterly taken by surprise once in a foreign city by being invited out to breakfast, as she supposed privately, and finding herself suddenly in a large hall, upon a raised platform crowded with local dignitaries, and greeted before she could get her breath by a chorus of children's voices singing an anthem in her honor, especially composed for the occasion. Her love of fun was greatly excited by this unexpected situation, and she used to relate the anecdote, with details about her unprepared condition which were irresistibly amusing.

The sense that a great work had been accomplished through her only made her, if possible, less self-conscious. Late in life (when her failing powers made it impossible for her to speak as one living in a world which she seemed to have left far behind) she was accosted, I was told, in the garden of her country retreat, in the twilight one evening, by a good old retired sea-captain who was her neighbor for the time. "When I was younger," said he respectfully, holding his hat in his hand while he spoke, "I read with a great deal of satisfaction and instruction ' Uncle Tom's Cabin.' The story impressed me very much, and I am happy to shake hands with you, Mrs. Stowe, who wrote it." "I did not write it," answered the white-haired old lady gently, as she shook the captain's hand. "You did n't?" he ejaculated in amazement. "Why, who did, then?" "God wrote it," she replied simply. "I merely did his dictation." "Amen," said the captain reverently, as he walked thoughtfully away.

This was the expression in age of what lay at the foundation of her life.

Her absent-mindedness grew upon her with increasing

years. It was only by an effort that she was able to restrain herself sometimes after a brief conversation from lapsing into a calm world known only to herself; but this condition approached gradually. As she explained to her husband in the early years of their life together, this habit of mind was frequently the result of fatigue even while she was still in the prime of life. Perhaps a dinner-table of invited guests were eagerly listening to her conversation, when at some suggestion of a new train of ideas, either from within or thrown out in response by another, she would become silent and hardly speak again. Occasionally at a reception she would wander away, only to be found strolling about in the conservatory, if there were one, or quietly observant in some coigne of vantage where she was not likely to be disturbed.

There is an anecdote given to me by a friend which illustrates her shortcomings in this direction. Once when she was at the height of her fame and popularity she was expected on a certain day to dine at the old President Quincy house in Quincy. The ladies, his daughters, received their guest with the great dignity and courtesy which were native to them, and she was shown to an upper room to arrange her dress after the journey. The ladies waited in the drawing-room below; but presently there seemed to be unnecessary delay in Mrs. Stowe's joining them. They waited more and more impatiently; they began to watch the clock while the minutes passed, but still there was no step on the stair. At last dinner was announced and still they waited, and the maid who was sent up to speak to Mrs. Stowe returned to say that she had knocked at the door but there was no answer. Then the hostesses became anxious, and hurried to her room in person to see what the serious reason might be. They opened the door; there stood Mrs. Stowe just as they had left her, her bonnet and shawl still on, standing before a bookcase reading a volume which she had taken down. " Oh," said she, returning suddenly to the present scene of things; "do forgive me ! I found this dear old copy of Sir Charles Grandison just like the one I used to read. I have n't seen it for years and years ! "

Among the responsibilities of the later period of her life was that of getting Professor Stowe to consent to publish a book. This was no laughing matter; at first the book was planned merely as an article on the "Talmud " for the "Atlantic Monthly." Afterwards Professor Stowe enlarged the design. Later, in speaking of his manuscript, she says: "You must not scare him off by grimly declaring that you must have the *whole manuscript complete* before you set the printer to work; you must take the three quarters he brings you and at least make believe begin printing, and he will immediately go to work and finish up the whole; otherwise what with lectures and the original sin of laziness, it will all be indefinitely postponed. I want to make a crisis, that he shall feel that *now* is the accepted time, and that this must be finished first and foremost."

And again she says: "My poor *Rab.* has been sick with a heavy cold this week, and if it had n't been for me you would n't have had this article, which I send in triumph. I plunged into the sea of Rabbis and copied Mr. Stowe's insufferable chaldaic characters so that you might not have your life taken by wrathful printers. . . . Thus I have ushered into the world a document which I venture to say condenses more information on an obscure and curious subject than *any* in the known world — Hosanna ! "

In 1881 she wrote to her son Charles: "I send you a newspaper clipping showing the disposition of educated Christians to return to the primitive basis of the great facts of Christianity. . . . I have so rich a blessing from my own keeping of Lent and Holy Week that I cannot but

rejoice when I see the minds of our pious people turning
in this direction, for it is turning from all controversial
issues to the *one* spot where Christian union becomes a
verity.   At Gethsemane, the Cross, and the Sepulchre,
Christians *feel* together.   They *feel*, not *know*, they are
one.   Nicodemus, Joseph of Arimathæa, Peter, James, and
John were all disciples together at the sepulchre.

"I have just heard of the sudden death of my friend
Mr. Fields, . . . and now we all ask, What has he left
of all his life's accumulations?   Houses, lands, pictures,
literary reputation, all that gone — dreams, things of the
past.   Had he any treasure laid up in Heaven?   I think
from my remembrance of him that *he had just what Jesus
meant by treasure laid up in Heaven.*   He had a habit
of quiet benevolence; he did habitually and quietly more
good to everybody he had to do with than common.   He
favored with all his power ——'s charitable work, and such
habits as these are, I think, what Christ meant by laying
up treasure in Heaven.   A spirit sympathetic with Christ's
spirit, prepared to appreciate and enjoy Christ's work, is
what He Himself, in the only account He gives of the
last award, makes the *test* of fitness for eternal life.   I
find many traces of childlike faith in his last pieces. . . .
When a friend is gone to the great hereafter how glad we
are that he *did* believe."

Mrs. Stowe's last public appearance was in June, 1882,
when her Boston publishers arranged a reception for her at
the beautiful country-seat of Ex-Governor Claflin.   Henry
Ward Beecher accompanied his sister and responded to the
address of welcome in his own natural and touching manner.   After poems by Whittier, Holmes, and others had
been read, Mrs. Stowe herself came to the front of the
platform.   The whole company rose and remained standing
until she had finished.   In her quiet, modest way, and yet
so clearly as to be plainly heard by all, she said: —

"I wish to say that I thank all my friends from my heart, — that is all. And one thing more, — that is, if any of you have doubt, or sorrow, or pain, if you doubt about this world, just remember what God has done; just remember that this great sorrow of slavery has gone, gone by forever. I see it every day at the South. I walk about there and see the lowly cabins. I see these people growing richer and richer. I see men very happy in their lowly lot; but, to be sure, you must have patience with them. They are not perfect, but have their faults, and they are serious faults in the view of white people. But they are very happy, that is evident, and they do know how to enjoy themselves, — a great deal more than you do. An old negro friend in our neighborhood has got a new, nice two-story house, and an orange grove, and a sugar-mill. He has got a lot of money, besides. Mr. Stowe met him one day, and he said, 'I have got twenty head of cattle, four head of "hoss," forty head of hen, and I have got ten children, all *mine, every one mine.*' Well, now, that is a thing that a black man could not say once, and this man was sixty years old before he could say it. With all the faults of the colored people, take a man and put him down with nothing but his hands, and how many could say as much as that? I think they have done well.

"A little while ago they had at his house an evening festival for their church, and raised fifty dollars. Every one of his daughters knew how to cook. They had a good place for the festival. Their suppers were spread on little white tables with nice clean cloths on them. People paid fifty cents for supper. They got between fifty and sixty dollars, and had one of the best frolics you could imagine.

"That is the sort of thing I see going on around me. Let us never doubt of the result."

During the year Mrs. Stowe busied herself with the labor

of putting her letters and papers in some order.   She had written to her son Charles at the beginning of this task: —

MY DEAR CHARLEY, — My mind has been with you a great deal lately.   I have been looking over and arranging my papers with a view to sifting out those that are not worth keeping, and so filing and arranging those that are to be kept that my heirs and assigns may with the less trouble know where and what they are.   I cannot describe (to you) the peculiar feelings which this review occasions. Reading old letters, when so many of the writers are gone from earth, seems to me like going into the world of spirits, — letters full of the warm, eager, anxious, busy life, that is *forever* past.   My own letters, too, full of bygone scenes in my early life and the childish days of my children.   It is affecting to me to recall things that strongly moved me years ago, that filled my thoughts and made me anxious, when the occasion and emotion have wholly vanished from my mind.   But I thank God there is *one* thing running through all of them from the time I was thirteen years old, and that is the intense unwavering sense of Christ's educating, guiding presence and care.   It is *all* that remains now.   The romance of my youth is faded; it looks to me now, from my years, so *very* young — those days when my mind only lived in *emotion*, and when my letters never were dated, because they were only histories of the *internal*, but now that I am no more and never can be young in this world, now that the friends of those days are almost all in eternity, what remains?

.   .   .   .

I was passionate in my attachments in those far back years, and as I have looked over files of old letters, they are all gone (except one, C. Van Rensselaer), Georgiana May, Delia Bacon, Clarissa Treat, Elizabeth Lyman, Sarah Colt, Elisabeth Phenix, Frances Strong, Elisabeth Foster.

I have letters from them all, but they have been long in spirit land, and know more about how it is there than I do. It gives me a sort of dizzy feeling of the shortness of life and nearness of eternity when I see how many that I have traveled with are gone within the veil. Then there are all my own letters, written in the first two years of marriage, when Mr. Stowe was in Europe and I was looking forward to motherhood and preparing for it — my letters when my whole life was within the four walls of my nursery, my thoughts absorbed by the developing character of children who have now lived their earthly life and gone to the eternal one, — my two little boys, each in his way good and lovely, whom Christ has taken in youth, and my little one, my first Charley, whom He took away before he knew sin or sorrow, — then my brother George and sister Catherine, the one a companion of my youth, the other the mother who assumed the care of me after I left home in my twelfth year — and they are gone. Then my blessed father, for many years so true an image of the Heavenly Father, — in all my afflictions he was afflicted, in all my perplexities he was a sure and safe counselor, and he too is gone upward to join the angelic mother whom I scarcely knew in this world, who has been to me only a spiritual presence through life.

Mrs. Stowe and her husband passed some time in Boston at this period with her married daughter. She wrote of the pleasure they had in reading: —

"Your father enjoys his proximity to the Boston library. He is now reading the twelve or fourteen volumes of the life and diary of John Quincy Adams. It is a history of our country through all the period of slavery usurpation that led to the war. The industry of the man in writing is wonderful. Every day's doings in the House are faithfully daguerreotyped, — all the mean tricks, contrivances

of the slave-power, and the pusillanimity of the Northern
members from day to day recorded. Calhoun was then
secretary of state. Under his connivance even the United
States census was falsified, to prove that freedom was bad
for negroes. Records of deaf, dumb, and blind, and insane colored people were distributed in Northern States,
and in places where John Quincy Adams had means of
proving there were no negroes. When he found that
these falsified figures had been used with the English
ambassador as reasons for admitting Texas as a slave State,
the old man called on Calhoun, and showed him the indus-
triously collected *proofs* of the falsity of this census. He
says: ' He writhed like a trodden rattlesnake, but said the
census was full of mistakes; but one part balanced another,
— it was not worth while to correct them.' His whole
life was an incessant warfare with the rapidly advancing
spirit of slavery, that was coiling like a serpent around
everything.

"At a time when the Southerners were like so many
excited tigers and rattlesnakes, — when they bullied, and
scoffed, and sneered, and threatened, this old man rose
every day in his place, and, knowing every parliamentary
rule and tactic of debate, found means to make himself
heard. Then he presented a petition from *negroes*, which
raised a storm of fury. The old man claimed that the
right of petition was the right of every human being.
They moved to expel him. By the rules of the house a
man, before he can be expelled, may have the floor to
make his defense. This was just what he wanted. He
held the floor for *fourteen days*, and used his wonderful
powers of memory and arrangement to give a systematic,
scathing history of the usurpations of slavery; he would
have spoken fourteen days more, but his enemies, finding
the thing getting hotter and hotter, withdrew their motion,
and the right of petition was gained.

"What is remarkable in this journal is the minute record of going to church every Sunday, and an analysis of the text and sermon. There is something about these so simple, so humble, so earnest. Often differing from the speaker, — but with gravity and humility, — he seems always to be so self-distrustful; to have such a sense of sinfulness and weakness, but such trust in God's fatherly mercy, as is most beautiful to see. Just the record of his Sunday sermons, and his remarks upon them, would be most instructive to a preacher. He was a regular communicant, and, beside, attended church on Christmas and Easter, — I cannot but love the old man. He died without seeing even the dawn of liberty which God has brought; but oh! I am sure he sees it from above. He died in the Capitol, in the midst of his labors, and the last words he said were, 'This is the last of earth; I am content.' And now, I trust, he is with God.

"All, all are gone. All that raged; all that threatened; all the cowards that yielded; truckled, sold their country for a mess of pottage; all the *men* that stood and bore infamy and scorn for the truth; all are silent in dust; the fight is over, but eternity will never efface from their souls whether they did well or ill — whether they fought bravely or failed like cowards. In a sense, our lives are irreparable. If we shrink, if we fail, if we choose the fleeting instead of the eternal, God may forgive us; but there must be an eternal regret! This man lived for humanity when hardest bestead; for truth when truth was unpopular; for Christ when Christ stood chained and scourged in the person of the slave."

Meanwhile, the comfort Mrs. Stowe drew in from the beauty of nature and the calm around her seemed yearly to nourish and renew her power of existence. Questions which were difficult to others were often solved to her mind by practical observation. It amused her to hear persons

agitating the question as to where they should look to supply labor for the South. "Why," she remarked once,
"there was a negro, one of those fearfully hot days in the
spring, who was digging muck from a swamp just in front
of our house, and carrying it in a wheelbarrow up a steep
slope, where he'dumped it down, and then went back for
more. He kept this up when it was so hot that we thought
either one of us would die to be five minutes in the sun.
We carried a thermometer to the spot where he was working, to see how great the heat was, and it rose at once to one
hundred and thirty-five degrees. The man, however, kept
cheerfully at his work, and when he went to his dinner
sat with the other negroes out in the white sand without
a bit of shade. Afterward they all lay down for a nap in
the same sheltered locality. Toward evening, when the
sun was sufficiently low to enable me to go out, I went to
speak to this man. 'Martin,' said I, 'you've had a
warm day's work. How do you stand it? Why, I
could n't endure such heat for five minutes.' 'Hah! hah!
No, I s'pose you could n't. Ladies can't, missus.' 'But,
Martin, are n't you very tired?' 'Bress your heart, no,
missus.' So Martin goes home to his supper, and after supper will be found dancing all the evening on the wharf near
by! After this, when people talk of bringing Germans
and Swedes to do such work, I am much entertained."

Many were the pleasant descriptions of her home sent
forth to tempt her friends away from the busy North.
"Here is where we read books," she said in one of her
letters, written in the month of March. "Up North nobody does, — they don't have time; so if —— will mail
his book to Mandarin, I will 'read, mark, learn, and in-
wardly digest.' We are having a carnival of flowers. I
hope you read my 'Palmetto Leaves,' for then you will
see all about us. . . . Our home is like a martin-box.
. . . I cannot tell you the quaint odd peace we have here

in living under the oak. 'Behold she dwelleth under the
oak at Mamre.'   All that we want is friends, to whom we
may say that solitude is sweet.   We have some neighbors,
however, who have made pretty places near us.   Mr.
Stowe keeps up a German class of three young ladies, with
whom he is reading Faust for the nine hundred and ninety-
ninth time, and in the evening I read aloud to a small
party of the neighbors.   We have made up our home as
we went along, throwing out a chamber here and there,
like twigs out of the old oak. . . .   The orange blossoms
have come like showers of pearl, and the yellow jessamine
like golden fleeces, and the violets and the lilies, and azaleas.   This glorious, budding, blossoming spring, and we
have days when merely to breathe and be is to be blessed.
I love to have a day of mere existence.   Life itself is a
pleasure when the sun shines warm, and the lizards dart
from all the shingles of the roof, and the birds sing in so
many notes and tones the yard reverberates; and I sit and
dream and am happy, and never want to go back North,
nor do anything with the toiling, snarling world again.   I
do wish I could gather you both in my little nest."

"This was the last winter passed in their well-loved
Southern home," writes Rev. C. E. Stowe, "for the following season Professor Stowe's health was in too precarious
a state to permit him to undertake the long journey from
Hartford.   By this time one of Mrs. Stowe's fondest
hopes had been realized; and, largely through her efforts,
Mandarin had been provided with a pretty little Episcopal
church, to which was attached a comfortable rectory, and
over which was installed a regular clergyman."

In January, Mrs. Stowe writes: —

"Mandarin looks very gay and airy now with its new
villas, and our new church and rectory.   Our minister is
perfect.   I wish you could know him.   He wants only physical strength.   In everything else he is all one could ask.

"It is a bright, lovely morning, and four orange-pickers are busy gathering our fruit. Our trees on the bluff have done better than any in Florida.

"This winter I study nothing but Christ's life. First I read Farrar's account and went over it carefully. ·Now I am reading Geikie. It keeps my mind steady, and helps me to bear the languor and pain, of which I have more than usual this winter."

But in the spring she wrote from Mandarin to Mrs. Howard: —

"I have been very unwell the season past. I have suffered more pain, more weariness and weakness, than ever in my life before. . . . But one thing, dear, precious friend, I cannot do, while my husband lives, I cannot visit and leave him, neither can I take him. He requires personal attentions that only a wife ought to render. They are not fatiguing nor exhausting, but require that I should be constantly with him. I think we have never enjoyed each other's society more than this winter. His mind is still clear and bright, and he is competent as ever to explain a text or instruct me in the merits of a verse. At our home in Hartford everything is arranged with reference to his comfort and he *is* perfectly comfortable, but my friends must come there to see me. I cannot leave him to go to them."

In December of the same year she writes again from Forest Street, Hartford, Connecticut: —

DEAR SUSIE, — Instead of the annual fuss and rumpus of this time of the year, the packing of trunks and the writing for passage tickets and arranging for a sea-voyage, I am quietly settled down for the winter in my Hartford home, and devoutly blessing my dear Father in Heaven that I have so quiet a home to settle down into.

It has become clear that Mr. Stowe cannot take the

journey. We dare not undertake it Our Southern home has no such conveniences as an invalid needs. It was charming while Mr. Stowe was well enough to sit on the veranda and take long daily walks, but now it is safer and better that we all stay with him here. . . . I can make him happy, and I look on this as my appointed work, and hope to do it faithfully. . . . H. and E. aid me heroically in everything. I have *no* household cares.

Pray for me, dear sister, and believe me ever your loving and true friend,   H. B. STOWE.

Susie, *do, do* write to me.

Again she writes to Mrs. Howard in January, still in Hartford: —

"You could not do a more generous deed than to enrich me with one of your precious letters. I am watching the slow sinking of my dear husband under an incurable disease, and only praying now that he may be spared pain. I do not feel strength within me to see him suffer.

"I have many things to be thankful for: a comfortable home, with every convenience for the care of the sick; two daughters, who relieve me of every household care, and a trained hospital nurse, who knows how to do everything and *does it* with neatness, order, and efficiency. . . . So I live day by day. I feel myself rather weak and weary, not with physical labor, for of that I have none, but you know all about it, just how it would be. . . . Please ask Henry to write me a few lines that I can read to my dear husband; his mind is clear, and I read all my letters to him, and nothing would please him more than a few lines from Henry, whom he always loved peculiarly from the time he was a student onward."

"For nearly a year now," she writes in December of the same year, to Mrs. Howard, "I have been a watcher and a waiter by my husband's sick-bed; caring for my

own health and spirits that I might always show a cheerful
and hopeful face to him, and have something cheerful to
say to him when he feels cast down and discouraged."

Mrs. Stowe always insisted that no small proportion of
her success in literature should be attributed to her husband. But her love for him made her see, not what was
untrue, but what was secondary in her work, as if it were
of primary importance. He appears to have been a genuine
scholar, one of a race rare enough at any time, nor was his
mind confined to any narrow groove. He was first, above
all, learned in the Scriptures, but his mind was a strange
storehouse of an endless variety of things which his vigorous
memory never suffered him to forget. Professor Stowe
died in August, 1886.

A period of rest now opened before Mrs. Stowe, who,
bending under the weight of seventy-six years of unremit-
ting toil, seemed to be possessed by a great calm. She
had written thirty books, beside an incredible number of
magazine papers, journals, short stories, letters, and charitable missives. There are few lives which can approach
such a showing of industry. She continued to write a
few, a very few, notes to her friends. She says in one of
these : —

"I have thought much lately of the possibility of my
leaving you all and going home. I am come to that stage
of my pilgrimage that is within sight of the River of
Death, and I feel that now I must have all in readiness
day and night for the messenger of the King. I have
sometimes had in my sleep strange perceptions of a vivid
spiritual life near to and with Christ, and multitudes of
holy ones, and the joy of it is like no other joy, — it
cannot be told in the language of the world. What I
have then I *know* with absolute certainty, yet it is so
unlike and above anything we conceive of in this world
that it is difficult to put it into words. The inconceiv-

able loveliness of Christ! It seems that about Him there is a sphere where the enthusiasm of love is the calm habit of the soul, that without words, without the necessity of demonstrations of affection, heart beats to heart, soul answers soul, we respond to the Infinite Love, and we feel his answer in us, and there is no need of words. All seemed to be busy coming and going on ministries of good, and passing each gave a thrill of joy to each as Jesus, the directing soul, the centre of all, 'over all, in all, and through all,' was working his beautiful and merciful will to redeem and save.   I was saying as I awoke: —

> " ' 'T is joy enough, my all in all,
>   At Thy dear feet to lie.
>   Thou wilt not let me lower fall,
>   And none can higher fly.'

"This was but a glimpse; but it has left a strange sweetness in my mind."

To Mrs. Howard she wrote: "Your note to me since brother Henry's exaltation was exactly *word for word* what I can send back to you. . . . If you dreamed I was in trouble the other night, you dreamed the truth, for I have been suffering. . . . I see that almost all your family have crossed over Jordan, leaving you still here. . . . I had written thus far " [she says, and it is a very brief note, alas!] "when I was obliged to stop through fatigue. It is long since I have tried to write *any*thing, and my strength gives out quickly; but I hope this imperfect scrawl will show you that I am still your ever affectionate

H. B. STOWE."

This was almost the end; occasionally she was known to write an exceptional note, but, as she says to Mrs. Howard, "My mind wanders like a running brook, and I do not think of my friends as I used to, unless they recall themselves to me by some kind action. . . . I think I am in something of the condition of a silkworm who has spun out all his silk, and can spin no more, unless he has some fresh mulberry leaves. When I reach the 'golden shores,' where grow the trees of life, there I may be able to renew the happy friendships with those who have gone before and may come after me to that happy land."

Finally, she says to Mrs. Howard: —

"My sun has set. The time of work for *me* is over. I have written all my words and thought all my thoughts, and now I rest me in the flickering light of the dying embers, in a rest so profound that the voice of an old friend arouses me but momentarily, and I drop back again into repose. . . . Since the going home of my dear brother Henry, our country has not sustained such a loss as this of Phillips Brooks. He was one of the truly great ones of this earth, — great in the noble simplicity of his life and character."

As I have said, she was like her father, Dr. Lyman Beecher, in many things. The scorching fire of the brain seemed to devour its essence, and she endured, as he did before her, some years of existence when the motive power of the mind almost ceased to act. She became "like a little child," wandering about, pleased with flowers, fresh air, the sound of a piano, or a voice singing hymns, but the busy, inspiring spirit was asleep.

Gradually she faded away, shrouded in this strange mystery, hovered over by the untiring affection of her children, sweet and tender in her decadence, but "absent."

The tenderness and patience of her waiting years could only be told perfectly by the daughters who hung over her. She knew her condition, but there was never a word of complaint, and so long as her husband lived she performed the office of nurse and attendant upon his lightest wishes as if she felt herself strong. Her near friends were sometimes invited to dine or to have supper with her at that

period, but they could see even then how prostrated she
became after the slightest mental effort. It was upon
occasion of such a visit that she told me, with a twinkle
of the eye, that "Mr. Stowe was sometimes inclined to be
a little fretful during the long period of his illness, and
said to her one day that he believed the Lord had forgotten him." "Oh, no, He has n't," she answered; "cheer
up! your turn will come soon."

She was always fond of music, especially of the one kind
she had known best; and the singing of hymns never
failed to soothe her at the last; therefore when the little
group stood round her open grave on a lovely July day
and sang the hymns she loved, it seemed in its simplicity
and broken harmony a fitting farewell to the faded body
she had already left so far behind.

She died July 1, 1896, at the age of eighty-five years,
and her body was buried beside those of her husband and
the children who had preceded her, in the burial ground at
Andover.

A great spirit has performed its mission and has been
released. The world moves on, unconscious; but the
world's children have been blessed by her coming, and
they who know and understand should praise God reverently in her going. In the words of the prophet we can
almost hear her glad cry: —

"My sword shall be bathed in heaven."

INDEX

ABBOTT, Dr. Lyman, his statement of the Henry Ward Beecher scandal, 352 ff.

Abolitionist, Abolitionism, see Slavery.

Absent-mindedness, in Mrs. Stowe's grandfather, 2; in Mrs. Stowe, 2; a physical infirmity with Mrs. Stowe, 106; increases with age, 378 f.

Adams, John Quincy, his life a warfare with slavery, 383 ff.

Address to the women of America, containing 562,448 names of Englishwomen, 158 ff., 263; reply to, 263.

"Addresses" presented to Mrs. Stowe at English public meetings, 158, 159.

"Agnes of Sorrento," conception of, 283 f.; interferes with "Pearl of Orr's Island," 285; pleasure in writing, 285; published, 294.

Amherst College, Henry Ward Beecher graduates from, 88.

"Analogy," Bishop Butler's, 49.

Ancestry of Mrs. Stowe, 1.

Andover Theological Seminary, calls Professor Stowe, 166.

Anti-slavery, see Slavery.

Appeal to the women of England, Mrs. Stowe's, 263 ff.; replies, 268.

Appeal to the women of America, Mrs. Stowe's, 210 ff.

"Arabian Nights," Harriet Beecher's solace in childhood, 23.

Argyll, Duchess of, letters to, 269, 274.

Argyll, Duke of, defends Northern States, 160.

"Asia, Researches in," Buchanan's, read by Mrs. Foote, 19.

Bailey, Dr., edits anti-slavery paper in Cincinnati, 94; the "Press" is destroyed by mob, 94 ff., 143; editor of "National Era," 133.

Batavia, N. Y., Mrs. Stowe visits, 108.

Beecher, Catherine, sister of Harriet Beecher; the eldest child, 9; "makes fun for everybody," 26; her school in Hartford, 42; assumes care of Harriet's education, 42; fears Harriet's conversion is irregular, 51; her influence on Harriet's character, 52 f.; her engagement and loss, 52 f.; her bravery, 53; letters to Dr. Beecher, 63; to Edward Beecher concerning Harriet's health, 64; her refutation of Edwards "On the Will," 64; character somewhat stern, 66; goes to Cincinnati, 73; writes "Emigrant's Farewell," 76; with Mrs. Stowe at Brattleboro, 112; letter from Mrs. Stowe, 243.

Beecher, Charles, brother of Harriet Beecher, "a mischievous little fellow," 26; plays flute, 42; letters from Mrs. Stowe, 303, 349, 351, removes to Florida, 304; charming character impressed on region, 305; minister in Saco, Me., 374.

Beecher, Edward, discusses with Mrs. Foote, 19; plays flute, 42; strong influence over Harriet Beecher's mind, 54; letters from Harriet Beecher, 60, 66, 68; preaches for his father, 103; Mrs. Stowe's visit, 130; reported to have been killed at Alton, Illinois, by pro-slavery mob, 144.

Beecher, Mrs. Edward; her suggestion the cause of "Uncle Tom's Cabin," 130.

Beecher, Esther, aunt of Harriet, at Litchfield, 37 ff.; her fund of information, 37; "nineteen rat stories," 38; Lord Byron, 38; takes Charles and Thomas into her home, 52; goes to Cincinnati, 73; care of home, 87.

Beecher, Frederick, "an interesting little fellow," 26.